LAST CARAVAN TO CARMELSARA

ADVENTURE, MAGIC AND A SLOW BURN
ROMANCE BETWEEN TWO PEOPLE WHO
CAN'T STAND EACH OTHER

JACK GARRETY

FOR'SAIL PTY LTD

First published in 2018 by For'sail Pty Ltd Tugun Qld 4224

Garrety, Jack

Last Caravan to Carmelsara

Cover design by Andrei Bat

ISBN 978-0-6482548-0-5

Copyright © 2018 by Paul Garrety

To Annie
Always and in all ways

Last Caravan to Carmelsara

ONE

Roganshah was a city swollen with greed.

Beneath it was the familiar sweet-rot stench of Death, silently stalking, gorging on desperation.

Neah's sensitivity was so high she could almost taste it. She blocked her nose and inhaled through her teeth, wrapping the reins tighter about her fingers. The horses were skittish amidst this crowd, making the gypsy wagon even more unwieldy.

"A gap is due to open. Through there." Deva's worn gold bracelets clinked together as she pointed.

Neah shaded her eyes against the noon glare. She could see nothing other than the seething mass of bodies.

"Far sight is your gift, Mother, not mine. Whereabouts?"

"Over there. Near the watering troughs. Hurry."

Neah flicked the reins, but the horses, like them, were tired.

The gap opened.

And closed.

"Shishkah!" Neah slapped her thigh, their wagon now marooned like a red-and-green island within a surging sea of bodies.

"Roamen." The voice was coarse, loud, and vaguely threatening.

Neah followed it down to a Commonwealth soldier standing beside their wagon looking up at her.

"You speak in Shaylene?" He spat the final word.

"I curse in many languages. It is a habit. No more."

Without averting his gaze, he reached up and snatched the reins from her. His once white uniform was torn beneath the shoulder and stained with what might have been blood.

"Habits like that could get you killed. What is your business here?"

Neah's chin lifted; she sensed both the threat from the soldier and unspoken caution radiating from Deva beside her.

"The market." Neah forced her voice into the strong melodic accent of the high steppes. Roamen were more common there. "If you will return my horses to me." She held out her hand.

His close-set eyes flicked back and forth. They looked greedy. She could feel his gaze scuttle across her skin. She knew that look, that feeling—intimately. The skin beneath the scarf at her neck and the scars it covered quailed in response.

"The square is closed to wagons," he said finally.

"But I have seen other wagons go through—"

"I said it's closed."

"To everyone, or just *Roamen*?" The hotness bubbled up, forming unedited

words that spilled from her mouth.

The soldier's eyes narrowed, the fingers of his other hand firming around the hilt of his sword.

Deva gave sharp intake of breath and leaned across, shushing Neah with a cluck of her tongue, and addressing the man. "Forgive us, sir, my daughter is tired and a little sun touched." She tapped the side of her head. "We've been travelling many days, trying to avoid the Shaylene army. We need only to buy food and find water, then we'll be on our way."

"There's water in the trough." He indicated a group of horses gathered around a hollowed-out tree trunk behind him. Its inside walls were slimed with green. "Five coppers." He held out his hand.

Deva smiled and shuffled through a pocket stitched into her shawl. Both knew the water was free. Counting out the coins, she muttered to herself. Neah recognized the incant for fear, and felt the whisper of energy shift as it was absorbed by the coins.

Deva reached across to tip the fear-charged coins into his filthy palm.

He tossed the reins back at them, stuffing the coins into his pocket.

Deva leaned closer, catching his eye. "Is the Shaylene camp far from here?"

His eyes widened to whites as the incant took root with the mention of the enemy. He backed away, the crowd slowly absorbing him.

"Thanks," Neah said. "Sorry."

Deva patted Neah's leg. "There'll be more of his kind along directly. I'll take care of them too. Fear is a powerful weapon in times of war. Why don't you ride Magic through to the marketplace? I'll water the other two horses, seeing as how we've paid for the privilege."

Neah nodded. Handing Deva the reins, she slipped through the frilled curtain into the dim coolness of the wagon.

Traces of nutmeg and garlic lingered from the meal three nights before. Neah licked her lips; they hadn't eaten a proper meal since then.

She gathered her billowing skirt, hooked the bunched material back through her legs, and tucked it into her wide belt. The myriad of tiny bells sewn into the skirt's fabric trilled softly. Opening the wagon's rear door, she tugged on the tether and drew the horse closer, taking one of the last sugar cubes from the jar. Magic snickered, her muzzle soft against Neah's palm.

"Good girl, Magic," Neah whispered, using the wagon's rear steps to launch herself up onto the horse's back. The hitched skirt and knee-length boots now looked like midcalf leggings. Without the saddle, Magic's coarse coat was warm, soaked with sun, her scent familiar and strong. Neah reminded herself to give the mare a good brushing tonight.

Squeezing her thighs, she urged Magic forward, pausing to let the horse drink deeply from the trough before threading their way through the crowd and into the adjoining square.

Here, there had been some attempt at organizing the chaos. Stalls were crammed along all four sides, while in the middle a series of colorful tents were selling bladders of new wine and slabs of meat cut from spit-turned beasts. Neah ignored the catcalls and whistles from red-faced men at the long makeshift tables, guzzling bravado. Courage came in tankards during wartime.

And swarming amidst it all were the people. Survivors and refugees of all color, culture, and shape. It was as if a giant hand had scooped up samples from all the scattered lands of the Common-wealth and dumped them here, in what only months before had been a sleepy regional center—before the Shaylene had invaded.

Urging Magic along the row of market stalls, Neah noticed a group of soldiers clustering around a doorway further down. The sign above it read Sheriff. She eased Magic back and brought her around, watching the soldiers out of the corner of her eye. She felt a bump against her leg and looked down.

A man was sprawled on the ground amidst a scattered selection of tired-looking vegetables. He shot her a foul glance and shuffled to his feet. Despite the heat he was dressed in the long flowing robes of the steppes.

"I'm sorry, I didn't see you." She swung one leg over the top of Magic's neck and slid down the mare's side in one easy movement. The smell of overheated and unwashed bodies closed in on her. She tapped a bunch of withered greens. "How much?"

He brought up a hand, shielding his eyes from the sun. "One silver." His accent was heavy and thick.

Neah asked again, this time using the man's native tongue.

"Still one silver." He shrugged, showing his palms. "Food is in short supply. Everyone is trying to make enough to get away from here before the Shaylene come. I'll give you two bunches for one silver, and throw in some of the tubers," he added.

She was tempted to move on, then remembered Deva was waiting. Neah didn't want to leave her alone for too long.

"I'll give you two silvers for everything you have here."

"Three," he snapped back.

"Two and a half."

"Done." He bundled the poor offerings into a hessian bag. He seemed relieved.

"What will you do now?" she asked.

"There is a caravan forming tomorrow. This will help my family get ready to join."

"A caravan? To Carmelsara?"

He nodded. "It is the only safe place left."

"Who leads this caravan?"

"His name is Hawke."

A small thrill ran through her. *The prophecy is proving to be true.*

She counted out the coins and slung the bag of vegetables across Magic's neck before springing up onto the mare's back.

When she looked around the man had already rolled up his belongings and disappeared into the crowd. The space where he'd been was now bare.

Neah was about to return to the wagon when she noticed a flicker of sorcery off to the left. Wary, she scanned the crowd. It seemed to be coming from behind a fruit stall near the sheriff's office. Yes, there it was again, the telltale shimmer of illusion, as if a patch had been sewn over the surrounding air. It caught the light—obvious for those with the eyes to see.

Few, it appeared, had. No—there was one. A small boy, his head cocked to one side like a puzzled puppy.

The shimmering patch faded and from behind it stepped a man, ordinary-looking but determinedly so, as if he'd taken pains to blend in, except for his boots. They were different. One was an ankle-high maroon, once favored by gentry, while the other foot sported a scuffed brown hunting boot. The man crunched into an apple as he looked about, then reached over and palmed the purse from the fruit vendor's takings box, slipping it into his waistcoat pocket.

A thief as well as a magician.

The man looked around, saw the boy watching. Picking another apple from the stand, the thief lobbed it over to him. The boy caught it. From her vantage point Neah foresaw the chain of events that would now unfold: the fruit vendor's eyes would follow the movement of the apple, then return to glance at his takings box, realize the bulging purse was gone and, with the help of the magician, make the obvious connection with the boy and the apple. The real thief would then simply step back and fade into the ensuing confusion while the boy would be taken by the soldiers. There was little tolerance for thieves—or illusionists—under martial law. Despite her own gifts, Neah nursed a deep distrust of wizards—manipulators all—and she really hated thieves.

Using her heels to urge Magic forward, she bent down, gripped the child's arm, and hauled him up, settling him next to the sack of vegetables. Magic snorted at the extra weight. "Quiet, girl. It won't be for long," she whispered.

The boy looked up at her with wide eyes and then across to the still shimmering man. The magician's eyes locked on hers. His sequencing had been disrupted. Before he could retaliate, she raised herself up, yelling and pointing.

"Fruit vendor! That man there! He's a thief. He took your money. I saw him."

The fruit vendor looked into his empty takings box and then grappled with the magician, calling for help. The nearby soldiers rushed over. Neah rode over to where the soldiers had been standing and set the child down beside a barred window at ground level. She dimly registered the shape of a man's head peering out.

"Stay here," she told the boy. "Tell them what you saw. You'll be safer here than anywhere." She smiled down at him before riding off.

CALEB WATCHED the back of the woman ride away. His view through the small barred window was limited, visible only in chunks between busy passing feet. Up on the horse she'd been above the crowd, and while he hadn't been quick enough to make out her face, something about the toss of her hair seemed familiar, a sort of contained wildness of the dark curls and the tiny bells.... No, it was gone. Hopeful thinking in a place weary with despair.

His arms shook with the effort of holding himself up at the cell's window. He used his boots to clamber up for a better toehold against the roughened walls. Breathing in, he tightened his grip on the bars, elbows digging into his rib cage for greater leverage as he willed more strength into his biceps and forearms, searching for his adjutant, Arrowsmith. He cursed his own weakness. The battle had been days ago.

And where the hell is he?

He did his best to peer along the street. Nothing. Arrowsmith was never late. Caleb wouldn't allow himself to think his adjutant wouldn't answer a Sworn summons. It was inconceivable.

He drew on the deep-seated anger that boiled in his gut to keep him in place at the window.

A shadow fell across his face, and two small, dirty feet appeared.

"Hey, boy, get out of my way."

The feet jumped back, then slowly a child's face appeared, a boy, his thick mop of curly black hair filling the space. His amber eyes were wide with both fear and curiosity. They stared at each other for a beat, then the boy asked, "Are you in the army?" pointing at Caleb's tattered uniform.

Caleb nodded.

"Why are you in there then? They say the Shay-lin," he stumbled over the unfamiliar word, "are less than two days' ride away. The army is supposed to be getting ready to hold them back. If you're in the army, you should be there."

"Well, that makes two of us who think that. Now get out of the way, I'm looking for someone."

The boy moved to one side and sat in the dust beside the barred window, his back against the wall. He looked to be an urchin, with only a threadbare tunic covering his skinny brown body, yet there was something canny about him. Caleb remembered a time when he was that age, that boy, alone on the street. When food wasn't provided, but scrounged or stolen. He remembered the taste of denial.

"What's your name, boy?"

"Chea." He took a huge bite from a large green apple.

"What else do 'they' say about the army, Chea?" Caleb asked, eying the apple.

"That the army won't hold. They'll break and run—like the last time—and this city will be overrun, just like the others."

"Well, don't believe any of them." A prickly memory of the recent routing by the Shaylene flickered across Caleb's mind. He slammed the lid on it. "How about sharing some of that apple?"

"Why?"

Good question.

"Because I'm hungry—and I'll give you a copper."

The boy grinned, apple juice trickling from the corners of his mouth. Taking two more bites, he held the apple up in front of his eyes, turned it, then with his front teeth fastidiously nibbled at some nobbly protrusions until it was exactly half. He handed it through the bars. Caleb snatched it and dropped lightly back to the floor.

Crunching up the remains of the apple, he tried to remember the last time he'd eaten. He couldn't recall much of yesterday at all.

"Where's my copper?" Chea asked from above.

Caleb smiled and dug through his pockets. Empty. The guards had taken everything. Then he remembered his stash. He picked up the bottom of the ragged cloak and tugged the hem apart, digging out the single coin. He held it up.

"Here, use this to go get us both some real food. You look like you could do with a bit of fattening up. When you come back, I'll give you a copper out of the change."

The light in the cell shifted as the boy changed positions to take a closer look. His eyes widened when he saw the gold coin.

"How do you know I won't take the money just for me?"

Caleb laughed, the sound overly loud and unfamiliar in the confined space. It was exactly what he'd been thinking.

"You have an honest face," he said finally. "And besides, the guards will only steal it from me. I need food and water now, otherwise I'll be in no fit state to leave when my men arrive."

"Your men?"

Caleb realized he'd said too much, so ignoring the question he went over to the wall and held up the coin. The boy reached down, stretching his arm, shoulder tight against the bars until his small fist closed around it. Sitting back on his heels, Chea held the coin in his palm and lightly, even reverently, traced the intricate raised impressions on both sides. Caleb suspected the boy had never seen this much money before, and wondered again at the wisdom of handing it over.

"Boy."

Chea snapped back as if caught doing something he shouldn't.

"Get me some pies. They must be just up the road because I could smell them earlier—and some more of that fruit. A flask of wine too—if you can find it—and whatever you want."

Chea nodded once and stood, his filthy, bare feet visible for a brief moment before they ran off.

CALEB SLUMPED BACK against the wall and slid to the floor.

Five months earlier he'd been free. Five months earlier he'd had a career, and five months earlier Roganshah was just another shithole on the map that he couldn't spell. Now Roganshah was a hastily scrawled line on a map that delineated the Commonwealth's shrinking borders.

If the boy was right and the Shaylene were preparing for another offensive, then the army would be in lockdown readying itself to face them. Arrowsmith, while sworn to Caleb, wouldn't be able to come.

The curse of it was that Caleb still didn't know why the hell he was here. The last thing he remembered was being in a tavern after the battle, and then being arrested.

He stood, impatient for movement, and paced from one diagonal corner of the cell to the other, his stained and bloody cloak swirling about his boots as he turned.

Eight.

Eight steps one way; eight and a half back. Three hours ago it had been four—stalking, angry strides—that had frustrated him even more. Smaller steps forced him to slow mentally, to concentrate on something other than the four walls and his simmering anger that threatened to boil over with every step.

Nine.

Weak afternoon light and isolated cries from the street above filtered down. Barely a hand's breadth high, the barred window provided the cell's only light and ventilation. He didn't know what would happen when the sun went down. There were no candle sconces. He'd hoped that Arrowsmith would have arrived before then.

Ten.

As he reached the far corner he spun, tensing his thigh muscles, and crossed the room in two determined bounds, using the momentum to launch himself back up the opposite wall. Stretching, he caught hold of the bars of the small window and hauled himself up until he was able to see out once more.

The boy was nowhere in sight. While he was miffed at his own foolishness in giving the coin to him, at the same time he wished the boy well.

Footfalls and muffled voices from the sheriff's office above were followed by a commotion on the stairs. More voices, becoming louder. Caleb dropped back down.

Someone was shuffling at the door. He readied himself to tackle whoever came through, desperate for release and answers.

The eye slit slid across and the guard's guttural voice barked, "Into the far corner." Caleb exhaled the tension away and took a step back, then another until he felt the two walls against his shoulders. "Now turn around. Hands behind you."

Caleb hesitated, mentally calculating the distance between his corner and the door. Facing it he had a chance, turned this way he'd have to do a backward flip....

Something crashed into him, and his face sprawled against the walls. He pushed himself away. Whatever had hit him was now down by his feet, tangling them. He felt himself falling, punctuated by the guard's harsh laugh as first one boot then another thudded into his unprotected ribs. Curling into a ball he rolled away. Fleshy fingers with long nails scraped the back of his neck to firmly grip the back of his cloak, tugging up, drawing the thick fastening chain tight against his throat.

"Hands behind you."

With a rattle of chains they bound him, the iron sharp-edged and cold around his wrists.

"Feet too. Ankles together."

Shackled? Who do they think I am?

"Up, coward."

Another kick. This time to his head. White light exploded against his skull, followed by a ringing, as if he'd stood too close to the battle bell when it sounded. Grunting, he tried to roll further but he was already against the wall. "Coward" rang with each aching throb.

Have they confused me with someone else?

He'd been called many things. Coward? Never.

"Get *up!*"

Using the wall to steady himself, Caleb shuffled to standing, sight blurred, nausea surging against the back of his throat. At his feet he could make out another manacled figure. He was struggling to get up as well. It seemed to be even harder for him, as his head was completely covered by a black witch-hood. He was wearing odd boots, one reddish and the other scuffed brown.

Caleb spun to face the guard, who took an involuntary step back. "Why am I imprisoned here? I am a full commander of the Commonwealth and I demand to see General Amos. You have no jurisdiction over me."

"Oh, don't worry, *Commander,* the general wants to see you too," another voice said from the doorway. Caleb glanced over. A corporal and several other uniformed men were snickering at the open door. All were armed. The corporal continued. "He went and made a special trip back from his important duties and such, just to watch your ex-e-cution."

TWO

Neah tumbled the vegetables onto the small bench that served as the wagon's tiny kitchen. Deva poked through them. Her left nostril flared, quivering slightly with what might have been distaste.

"Two silvers, you said?"

"Two and a half." Neah bit into one of the greens. It was soft but still tasted delicious.

"I always say, the tastiest dish starts at the market. These started out old—and were overpriced," Deva muttered.

"Don't you also always say hunger is the best spice, and need always comes before price?" Neah smiled, opening the grate on the small potbelly stove to light the kindling. The potbelly served as their combined oven, hotplate, and heater. Unfortunately, they all worked at exactly the same time, and coupled with the heat of the afternoon, caused sweat to stream from their faces.

Deva grunted, rolling one of the tubers between her fingers. "And I also remember saying a good memory can be a curse on all your relatives. Especially mothers. Now, why don't we make the best of this? You get the fire going and I'll chop. A few spices and seasonings—we could still call it soup, anyway."

Neah glanced out the window. "Let's go outside. There's some shade beside the wagon."

Deva, bending over the pot, inhaled deeply, smacking her lips four times as if tasting the steam. The corners of her mouth turned down.

"All right. This is a ways off ready yet."

Outside, the afternoon sun was still blisteringly hot. Neah spread a blanket in the square of shade cast by the wagon and reached up to unhook one of the hessian water bags. Its damp exterior was soothing, the water inside cooled by evaporation.

She drank, and wiped the back of her hand across her lips. "The man who sold me the vegetables is hoping to take a caravan that is forming tomorrow."

"Did he say who—"

"It's him. Hawke is the wagon master."

"Thanks be. Even I was beginning to doubt. We've travelled so far. Gone through so much. Especially you."

A prickly sensation flickered beneath the tiny scars around Neah's upper chest and torso, and a memory broke free, jagged and sharp. She crushed it and crammed it down with all the rest.

"There was a wizard in the square as well."

"What grade?"

"I couldn't tell. I was too far away. All I saw was an illusion, poorly projected. He tried to blame it on a child."

"And you stopped him," Deva finished, sighing. "Neah, our mission will only work if we don't bring attention to ourselves. People are looking for us. The incident at the tavern the other night created enough of a stir."

"A stir? Is that what you call being drugged and dragged upstairs by a man I only just met?" Neah's voice pitched higher, bringing moisture to her eyes. "I just want this all to be over. Ended—all of it. I just want it to stop."

Deva squeezed Neah's hand. "It will be soon. Don't worry. We've come too far. Now we just need to find a way of joining that caravan tomorrow."

THREE

The corporal seemed to derive some perverse pleasure from shoving Caleb. It occurred to Caleb that it must be every enlisted man's fantasy to have it over an officer in this way. It wouldn't have been quite so bad if the little man hadn't punctuated each jab with "coward" or "traitor." Caleb knew it would only get worse if he resisted, so he tried to keep moving. The streets were crowded, made more so by people stopping to stare. The corporal stamped on the chain trailing between Caleb's ankle shackles. The suddenly taut chain snatched his feet away and Caleb fell, turning his face at the last second to avoid it smashing against the cobblestones. His torso squelched onto a pile of horse shit. It was still warm.

Above him the corporal laughed. "That'll give the general something to remember you by." He ordered two of his men forward to clear the way through the bystanders. The other two guards dragged Caleb up by the arms. The stench wafted up. When he looked down, the front of his uniform was thickly soiled. Caleb did his best to scrape the worst of it away.

This has to be some sort of grandiose military mix-up.

The corporal called a halt in front of an official-looking sandstone building. The Commonwealth flag fluttered from a makeshift pole outside. Requisitioned headquarters.

Two guards wearing the uniform of Sworn men appeared from the alcove flanking the stone steps leading inside. Both were battle armed and wore the personal insignia of General Amos. The corporal produced a crumpled order and the guards stepped to either side to allow the detail to mount the stairs.

"Through there." The corporal pointed at a set of double doors off to the right.

As he turned, Caleb noticed the corporal raise his foot, the boot poised to shove Caleb forward so he'd sprawl through the swinging doors and fall to the floor at the feet of whoever was waiting on the other side. Taking a step to the left, he lifted one of his shackled feet and moved his weight onto the ball of the other. The kick, when it came, struck his right buttock, swiveling him so that he ended up facing the corporal.

Raising his manacled hands, he pointed one finger directly at the corporal's nose. "Touch me again, son, and you'll regret it. Otherwise, once this misunderstanding is sorted, I'll make *sure* you are transferred to my unit. Take it from me, you really don't want that to happen. This," he indicated the manure stain on his chest, "is *nothing* compared to what will happen to you." He waited, watching the little man's eyes narrow and flick from side to side, weighing the risk.

Caleb took another step closer and lowered his voice, the words slow and measured. "Do-you-under-stand-me, Corporal?" The little man's face reddened. Nodding, he motioned for one of the men to open the doors. Caleb turned, straightened his cape, and entered, boot heels clicking against the stone floor, the chain between them dragging behind.

Inside, a long table had been set up facing the door. General Amos was seated near the middle. To his right was an impeccably turned out staff officer who Caleb remembered the men nicknaming Major Bum Shiner, and on the other a full colonel whom Caleb vaguely recognized—something about the Eastern frontier. His face was scored by scars from old battles and he had the look of someone you could count on in a fight, but not cross. From the expression on his face, Caleb had the distinct impression he might have done the latter.

General Amos glanced up as Caleb approached, immediately returning his attention back to the document he was writing.

Caleb saluted and waited for it to be reciprocated. It wasn't.

This must be bad. Really. Bloody. Bad.

"Stand easy, Kane," General Amos said, running a practiced eye from Caleb's muddy boots to the bloodied and soiled white uniform. "You're a disgrace." His nose twitched at the smell before returning his attention to the document. He signed it with a flourish and slid it to the staffer beside him, instructing, "Read out the charges, Major."

The dapper officer cleared his throat. "Commander Caleb Kane, it is alleged that on the eighth day of—"

General Amos waved his hand, interrupting. "We don't have time for all that. The charges are treason, desertion of your post, and mass murder. What do you have to say for yourself, Kane?"

To Caleb it was like the ground beneath his feet had caved in. This was more than a stuff-up. Surely he must be dreaming. This was... this was a nightmare.

"Kane? Commander? I repeat, how do you plead?"

Caleb, mouth dry, stammered a reply. "N-n-not guilty... sir. Sir, I don't understand any of this. I—"

"Silence." General Amos glanced at the oversized clock on the wall. He motioned to the grizzled officer on the other side of him. "Colonel Wright here has already provided a sworn affidavit of what he—and many of your surviving fellow officers—witnessed, yet you seem intent on pursuing this charade?"

Gathering his wits, Caleb straightened. "I do, sir. I refute these charges absolutely."

General Amos sighed. "Very well. Tell us your version of what transpired when we engaged the Shaylene on White Stone Ridge three days ago."

"Sir, my one hundred Sworn were positioned along the ridge. Our orders were to hold the line and then advance in support of the mounted Cossars once they were deployed from the right flank."

"And did you?"

"Indeed we did, sir. The battle was fierce and bloody, however, the Shaylene did not breach the line. The body count was huge as we moved out behind the Cossars."

The colonel's chair overturned, thudding against the wooden floor, as he lurched to his feet. His face flushed, highlighting the raised white scar tissue. "It was huge, all right. You bloody butcher. Traitor! I can't bear to sit here and listen to this."

"Colonel Wright. Contain yourself," Amos warned, turning to the clerk of courts who was off to one side, recording the transcript. "Let's not drag this on unnecessarily. Is there a Clarity Ball nearby?"

"There is, sir. Every courthouse has one. However, the prophecisors who power it have all been seconded and taken by the Army."

"All? Surely there must be someone here who can energize the thing?"

Caleb heard a sound behind him. He glanced around. The corporal who'd brought him in had stepped forward.

"Yes, Corporal, do you wish to say something?" Amos barked.

The corporal cleared his throat, his voice squeaky and unsure. "Sir, there's a man, I seen him in the cells with the commander here. He was wearing a black witch-hood. He might be able to help."

"See to it—and hurry. Unmanacle Commander Kane before you go."

The corporal returned some time later, leading the man with the different-colored boots. As soon as they stood before the general, the clerk of court disappeared through a side door and came out cautiously wheeling a trolley. It supported a massive crystal dome. He positioned Colonel Wright on one side and Caleb on the other, instructing both to place their hands flat on the crystal. The surface was cold and smooth beneath Caleb's roughened hands, his wrists free but worn raw from the tight manacles.

"What is your name?" General Amos asked the man with with mismatched boots.

The hooded man turned in the direction of the voice. "I assume you're speaking to me? My name is Mohar. I am from the north."

"I don't give a damn where you're from. I'm told you may be able to power a Clarity Ball, is that right?"

"I might. If I could see it."

"Take off that damned hood."

"But General," the clerk said. "If we uncover his eyes he may bewitch us."

"Superstitious claptrap. Take it off."

The clerk undid the tracer from around the man's neck, averting his eyes as he lifted the hood off. Mohar shook himself like a large dog, blinking against the afternoon light beaming in through the high-set windows.

"Well?" the general asked. "Now you can see. Can you work it?"

Mohar made a show of inspecting the crystal, the fingers of one hand scratching at the close-cropped beard on his chin. "It will be difficult. Perhaps, if....'

"If? If what?"

"Well, General, forgive me, I thought that would be obvious. I am charged with using magic for theft. If I do manage to power up this ball, then I'll also be incriminating myself in front of the very person who is to hear my case. How could I plead my innocence then?"

The general waved his hand. "Do as I ask and the charge will be reduced to petty theft."

Mohar extended a leg and bowed. Caleb sensed a mocking quality to it.

The clerk positioned Mohar between Caleb and the colonel. "Now, sir," the clerk said, "please cup the back of each man's head. Palm flat against their skull. That's it. Make a tight connection."

"What witchcraft is this?" Caleb blustered, pulling his head away from Mohar's hand. "This man is a thief. I don't trust him."

"Silence," General Amos snapped. "Thief or no, he cannot influence the outcome. He only provides the energy to power the dome, is that right, clerk?"

"That is true," the clerk said. "The prophecisor is powerless to influence what is shown. Once he activates the crystal, the memories of each of the two men touching the globe will be extracted and projected inside for all to see."

A low humming began. It seemed to be thrumming up from the floor through the soles of Caleb's boots, into his legs, trunk, and finally down his arms into the cold, hard surface of the crystal. At the same moment he experienced a flashing in his head, as if a strong light was being shone into dark, shadowy recesses.

The clerk checked the eyes of Caleb and the colonel, and turned to face the general, bowing. "We are ready to begin, General."

Amos waved his hand as if to hurry him along, and the clerk returned to his bench, speaking from there.

"Think of the battle, the smell of it, the heat of the day, the weapons in your hand." Caleb felt something stir, then flow through him into his hands. The crystal seemed to be trying to pull him in, absorb parts of him somehow. A grunt from the old soldier opposite indicated the same thing might be happening to him.

A memory of the day returned. When he opened his eyes, what he was remembering was being projected inside the crystal, seen from his own perspective, as if he was both watcher and creator of the image. Even stranger, through the clear crystal he could see a similar image of the pre-battle preparations displayed on the opposite side. The same scene, from a different viewpoint, drawn from the old colonel's memory relative to where he was on the line. Caleb even caught a brief glimpse of himself on his stallion, inspecting his hundred Sworn, readying them. The attack at that stage would have been only minutes away.

"Amazing," General Amos said. "Move it forward to the battle. Kane, you first."

Caleb brought the memory up of the howling approach of the wild Shaylene with their painted battle faces and bloodred armor.

The clash came; Caleb's hundred Sworn swayed, recovered, and pushed back. There was one small breach in the line, hastily filled, Caleb himself leading it, his two battle cutlasses twirling, hacking, heads flying. The Shaylene were pushed back.

How could that really be? Caleb remembered the Commonwealth's stampeding, inglorious retreat back to Roganshah.

"Curious," the general muttered. "Colonel, your turn."

Caleb removed his hands from the crystal and looked over to the colonel's side, his breath catching as the scene unfolded. The battle was the same but instead of fighting the Shaylene, Caleb was leading the charge—*against his own side.* The Shaylene flowed through the huge gap that Caleb's men had left on the ridgeline. Commonwealth men were falling before the frenzied attack. There was Arrowsmith cutting and slashing to Caleb's right flank. He could feel the link to his hundred Sworn, channeling and commanding their advance by thought alone. His own two battle cutlasses cut a ruthless swathe through the confused throng of Commonwealth defenders.

He turned his head away, unable to watch any more. "Enough," he grunted. "I've seen enough, what trickery is this?" Legs trembling, he sank to his knees. His eyes were drawn irresistibly back to the scene still playing on the colonel's side. There was the routing and the forced relinquishment of the ridge, followed by the desperate, panicked retreat.

And there he was, cutlasses still swinging, jumping up and down as if this was some massive victory, surrounded on all sides by dead and bleeding Commonwealth soldiers.

How could that be even possible?

"I think we've seen enough, Colonel," Amos said quietly, his voice tight with emotion. "What do you have to say, Kane?"

"Sir, this is witchcraft. You saw for yourself what happened on my side... that... that other thing," waving at the colonel, "is a fabrication to somehow discredit me and my men—"

A scuffle and muffled shouting from outside interrupted. They all turned as the doors burst open. The major leapt to his feet, sword gliding smoothly from its scabbard.

A big man with thick white hair and large weathered hands pushed past the two guards and strode to the table. Following, the guards swarmed over him, and he used his bulk to shake them off like bothersome flies.

"Who the hell are you?" the general snapped, waving the guards away.

"Hawke," the man said, straightening his fleece vest. "Nathan Hawke. Master Caravaneer."

"Ah, the infamous caravan master. Wait over there, I'm about to sentence this man to death."

Hawke glanced briefly at Caleb before taking a wide stance in front of the table.

"General, with respect, I have no time to waste waiting. I have a caravan to put together, and I have just been told that the standard military escort has been withdrawn—on your orders. Sir, need I remind you that it was the Torian himself who instructed that the army would protect all caravans to Carmelsara. Now I really need—"

"What you need, sir, are manners—and respect. In case you hadn't noticed, there's a war underway less than two days' ride from here, and I need every one of my men to help fight it otherwise there will be no Torian and certainly no Carmelsara, much less the need for a caravan to travel there. Do I make myself clear?"

Hawke's lips compressed, the corners of his mouth turning down as if trying to swallow something distasteful. Finally he nodded.

"Excellent. Now go take a seat by the clerk and wait your turn. Mind, I can't promise anything."

Hawke stomped off and flopped down on a bench beside the clerk's stool.

"Kane, the colonel's recollection has been corroborated by others. Where are your witnesses? I will hear them."

"Might I say something?" Mohar asked, stepping out from behind Caleb and the colonel.

"No."

Mohar continued anyway, his voice rising and falling in a curious lilt that Caleb vaguely recognized, like a familiar face glimpsed across a crowded room, and for some reason that thought brought up the face of the girl on the horse once more.

"It appears that there are two versions of what happened, and while the colonel's view can be corroborated it may mean that the commander here could be the unwitting victim of sorceric persuasion. We all saw his version of the events. The Dome cannot display falsely. Kane honestly believes that's what happened. Were it not for the testimony from the colonel and his fellow officers, you may as well."

"What are you on about, man?" the general asked, his voice still impatient. Caleb noticed that its former vehemence had dissipated.

"It's possible that the commander was bewitched into behaving as he did."

"Bewitched? To do what? Switch sides and slaughter his fellows? If that were true, then no one would be safe and there'd be no need for a war at all, would there? There'd be riots instead."

Mohar held up his hands, the same lulling singsong quality returning to his voice. "All I'm saying is that it's possible. Technically difficult, granted, though someone who was very, very skilled could manage it."

"Someone like you?" the general said quietly, voice syrupy and dangerous.

"Me?" Mohar took a step back, shaking his head. "No, no. Definitely not, I'm a simple tinker with a few basic tricks. Nothing like that." He pointed back at the globe, pausing before adding, "I would venture a guess who might."

"Enlighten us."

Mohar opened his arms, palms up, as if the answer were obvious. "Who had the most to gain in that attack? And of those, who has the skills required to carry it out? It would be a very short list. The Shaylene at the top of it, or their queen, Shayla—a skilled sorceress, to be more precise."

"Shayla— Are you insane?"

"Quite possibly, but irrelevant to this situation, I think... er, with respect."

"She is said to have extraordinary powers, sir," the major muttered, loud enough for Caleb to hear. "It is said each and every man in the Shaylene army would die for her."

"Many things are said of Shayla, Major, that does not mean we need to swallow each of them whole and untasted. How could she have done this... this... possession?"

Mohar shrugged. "For something of this magnitude? Physical contact would be best. Then ideally something of the commander, hair or nails or... intimate body fluids...."

"Kane? What do you say to this?"

Caleb felt the blood rush up his neck. "Well, there was a woman, sir. A couple of nights before the battle, but many of the men—"

"Who was she?"

Caleb shrugged. "A girl, I don't know. I can't remember." As he spoke a flash of dark curly hair appeared in his head and vanished again. Then a rush of lurid memories: wide dark eyes, unbound cascading black hair, gold hoop earrings, and strong thighs, as if they'd spent a lot of time across a horse. Her hands were not those of a maid either. He remembered their coarseness rasping across his back. It had excited him to—

"Commander Kane!"

He straightened. "That night is all a bit of a blur, sir, I'm sorry. The girl may have been a Roamen. I remember being at the tavern and she just seemed to arrive. Sir, can you tell me about my men? How many of my hundred are left, after—?"

"Seven." The colonel spat the word out before the general could reply.

The number cut through Caleb like a knife. Ninety-three dead? All of them his responsibility. If what the colonel had showed him in the Clarity Ball was true, then the seven who were left would be branded as traitors along with him. The dead would be shamed, their families denied pensions, any prizes forfeit. Caleb deserved to die, ninety-three times over. When he spoke, his voice was rough. "Sir, might I plead for my men?"

"They are Sworn, Commander. They are bound to follow your lead wherever you go—including the execution block. You know how it works. They share your glory as well as the shame."

"They had nothing to do with... whatever happened. I don't even remember, damn it. How can they be blamed?" He paused, his mind racing before he blurted, "I demand a full board hearing. It's my right as an officer."

Caleb was gambling. He had nothing left in play other than the lives of his men, whose only crime had been to follow him, unquestioningly, to infamy. A full board hearing would be a stretch, but it would at least give him time to try and work something out to help them.

Mohar spoke again, his voice lilting. "From what little I saw of this city, General, it is in turmoil. Refugees are pouring in from the outer provinces. If word got out that the army was susceptible to psychic attack, capable of killing its own...." He let the words drift unspoken.

The major cleared his throat and leaned in toward the general, whispering earnestly in his ear for several moments, glance flicking over at Caleb several times.

When they separated, Caleb saw from the expression on the general's face that a decision had been made.

"Step forward, Kane. The thief makes a point. The major has also reminded me that an execution of Sworn men and their commander, particularly someone as popular as you, will raise serious questions within the ranks. Rumors will spread like fleas on a dog. It doesn't matter if Shayla was behind this or not, I can't take the chance of other officers believing possession may be possible. We'd have a rush of deserters."

"But sir," the old colonel protested, taking a step toward the general. "You can't seriously be suggesting that—"

"Stand down, Colonel."

"Sir! I must protest."

"I said stand down and resume your seat." They waited for the colonel to walk back around the table, pick up his chair, and slam it back into place. When he sat, his back was stiff with held tension.

"Commander Kane, I am granting your request for a full board hearing. However, as we are in a state of war I will instruct that it be heard by the Officers' Board in Carmelsara. In the interim I am placing you in the charge of this man." He motioned for the caravaneer to come forward. "You and your remaining seven Sworn will, in turn, provide the military escort for his caravan."

Hawke stalked back to the table. "What? You expect me to lead two hundred people for three months—or more—with just eight men to protect them? The whole damn Commonwealth is in revolt from here to Carmelsara. With the army bailed up, every bandit and warlord will see my caravan as an easy target. You're sentencing two hundred people to death, without a proper escort."

"Not two hundred, Master Hawke. You'll have at least four hundred, possibly five, under your care. And you'll not just have eight Sworn. There'll be nine."

He exchanged a smug look with the major before addressing Mohar. "Surely a *simple* magician like yourself must be worth two, even three in a serious engagement with mere bandits."

"Me? I'm no Sworn. I'm a free man. I'll never bend my will to another."

General Amos made several notations on the orders he'd signed earlier, and looked up with a smile. "I've learned that 'never' is 'never' a reliable measure. Neither of time nor destiny. I would have thought you'd have known that already, magician. Major, I'm putting you in charge of ensuring that these arrangements are carried out to the letter. Whatever it takes."

FOUR

Roganshah was the nexus of two trade routes, at the bottom of a shallow valley. The surrounding hills provided a gusty conduit for the unseasonably cold autumn winds. A tenuous dawn only hinted at later warmth.

Hawke hunkered further into his knee-length coat, breath misting in puffs before him. He hated the cold, and his age only seemed to accentuate it.

Rounding the final corner that opened into Roganshah's market square, he stopped. A ragged queue, four deep in places, spread around three sides of the large square. The queue ended in front of a small red door. The faded words of Caravan Registry could just be made out in the faint light.

"Shit," he muttered. At a quick estimate there had to be a thousand people lined up. The interviewing alone would take all day and most of the next, unless he could find some way of narrowing it down. With this many people and so few spaces available, there was bound to be trouble.

"Master Hawke."

He spun around, his fists bunched and ready.

Something tugged at the hem of his coat. "Down here." The child was not much higher than his thigh, unwashed and underfed, exposed skin prickling from the cold, his voice timorous.

"What do you want, boy?"

"Is it true that the commander from the cells will be travelling with you to Carmelsara?"

"What of it?" His voice sounded harsh even to his own ears.

The boy took a step back, holding up a grubby package. "Then this is for him. Can you give it to him?"

Hawke reached out. The contents were squishy, the cloth stained and wet.

"What is it?" he asked, sniffing it suspiciously. The smell of congealed meat sauce wafted out.

"His food, and... this is his too." The boy reached out with his other hand. Hawke opened his massive paw and felt warm coins tinkle into his palm. "Can you tell him I stopped to eat mine and fell asleep. By the time I came back to his cell he was gone. Oh, and I spent some of the money on a blanket last night and someone stole the wine while I was asleep."

"Who are you, boy?"

"My name is Chea."

"And how do you know me?"

He shrugged. "I hear things."

"Like what?"

"Like... you're the best caravaneer in all the Commonwealth." The words came out in a rush. They had the flavor of being rehearsed.

Hawke grinned anyway. "And who did you *hear* that from?"

"My father. He said you had old hair. It made you wise before your time."

Hawke grunted, running his hand back through his unruly white mane. Old hair was a caravaneer term.

"Your father, you say? Who might that be?"

"His name was Dirk. Master Dirk. He was a caravaneer too."

"Dirk? I didn't know he had a son. Not your age, anyways."

Chea shook his head. "My mother was not his wife. Master Dirk allowed me to work with him. I learned much."

"So why aren't you with him now?"

"He's dead. Everyone from his caravan is. Except me. We were attacked—big men with pointy teeth, riding small horses, surprised us a week into the road."

"A week into?" Hawke asked. The bandits sounded like Nuttals, but they were natives of the desert. They'd never ventured this close to a Commonwealth settlement, particularly one as strongly garrisoned as this.

What does that mean?

"I was hit here," Chea said, turning his head, pointing to a crusted wound thick with matted black hair. "It was from a hammer throw. I seen it coming and ducked, but not quick enough. When I woke up I was lying in a big pool of blood and everyone was dead—or gone. My father too."

"What about your mother?"

"Dead—of the pox last year. That's why my father took me. To look after the horses."

"Did the bandits come back?"

"No. Everything was on fire. They took all the animals and most of the food. I packed up what I could find and walked here. Travelling at night. It took me three weeks."

"You walked? On your own? Did you report all of this to the army?"

Chea shook his head. "I tried. They chased me off. Will you take me to Carmelsara, Master Hawke? I have an uncle there."

Hawke rubbed at his face. Bastard children bred like maggots among the Caravaneers' Guild. Three months was a long stretch to be without a woman's comfort, and much could happen on the road. Hawke left all that to the younger men. He had no real need of it. Not now.

"We'll see," he said, placing his hand on the boy's shoulder. "I'm

going to need some help processing all these people in the square."
He reached into his jacket and pulled out a sheaf of crumpled paper.
Selecting a scrap that was reasonably blank, he wrote a short message,
and gave it to Chea. "Take this note to Commonwealth headquarters
—you know where that is? Good. Give it to the guards outside; they'll
know what to do. Then meet me over there in that building with the
red door. All right?"

Chea grinned, a full mouth of white teeth splitting the dirty face.
His body, though, was still shivering. Hawke slipped out of his coat
and then removed the fleece underjerkin, handing it to the boy.

"Put this on." Passing over the linen-wrapped package, he added,
"You may as well eat this too, it'll be a long day—and get yourself
some boots." He handed some of the coppers back. "Kane won't have
need for coin where he's going."

None of us might.

Caught between the Shaylene and the monstrous Nuttals,
Hawke felt that the security the Commonwealth had provided for so
long was fraying from all sides.

"KEEP HIM STILL. MORE MEN HERE."

Additional guards clattered in, throwing their weight against the
thrashing Mohar. He was manacled to a stone wall by his ankles and
wrists, arms and legs spreadeagled.

"Secure that neck brace. His head's floppin' about like a landed
fish," the sergeant snapped.

Two of the men fitted it to Mohar's neck, threading a long spike
through the hole on either side of the thick metal plates so that the
center of it crushed into his Adam's apple, effectively silencing him.
From across the room Caleb felt the man's blue eyes bore into him,
pouring out resistance. He ignored them, his own recriminations too
strong.

"Bring the commander over," the sergeant called.

Caleb allowed the men to haul him up from the bench and drag him to the transfer point. Forced swearings, along with slavery, had been outlawed decades before. In Caleb's case it would never have been necessary anyway, as there'd always been a waiting list of men to join his hundred Sworn. They'd had the highest prize split and the lowest casualty level—up to now.

The guards removed his cloak and shirt and positioned his bare back against the marked position on the wall beside Mohar. The stone was cold and damp. He pushed himself against it, relishing the discomfort, trying to numb the sounds of the accusing dead in his ears. Images from the Clarity Ball kept exploding across his mental screen, superimposing themselves over his own recollection of what had happened. It felt like he was at war with himself.

He didn't really believe the fool magician's claim that it was Shayla in his head—or his bed. His memory of the woman was clearer now. Roamen, homeless like all of them, overly flashy and loud to compensate. She was no sorceress. Caleb's tolerance for magicking was high, his mental walls vigorously defended, supported by a high level of sensitivity to the aura of the magic. No, if the Roamen girl had tried to seduce his mind as well as his body he'd have known it, despite how drunk he'd been.

Yet, if she hadn't, what was behind the massacre and why don't I remember?

"Do you have a signal, Sergeant?" The major's clipped voice intruded. He'd led the detail from the courtroom across to Roganshah's primitive transfer facilities, ushering Mohar and Caleb into separate holding cells while they made ready.

"Not yet, sir. The thief is resisting."

In a voluntary transfer the men would simply exchange blood and vows and then a prophecisor would use energy to meld the two consciousnesses, subjugating the transferee to the other. Forced transfers were much more difficult and required a great deal of energy. As there were no prophecisors left in Roganshah, the major was trying to use the receiving wall to tap into Mohar's own reserves to power it.

So far it was not working, and Caleb doubted it would, not with Mohar resisting the way he was.

"Light the fire," the major said finally. "Let's see how the thief likes that."

The guards fired a torch and touched it to the tinder in the hollowed-out section of wall between Mohar's spreadeagled legs. Caleb heard it catch, the flames eagerly crackling as they consumed the dry wood. Gradually, the men fed in larger logs, and slowly the wall began to warm from the base up. Caleb ground his back against the stone, unwilling to relinquish the cold discomfort and accept the creeping warmth, replacing it instead with the sharp grain from the rough-hewn rock.

From the speed at which the heat travelled up the wall, Caleb realized the rock surface must only be thin, chosen specifically for superconduction. It was already hot against his own back and he was some distance from the fire. He could only imagine how the heat might be affecting the magician. He glanced over. Mohar's eyes were squeezed shut, his close-pressed lips grim and deter-mined. Sweat streamed from his forehead, coursing down the deep lines on either side of the man's face, spilling from his chin and matted beard. He looked older, as if something had been sucked from him.

"So would you with a fire against your back."

Caleb started at the sound of a strange voice inside his head. It sounded like.... He looked back at Mohar. The wizard's the eyes were open, staring back, then one winked and Caleb's head snapped back to the front as if he'd been struck.

This wasn't the way transfers were supposed to work. They were one-way channels—or they were supposed to be.

Surely these fools haven't got it back to front and subjugated me to him?

Reversed flows in forced transfers had happened in the past. Caleb felt the words of protest form behind his lips, but something held them back. So what if it had been done ass about? It couldn't be any worse than what he was feeling or going through right now. Maybe the guilt and pain would be shared as well?

"Don't bet on it, Comm-an-der."

That voice again. This time Caleb felt pain through the words.

Gods' blood, is this what it's like for all transfer supplicants?

"Is there a signal, Sergeant?" The major's voice again. Was that in his head too? No, the sergeant was replying.

"Yes sir, the wall is live. Resistance has been modified. Transference can now begin."

"Very well. Make the incision."

The sergeant looked back blankly. "Sir?"

"The cuts, man, make the cuts."

The sergeant reddened, embarrassed in front of his men. Caleb found himself disliking Major Bum-Shiner even more. Odds were the major had never even been in a battle, and Caleb wouldn't like his chances if he expected the sergeant to be covering his back in a few days' time. Or maybe staff officers didn't have to fight?

Brusquely the sergeant gestured at the two guards, who moved forward and

unsheathed their daggers. Caleb felt the tip of the blade nick the skin along the top of his shoulder and slice across it. Warm wetness swelled, then dribbled down his back, seemingly drying immediately. It felt as if it were being sucked into the wall. The heat against his back increased.

Has the flow of blood from grinding my back into the wall caused the strange reaction with the wizard?

"*A little, not much.*" Mohar's voice invaded his head once more, clearer this time. The words seemed less painful, leaning more toward the easy drawl he'd used in the courtroom earlier.

How are you doing this? Caleb thought back, wondering if he'd get a reply.

"*Magic.*" And the thief laughed inside Caleb's head.

LATER CALEB WOKE, taking in the low ceiling of the cell and roughened walls. He was lying on one of the two benches, his back still bare and on fire. Despite that, he shivered. They hadn't returned his cloak, and he was bizarrely pleased that his last coin had gone to some use other than paying for a jailer's drunken binge.

He sat up, rubbing his arms. *The cold down here would keep killed meat fresh for a week.*

Mohar was sprawled facedown on the bench opposite. It looked like he lay where they'd dumped him. His back had been dressed with foul-smelling ointments. In between the strips of bloody linen, the skin was blistered and red.

Standing, Caleb looked up at the small window at the top of the wall. The cell was similar to the one he'd been in earlier, where he'd given his last coin to the urchin. He wondered if the child had ever come back. His stomach growled in response.

"You worry a lot, do you know that?"

Mohar was still facedown, his eyes shut.

"Some of us have things to worry about."

Mohar grunted with pain as he tried to get up.

Caleb hesitated, then went over, helping him into a seated position. Mohar slumped on the edge of the bench, head down, his long hair curtained around his face.

"What happened back there? Were you speaking in my head?" Caleb asked.

"You were there. You tell me."

"I need to know, damn it."

Slowly Mohar lifted his head, painfully raising his arm to flick a straggly lock of black hair from his eyes.

"You need to know what? That you're blameless? That you're crazy and don't hear my voice in your head? Well, you're not, Kane. On both scores."

Mohar eased himself to his feet. He tried to turn his head to see over his shoulder, and was pulled up by the pain.

"How bad is it?" he asked. "My back. It feels like I've been flogged."

Caleb tentatively lifted one of the bandages. "It'll heal. There'll be some scarring. No worse than you would have come back with from a war."

"Encouraging bugger, aren't you?"

"Stop that. I order you to stop it."

Mohar's mouth moved back toward its customary smirk. "You order me?"

Caleb straightened. "Yes, of course. You are the supplicant. You are bound to me and so are subject to my will."

"Oh, is that how it works? And what if I don't want to?"

"Don't want to?" Caleb laughed. "You're serious, aren't you?"

Mohar said nothing, just stared quietly back, eyes daring.

Caleb focused, preparing a mental command, his mental doors opening as he projected it. He felt the power of the words slide away, as if his command had hit a barrier, deflecting them. He tried again, concentrating harder this time. Mohar smiled.

"Knock, knock." Caleb heard the words as if spoken inside his head. Hastily he slammed the connection shut.

"How are you doing this, wizard?" His voice sounded ragged. He was shaken that his own commands were not penetrating. The power tables had been turned. He didn't like the feeling.

"Now that would be telling, wouldn't it? But I will tell you how this will play out from here. We will both pretend that the transfer has worked as it should and I am in your *thrall*." He wriggled his fingers at the side of his head, eyes wide. "Then, once we can't see good old Roganshah for the dust of that stinking caravan, I shall fade quietly away, into the night. After that you can do whatever you damned well please."

"Just like that? And the—interference?"

"If you mean will I be able to manipulate you from a distance, sadly, no. Will you miss me?" He tapped his index finger against the side of Caleb's head and laughed. "No, Commander, regrettably my talents, such as they are, are basic. Short-range only. Not that you'll be relieved for very long. Between the bandits and the Shaylene, your little caravan will be lucky to last the week. However, you and your inglorious seven can die like heroes defending it. You may even get a posthumous pardon, what do you think of that? If the Commonwealth survives, of course, which is equally unlikely."

"Why do you say that?" Caleb was curious, even a little relieved about what Mohar had just said. Death—an honorable death! Was it too much to hope for in the wake of his immense guilt and shame?

"The old Torian is dying. Why do you think the Shaylene decided to attack now? If the old boy dies without a successor, then the Commonwealth will burst apart like a rotten fig. Old factions will re-form and fight each other rather than the common enemy."

"The Torian's successor is due to be named any day now. It has been announced."

Mohar made a scoffing noise. "You can't just appoint a Torian. He, or she, must declare themselves by revealing the Torian's mark, and then be confirmed by the Council of the Commonwealth. After that they need to be groomed for the role in a thousand different ways. The announcement was propaganda while they wait for the war to be decided... which may not be too far off—thanks mainly to you. The army has suffered a major defeat—they're just not all dead yet."

"You underestimate us. The army will recover."

Mohar made a *phat* noise. "They're demoralized and confused. You know better than me what that can do. No, this is a time of flux, and if the signs are anything to go by on your side, Commander, the Commonwealth is under pressure, and I have no intention of being caught in the middle when it implodes."

Mohar returned to his bench and gingerly eased himself back down with a grunt and grimace.

Caleb paced, frustration and anger seething through him. He stopped in front of Mohar.

"Did you see her when you were inside my head?"

"Who?" Mohar replied, easing himself back, wincing as his dressings touched the rough cell wall.

"The woman—Shayla."

Mohar shrugged and grimaced again. "I took the opportunity to have a peek inside, however, I have no idea what Shayla looks like so I can't say. The woman I saw though was comely, quite comely. A Roamen I'd say, curly blackish hair, wild dark almond-shaped eyes. Overall, very... shapely. Come to think of it, she looked a bit like that damned girl on the horse who landed me in here."

Caleb seized on it. "Yes, that's her. That's her exactly! The girl in the square. I knew she looked familiar. But how could that be the great Shayla? A Roamen?" He laughed. "Come on."

"Shayla is a sorceress. She can be many—or any. Don't dismiss what I said just because it makes you feel better. My explanation is the only one that makes any sense. Unless, of course, you truly are insane and slaughtered all those men for no good reason. Then I have a real problem, if I'm to share your head space for a few more cursed days."

Caleb felt the rage and powerlessness rise. He closed his eyes and breathed deeply, allowing the surging waves of emotion to settle. Beating the man senseless would do little—other than give him a brief release. He seriously pondered whether it would be worth it before asking, "Who are you, anyway? Is Mohar your real name?"

"Knowledge is power, my friend, and right now you have a shortage of both." He attempted to place his hands behind his head and was checked by pain. He feigned a smile and closed his eyes.

There was a scrape at the door and a pair of eyes appeared at the slot, then with a rattle of keys the door opened and a guard slid a tray across the floor with two bowls of porridge and rough-cut bread. Another man ladled water into two wooden cups.

"Get it down, quick. There's a riot brewing down at the caravan office and you two are being sent to sort it all out." He laughed as he slammed the door once more.

FIVE

Hawke glanced up as the door creaked open, his voice thundering, "No one yet, I told you. Not until the damned army gets—"

Caleb stepped over the raised threshold.

"I'm all the army you seem to be getting."

"What, not the whole *eight* of you?" Hawke fired back, throwing down the quill. Blobs of red ink splattered across the open ledger.

"Nine is the latest count. The wizard is outside."

"Ah, of course. What's he doing? Casting a spell on the hordes? The clattering out there does seem to be less."

"Regrettably, he doesn't share *his* secrets with me." Caleb looked around the small room. There was another door at the back. It too was closed. "My cell was bigger than this."

"I chose it deliberately. A lot of people want to get out of Rogan-shah right now. Having a small space restricts how many can get into it at one time. Less room for trouble."

Caleb nodded. "Makes sense."

Hawke used his foot to shove one of the stools over toward Caleb. It scraped against the bare wooden floor, sending a flurry of dust into the air. "Here, take a perch. We've still got a few minutes before we start."

"Start what?"

"The interviews. I've decided that you should be part of the selection panel. This will be a hard crossing, dangerous too. We can't afford to take anyone who can't pull their own weight, or more importantly is likely to make trouble for the rest. Got it?"

Hawke dug out a pouch of rough-cut tobacco from the pocket of his coat. He emptied a quantity into the palm of one hand, then used the heel of the other to grind it. The rich aroma of crushed, marinated tobacco leaf permeated the room.

Caleb straddled the stool, springing back to his feet as the door behind him opened with a bang. His nerves were shot.

"Ah, here's the tea." Hawke cleared a space on the table before him with his elbow. "Deva, this is, er... can't remember your name. Anyway, he's heading up the military escort. Deva's agreed to be our camp cook, plus she's a healer as well. She and her daughter. They were a rare find."

Deva set down the steaming mug in front of Hawke and cautiously nodded at Caleb.

"Caleb," he said simply.

The woman stared back, her deep brown eyes widening briefly before retreating back behind their hooded lids. He felt like she'd looked into his head the same way Mohar had.

"Tea?" she asked.

"Yeah. Thanks."

Turning her head, she called back through the door. "Another mug, Chea."

"Chea?" Caleb repeated, sitting straighter. The boy's head appeared around the edge of the doorway. He grinned sheepishly at Caleb.

"I told him to keep the money you gave him," Hawke said. "I daresay he'll return what's left of it later. He's an honest lad. Canny too." Hawke leaned to one side so he could access another pocket in his voluminous coat, tugging out a curved pipe. He proceeded to pack its oversized bowl with the crushed tobacco strands.

"That was generous of you. That coin was all I had."

"Then it's a good thing you entrusted it to someone like Chea. There's not much integrity left in this town. That much I do know."

Chea placed a mug on the floor beside Caleb and scuttled over to sit cross-legged at Hawke's feet.

"Deva, you sit there next to Caleb. Now, I'll have final say on who we take, however feel free to make any comments after they've gone. You too, Chea. Each of you will have a different perspective. If this caravan is to get through we'll all need to work together, so let's start now. Ready?"

Hawke struck a match against the wall behind him and fired up the massive pipe. Fragrant blue smoke billowed from it, filling the room. Caleb waved his hand through it. Deva, her bulk balanced on another small stool beside him, coughed delicately.

There was the sound of an argument outside, followed by a scuffling sound against the ancient wooden door.

"Should we open up now?" Caleb asked.

Hawke sighed. "It'll be that, or they'll break it down. One at a time, mind."

Caleb crossed the floor and opened the door, nodding at Mohar. The wizard looked harried, as if he was juggling one too many balls.

Good.

A fat merchant pushed his way past and into the room. Caleb latched the door and returned to his seat.

The overdressed man mopped at his sweating brow with a soggy linen cloth. "Finally. Do you know how long I've been waiting out there in the heat—"

"I'm guessing a lot less than anyone else," Hawke said drily, taking in the man's fur-trimmed britches and gold-buckled shoes. "What do you want?"

The man puffed himself up and tugged out a leather purse from his oversized belt and dumped it on the ledger. "To join the caravan, of course. There are four of us—three wagons."

"Only three wagons?" Hawke said, eyeing the purse like it was an overfull chamber pot. After a time he said, "And this is what? Your idea of a bribe? There is no fare to be paid, not until I bring you to your destination anyway. That is the caravaneers' tradition."

The fat cheeks reddened and some of the bluster leaked away. Caleb had the feeling that this was a man used to talking directly to other people's greed.

"Call it a donation towards expenses," he said finally, his smile greasy and knowing.

"You can call it whatever you like. It's still a bribe and I don't accept them. Now take it and get out."

"What?"

"Are you deaf as well as fat? I said you're not coming. Get out!"

"How dare you? This letter is from the Regional Consul. It instructs you to—"

Hawke threw the purse back at the man and said to Caleb, "Get this fool out of here. And send in the next one."

THE DAY PROGRESSED SLOWLY. By midmorning the predawn chill was a distant memory as the tiny room heated. Caleb tugged open the collar of his uniform. Another trickle of moisture dribbled from his hairline and tracked down his cheek. This selection task was proving to be both tedious and long, qualities he had little liking and even less tolerance for. At least he was better off than those waiting outside in the sun.

Gulping back another cup of water, Caleb caught Chea's eye and winked. The boy had sat at Hawke's feet for most of the morning. He smiled back tentatively, noticed Caleb's empty wooden cup, and scampered into the room behind, returning with a pitcher. He refilled Caleb's, and then went round everyone else. Deva smiled and ruffled his hair, muttering something at him. He grinned back.

So far they'd only accepted thirty families out of almost two hundred through the door. Apart from the fat merchant, Hawke refused to tell anyone whether they were in or not. He simply thanked them and said all the names would be posted on the board tomorrow. True to his word, Hawke gave the other three on the panel their say, after which he made a mark in one of the columns in the big ledger and bellowed, "Next!"

"Next!"

Caleb's attention snapped back. His mind had been drifting with the stifling heat and boredom. He couldn't remember what the last person interviewed had even looked like, much less the decision they'd taken afterwards. Disturbing, bloody images of what he'd seen in the Clarity Ball kept intruding, subverting his attention as he stewed on what possibly could have happened. The guilt was a mudflow, relentless, heavy, and suffocating, yet he still couldn't remember. It was like waking up with a stinking hangover and no memory of what had happened the night before, the only clue third-party anecdotes that seemed to become grosser with each retelling.

"Will you stop thinking about that stuff—it's disturbing. Remember, I'm hooked into your head."

"Stop that!" he shouted.

The others turned toward him.

"Is everything all right, Commander?" Hawke asked.

"Fine. Sorry, thinking about something else. Probably the heat."

Damn the wizard.

Caleb rubbed his chin, as if this might rectify something. He could feel Deva's gaze on him.

If she's a cook, then I'm a prince. There's something about her. Cook indeed.

"All right, Caleb. Fair warning. Another one coming in. Watch out. He could be trouble." Mohar again. This time Caleb managed not to flinch.

Action, at last.

Caleb readied himself. The door swung open, slamming into the wall behind, dislodging a large lump of plaster from the wall. A man's large frame filled the doorway. With the sun behind him, he looked like a shadow, and so tall he had to duck to enter. He stood before Hawke's table, legs apart, one hand resting on the pommel of a large broadsword at his side. Something about him seemed familiar.

"And you are?" Hawke asked, his white bushy brows drawing close. One of his great nostrils quivered, as if he were sniffing the air and wasn't quite happy with the result.

"Quayle. Major Quayle, retired."

"And what can you offer our caravan, Mr. Quayle—if indeed we were able to offer you a space?"

"Men." He glanced at Caleb. "I hear you're ninety-three short of the usual complement." His mouth curled, almost daring.

Caleb sprang to his feet, reaching for his cutlasses, but finding only space where they used to be.

"Lost something *else*, Commander?" Quayle asked, his black eyes amused.

"Caleb. Sit down." Hawke turned his head and spat in the corner before firing up the great pipe again. The room was once more thick with blue smoke. "You were saying, Quayle?"

"Forty of the best. Armed and ready to guard your party in return for passage to Carmelsara."

"Sworn or hirelings?"

"Sworn men are hard to find these days. Even harder to trust a leader who won't lead you to your death," he said, shooting a knowing glance at Caleb, his voice goading.

Caleb forced himself to remain glued to the stool.

"Hirelings then. Mercenaries," Hawke said.

"Your term. I prefer to call them professional soldiers. All Commonwealth trained."

"Who pays them?" Hawke went on.

"Does it matter?"

"It does to me, and it's my caravan."

Quayle shrugged. "A merchant. He travels with a family and

some retainers."

"How many?"

"Ten, plus me—and my men. Four wagons in all."

Hawke grunted. "And at least forty horses, I assume, all of which have to be fed. There's little natural feed for much of this trek. Everything we and the animals eat has to be carted. The army usually bring their own."

He darted a glance at Caleb. "What do you say, Commander? Could you do with some help from this fellow's merry band?"

"Yes, to the help, but not from this man—or his cutthroats. I remember you now, *Major*. You weren't so much retired as cashiered, I recall. Black marketeering, wasn't it?"

Quayle sneered. "Among other things. It sounds like with my cutthroats and your murderers we'd all be in good company."

Caleb launched himself off the stool. The big man was ready for him. Gripping one of Caleb's outstretched arms, he ducked and with a neat sidestep used the momentum to send Caleb sprawling against the wall. Quayle pointed.

"Surely you can't tell me this is the one you'll be relying on for protection?"

"Yes." Hawke made a mark in his ledger. "Yes, this is the man I'm relying on, and not you—or your men, or the fat merchant who hired you. I'm guessing it's the same oaf I refused earlier, trying to get in the back way, so I'll tell you what I told him. Get out. Caleb, you go sit back down. At least that rumble will have woken you up."

Quayle's eyes narrowed, gaze hardening. "It's a long way to Carmelsara, Master Hawke."

"Then you better get started," Hawke said.

Quayle stalked from the room, slamming the door behind him.

Caleb eased himself back onto the stool.

"What did you think about that one, eh, Chea?" Hawke asked, peering down at the frightened face of the boy.

"A bad man, I think."

"That's-a-boy, you've got good instincts." Hawke patted Chea roughly on the head. "A caravaneer needs to use his nose as well as his eyes if he's not to wake up one night with a knife halfway through his throat. With forty armed men against the commander's seven— sorry, eight—most everyone would end up barefoot by the side of the road inside a week."

"Hirelings." Caleb spat the word. "They'll change sides in a blink if there's an extra copper on offer."

Deva stirred beside him. So far she'd said little, seemingly satisfied to leave the decisions to Hawke. When she spoke now, her voice was heavy with portent and more eloquent than she'd so far been, as if the words weren't hers to say.

"Sometimes it's better to keep snakes close, where their venom can be milked and guile contained, rather than freed and expected not to strike. A snake cannot go against its nature, so it must be we who flow with it, not the other way."

AT SUNSET HAWKE put down his quill. "There are no tapers in here, nor lamps. None to be had in the whole of Roganshah, Chea tells me. I suggest we break for a meal and resume first thing tomorrow."

He closed the heavy ledger with a thud, puffing fine dust into the air, and stood. "Is there anywhere close by that offers a decent meal?"

Deva looked up. "My daughter is working tonight in a tavern just down the road. She said the food is reasonable."

"Reasonable is probably the best we can expect at times like this."

"How many did we sign up today?" Caleb asked, bending forward to stretch his cramped muscles.

Facing the window, Hawke stared out. "Too many and not nearly enough. Technically we're full, and there are still hundreds outside waiting to be seen. Some may have better skills than those we've seen so far. I'm not deciding finally until tomorrow."

"That decision will mean the difference between life and death for many of them. All who remain will die at the hands of the Shaylene," Deva said, her voice weary. "We are notI am not Gods old man. We cannot make such choices."

Hawke snorted and turned back to face the others. "Given a choice between taking a God on this caravan, or a man from Ore who could forge sound weapons, I have no doubt who I'd choose. Anyway, if we're caught in the desert with the Shaylene behind and the Nuttals in front, I'm not sure we'll be doing anyone any favors taking them with us."

He opened the door and stepped outside. Taking a wide stance, settling his fists on his hips, he called for quiet, his deep voice carrying even to the back of the large square.

"Go to your homes and come back in the morning. Do not be concerned. There are still thirty wagon spaces within the caravan yet to fill."

There were grumblings from the front, but for the most part people understood and broke into small groups as they moved away.

"Deva, you lead the way to that tavern of yours. My throat is as dry as baked clay."

They fell in behind her, Caleb beside Hawke.

"Thirty families still to come?" Caleb queried, glancing at Hawke.

Hawke allowed the hollow tromp of their boots against the wooden foot passage to fill the space between them before answering.

"They don't know that—and won't even after the list goes up tomorrow. Thirty spaces gives a man hope. He can look to either side and believe he is a better choice than either of his two neighbors. Anything less than thirty, and men get desperate. Do desperate things. I've seen it before."

Deva paused outside an open door covered by heavy burlap sacking. Mohar poked his head through the central slash and spoke to someone inside, the sound of his voice just audible above the noise leaking out.

"Interesting door," Hawke said.

"Easier to throw people out that way," mumbled Caleb. "They're popular in Shore; the sailors down there get pretty rowdy."

Mohar's head reappeared.

"They're full—however, for a small price they'll set up a table for us near the back." He raised an eyebrow. "As long as someone is able to pay." He patted his own empty purse.

Hawke counted out silver pieces and gave one to each of them. "An advance on all your wages. You too, Chea. At least I won't have to worry about keeping one of my team away from the ale." He winked and, keeping his hand lightly on the boy's shoulder, followed Deva inside. They all paused just inside. Hawke ran a practiced eye across the room, assessing risk

The room was thick with smoke and loud talk, layered with the smell of roasted meat and stale, spilled ale. At the far end of the room was a hearth with a decent fire. It was here that they were clearing a space. A rounded tabletop was being rolled out from a back room, men carrying extra stools following.

Hawke pointed, then prodded Chea forward, keeping the boy close as they wove through the drunken, noisy crowd. By the time they reached the other end, five small stools had been arranged around the table. Caleb chose one for Chea and sat beside him, leaning on the tabletop to test its stability. It wobbled. The end of the upturned log that it rested on hadn't been squared. The surface of the table sloped.

Toward Mohar.

Caleb imagined brimming tankards slopping onto the table and down into Mohar's lap.

"I heard that."

I wager you'll feel it too. Soon enough.

Deva remained standing. She surveyed the room, as if looking for someone. Finally her face brightened and she waved.

"Here she comes. My daughter, Neah," she said, nudging Caleb.

There was a moment of disbelief before Caleb leaped to his feet, the tabletop wobbling with the sudden movement.

"You!" He pointed at the woman across from him. "It's her. She's the one—"

Neah cursed and threw a full carafe of wine directly at him. It hit him on the side of the head and he fell to the floor. Hawke grabbed Chea and hauled him out of the way.

Caleb lurched back to his feet, blood and wine mingling to drip from his nose and chin. Claret spread across his uniform like arterial blood, its cheap stench filling his nostrils.

"Witch!" he yelled, pointing an accusing finger across the table.

"Rapist!" she yelled back, her voice pitched to cracking. She raised her hand, fingers weaving into a knot. "I curse you." And spat.

The globule arced high across the table and landed squarely on Caleb's forehead. He felt a wave of rage rise from his feet and sweep through him. He swiped the spit with the back of his hand and flicked it away before launching himself across the table, arms outstretched, reaching for her neck. She screamed, leaping away as Caleb landed heavily across the tabletop, his weight overbalancing it. He slid to the floor with a crash.

The others gathered around him as he struggled to find his feet amidst the slippery mess on the floor, Deva slapping at him, shouting, "Leave her alone."

Over the noise he could also hear the tavern owner, a busty matriarch at the front door, yelling repeatedly for the guard.

It was Hawke who pulled him up, gathering Caleb beneath one massive arm while fending off the girl with the other. Mohar was laughing, which made Caleb all the more determined to wriggle free and—

"Stop!" Hawke roared, his voice cutting through the noise to silence the whole tavern. "Now, one of you tell me what this is all about. *Before* I let you go."

They both started yelling at once.

"Quiet!" Hawke yelled again, tightening his arm around Caleb's ribs, forcing the air out. "You first, girl. Tell me, quick now, before I have to crush him."

"You can kill him twenty times and still it wouldn't be enough for what he did. He raped me. Four nights ago."

"I've never raped anyone—"

"Cocky officer shit! You were so drunk you don't even remember drugging and raping me after I finished work for the night."

"Is this true, Caleb?" Hawke's voice thundered through the room, which had gone strangely quiet.

Caleb shook his head vehemently, creating enough space for his constricted ribs to drag in a breath. "I'm telling you she's lying. I've never drugged or raped anyone. She was the one who seduced me, not the other way around. She got me drunk and took me upstairs."

Deva snorted loudly. Several broken cheers erupted from a nearby table. Caleb wriggled free of Hawke's grip.

"Plus, she stole my purse while I was sleeping. She's a witch, I tell you. The horse-witch Shayla rode in on her that night and filled my mind with illusion."

A mumbled wave rolled across the tavern at the mention of Shayla. Some made the sign against the evil eye.

Neah unreeled another round of curses at him.

"Deva," Hawke called, eyeing the unrest in the room. "Get her out of here. Hurry."

Deva placed her arm around Neah, weaving her through the tangle of tables and chair toward the exit. Those standing reluctantly parted before them, like a bow wave, Deva a diminutive but determined frigate under full sail.

As they neared the door a scuffle broke out as some off-duty soldiers blocked their way, though it was short lived as the guards from the jail burst in. They hurried to the back, intent on securing Caleb and Mohar.

Hawke repositioned the table and overturned stools, patting Chea reassuringly on the head. "You all right, son?"

Chea nodded, his smile gap-toothed and wide.

Hawke called for more food and ale, before mumbling, "I always feared hell was a place I'd end up. It seems I'm already there."

SIX

The list was posted at noon the next day. Caleb watched the crowd searching for their names amidst the sweeping red-inked letters of the jagged-edge page torn straight from Hawke's ledger. Most were disappointed, melting away, as if they'd expected nothing more.

At the edges of the milling crowd, opportunists waited, studying the expressions of those who pushed their way from the crush, approaching the successful with whispered, extravagant offers of exchange.

"Enjoying the show?"

Caleb jumped, and Hawke laughed.

"For a big man, you move quietly."

"Or maybe you were preoccupied," Hawke said, stopping several paces away. His nose quivered, and one of his oversized nostrils lifted in distaste. "Doesn't that army of yours have any spare uniforms? I can smell you from here."

Caleb looked down, pulling on the puckered shirt stained with memories of last night and cheap red wine. "It's not my army. Not anymore. I'm suspended, so no pay or benefits for me—or my men—

until the hearing. My Sworn are due here soon though. Arrowsmith, my adjutant, will have my spare kit with him."

Hawke paused, then said quietly, "I imagine that meeting will be difficult for you."

Caleb folded his arms. "I'm not looking forward to it." He pushed himself away from the wall. "If it hadn't been for that... witch or whoever—whatever—she is.... I still hold her responsible for the deaths of my men."

"Let's not start all that again. You have your version of what happened and she has hers. They'll both be heard in Carmelsara."

Caleb snorted. "You can't honestly say you believe her? She's Roamen! They lie to live."

"And the army doesn't? All I know is that for the next three months we'll all be living in close quarters. A caravan is not just a means of transport, it's a community that relies on each other for survival. I can't afford to have two key members of it at each other's throats. It will create tension and division. Your job—and that of your men—is to get us to Carmelsara. Put it aside until then."

Caleb swung around to face Hawke, his fists bunching. "Put it to one side? That witch has cost me my career. Ninety-three of my men are dead—because of her. The remaining seven are facing a death sentence for treason—because of her. My men are Sworn. They believed whatever I saw that day. They felt what I felt, that's the way the Sworn link works. And I say she's responsible."

"That's not the point right now, is it?" Hawke stepped in close, his face only inches from Caleb's. He jabbed a stubby finger against Caleb's chest. "You have over five hundred souls relying on you to protect them. We have little enough chance of making it through without you infecting your remaining men with bitterness and revenge. Can't you see that?"

Caleb took a deep breath and closed his eyes. Conflicting emotions surged through him, battering at the sharp edges of his guilt.

Finally he opened his eyes and exhaled, nodding. "Very well. Just keep her out of my space."

"I can't do that. I told you, we're to be a community. Like any family, all space is shared. There will be none to spare to keep you two apart. Now, I've already spoken to the girl and she has agreed, for the good of all, to do the same. But only if you will as well."

"She's making ultimatums? To me?" Caleb spluttered.

Hawke sighed and swung his arm in a determined arc, the back of his hand catching Caleb under the jaw, sending him sprawling onto the boardwalk.

"Now, I can do this with either honey or vinegar, Commander, but I swear I will do it. We're all stuck with each other. If you cannot put this aside, I will kill you myself and no one will say a word. And when it's over your men will still have to face treason charges and they will still have to protect the caravan, but without you. They have their orders and they will follow them. So tell me now, before they ride through that gate, which way will you have it?"

Caleb pushed himself to his feet and dusted down his uniform. That was the second time the old man had bested him in less than twenty-four hours. Caleb was an able officer, nimble and quick, but his real strength was in strategy, and everything told him now there was no advantage in pursuing this any further. Not yet, at any rate.

He extended his arm, meeting the older man's eye. Hawke's massive hand gripped Caleb's forearm in return.

"It is done," Hawke said, nodding. "Thank you. I know that wasn't easy."

"Little seems to be these days." Caleb turned away, squinting out into the sunlit square.

In the middle another group was forming. At its head, facing them, were two bulky figures. They appeared to be addressing the rest.

"That's Quayle, the mercenary, and that fat merchant. What are they up to?" Hawke asked.

"I hear they're putting together another caravan. Auctioning the places off. I'm told they'll have at least four hundred by day's end."

"Auctioning places off? That would be right. All roads lead to the market for a merchant. That won't be of much help for those who can't keep up, or don't think to bring enough to feed their horses."

"Much less rely on Quayle and his thugs to protect them," Caleb muttered. "I wouldn't have thought there would be enough supplies left in Roganshah to outfit two caravans."

"There aren't. I'm on my way to resecure my supply contracts. A few of them are threatening to go to the highest bidder for what they have left, but I haven't been a caravaneer all these years without having a few tricks tucked away for times like this."

"Good luck with that."

Hawke pulled on his nose, then pointed at a group of uniformed horsemen trotting into the square. The one at the front was leading a spare horse. "I don't think it's me that will be needing the luck, Commander. After you've briefed your men, bring them over to the old city gates on the Carmelsara route. The caravan is assembling there. It will help if the uniforms are visible while my ostler is organizing the wagons."

THE NIGHT WAS COLD, and several large fires were crackling high and hot between the jumble of wagons and beasts, their flickering light creating oversized shadows against the craggy surface of the city wall.

Caleb picked his way through the tangle of equipment and people. No one seemed to have heeded the instructions about packing away their gear. Bags of grain, blankets, blackened pots, and all manner of travelling trunks and chests were heaped haphazardly around each wagon, their owners perched atop the goods as if to lay claim to a small island of certainty. Two Sworn, on first watch, guided their mounts along the open perimeter of the bunched-up wagons, saluting as they passed. Caleb bunched his fist and brought it to his chest in acknowledgement.

Predictably the meeting with his Sworn had been difficult. Of course they already knew everything, even down to the mission to Carmelsara, yet being Sworn they'd refused to blame him, which only served to gouge his own feelings of guilt even deeper.

He hadn't spoken to the witch. Earlier she'd caught him staring at her, inadvertently catching his eye when she'd glanced up from overseeing the stacking of crates into the supply wagon. The implacable hardness and hatred emanating from those eyes matched his own. Not for the first time he wondered whether Hawke had actually spoken to her first, or had he gone to her afterward saying he would behave if she would?

"Ah, Commander, there you are. Everything ready, is it?"

Caleb spun around, feeling his face flush, fearing that Hawke could tell what he'd been thinking. Chea, beside him, was grinning, his white teeth gleaming, as if he was in on it too.

"Well enough—with this wall at our backs," Caleb said, recovering. "Once we get on the road though I'll have to roster some of the fitter men to fill out the night patrol. Seven won't cover a group this size."

The old man nodded, looking around. "Plenty to choose from. Your men seem... engaged. Your meeting with them went all right then?"

Caleb nodded. "They're good men. Better than I deserve."

"They're your men; take the credit. There's little enough of that around these days. Come with me now. It's time to get this lot into order."

Hawke strode off, threading his way through the chaos, Chea bobbing in his wake like a cork following a strong current. Caleb followed. When they reached the biggest of the fires, Hawke stopped and clambered onto an upturned barrel, pulling a large ivory whistle from one of his greatcoat pockets. He blew on it, the sound penetrating and shrill. The multitude of sounds around the camp stopped abruptly. Hawke blew the whistle again, longer and louder this time.

More people appeared, pushing others toward the center, better to see what the shrill noise was all about.

Hawke held up the whistle. "Think of this whistle as me. If you hear one blast, it means get ready to make camp, or move out. Two blasts, just like now, tells you to stop what you're doing and come in close, as there is something important to discuss, and three... well, let's hope we don't need three, as that will mean we're all in danger. For those who haven't heard, we'll be pooling all the food for this journey. That way no one will go short. So, if you haven't done so already, bring all your food up here to the supply wagons. All of it, mind. I'll not have some people feasting while the wagon beside them goes short. Not on my caravan. There is a list of pooled duties. My ostler, Turps, has nailed it up in a few places. Where are you, Turps? Ah, there you are, stand up will you so everyone can see you. Oh, you are standing."

Hawke paused for the scattered laughter to subside. Caleb got the impression that it was an old joke between the two men. Turps was a midget who moved with the frenetic pace of a man who had too much to do within too little time—which may have been true.

"Turps is my second in charge. He is mute, not deaf, and certainly not dumb. He speaks with his hands. Let him touch you and he'll be able to communicate simple instructions—you'll just know what to do. Works wonders with the animals too. Remember this. Caravans only survive if there are rules. My rules. The one you have to worry about most is keeping the nose of your lead animal—whether it's a horse, camel, or ox—aimed directly at the back of the wagon in front. If the wagon in front of you stops, then it's up to you to let me, or Turps, know. One of us will always be at the front or the very rear. Or find Chea—get up here, son." Hawke bent down and effortlessly hauled the boy up onto the barrel.

"Chea is our runner. If you give him a message, he'll bring it to me. When we set out, this caravan will be a five-minute hard ride from one end of it to the other , so even communicating is going to be a challenge. I can't emphasize enough that for us to get through, we all have to work together. All right?"

There were a few nods and isolated mumbles.

"There are a few more rules, but you can pick up on those along the way. Any questions?"

A woman spoke from the back. Her voice carried right to the front of the crowd.

"Word is there's another caravan leaving tomorrow that's bought up all the spare supplies. How do we know there'll be enough to get us to Carmelsara?"

Hawke frowned. "In better times I wouldn't leave here unless there was enough to feed the people and the beasts for however long the crossing takes. The simple fact is, these aren't better times. We either leave and live on what we can share, or stay and face the Shaylene. If any of you are concerned, go join the other caravan—if you have the food—and the coin. There's no food pool there. The merchant bought up everything he could and is selling the supplies back to those who have purchased places. If that's the sort of man you want to lead you across the mountains, there's still time. Anyone else?"

Another voice from the back. A man this time. Caleb couldn't see who it was.

"Word is the army is pulling out of Roganshah tomorrow. Why aren't we leaving at first light as well?"

"We're not ready." Hawke indicated the chaos of belongings spread around each wagon. "I spoke to the general this afternoon, and yes, you're right, most of the army is moving out tomorrow. The Shaylene are a two-day ride from here and this city is indefensible. Its walls were built before I was born and neither they—nor I—are any match for modern warfare. The army will, therefore, meet the Shaylene on the hills behind us as they approach from the Shore road. We will have ample time to move out before then."

A murmur flickered then flared, spreading like a hungry grass fire.

"Quiet!" Hawke roared, his voice reverberating within the stillness that followed. "As I was saying, *most* of the army is moving out. A garrison will remain here until we leave the day after tomorrow. Even if the Shaylene break through the Commonwealth line, they will have many casualties and will probably regroup here in Roganshah to stabilize their supply lines. They won't be interested in following us. Why would they? A bunch of farmers and merchants?"

He stared into the crowd. No one answered. Finally he nodded.

"Finish loading your wagons tonight. Anything that doesn't fit, or you don't absolutely need, leave behind. Be ruthless. If you aren't, I will be. Turps and I will be checking each wagon and the health of each beast from first light tomorrow. Remember, everything you bring has to be pulled. Old and sick animals simply won't make it, and there are no spares to take their place. So help them help you by keeping your wagon light. Tidy and tight, you'll hear me say it time and time again. Tidy and tight. Anyone's wagon—or beast—not ready by inspection time tomorrow won't be coming."

"Nice pep talk. Very reassuring."

Caleb turned at the sound of Mohar's voice.

"If you don't stop sneaking up on me, the only reassurance you'll get is knowing my blade will end up against your throat."

"If it's that easy to catch you unawares then my money will be on the Shaylene way before then." Mohar stepped around a large crate of squawking fowls to stand in front of Caleb, the usual smirk tugging up one corner of his mouth.

"What are you doing here anyway? You're on first watch with Williamson, aren't you? Where's your horse?"

"With Williamson. He sent me to find you."

"What for?"

"Something you need to see."

"Can't it wait? I have to help Arrowsmith sign up the extra patrols—"

Mohar glanced down at his scuffed mismatched boots before

saying, "I've found that most everything in this life will wait—except death."

"Someone is dead?"

"Murdered, if the knife in his chest is anything to go by. But then I'm just a simple tinker, what would I know?"

HAWKE TURNED his head and spat, then fired up his pipe. He waited until it was burning fiercely, the smoke billowing, before speaking.

"What did you do with the body?"

"Buried it." Caleb said. "Over by the stables. With all that's going on, the army won't be interested in hearing about it, and whatever civilian authorities there might have been in Roganshah before...." Caleb's voice trailed off.

"Do we know who he is—was?" Hawke asked.

"Only that he was from wagon fourteen. The woman there finally broke down and admitted he wasn't with her. She hardly knew him."

"What was he doing with her then? Who is she?"

"A single mother to three kids. Daughters. She knew she'd have no chance of getting a place in the caravan without someone to handle the horses and the manual work, so she convinced a young man she met in the interview line to stand in as her husband. The kids went along with it. Thought it was a good game."

"And it seems he lost. Any idea who—why? Any of that?"

"It could have been anyone, for any reason. People do strange things at times like this. Take things to extremes over nothing: gambling, looking at another man's woman the wrong way, theft. Take your pick." Caleb paused. "There was one strange thing though. He was wearing this odd set of beads around his neck. I had the woman in wagon fourteen identify him, and she commented on them. Said she'd never seen them on him before."

"I assume you have these beads with you?" Hawke asked.

Caleb dug around in his pocket and tugged them out. They were black-and-white polished stones strung onto hide, with what looked like a large red crystal as a heavy central feature. He handed them to Hawke, bizarrely relieved to be rid of them. He wasn't superstitious, but his men were. Several had made the sign against dark magic when they'd sighted the beads on the dead man. Caleb had even over-heard a couple of the men speaking in hushed, urgent tones about the surviving Sworn being cursed. He'd crushed that one immediately. All the same, it was a bad omen. The beads meant something.

Something shifted inside Hawke's wagon. The old man didn't seem to hear it; instead he hefted the beads in his hand, as if assessing their worth.

"They look ceremonial," he said at last, placing them atop a crate beside him. Caleb noticed Hawke wipe the palm of the hand that had been holding them against the fabric of his greatcoat, as if trying to remove something. Caleb had felt the same when he'd held them.

They sat in silence, thoughts about the beads hanging in the air between them like the thick blue smoke from Hawke's pipe.

The sound from inside the wagon came again, like the shuffling of something large trying to get comfortable.

"What's that noise?" Caleb asked. "Do you hear it? It's coming from inside your wagon."

"It's probably Chea. How many others know about the murder?"

Caleb glanced uncertainly at wagon's back door. It hadn't sounded like a boy moving around in there, more a fluttering.

"Only me—and my men. Oh, and the wizard, of course. I don't count him." "Keep it that way. Hopefully this is an isolated incident, however, keep an eye out. Especially on Mohar. I don't trust him. Does he know what these beads signify?"

"He didn't say. I'll ask him."

"No, don't. Let it lie. We have to be ready to leave and I don't want to start any superstitious rumors if we can help it."

"What about the woman and her three daughters? She is

concerned that without the dead man you won't take her," Caleb asked.

"She's right, I won't. A young woman on her own can become a threat to the other women and a temptation to the men. In short, they cause trouble. I try and avoid trouble wherever I can."

"But you can't leave her here," Caleb said. "Not now, with the army pulling out and the Shaelene coming. Do you have any idea what the Shaylene do to women? It'll be slavery at best for her and the girls."

"And will you be the one to protect them all day and every night if we take them with us? Be responsible for anything that might happen because of them? How will you do your own duties if you have to keep one eye on that family? Will others be hurt as a consequence of your divided attention, and what will that mean? These are all questions that I have to ask myself. My responsibility is to the caravan, not one woman and her children. She'll have to take her chances here. The army will do what it can for those that remain."

"I was thinking of the cook, Deva. Couldn't you assign them to her permanently? They're women on their own too, and they could look out for each other, plus the daughters could lend a hand with the kitchens," Caleb suggested.

Hawke pursed his lips as if tasting something sour. "It might be a solution, and having a larger permanent kitchen team might work better. I'll speak to Deva," Hawke said, swinging shut the back door to his wagon and easing himself down onto one of the steps. He grunted as if in pain.

"Are you all right?" Caleb asked.

"Yes, unless you've discovered a cure for old age."

"Death usually works."

Hawke looked up at him from beneath his bushy brows. "You're cynical, Commander, did you know that?"

"Is that against one of your rules?" Caleb snapped back. Then quieter, "Sorry, I haven't slept."

"No apology necessary. Particularly as you're right. The *rules* are only there to give the illusion of certainty, where there can be none. Anything can, and probably will, happen on this trip. It's dangerous. People will get hurt; others will, almost certainly, die. But no one wants to hear that. Rules encourage compliance, nothing else. That's why armies bristle with them—you're clever enough to have figured that one out, son. That's why you're cynical."

"Is that a fact?" Caleb said, feeling unsettled and exposed.

"Yes, it is. Because you still desperately want to believe, to buy back into the fantasy that the army—the generals—have all the answers. That bubble has already burst for you though, and now it's too late. It can't be sealed even if they find you innocent at Carmel-sara. No, like me, Commander, you're adrift in that dark sea of uncertainty." He pointed to the beads on the barrel. "You felt something on them, didn't you?"

Caleb nodded. A puff of wind came from the east, and Hawke's fragrant blue smoke circled around them like mist. It had a peculiar smell to it, familiar yet not pleasantly so. Caleb had thought that yesterday too.

Hawke continued. "There are forces that are totally beyond our understanding. They have their own rules too. Ritual magic is steeped in it. Do you see? True freedom is to know all this and yet be prepared to move forward without expectation or fear of what might —or should—happen. To accept and adapt."

"You make it sound easy," Caleb said, surprised at the bitterness in his voice. He took a small step to the side, away from the smoke. Hawke removed the pipe and stabbed the air with the mouthpiece, making a point.

"Like many of the ancient internal practices, it is both the easiest and most difficult thing that any of us will ever attempt. And not just once. For us to truly be aware of what is happening, you and I must practice it every moment of every day until the only real certainty catches up with us."

"You mean death—again," Caleb finished for him.

"Yes, and by then we may be more ready to face it. Or, more

precisely, to have a good death." Hawke inhaled deeply, holding the smoke in.

"That sounds like a hope."

Hawke's eyes glittered in the gathering light. He wagged an index finger at Caleb. "Ah, hope, yes. But not an expectation."

SEVEN

The second body appeared a week after the caravan departed.

Hawke called an immediate meeting a short distance from the camp. When Caleb arrived, the others were already clustered together in a loose circle. Hawke and Turps shuffled aside to make room. Deva, squatting opposite, nodded, while Neah chose to ignore him.

"What do you have there, Commander?" Hawke asked, eyeing Caleb's closed fist.

Caleb tossed a set of beads into the center of the circle. They were identical to the ones they'd found on the first body.

Hawke poked them with the toe of his boot as he might a dead serpent. The lamplight flickered weakly against the facets of the red crystal. "These were found on the girl?"

Caleb nodded.

"Do we know who she was?"

"The seventeen-year-old daughter of a smith. Wagon thirty-two."

"I know her," Deva said. "Nice girl. Long dark hair and a lovely smile. She helped us prepare the evening meal just two nights ago. You remember, Neah?"

Neah, her gaze fixed, started as if prodded. "Yes. Yes, of course, I remember her."

"You're staring at those beads as if you recognize them." Caleb's tone was accusatory.

Neah glanced up, eyes narrowed and flashing dangerously. Patently ignoring Caleb, she spoke instead to Hawke.

"The beads are significant," she said, then glanced at Deva as if she'd heard the old woman say something. "Mother?"

Deva's brow was furrowed, and her lips poised midway between a spit and a kiss. Caleb had the impression that if the old woman had a stick she would have hit the beads just to make sure they were dead.

Finally she said, "They reek of dark magic. That large red crystal represents transformation; the small stones surrounding it amplify energy that in turn feeds the crystal. Their power has been expended. They should be buried to be sure. Somewhere deep."

"What do you mean, 'expended'?" Hawke asked.

Deva drew in a deep breath and expelled it slowly. "They have been used in a ritual. You may be able to still smell it, like something acrid and burnt?"

Hawke bent closer and sniffed suspiciously, then leaned back and nodded slowly.

"This is the second body, you said, Commander?" Deva asked, looking up and squaring her shoulders.

Caleb nodded. "The first was a young man, similar age. He was the one travelling with the family we sent to you at the start of the trip."

"Julia and her daughters?"

"Is that her name? Sorry, there are a lot of people on this caravan. We asked her not to say anything about how he died. He'd been stabbed. The knife was still buried in his chest. There are no visible wounds on this girl's body though. Nothing really to indicate how she died."

"What about you, wizard? Do you sense anything more?" Hawke asked.

Mohar squatted down beside the beads, sniffing the air above them, his mouth curling with distaste. "I agree with Deva, but no, I have not seen their like, other than they are identical to the first." He stood again. "It's obvious, though, that we have a murderer amongst us."

"Who found her?" Hawke asked.

"Her mother, I think," Mohar continued, glancing at Caleb, who added, "Yes, she'd been sent to fetch water for the horses. When she didn't return, the mother went looking and found her in a patch of spinifex about fifty paces from the water barrels. The marks in the sand look like she was dragged there."

"There was no attempt to hide the body?" Hawke asked.

"No. I got the impression that whoever did it wanted the body found. It had been laid out carefully."

"Positioned purposely?" Deva asked.

Caleb glanced at Mohar and nodded. "I suppose you could say that. She was on her back, arms outstretched. An odd way to fall otherwise. Why? Is that important?"

Before Deva could answer, Hawke interjected. "What about footprints?"

Caleb shook his head. "Nothing definite. There were none leading away, which means the murderer is likely to have come from the camp—"

"How many others know?" Hawke interrupted again.

Caleb pursed his lips, blowing out in a silent whistle. "By now? I'd say just about everyone. These things have a way of spreading. The family is raising some heat, as you'd expect. I left Arrowsmith down there with a couple of men, in case there's any trouble."

"It's best we try and return to routine as soon as we can. Deva, are you and your team ready to serve the evening meal?"

She nodded, her hooded eyes revealing little. Caleb suspected the old woman knew more than she was saying.

"*I agree. The old witch is cunning, but I don't feel like this is her work—or the daughter's,*" Mohar's voice intruded. After more than a week of sharing his headspace, Caleb barely jumped now when the wizard's voice slipped through.

You were going to leave the caravan, and me specifically, after we quit Roganshah? he fired back.

"And go where? With what? I can't go back, and there's just desert around us. At least here I can eat and drink in relative freedom, even if you do insist on me doing those accursed nighttime patrols."

"Commander?" Caleb realized Hawke had been speaking to him. "Yes? Sorry."

"I said get rid of these." Hawke flicked a finger at the beads. "Bury them, as Deva suggested. Preferably while everyone is at meal tonight so no one sees you. Is there any chance we can increase the watch too? At least for the next few nights."

Caleb nodded, smiling to himself as he looked over at Mohar. "Already underway. Mohar comes on in three hours' time with two of the auxiliary we selected, so there'll be a double watch. The men will all be tired tomorrow, but I agree it's important that we show a more visible presence. It will at least give the *illusion* of security."

Hawke grunted and turned to the ostler, who had appeared at his side. "Turps, from tomorrow night make camp in a defensive ring, though with this many wagons we'll probably need two."

The little man made the shape of a large "eight" with his hands, raising his eyebrows in question. Hawke grunted.

"Good idea. Turps says a defensive eight will work best for that."

"Which means...?" Caleb asked.

"We'll form a figure eight with the wagons. When it's done correctly, the galley ends up in the junction of the two circles, providing access to both. We'll corral the beasts in the center of each ring."

Caleb nodded, imagining the clear surveillance fields inside the circles of the eight. "That'll make it easier to patrol too."

"Good. I'll leave enough daylight tomorrow for Turps to lead the wagons into shape," Hawke went on. "In the meantime, let's officially call the girl's death a snakebite. I'll make an announcement after dinner warning parents to be mindful. Remind them that the desert has many dangers and so forth. I saw a few snakes on the trail today, so it should make for a reasonable explanation. What can we do to find who this is?"

"It could be anyone," Caleb said. "Even one of us." He looked pointedly at Neah. "These two obviously know more than they're letting on."

"You dare to suspect that we would do such a thing?" Neah erupted, taking a step forward, her hands bunching into fists.

"Neah." Deva's voice was like a whip crack. She placed a placating hand on her daughter's forearm and gently drew her back. Deva looked directly up at Caleb. "We do not engage with this," she said, pointing at the coiled beads on the ground. "Dark magic is like acid to the soul." She turned away and spat, making a complicated gesture with her hand as if shaking something from it. "You are right though," she continued, wiping her mouth with the back of her hand as she faced him again. "I feel there is a larger intention here, and death is simply a consequence of it. He does too." She nodded at Hawke, and the old caravan master gave a begrudging nod.

"So you're saying that these killings will continue?" Caleb asked.

"That is my feeling. Do you still have the knife that killed the first man?"

Caleb nodded.

"Bring it to me, wrapped in cloth, after the evening meal. There may be some traces of the user, or their intent, that Neah and I can detect. These beads are useless for that. They are too contaminated."

"Let's regroup tomorrow then," Hawke butted in. "I want this murderer found. We can contain the situation for now, however, the more deaths we have the harder that will get. Turps, get a few of the men to help you organize a grave, and we'll bury the poor girl before we break camp in the morning. I'll announce that tonight as well."

He stretched, looking up into the star-studded sky, adding, as Caleb crouched down to collect the beads, "Commander, you may want to send out a small advance party in the morning. Two men should do, as long as they're handy hunters. I sighted a pod of elk earlier. They'll be heading west toward the well where we'll be making camp tomorrow night. If your men ride ahead they should intersect them. Nothing like fresh meat to take everyone's mind off unpleasantness. Now let's get on back."

NEAH WATCHED Caleb bundle the beads into his coat as the group broke up.

Fool! After all we said, he still handles them. Imbecile!

"Your thoughts speak loud." Walking back to the camp, Deva quietly tucked Neah's arm under hers, slowing their pace.

Neah felt her mother's quiet energy steal over her.

"Best keep them close until we know who is behind this," Deva added. "You know what I always say: Raging against blind ignorance hurts no one but you. They don't know any different."

Neah took a deep inhale. She both hated and loved her mother's pithy sayings. She soothed herself with the thought that he already carried the curse she'd placed on him.

"Speaking about blind ignorance, can you believe he tried to make out that we were responsible for that poor girl's death? Him, the one who compelled his own men to murder, tries to paint me as a butcher. Ha."

"He's a man," Deva said. "They always go for the obvious. Remember, he hates you as much as you do him—plus, you're my daughter. Obvious. However, everyone will be looking at us sideways if the killings continue—at anyone with a touch of the old ways, for that matter. Master Hawke too. He knows more than he is letting on. Did you sense that?"

"The way he kept interrupting, as if he was scared we might say too much. Do you think he knows about us?"

"I wouldn't underestimate him. In any case we need to be watchful. Hopefully that dagger will contain some clue."

Neah looked up at the vast expanse above and took another generous breath, exhaling it along with some of the built-up tension. The surrounding silence was like a refreshing dip in cool water. Even the baked soil of the savannah had cooled. Neah kicked off her slippers, and in one smooth movement swept down and retrieved them, preferring as always to feel the earth beneath the soles of her feet, connecting her to the Mother's source.

A bright moon and the array of stars provided enough light for them to walk without the help of a lamp. The semidarkness allowed space for the question that had been swirling between them.

"Is it her, do you think, Mother? Can she have found us already?"

Deva didn't reply immediately, the crunch of the sand beneath their feet and the quiet clink of bangles at their ankles connecting them across the silence. Finally the old woman said, "No. At least, not directly. I don't feel her presence here. Do you?"

"Not really. But this must be her work. Those beads are—"

"I know." Deva sighed. "I know."

The clatter of ladles against pots and exasperated voices interrupted their musing.

"It sounds like we're getting back just in time. You can hear that foolish woman from wagon twenty-six all the way over here." Deva waddled over to the first of the cooking pots, lifted the lid, and peered in, sniffing and smacking her lips through the uprush of steam.

Neah took up her place at the serving table beside Julia and her three daughters. The sisters were lined up in descending height order: the first in charge of a stack of wooden bowls, the next an array of mugs—a water barrel on the opposite side of the trestle—and finally, the youngest, her chin barely above the table's edge, ready to pass across hunks of rough-cut bread.

"The girls seem to be all ready for the rush," Neah said brightly.

The young blonde woman beside her smiled, highlighting the fine lines radiating from the corners of her eyes.

"They enjoy it. It seems to give them a place, and Deva makes them feel like they're doing something important." She glanced away.

"I feel safer with you two as well. The girls and I haven't had much of that; not since their father died. Master Hawke was right, the way some of those men here look at me...."

"Was it the war that took your husband?" Neah's voice was gentle, suspecting Julia's deep wound at the loss of her security had scabbed while still too raw. She sensed an underlying infection there too, of loss and unjustified abandonment.

Julia shook her head and sniffed. "Just a stupid accident nine months ago. At our farm. He was so passionate, so proud of that place, and now it's all gone. The girls and I just managed to get out with the wagon and a few supplies before the Shaylene came. In a way, I'm pleased he didn't have to see that."

"How did you manage until then?"

"Neighbors and friends mostly. Honestly, though, I don't know how much longer we could have lasted, even if the Shaylene hadn't forced us off." She sniffed again and tried for a smile. "We're hoping for a new start in Carmelsara. I have people there. They'll take us in." Her voice wavered.

Neah wondered whether it hid false hope. Much as she disagreed, in this world a woman like Julia with three children needed a man. For protection, if nothing else. She needed to marry again. For a widow without means of her own and three extra mouths to feed, that would be difficult.

"I heard there was another death tonight," Julia said. "That young girl who was on cooking roster with us two nights ago."

"Word travels," Neah replied. "They're looking into it. Nothing like the last one with your protector, though. Master Hawke thinks she was bitten by a snake."

They were interrupted by two of the cooks struggling over with a large tureen between them. Neah and Julia helped them heave it up onto the tabletop, Deva hovering behind, snapping out directions.

"That's the first of them," one of the frazzled women said, brushing away a lank lock of hair from her streaming forehead. Neah removed the lid and a delicious smell of beef and aromatic spices wafted out, captured within the rising steam.

"All right, girls. Start the line," Deva called to the head of the table. The oldest daughter handed across a wooden bowl to the first in the queue, and the meal service began.

After the first night where they'd foolishly tried to feed all five hundred people at once, Deva had split the main evening meal into two sittings, an hour apart.

The morning meal was simpler, with bread, dried fruit, and meal porridge laid out on the trestle tables well before dawn for people to help themselves. All the servers had to do then was keep the tables stocked while Deva and her rostered team of helpers baked the bread that had been kneaded and left to rise by the fire's embers the night before. An additional round of bread and goat cheese would be distributed and eaten when the beasts were rested at lunch.

Neah focused on ladling out the meal, a hastily prepared stew. She allowed her attention to drift, ignoring the good-natured grumbles of those in the line. Truth was, after the live goats and fowls were gone, it would be variations on beans and dried meats until that too ran out. After that Deva had said it would stretch to "soup-anything" for as long as the rest of the ingredients held. Despite what Hawke had announced at the first meeting, provisioning in Roganshah had proven near impossible. Even after all the food had been pooled there was be barely enough to make it for the three months on short rations. Hopefully Hawke was right about the fresh meat tomorrow night.

How did he know about that herd of elk, much less where they were heading? He hadn't left the caravan all day and neither had that curious little man, Turps.

Julia's voice intruded. "Good evening, Commander."

Neah's senses snapped back.

Him.

Caleb looked uncomfortable. He managed a distracted smile at Julia, holding his bowl before him with two hands.

Like a beggar.

Julia gushed and heaped the bowl up with two servings' worth of the spiced mashed tubers, lightly touching the hair behind her ear as he made ready to move along.

Could she be flirting with this oaf? I know she needs a man, but this...?

Neah stopped herself from snorting, and stared hate directly into Caleb's eyes, ladling so much hot gravy onto his plate that it over-flowed and dripped onto his fingers. He jumped, managing to keep the bowl level, sucking at his bottom lip as if to prevent any stray words from escaping.

He remained in place, gravy dripping onto the table.

"Witch," he mouthed the word silently, though it was as if he'd said it.

She formed "butcher" with her lips and fired it back. At a nudge from the person behind, Caleb moved on. From the corner of her eye, Neah saw Deva approach him at the end of the table. Caleb stopped, put down the laden plate—sucking spilled gravy from his fingers—before reaching inside his cloak and withdrawing a cloth-wrapped package. He passed it across the table to Deva, who nodded and tucked it into the colorful sash at her ample waist.

The cursed brings forth the cursed.

NEAH DIDN'T GET a chance to speak to her mother until after the second cleanup. The rest of the women had gone to bed, and she was finishing off stacking the clean bowls and spoons. A man's voice startled her.

"It might be easier to give everyone their own bowl and spoon to look after. That way they would have to clean them, not you. It'd save you time after each meal."

Neah looked up, surprised. She hadn't heard him approach. "Or you could just decide to give us a hand, wizard."

"I am no more wizard than you are noble—Roamen," Mohar said, his dark eyes challenging.

"Mohar doesn't like being called wizard," Deva chided before Neah had a chance to reply. "And he's right about the bowls. Tomorrow we'll tell them to bring the ones they have back for every meal. If they lose them, then they'll go hungry. That should make sure they take care."

Neah dipped and dried the final bowl before returning her attention to Mohar. She wiped her hands on her apron. "I assume you're here to look at the dagger?"

"I've already seen it," he said, eyes narrowing with amusement. "In situ. No, I thought perhaps I might be of some assistance in tracing its source."

"Oh? And how would that be?"

Mohar crouched down beside them. "All right then. Let's just say I wanted to watch what you did. To learn something. Is that more palatable?"

Neah and Deva exchanged a glance.

"There is no mystery in psychometry," Deva said finally. "You either can sense something from an object, or you can't." She indicated his boots. "Take these mismatched old scuffed boots, for example. They aren't yours, are they?" Without waiting for an answer, she placed a hand on the leather uppers of both boots. "I sense these are from two different men. One had large feet, the other small."

"That's why I had to steal them. My feet are quite different sizes. A pair of matching boots just don't fit."

"So why not buy two pairs?" Deva persisted.

Neah recognized the tone in her mother's voice. She was baiting Mohar. From the look in his dark brown eyes he knew it too, and was becoming uncomfortable.

"The boots wear out too quickly. I need new ones every two weeks. I can't afford them. I'm only a poor tinker, after all," Mohar said, tensing himself to stand upright. Deva leaned heavily on his knees, examining the scuffed boot leather more closely.

"Every two weeks?" Neah joined in, her eyes widening. She knew where this was going now. "You must be very hard on them," she said innocently, and reached over to touch one of the boots herself. Like Deva she detected a ripple of energy from the previous owner. Of more interest was the strong throb of current travelling up through the soles of the boots.

Deva cupped her hand around the back of one of the boots and then the other.

"No, my guess is that the old boots help diffuse the energy you're drawing up. New boots wouldn't do that. You need them old. That's why you steal them, and that's why they wear out so fast."

Mohar struggled to rise. Deva leaned her considerable bulk against his knees, forcing him back until he tipped over onto the sand, his legs flipping into the air. Deva and Neah each grabbed one of the boots and tugged them off.

"What are you doing?" he spluttered, making a clumsy grab for one of them.

Neah swerved out of the way of his swinging arm, and tossed the boot aside, catching hold his bare feet. She held them securely to prevent him from standing while Deva carefully examined the soles.

"Enough, daughter," Deva said, stepping away. "Let him go."

Neah released him and Mohar scrambled clumsily to his feet, hands brushing dust from his clothes.

"You are not who you wish us to believe," Deva said. She paused before adding emphatically, "Wizard. These feet of yours have a particularly strong connection to the energy of the earth. She is our source-Mother too."

Mohar bent down and retrieved the discarded boots, hugging them to his chest. Deva shrugged and continued.

"Their difference in size also gives them a secondary affinity to water and fire, which to my mind would just about make you a Third Laurel wizard. That's about as close to a 'simple tinker' as a summer breeze is to a hurricane, wouldn't you think? So, do you want to tell me the real reason you came here tonight?"

Mohar bent each knee in turn to drag his boots back on. Neah could see his molars grinding beneath his cheeks, and she wondered if they'd gone too far. A pissed-off Third Laurel wizard could be dangerous.

He straightened up and faced them. "I wanted to see for myself whatever you discovered from handling the blade."

"Why? Don't you trust us?" Neah asked, her chin rising.

"It was obvious you were both hiding something at the meeting. Hawke too. If I'm to be stuck in this godforsaken caravan, mind-wed to an imbecile with a death wish for glory, I want to know what else I'm up against."

"Have you tried to sense the blade yourself?" Neah asked.

"Psychometry is not one of my gifts," Mohar said.

"Yet you are a Third Laurel. How is that so?" Deva persisted.

Mohar shuffled his feet. "That talent along with others was… taken from me. My left foot was shrunk to unbalance my energy. The vibration from used shoes helps to even it out as best it can. The rest is dissipated."

Deva grinned, nodding. "Aha. You have transgressed. That explains much. It must have been something big—and upset someone very powerful." She waited, but Mohar added nothing further. "Very well. These are your secrets to hold, not mine to pry free. We, on the other hand, have nothing to hide."

"That, I seriously doubt," he said.

Smiling, Deva undid the sash at her waist and allowed the cloth-wrapped package to fall to the ground.

"Unwrap it for me," she instructed Mohar.

He bent down, and without touching the knife tumbled it from the cloth. It lay in the dust, its highly polished blade catching the light.

"Tell me what you see first, Mohar."

He crouched down, examining the knife, then pointed with his pinky. The nail on the finger was abnormally long, its curve painstakingly shaped. Neah glanced at her own work-worn nails. Two were still grimed from the cleanup. She curled the grubby fingers into her palm and hid the bunched fist away in the folds of her skirt.

Finally he spoke.

"This blade, as you can see, is double-edged. This deep forefinger quillon here"—he traced the outline of the curved metal separating the handle from the blade—"indicates it was probably forged to order. Tailor-made expressly for an assassin's hand, I'd say. A small hand, judging by the distance between the forward quillon and the curve at the butt of the handle."

"You seem to have a lot of knowledge about knives," Neah said, still preoccupied with the carefully groomed nail. She could almost swear it was lacquered as well, and felt an unreasonable resentment, remembering a time when she too had enjoyed such indulgences.

"I lived in Forge for a while. Weapons are the main industry there," he answered simply.

"The design on the handle is interesting." Deva leaned in to take a closer look. "What are these silver strands that are wrapped around the shaft? They look like decoration, but have a feel of something to them."

"They facilitate the transmission of energy. Like the round black-and-white beads we found on the bodies. My guess is that the beads and knife all stem from the same lineage."

"So you're saying this is a wizard's knife?" Deva asked.

"Probably," he said vaguely. "However, we don't know whether whoever wielded it was the original owner. Given the work and cost of such a knife, it's unlikely he—or she—would have left it behind, unless...."

"Unless what?"

"Someone wanted us to know that the killing was more than the end result of a violent argument."

"Let's see if we can find out." Deva picked up the knife. She held out her other hand to Neah, who took it firmly in her own.

Immediately a rush of images ran across the screen of Neah's eyes. Isolated snatches of contact, some stronger than others. There was blood too. A lot of it, springing from a ritual. However, it was indistinct, scattered. It felt like she was inside a busy packed market, where only the odd word became clear amidst a buzz of surrounding noise.

"Center me," Deva commanded. Her voice had deepened. Neah recognized it as the one she used after she'd dropped into a light trance. It helped her connect more directly. Focusing on her feet, Neah grounded herself into the earth, drawing up on the source-Mother to assist them both to stabilize.

The flow of images steadied and Neah drew in a deep breath, gradually exhaling it in three distinct stages, pausing between each. She repeated this several times. The contact between Deva's hand and her own warmed, then heated until it felt like she held a blazing coal against her palm. Neah directed her awareness away from it, knowing from experience that there would be no burn mark after they released.

"Do you see it?" Deva asked, her words slow, measured, and deep.

"Yes."

"What is it?" Mohar demanded.

Neah was finding it hard to concentrate on anything else, and whilst she could hear Mohar the effort of trying to formulate a response to him was beyond her.

"What do you see?" he persisted, the words seeping into her consciousness one at a time, like slow drops through a small hole.

With an effort of will Neah raised her free hand and clamped it onto Mohar's shoulder, allowing the images streaming from Deva to pass directly to him.

"It can't be," he said, jerking beneath her hand.

Neah could only stare, her eyes wide and transfixed. The knife was only the instrument here. No wizard had physically killed with it. Instead, it had been used to wield a human.

EIGHT

Dawn was cold. And lonely, despite the crowd clustered close around the shallow grave.

Death had a way of doing that, Hawke pondered. Seemingly uniting the survivors, yet simultaneously reminding them that once through its narrow gate, they would be utterly alone.

He closed the Book of Blessings and, mindful of the loose pages, tucked it into a pocket of his greatcoat. He turned to face the sun, its brightness already tracing the outline of the distant peaks. In another few weeks they'd be in those purple-tinged foothills, and the real journey over the mountains would begin.

Behind him Turps was directing some of the men to fill in the grave. They'd used wooden staves broken down from empty water barrels to cover the body. It would deter the scavengers.

For a while.

Hopefully time enough for the girl's spirit to be uplifted. It was the best they could do with what they had.

The family's father came up to Hawke and mumbled his thanks for the service. Hawke gripped the man's forearm and stared deeply into his red-rimmed eyes. It wasn't easy to lose a child, and Hawke had seen too many fathers with eyes like these over the years, the pain raw, almost as hard to witness as to bear. He drew himself up, releasing the man back to his family, and spoke quietly to Turps.

"You take the lead wagon again today. Chea and I will do the rear."

The little man looked up, momentary surprise on his face. He nodded, and with a final energetic gesture at the shoveling men to hurry up, he bustled off. Turps and he each drove their own wagons— one to the front and the other as vanguard at the tail of the caravan. Topping and tailing, Hawke called it. He'd adopted this practice after once losing both supply wagons to a wall of water that had swept down what was supposed to be a safe river crossing. Lack of supplies threatened individual survival, and that, in turn, was the single largest threat to a cohesive community. He'd seen starving men fight over food.

Been one.

He wasn't proud of that.

Normally he and Turps took it day about, because tucking in at the back meant swallowing everyone else's dust. Hawke was still coughing up red-tinged globs of phlegm from yesterday. The discomfort, though, was a trade-off for being unobserved. Sometimes, like yesterday and today, that was necessary.

Making his way to the rear of the caravan, he nodded in response to a few greetings, but mostly all were too busy getting ready to break camp. That was as it should be. Work and focus kept trouble at a minimum.

Another of his maxims.

Hawke's wagon was green and square, fashioned after the Roamen design of a high-shingled red roof and leadlight glass windows at either side. At the rear, a full-sized door provided access and ventilation. From a distance it looked like a small cabin on large wooden wheels. Hitched to the back was one of the open-topped supply wagons, its cargo tied and secured by strong waterproofed canvas.

Apart from his animals, the quaint green wagon contained everything he owned. Whatever didn't fit inside one of the cleverly engineered drawers and space-saving compartments was simply left behind—or gifted, if someone else had a use for it. Fewer possessions made his life less complicated. Relationships seemed to work the same way, forming from necessity and then, when the journey was over, he'd allow them to unravel, dissipate. If they were sticky, he'd have to sever them as kindly as he knew how. It didn't ease the pain, but it cut down on the suffering. Those left behind would either quietly watch, cry, or curse the back of his wagon as it slowly rolled away. Deva had hinted at this two nights ago over the remains of the fire, probing his aloneness in the pre-dawn—the loneliest time of all— before the rest of the camp had fully stirred. Neither of them slept overlong.

He'd meant to speak with Deva this morning after the service to see what they'd discovered from the dagger; however, she'd already gone to oversee the breakfast when he searched for her.

Approaching his wagon, he saw that Chea had already brought the team of horses from the overnight corral, and was waiting for Hawke to hitch them up. The boy was willing, lacking only the height.

"Good lad. Best get the poultry rounded up and into their travelling pens; we'll be moving out soon. Have you done the supply manifest for the morning?"

Chea grinned, standing straight as if reporting. "All the chickens done, Master Hawke. Manifest too. Nothing missing."

"That's what I like to hear. Better climb on up then."

Chea scurried round the back and clambered into the wagon.

Supply theft was sometimes a problem with food pools. It was probably too early to be worried about it, but having the boy perform a daily check meant people would see it being done. When they finally reached the mountains and the supplies ran low, it might make them think twice before trying to pilfer.

As he bent down to hitch the lead team to the shaft, a sharp pain blindsided him. He grunted, staggering slightly, his hand moving automatically to his abdomen as if this might ease the throbbing. He breathed in and out several times before cautiously easing himself back to an upright position.

Foolish old man.

Pain was inevitable and even necessary. That's what he told himself. It helped keep his mind on the job. Once he let his attention drift, he forgot to be mindful of how he moved, and then the pain always brought him back. Like a well-trained but savage flock dog retrieving an airheaded sheep.

He finished hitching up the horses, giving the lead mare a quiet pat on the neck. She snorted in response, the skin on her neck quivering like tiny ripples on a lake. Animals responded to Hawke, always had, which, like many sensitivities, was simultaneously his curse and blessing. When employed fully, such as with Valiant, it always came with a price.

He could hear Chea clattering around inside the wagon, tying down and securing everything. He didn't seem to have to tell him much. The boy just seemed to know what to do instinctively, probably from his father.

Keep mindful.

He approached the wagon and slowly raised one foot until it rested on the step. Then, keeping tabs on the dull throb radiating from the side of his ribs, he carefully hauled himself up and onto the bench seat. The wagon moved, settling deeper on its springs. A sprung wagon was one of his few indulgences. Nowadays he preferred the wagon to his ageing gray gelding.

Chea emerged from behind the curtain and climbed up beside him, his mouth full of one of the sweet cakes that Deva fed him constantly "to build him up."

"All set, Chea?" Hawke said, automatically leaning out to make sure his horse and the supply wagon behind it were secured and attached.

"All set, Master Hawke."

To the front he could see the lead wagons moving into line, others falling in behind as the space opened up. It took time for all the wagons to start moving. Eventually the wagon directly in front of his lurched into motion. He clucked the lead mare into action. She tested the weight and took the first step forward, the other horses in the team taking up the strain as well. Hawke wrapped the reins around the long shaft of the hand brake, and dug around in his voluminous pockets for his tobacco pouch. The mare knew what to do from here.

"So, Chea, we'll be making camp at a well tonight."

The boy stopped chewing and looked up at him. He swallowed before he spoke. "Which one?"

"I think you know the one I mean. It's the first one out of Roganshah. Strophos Well." Hawke waited for the boy's face to register understanding.

He continued to look blank.

"All right then. It's probably the one where your father's caravan was attacked. What's left of his wagons are likely still there because no one has been out this way since—apart from the caravan that left before us, and I can't see that fat merchant doing much about it."

After a time Chea nodded and began nibbling what was left of the sweet cake, staring down at his bare, dusty toes.

"Chea?" Hawke tried again.

"Yes, Master Hawke," he said, looking up.

Hawke felt awkward and tried again.

"I want you to know that if whatever you see there tonight upsets you, you can come to me—or Deva, if you prefer. I've let her know. She said you can go over to her wagon anytime. You know that, right?"

"Yes, Master Hawke."

Chea looked away. It was as if he hadn't understood. Sometimes Hawke felt that Chea wasn't really there. It was a curious sensation, and seemed to evaporate as quickly as it formed, like trying to make meaning of an object just out of focus.

Hawke sighed and packed his pipe. It would probably sort itself out. Deva said it was likely that Chea would have a reaction. The burnt-out caravan could—and probably would—bring back the memories the boy had suppressed in order to cope. It was a miracle that he'd made it back to Roganshah at all—three weeks on the trail alone. Hawke still didn't know how he'd done it. Well, there was nothing else for it—if Chea was suppressing everything and he had a reaction, they'd have to deal with it. Together.

He fired up his pipe, drawing deeply on the smoke, holding it down in the base of his lungs to allow the small amount of poppy in the aromatic mixture to move into his bloodstream. He monitored its use and always ensured he remained sharp. Just enough poppy to take the edge off the pain. He could deal with the rest. Besides, it helped with the transitioning with Valiant.

"I'm going into the back for a few moments. Mind the reins, boy."

Chea glanced up at him nervously. "Are you going to see Valiant?"

"We won't be long today—you stay here and watch that fool in front. He's just as likely to pull up sharply if one of his nags decides to stop for a mouthful of sage bush." Hawke grunted as he stood and stepped over the bench into the wagon.

Inside it was cool and dark, the leadlight windows still shaded from the previous night. Valiant would still be asleep. Hawke moved quietly, gently tugging the curtains open and securing them with the scarlet ties his late wife had made decades before. Light filtered in through the opaque glass, touching on polished wooden drawers with bone handles worn smooth and thin with use. Warmth from last night's fire still lingered in the potbelly's thick iron as he brushed past.

From the far corner, adjacent to the door, Hawke heard the familiar shuffling behind the draped cloth.

"Yes, it's me," Hawke said, his voice light and conversational.

More fluffing. Despite his heritage, Valiant didn't particularly like mornings. Carefully Hawke slipped off the cover to reveal a large iron cage. A grumpy-looking, large winged bird stared back at him from red-tinged orange eyes. He shook himself, shrugging off the stubborn remnants of sleep.

"Yes, it's me," Hawke repeated. He continued to make soft comments as he slipped on the stiff leather glove and sleeve before removing a strip of dried meat from a nearby box and dangling it through the bars at the top of the cage. The bird shuffled over, tugging it free before gulping it down.

The ritual completed, Hawke snapped open the lock of the cage door and placed his gloved hand near the entrance. Gingerly the bird reached out with one yellow foot, its three talons dangerous with long, sharp points as they curled around the glove. The other foot followed. Even through the thick leather Hawke could feel the power of those feet. Once out of the cage, Valiant scampered sideways up the sleeve until it reached Hawke's forearm. He gave the bird another strip of meat, grooming the long brown feathers with the back of his fingers, making curious clicking noises at the back of his throat until the bird dipped its head. Gently he scratched around the crest of fanned yellow feathers at the top of his skull.

It was time.

"Ready, my beauty?"

Reaching up, he released a latch on the roof, flipping back a trapdoor. It thudded onto the roof, and the weak light of the early morning flooded in. Slowly, Hawke eased his arm up until the bird's body was fully through the hatch. It stretched its wings, gave several test flaps, and finally with a push through its feet, Valiant launched.

Hawke watched through the trapdoor as the bird swept up, its broad wings sweeping, as if catching the air, using it like handholds up a steep surface as it climbed. He shut his eyes, concentrating as he made the mental connection with the bird, startled, as always, at the rush of contrasting peripheral signals: the cold air against his face, warm sun on his back, the almost subconscious tensioning of tiny muscles making corrections to counter crosswinds or take advantage of any spiraling thermals, the massive whooshing power of the wings. He felt the bird's awareness behind his, and then a reluctant and gradual relinquishment, as if Valiant were stepping aside to allow Hawke fully in. The vista below opened like a wide door as he saw through Valiant's keen eyes. Miles of reddish-brown plains stretched away to the mountains, the caravan below looking like a sinewy worm wending its way.

He circled his wagon once, Valiant's expansive wings scooping up more height. Hawke applied his will, and the great bird banked out of the upward spiral and made ground, following the general direction of the road toward Strophos. Normally he wouldn't have transitioned to Valiant two days in a row—it took too much out of both of them—but something was niggling at him. He'd ignored such feelings in the past and always regretted it. Experience was an unforgiving teacher, and only a fool would choose to continue to ignore her.

Ahead he could make out the scattered, dusty palms that clustered around the small well. Surrounding them were the burnt-out skeletons of caravan wagons and men frozen in ragged disarray of either fight or flight. It looked like Chea's father hadn't even had time to organize a defensive circle. Taken by surprise then—a Nuttal specialty.

Swooping in low over the deserted wagons, he extended his senses. This was a place of the dead. Which of these was Chea's father? Possibly none. The Nuttals were slavers, and healthy, strong bodies were more valuable alive and intact. Nuttals only killed to subdue. The survivors would have been taken and chained, ultimately to be sold to the Shaylene.

He wondered at the wisdom of bringing his own caravan this way. The sight of this on top of the recent deaths might make things worse for everyone, not only Chea. Perhaps he'd get Turps and some of the men to ferry over the water barrels to fill, and keep the caravan away—

What was that?

Something had flickered at the very edges of his awareness. He gained height once more, casting wider, and caught it again. The feeling was light, like a brief puff from a cool breeze on a hot plain. He overlaid the feeling against the trajectory of his flight, and tracked the likely direction it had come from. The surrounding country was flat, save for a set of ochre-colored bluffs a league or so to the west—

That's it.

Hawke fed an impulse into Valiant's nervous system, and felt an immediate response as the powerful muscles guided him toward the outcrop. The feeling grew. There was life behind the rocks, but it was dampened down, as if covered by a thick blanket. Nearing the sheared rock face, he felt the rush of a thermal and spiraled into it, rapidly gaining height. On the other side, another caravan of a similar size to his was drawn close into the lee of the rocks. The wagons were in a line. Golden light reflected off one of them. Hawke recognized its impractical, ostentatious shape as belonging to the fat merchant, leader of the caravan that had left Roganshah just before them. Oddly, he could detect no sign of life even from the riders stationed around the perimeter. He sharpened Valiant's focus, zooming in. He swore silently, recognizing the shaggy mountain ponies of the Nuttals.

The fat merchant's caravan had been taken.

Hastily he withdrew his awareness. The Nuttals were extremely sensitive to energetic shifts, and absolute masters at concealment. He had no doubt that there would be more of them at the well, dug into the sand like dust devils, waiting for his caravan to arrive. At the appropriate time they would spring up in showers of dirt to surround and surprise them. It would be the perfect moment. With so few guards, and the focus on circling in for the night, the caravan would be an easy target, a fat plum to round out the Nuttals' slave drive.

He imagined returning, and Valiant banked back the way they'd come.

As the bird drew closer, Hawke gradually withdrew his aware-ness. This was always the tricky part. If he pulled out too quickly, Valiant could injure himself in the changeover; linger too long, and

Hawke risked getting trapped, his awareness split for days. Both had happened in the past, and he was anxious to avoid either.

He nudged Valiant's attention and felt the bird's consciousness slide over and settle back in charge. Hawke exhaled and withdrew fully just as Valiant thumped onto the roof.

From inside, Hawke approached the open trapdoor and extended his gloved hand, arm trembling with the aftermath of the meld and the bird's weight. Hawke contracted the muscles in his shoulder and forearm, then lowered the bird down and into the cage.

Valiant made a noise midway between a squawk and what might have been a curse as he settled onto his perch. Hawke hand fed him some more of the meat strips. Later, he'd release him to hunt. On his own.

Sighing deeply, Hawke sank into a tattered armchair beside the iron stove. Both had belonged to his father. Covered with odd-colored patches, the chair was still the most comfortable piece of furniture he owned.

He reached down beside the chair and retrieved the bladder of water, tilting back his head to squirt a generous amount down his throat. Two transitions in two days was definitely too much for his constitution, and Valiant's too, he wagered. Both of them were getting older. The transition left him feeling like he'd been drinking white spirit for two days and this was the morning of day three.

The bright light from the open trapdoor framed the huge cage. He brought his hand up over his eyes and groaned. Everything hurt, even the light.

"Master Hawke?" he heard Chea call to him softly through the curtain.

"What is it, boy? I've told you not to disturb me when I'm with Valiant." His voice was gruffer than he'd intended, and he immediately regretted it. He swore and pushed himself to his feet, taking one last gulp of water before parting the ragged curtain to rejoin Chea.

"Everything all right?" Hawke clapped Chea on the back.

"Everything is good," Chea said, eyes bright, smile brilliant. "I saw you. You and Valiant. Up there," he said, pointing.

Hawke nodded, unwrapping the reins from the hand brake. "Well, just remember that's our little secret. We don't want everyone knowing everything, now, do we?"

He flicked back on the reins and made a low whistle between his teeth. The lead mare stopped immediately.

"I'm going up to see Turps. We'll be pulling off the road soon." He resecured the reins on the hand brake.

"Not going to Strophos?"

"No. Not today." Hawke lowered himself to the ground, gritting his teeth at the stab of pain before pulling the saddle from its space beneath the wagon's seat. The gelding watched him, ears pricked, as Hawke unpacked the bridle.

"Yes, we're going, we're going," he said, fitting the bit, then hoisted the saddle up onto the horse's back, cinching it tight. He placed one foot in the stirrup and with a grunt swung up into the saddle. Pausing at the front of the wagon, he held his hand out to Chea.

"Coming?"

The boy leaped over and onto the horse in front of Hawke. The gelding set off in an easy canter down the long line of wagons, Chea waving at the wagon drivers as they passed.

Hawke spotted Caleb on the other side of wagon twelve and called out to him, pointing toward the front of the caravan. Caleb nodded and nudged his horse forward, matching Hawke's pace. They both reined in, walking their mounts, when they reached the front.

Taking the bone whistle from the looped twine at his neck, Hawke gave two long blasts. The signal for an announcement.

Caleb trotted around Turps's team to join Hawke.

"Trouble?" Caleb asked.

"I'm hoping to avoid it. The Nuttals are waiting for us at Strophos."

"Nuttals?" Caleb said, disbelief hanging from the end of the word. "How do you know that?"

Hawke ignored the question, his attention focused on the confusion swirling up from behind.

A caravan takes time to start rolling, and even longer to stop. The neat line of wagons was in disarray as each hastily pulled out to the side in an effort to avoid running into the back of the one in front.

Shouting and the frightened whinnies of horses slashed through the silence of the surrounding plain. Slowly the confusion settled as the occupants tied off and jumped to the ground, hurrying forward to gather in a loose semicircle around the front of Turps's wagon.

When the crowd seemed large enough, Hawke stood up in the stirrups, one hand resting lightly on Chea's shoulder, and gave another two long blasts on his whistle.

"I've just had a report from one of our scouts that there are Nuttals waiting for us at Strophos Well."

The muttering of the crowd swelled. Hawke's deep voice cut through it. "There's no need to panic. We just have to take another route, that's all."

"What other route? This is the only road to Carmelsara," a man close to the front yelled back.

"And what about water? My barrels are nearly dry," another said.

A few more shouted their agreement.

"Quiet," Caleb yelled, making a show of resting his hand on the hilt of his cutlass. "Let Hawke speak."

"You're both right," Hawke said nodding at the two men who'd spoken. "There is no other road, so we'll be going overland for a ways. It'll be hard, tough going, but the good news is that there is water at the end of it. There's a small spring Turps and I know of—less than a day's ride from here. If we're lucky we'll be there before sundown."

"Won't the Nuttals follow us?"

Hawke shrugged. "They'll be expecting us at Strophos tonight. When we don't show they may come looking, however, if we cover our tracks well enough they may not bother. Nuttals are basically lazy. Plus, they already have a large number of slaves with them, so they can't come after us in force without leaving them unguarded. The spring we're heading toward is in a canyon that is extremely well hidden. It's large enough to take our whole caravan. We can wait it out there. Now, go on back and secure your wagons; the going will be rough, and we'll need to look out for each other. It would be easy to break an axle out there."

A low rumbling began as the crowd broke up and drifted away. Hawke exchanged a glance with Turps, who nodded and made ready to lead the caravan off-road.

Caleb brought his horse closer to Hawke's.

"I didn't dispatch any scouts," Caleb said. "How do you know there are Nuttals waiting at Strophos?"

"You're forgetting the hunting party," Hawke countered.

"You mean the hunting party I didn't send out?"

"You didn't?"

Caleb shook his head slowly, his eyes never leaving Hawke's. "We've few enough men as it is without sending them out on some wild goose—"

"Elk, not geese, Commander," Chea interrupted, his expression innocent.

Caleb grinned, ruffling Chea's hair. "Are you trying to change the subject, young fellow? Maybe I should ask you how Hawke knew?"

"Oh, leave the lad be. It's quite simple, I saw them."

"Saw the Nuttals? How?"

"Through Valiant."

"Who?"

"Master Hawke's bird. Big, big bird," Chea chirruped again, his arms stretching wide for emphasis. "He flies."

"A bird?" Caleb paused, his brown furrowing. "So you're a what... a shape-shifter?" Caleb asked, the word catching in his throat even as he said it.

"Empath," Hawke replied. "But only with certain animals. I can share their senses for a time, so I can go where I need to. Valiant has been very accommodating, considering."

"Ah," Caleb said, nodding. "Now I get it. That was the flapping sound I heard coming from your wagon the night before we left Roganshah, wasn't it? And that's how you knew about the elk herd too."

Hawke nodded. "It's also why most of my caravans make it through when others do not. It helps to know what's waiting up ahead—as much as we ever can," he added. An unasked-for image of his wife's sudden death intruded, as if to mock his words.

He shoved the memory away.

Caleb looked pensive, then asked, "Have you been back? To Roganshah? Did you see what happened to the army?"

Hawke looked away. He'd been dreading this.

"Valiant and I went back the day after the battle was due to take place. The Commonwealth was defeated."

Caleb cursed and looked away. "I knew it. That damn fool general—"

"Commander," Hawke snapped. "I wouldn't have picked you for an armchair strategist. You know better than anyone that the Commonwealth was outnumbered three, possibly four to one. They had no chance."

"So they're all dead?"

"Not exactly, at least I don't think so. I didn't see enough bodies for that."

"What then? You're not saying they surrendered?" Caleb spat out the final word as if it were something bitter.

"All I can tell you is that there was a large encampment of Commonwealth soldiers on the outskirts of Roganshah. They appeared to be under Shaylene guard."

"That makes no sense. The Shaylene don't take prisoners."

Hawke shrugged. "You're the soldier, son, put yourself in Shayla's shoes. Carmelsara is impregnable. I've been there. Its massive gates are wedged between two tall mountains, impossible to climb. The ones surrounding the city and valley are even higher. What would you do?"

Caleb shrugged. "If I were her I'd use the lives of whoever is left to barter a surrender. Force the Torian to stand aside, or slaughter what's left of his army in front of the gates. No, wait, she'd probably use them as a human shield." Caleb said, nodding, the corners of his mouth curling down.

"There'll be civilians too. From those left at Roganshah." Hawke paused before going on. "But yes, I'd say that's the general idea."

"Master Hawke?"

He looked down. Deva was standing beside his horse. He hadn't heard her approach.

"Deva, I was looking for you at the service."

"I saw you, but I had to get the breakfasts organized. We need to talk, though, about the dagger."

"Very well. Let's meet at my wagon. Bring Neah and Mohar as well. Commander, can you organize one of your men to take Deva's team for her, and Chea as well? Then come on down and join us."

THEY CLUSTERED in a tight group on the shaded side of Hawke's wagon. Deva and Neah perched on low wooden stools, Caleb and Mohar standing to either side. Hawke's bulk completed the irregular circle.

He dug out a wad of dark tobacco and set about grinding it between his palms as he studied the faces before him.

"I told Caleb earlier, the Nuttals have captured the caravan that left Roganshah just before us. They were the slaves I was talking about."

Neah jumped to her feet. "Then we must do something. That could well have been us."

"But it wasn't, and there are some very good reasons for that. Those people knew the risks when they signed on to the merchant's caravan." Hawke methodically packed the tobacco strands into the blackened bowl of his pipe.

"They had no choice. You wouldn't take them," Neah shouted.

"No, if you recall, I couldn't take them. There's a difference, and what's more, we still can't. Besides that, I estimate there are upwards of a hundred and fifty Nuttals out there. We can only field eight men who are experienced in combat. What chance do you think they'd have riding against that many?"

"But we must do something," Neah persisted. "Those people will end up as slaves." Her hand moved to the multicolored scarf at her neck. "Don't you understand what that means?"

"I understand this, Neah. Those people are already beyond anyone's help, because the Nuttals perform the equivalent of forced general Swearings on their slaves immediately after capture. It makes them more compliant for transport, they say. Regardless of what you may feel, there's nothing we could do for them even if we were able to mount a rescue."

"Neah," Deva said quietly. "Hawke is right. Sit back down. Please."

Neah looked as if she might protest, but finally gathered her skirts and resumed her seat. Something wild and unbound still flickered in her eyes.

Hawke exhaled and struck a match against the sole of his boot. He puffed on the pipe a couple of times to get the burn going before continuing. "Were you able to pick up anything from that dagger last night?"

Deva nodded, speaking for the other two. "There's little doubt that the knife and beads are from the same magical lineage. As to who the energy originated from, well, Mohar has a theory about that. Do you want to tell them?"

The wizard was standing unevenly on the ground, or perhaps it just seemed that way because he was shifting his weight from one foot to the other, as if the earth was too hot to stay in one spot for long.

"There was quite a bit of residual energy left in the knife," Mohar said.

"Whose?" Hawke asked.

"More like 'what.' I—we—now believe"—nodding toward Neah and Deva—"that the knife was embedded with an entity that was activated by the blood of the first victim."

"An entity? What, like some sort of ghost?" Caleb asked.

"I'd call it more of a death spirit. Once released, it transitions to a host body and from there compels that person to kill. The host would have no idea it was present and almost certainly no memory of what it did while the entity was in possession."

"Do you know whose body it's using?" Hawke asked, not entirely surprised.

"No. It could be anyone."

"By anyone, you mean us as well?" Caleb asked.

"Of course," Mohar said. "You can see how difficult this will be, if I'm right? One thing I am certain of, it's powerful. In between killings it hibernates to shield its energy."

"Surely one of you three could pick up some sort of signal as to who it might be," Hawke suggested.

"Unfortunately not. Even those of us with the Sight can't detect it in the dormant state."

"We tried last night," Deva muttered, shaking her head.

"That's convenient. So this thing just eats and then sleeps until it's time to kill again, is that it?" Caleb said, chuckling.

Neah's voice slid into the interchange like a thin, oiled blade between two unsuspecting ribs. "I don't see why you find that so amusing, *Commander*. Isn't that what you do for a living?"

"Neah," Deva warned.

She tossed up her hands. "Oh, Mother, he's so closed. It's absolutely impossible. Why do you even bother trying to pretend it isn't so?"

Hawke cut in before Caleb could fire back a retort. "That's

enough, you two. And the beads," he said, returning to the central issue, "what do they have to do with the knife?"

"It's likely a new set of beads are manifested each time there's a killing," Mohar said.

"For what purpose?" Hawke persisted. "Have you found that out at least?"

"Not conclusively."

"But you have a theory?" Hawke probed.

Mohar sucked air in through his teeth, reluctant to voice the rest. Finally he said, "Well, as I told these ladies last night, I've witnessed something vaguely similar before, in Shrove. Identical amulets with similar beads were found on the foreheads of four women victims. They'd been murdered over a period of four weeks. The killer was never found. It turned out that the final victim had a raised sigil—a mystical design—between her eyes, directly beneath the amulet. It was as if it had been pushed outwards from the inside of the skull. The family of the woman said it definitely hadn't been there before."

"Meaning?"

"The amulet was used to reveal something that was hidden. In that case it was the mark of a witch. The killings stopped immediately afterwards. There are some similarities here. The beads, for one thing."

"If this is the same, then what would any hidden thing prove?" Caleb asked.

"That I can't speculate on."

Caleb spun around to face the women. "How about you two? I saw your faces last night. Both of you recognized those beads, don't deny it."

"I don't know what you mean," the old woman said, her eyes sliding away.

"Deva." Hawke's voice rumbled with impatience. "We have no time for games. If you know, or even suspect anything, now is the time to say it."

Deva, closed her eyes. Finally she said, "Very well."

"Mother!" Neah shouted.

"No, child, he's right. They have a right to know, especially with the Nuttals coming. You can be sure that the Shaylene army won't be far behind them. The beads are of Shaylene origin."

"How do you know that?" Caleb asked.

"They are part of a Shaylene ritual for calling out spirit. It's known only to Shaylene high priestesses."

"And you know this how?" Caleb asked.

Deva darted a glance at Neah before saying with a rush, "Neah and I are not really Roamen. We are from Shaylene, and I was part of their religious order."

"I knew it," Caleb muttered, his hand reaching for the battle cutlass at his belt.

Hawke stayed him with a strong hand. "Then why are you here? Surely you're not spies? If you are, you'd be mightily disappointed with what you've found so far." Hawke's mind churned with questions.

"I said we are *from* Shaylene. We don't support the invasion, or Shayla. Like everyone else on this caravan, we are simply refugees."

"But everyone else here isn't *from* Shaylene, are they? Why are you really here, old woman, and what are those beads for?" Caleb's words jabbed at her like spears.

"Before we managed to escape, we... heard... that the Torian's successor would be joining this particular caravan. It is imperative that we find whoever that is before Queen Shayla does."

"And you think these beads have something to do with identifying the Torian's successor?" Mohar asked.

"Without question. You were right about what you said before, Mohar. The beads have the power to force out what is hidden. The Torian's successor is always identified by the unique marks that appear on their body. The Torian's mark. That only happens when the time is ready for them to declare. The beads, however, have the power to draw those marks out prematurely."

"If that ends up killing the person, what would be the point?" Hawke asked.

"Shayla wants to assure herself that the Torian's successor is dead before her army reaches Carmelsara. Without an army, or a declared successor, the Torian will be forced to step aside, leaving the way clear for Shayla to seamlessly assume power over the Commonwealth."

"You haven't answered my question. How could you know all of this?" Caleb asked.

She turned to face him. Deva slipped her arm around the waist of her daughter and took a deep breath. "Because Shayla—Queen Shayla—is my daughter, and Neah is her sister."

NINE

No one said anything. It was as if their small group was suspended in disbelief, while in front of them the wagons groaned and creaked away, an oblivious, rolling backdrop to the drama.

Caleb spoke first, his voice incredulous. "You're Shayla's mother? So it was all true? The sorcery, the possession of my mind—everything?" He brought the heel of his hand to his forehead, senses swirling. Something red and hot bubbled up and surged through him. He lunged forward and grabbed Neah by the arm, dragging her to her feet. "You're going into chains until we reach Carmelsara, witch, and when we get there you will tell them exactly what happened that night and how it affected the battle. You will exonerate my men—"

"You pig!" Neah bunched her other fist and drove it into Caleb's cheek. Wrenching her captured arm free, she sprang away, rubbing circulation into the white pressure marks with her opposite hand. Caleb lunged toward her, and Hawke stepped between them, using his bulk to keep the younger man contained.

Neah continued to yell, ducking around Hawke's massive body like a barking terrier from behind a high fence.

"You dare accuse me of helping Shayla? Well, here, see here how highly my sister thinks of me."

She tugged aside the multicolored neck scarf and the top of her blouse to reveal deep scars running from her collarbone to sternum and radiating out to her shoulders. To Caleb's eye they looked like the deep welts from a horsewhip.

"These are the marks of a slave who will not bow. Shayla sold me to a man who then sold me on to many others, so do not doubt my commitment to bringing her down."

With a gut-tearing sob, Neah turned and ran.

Deva went to go after her.

"No." Hawke restrained her. "Let her be. She can't go anywhere, and I suspect she needs to be alone right now. I will hear the end of this wretched tale. Is what she said true? Those scars are truly terrible."

"Yes." Deva's eyes clouded as she continued. "Shayla wants to be queen, not just of the Commonwealth, but of all the known world. To bring that about she chose to use the left-hand path to power." Deva spat over her shoulder and made a pattern in the air with her fingers before going on. "She murdered her two older brothers as well as her father. The king. A man who'd never had a sick day in his whole life died within days from the canker."

"She murdered her sons as well."

"The rightful heirs. Both died in a tragic accident. Her work again."

"She admitted this?" Hawke asked.

"Not only that, she laughed about it following her coronation—as if she was proud—daring me to try and stop her. Well, I did try. So she had Neah's magic bound and sold her off as a slave, threatening to have her killed unless I helped her assemble an army."

"And did you?" Caleb asked, remembering the ranks of red-breasted charging barbarians he'd seen through the Clarity Ball, and his own deep guilt afterwards in inadvertently joining with them. He closed down the memory with difficulty.

"Much to my shame. Yes. All the while I scoured the ethers for a trace of Neah's location. I eventually found her six months later in the kitchens of a butcher. I was able to remove the binding that Shayla had placed on her, and together we made our escape via the high steppes, disguised as Roamen. The men she'd been sold to had treated her... very badly. The marks you saw are only the physical scars. The others go much deeper. I cut my ties with Shayla that very night. I should go to Neah now."

Deva made her way over to where Neah was standing. They exchanged murmured words that ended in a long hug. After several minutes, they returned to the group, arm in arm.

Neah gathered her skirts and sat back on the low stool.

Hawke, his brows drawn close together, asked, "Are you all right, Neah?"

"I'm fine. It gets to me sometimes."

"Understandable," Hawke said unnecessarily, then cleared his throat. "Deva, going back to what you said earlier. How do you know this new Torian is even part of our caravan?"

"It was told to us. It's a tradition for the Shaylene royal family to visit the Seeker—she's a prophet who lives high in the alps. I took Shayla and Neah there when their father was alive. Back then Shaylene was still a member of the Commonwealth. The Seeker told us that the fabled White Torian would be travelling with a caravan to Carmelsara during this year and lunar period. She even mentioned your name, Hawke. However, she also said this new Torian would be in great danger. If prevented from arriving at Carmelsara, then not only the Commonwealth, but the whole world would slide irretrievably into chaos. I thought it an odd thing to say. Later, it made sense after Shayla admitted to using dark magic to gain the throne."

"White Torian?" Hawke asked. "What is that?"

"Every hundred years or so a White Torian declares. They come at significant times, to head off threatened chaos, and have great power once declared and confirmed by the Commonwealth Council."

"That's all well and good, but why would Shayla knowingly murder her own family?" Caleb persisted, thinking of the burden of guilt he carried.

"The dark knight—our name for the guardian of the forbidden path—is seductive," Deva said. "He intuits our deepest desires—even those we are unwilling to acknowledge—and holds them up, draped in deception to tempt us. For those with the talent, temptations present themselves daily, even in the smallest and most innocent of ways. However, it is those temptations that we are unaware of or deny that are the most dangerous. Against those, we have no defense." She paused, took a breath, and continued. "I believe that is what happened to Shayla."

"I find this all very hard to believe," Caleb said.

Deva shook her head. "It is the choices we make in response to what happens that matters. Ultimately they determine the slipperiness of the slope. In your case, Commander, you have a choice to weigh yourself down with guilt, or respond to the duty before you and your remaining men. I don't blame Shayla for what she has done. She was morally weak, and that weakness was exploited through a series of choices she made. Had I honed her will sufficiently when she was a child, would this have happened? I don't know. Instead I poured all my energy into my sons. What has happened as a consequence of that is my responsibility. In accepting it, I have now sworn an oath to correct that shortcoming. Neah and I will locate the White Torian and protect him—or her—should they declare on this journey."

"And how do you expect to find this... person?" Hawke asked. "We have over five hundred souls travelling with us. I assume whoever this is doesn't know they are to be the new Torian?"

"The Torian's mark begins as a severe rash along with a high fever. Remember, Neah and I signed on as healers as well as cooks. We would be the first to know of anyone who presents with those symptoms."

"And then?"

"We protect whoever it is until we reach Carmelsara."

"That's your plan?" Mohar asked, suppressing a smile. "How do you propose to do that?"

"We have to trust the Mother," Deva said simply.

"Well, meaning no disrespect," Hawke added, "this Mother of yours probably already has her hands full with the Nuttals and this killer ghost in our midst, not to mention the entire Shaylene army that is due down this road very soon."

"We have our faith," Deva replied, taking Neah's hand, "and now we have all of you."

Mohar laughed. "Us? What do you mean by that?"

"Do you not think the circumstances that brought us all together are not curious? Commander Caleb, for example, would almost certainly be dead by now in one of those battles his army engaged in had not the events unfolded as they did. Even you, Mohar, instead of being Sworn to Caleb, you'd be enslaved or dead if you were not travelling with us now."

"You neglected to mention that the only reason either of us is here at all is because you two came to Roganshah," Caleb added, his voice strained, bitterness flowing over. "And how many more dead because of it?"

"But you are here, nevertheless," Deva said, her eyes beaming, hands expansive. "Because the Mother willed it so."

"You believe this is all some divine grand plan to save the new Torian, whoever that might be?" Hawke spluttered.

"Of course." Deva was adamant. "We will all have our part to play."

"Be that as it may, I don't see how getting the Torian to Carmelsara stops your daughter's army," Mohar said.

"It may not. If we manage to do so it will undermine the power of the prophecy. The exposed underbelly of the dark is superstition."

"How so?" he asked.

"The dark knight's rituals are built on it. The Seeker prophesied that the world would tumble into chaos if the White Torian did not arrive at Carmelsara. Well, what if he—or she—does get there? What if the new Torian is anointed after all? Shayla's confidence will be undermined, and doubt is the one thing that can erode will as surely as water and air rust iron. A strong will is vital for magic."

"Let's not get ahead of ourselves," Hawke said, checking the angle of the sun and the distance to the shrinking caravan. "We need to catch up with the wagons shortly, and we have yet to come up with a plan for dealing with this murdering entity of Shayla running loose in our camp. Any suggestions?"

"I'll increase the watch to pairs. Have the men monitor each other. It won't do much for morale, but that's the only way. I suggest we do the same for each of us," Caleb answered.

"Good point. You and Mohar watch out for each other, Deva takes Neah, obviously, and I'll team up with Turps. Mohar, any suggestions?"

The wizard was looking down when Hawke spoke, as if seeing his mismatched boots for the first time. When he glanced up he just shook his head.

"Neah, Deva?"

Deva looked back at him, her eyes shrewd. "We must all trust the Mother in this."

Hawke spat, knocking out the tarry dottle from his pipe against the heel of his boot. "All right. Let's get on back—and keep our eyes open. Mohar, can you take the women in my wagon? Commander, I suggest we cut some of those sage bushes and rope them to the back of the wagon, maybe even the saddles of our horses as well. They may help hide the caravan's tracks where they came off the road, should the Nuttals come looking."

NEAH IGNORED DEVA'S QUESTION, running her fingers lightly across the polished finish of the intricately fitted drawers in Hawke's bureau. "His caravan is much better than ours," she said.

"Neah," Deva repeated, frustration evident. "I asked are you feeling all right now?"

"I don't want to talk about it."

"Ah, that's what you always say. Even when you were a child. You can't hide from yourself forever, Neah. The last time—"

"Was the last time. This is now. And I'm handling it." Her attention was drawn to a rustling from the corner. "Mother, over here, look. It's—"

"Hawke's totem. I know. He's an empath. That's probably how he knew about the Nuttals being at the well."

Valiant blinked balefully at the intruders, then closed his eyes once more, swaying with the uneven motion of the wagon as it bumped across the open plain.

"We may as well make ourselves comfortable," Deva said, settling amidst the cushioning of the patchwork chair and closing her eyes.

There was nowhere else to sit. Neah sighed and made her way back to the front of the wagon, slipping between the curtained flaps and onto the seat beside Mohar. The sunlight after the dimness of the wagon was almost painful, and she held up a hand to allow her pupils to adjust.

From inside she recognized the low drone of Deva's snoring. That woman could sleep anywhere, and she smiled, a curl of love snaking through her. Deva was so predictable.

"It didn't take her long to nod off," Mohar said.

"She is tired, and won't bow to it most of the time."

"Like many women I've known," Mohar added, a cheeky twinkle crossing his cheek. Neah ignored it. She didn't feel like being cheered up. The encounter with Caleb had upset her more than she cared to admit. Deva was right—as infuriating as that was.

I don't like to look. So what? Who would want to look at what I've been through. Trouble is, only so much can fit where I stuff it. After that, the whole mess explodes—usually all over everyone else.

"Do you want to talk about it?" Mohar asked, seemingly reading her mind.

She shot him a vicious glance, ready to roar, but his eyes were locked on the distant dust trail from the caravan.

"No."

"I thought not," he replied quietly, still staring straight ahead.

They relaxed into the rhythmic sway of the horses' rumps. Joined with the creak and dip of the wagon beneath the rising heat of the day, it lulled them into their own reveries.

Finally it was Neah who spoke.

"What's he like, really? You're sworn to him, you know what he's thinking."

"Caleb? I'm not sure he'd like me telling you."

"I'm sure he wouldn't."

Mohar allowed himself a small grin. "I'll tell you this much. He's harder on himself than you could ever be—and that's saying something. Being privy to his thoughts is difficult sometimes."

"Do you have access to his memories as well?"

"I can only see what he remembers—stripped of its emotion. He's not lying about not remembering the night you and he—"

"But I remember. I remember everything. How can he not?" Neah shouted back, as if she might drown him out.

"The way I see it you were both used that night. What followed, therefore, cannot be laid at the feet of either of you. Like it or not, you were both victims to your actions and choices, just like your mother said. We all are."

Mohar's voice sounded bitter. When she looked at him his expression was still distant, as if he hadn't spoken at all.

TEN

"Master Hawke. Master Hawke. You better come quick."

Chea's brown eyes were wide with fear, his mouth gaping like a landed fish, the early sun behind him.

"What is it, boy?" Hawke squinted against the dawn, trying to struggle through the overgrown entrance to the canyon.

"More dead ones, Master Hawke. Two more."

"Dead? Who?" Hawke cursed as he dragged the saddle out from its space beneath the seat of the wagon.

"Man and woman. I think. Commander Caleb said for you to come quick."

"Yes, yes. I'm coming," he said, throwing the blanket then saddle over the back of his horse. He cinched it tight before fitting the bridle and mounting up. He reached out for Chea, who grabbed his arm eagerly, the tiny hand lost inside Hawke's massive paw. "Now, show me where."

The canyon had been hard to find yesterday. The narrow opening to the gorge had grown over since the last time Hawke had been here, and he'd had to take Valiant up to find it. As a consequence they'd made camp only as the sun disappeared behind the ochre cliffs at the end of the blind canyon.

"There. See?" Chea shouted, raising his skinny arm to point at three people clustered at one side of the pool. Further over was an even larger group that Caleb had cordoned off with some of his men. Approaching the roped-off area, Hawke could sense the fear washing back. Caleb saw him coming and hastily cleared a path.

As Hawke rode through, isolated words and snatched-off phrases floated up to him. "We're cursed," "Witchcraft," and "We'll all be murdered."

Guiding his horse carefully through the crowd, Hawke waved away the shouted questions, sliding Chea to the ground as soon as they were inside Caleb's cordon.

"You stay here with the men, Chea. I don't want you seeing this."

He switched his attention to the smaller group over by the pool: Deva, Turps, and another of Caleb's men, his adjutant, Arrowsmith.

Deva spotted him and approached as he dismounted.

"Who is it this time?" he asked as she came within hailing distance.

"A young man and a woman. Turps knows the wagon numbers they came from. There are two sets of beads this time. I left them where they were."

"Who found them?"

"One of the patrols. Arrowsmith was in charge. He's still here, if you want to talk to him."

Hawke nodded, noting the double sets of footprints in the sand leading to the corpses. It looked like they'd come out here to meet one another.

Budding lovers?

Turps looked up as Hawke approached, his hands and shoulders moving into an exaggerated shrug to reinforce the shaking of his head.

He patted the small man on the shoulder, receiving a succession of impressions from the contact. Turps was telepath who, when he wished, could project images of what he'd seen or done. It was obvious from the images Hawke had just reviewed that the two were already dead when Turps had been summoned. Wagon numbers and anxious faces of crying women floated in at the last. Relatives. Hawke recognized the families. Good people.

He squatted down beside the two bodies. They looked to be in their midtwenties, something akin to horror on their faces, frozen there permanently by death. That was new. The other victims had looked surprised, if anything. No other visible signs of violence. Just more of those accursed beads. He reached over and touched the forearm of the dead man. Not completely cold. He couldn't have been here long.

He looked up at Arrowsmith.

"When did you find them?"

"About twenty minutes ago."

He heard someone crunching through the sand behind him, and he turned to look.

Caleb.

Hawke stood, motioning at the growing group of onlookers, and asked, "Any trouble?"

"Not yet, however word is spreading fast. There are a few grumbles, but they're mostly scared. There's a lot of talk of witchcraft and this caravan being cursed."

Hawke grunted as he pushed himself back to his feet. "I'm starting to think that myself," he said dryly. "Did anyone see anything? Anything at all?"

"My men are still checking. So far, nothing. The patrols are on two-hour rotation. The murder occurred during the last one, between 4:00 and 6:00 a.m."

Hawke grimaced. "What a damn, bloody mess. After we've finished here, have some of your men wrap the bodies and return them to their families. I'll call by and speak to them later about the burial. Sooner is probably best, say, this afternoon."

Caleb nodded, motioning for Arrowsmith to organize it. The man saluted and went over to rejoin the other men.

"After breakfast I want the whole caravan interviewed," Hawke said. "Anyone who can't provide a witness to what they were doing between four and six, I want to see personally, got it? I don't care if it takes all day to get through them."

"That'll be a big job," Caleb said.

"We have to do something, and what's more important, we need to be *seen* to be doing something." He turned to Deva. "I'd like your and Neah's help in sensing those who don't have a witness. Better have Mohar in on that as well."

One corner of Deva's mouth crinkled. He recognized it as something she did when there was more to be said. "What is it?" he snapped.

"It's just that I'm not sure the killer will be among those who'll have no one to vouch for them," she replied.

"How so?"

The old woman stared down at the two lifeless bodies as if they might add something. Finally, she said, "I feel the same dank energy here, however, this time it's different. More concentrated. I almost get a sense of two different sets of energy."

"Two? What, murderers?" Hawke exploded.

"It's possible the entity may have replicated itself."

"What, you mean it's reproducing?" Caleb asked.

"Is that possible?" Hawke added.

Deva's eyes lost focus, as if she were tuning in to something. "More like dividing or splitting itself into two rather than reproducing, I'd say. And you know better than most, Hawke, that anything that can be perceived—"

"Can be received. Yes, I'm familiar with the saying."

Caleb shook his head. "If that's true there will now be two hosts—"

"Who will be able to corroborate each other, because they would have been together," Hawke finished for him, nodding.

"I've sent for Neah and Mohar to see if they can pick up anything else. Perhaps together we might do better."

"What if those two were to divide as well?" Caleb asked.

Deva sucked in her thin lips, reluctant to confirm what they all feared. "Then there'd be four. After that eight, then sixteen."

Hawke waved his large hand. "I can count. If that's true, then eventually the whole caravan will kill itself and just disappear, won't it?"

"Yes—if I'm right."

"How long before it spreads again?"

"Well, it's been just over a week since the first murder. It's likely that's the gestation period. The energy for the split is probably bled from the former victims."

"So we have a week?"

"Not necessarily. If the energy for this split was bled from the first victim, then the death of the girl the day before yesterday would mean we only have a few days before the energy of that starts the process over again. That period will probably get shorter as the number of victims increases."

"Surely there must be something we can do? Some way to detect them?"

"Neah and Mohar are here now. I'll go speak with them. There's a full moon tomorrow, it's a fortuitous time for a ceremony. Together we may be able to come up with a potion that will help identify those infected. But there is no guarantee."

She shuffled over to where the other two waited.

Hawke sensed Caleb had something else on his mind, so he resisted his first instinct to join them.

"Have you had a chance to use the bird to check whether the Nuttals followed us?" Caleb asked quietly.

"His name is Valiant, and no, I haven't. I meant to yesterday after he helped us find the entrance to this canyon, but there seemed to be a heaviness in him, or maybe it was me. Either way, we were stretching it even for that short joining time. He didn't have the energy to go far. Admittedly, I've been using him a lot lately. It takes a lot out of both of us."

Caleb looked up, surveying the rugged cliffs that ringed the blind end of the canyon. "This place makes me nervous. There's only one way in—and out. The Nuttals are excellent trackers. Even if we managed to fool them back at the road, it wouldn't take much to pick up our trail. There are too many wagons and beasts."

"Agreed. What's your point?"

"There's nothing to stop them from blocking off the only exit and then positioning archers on the cliffs up there to pick off my men. That done, they could just round the rest of the caravan up like so many sheep."

Hawke followed his gaze. It was possible. Archers in the right place could decimate the caravan from up there, and the Nuttals were second only to the Shaylene in their accuracy.

"You're saying I may have led us into a trap?"

"I could take a patrol out and check."

"No. If they are coming, there's no point advertising where we are." He looked around. Spotting Chea with the soldiers, he whistled to catch the boy's attention, motioning him over.

Chea ran toward him as if he'd been waiting to be called.

Hawke met him partway, shepherding him around the bodies to the rocky base of the cliff. Squatting down, he pointed up.

"Do you think you could climb up there, lad? I need to know whether you can see any riders coming this way. It's a long way. Can you do it?"

Chea nodded once, his face alight with the challenge.

"Then go. And be careful, mind."

Hawke watched as he scampered up the rock face past the spring that fed the deep pond at the base of the cliff. There were plenty of handholds, and Chea's limber young body made the most of all of them.

Nearing the top, one of his bare feet slipped, sending a spray of pebbles down to bounce off the jagged outcrops. Hawke inhaled sharply, holding his breath until Chea recovered and reestablished his hold. Using more caution, he navigated the last few meters, then hauled himself over the lip of the canyon wall. Hawke felt himself relax a little.

He cleared his throat and started packing his pipe. Minutes dragged by. Caleb joined him. Soon after, the other three came over.

"Is that Chea up there?" Neah asked, squinting at the small figure moving along the edge of the high cliff.

"Yes. Caleb's afraid the Nuttals might still be following us."

Chea moved out of their line of sight. "Where the devil has that boy gone now?" Hawke mumbled, firing up the pipe and puffing on it furiously.

"There," Caleb said, his arm stretching, finger pointing the way. Chea had appeared further along, his brown skin almost invisible against the dun color of the rock.

Soon after, he lowered himself over the edge and began the descent. When he was almost down, Hawke strode over and lifted him the rest of the way. The others trailed after him.

"What did you see, lad?" Hawke asked.

"Men on horseback, Master Hawke. Many men, maybe forty, coming this way. Very fast."

"How far away? Could you tell?" Caleb asked.

The boy shrugged, bringing his thumb and forefinger close together. "They were this big."

"Could you see the road from up there, Chea?" Caleb tried again, his voice patient. "How far between here and the road were the men?"

Chea grinned. "Half—they were halfway."

Caleb sniffed. "On fast horses they could be here in a matter of hours."

Hawke jammed the pipe into the corner of his mouth, leaving his words to slide around it.

"So, any suggestions?" His bushy white brows lifted hopefully.

"I say we take some men, pretend to engage, then break off, try to get some of them to follow. It might split their number," Neah said.

"And it might not," Caleb said. "Why would they chase a half-dozen men when they know there's a whole caravan to be had? You'd just be making it easier for them by splitting our own force."

"What do you suggest? Wait here to be killed off like rats?" Neah's chin jutted in defiance.

"No. I agree that going out to meet them is better than waiting here. This canyon is indefensible, particularly once the Nuttals realize they can deploy archers from those cliffs at our rear. And they will."

"You're saying we take them head-on?" Hawke blustered. "We don't have enough men for that."

"No. But we can lay an ambush for them where they least expect it."

———

THE SMALL GROUP SWUNG EAST, riding hard, Caleb at the front leading the eight heavily armed men.

"I think we have company." Mohar's voice intruded.

Caleb glanced back over his shoulder. A single rider was coming up
behind them fast.

Whoever it was rode well. He brought up the eyeglass that Hawke had loaned him, and muttered a curse, snapping it shut.

"Unbelievable!"

Neah reined in as she neared, slowing Magic first to a lazy canter then a determined walk. She was wearing a calico peasant blouse, the usual swirling skirt gathered into leggings and tucked into calf-length riding boots, her long unruly hair bound—far from tamed—by a red bandana tied behind her head. Across her chest were two broad bandoliers bristling with arrows, the fletching brightly colored in the Shaylene tradition. Caleb urged his horse over to intercept her, blocking the way. Mohar followed a couple of paces behind. The dust trail in her wake caught up and settled over them.

"What the hell are you doing? Is something wrong back there?" he shouted.

"No. I'm going with you." Her mare danced a little, and Caleb caught a glimpse of the distinctive shape of a Shaylene bow and more arrows in a quiver attached to the back of her saddle. It brought back unwelcome memories of the battle for the ridge. There had been too many brightly colored arrows that day.

"The hell you are. Turn around while there's time. I can't spare a man to take you back."

"I didn't ask for a *man* to take me anywhere. I'm here to help. The same as you," she said.

"I don't have time to argue this. Go back. Now. And take your toy arrows with you." Caleb tugged on the bridle, bringing his horse about.

He heard the familiar low whistle of a loosed arrow and its distinctive thunk. It landed between the front hooves of his stallion, the shaft trembling with the impact. The horse snorted, startled, and would have reared had not Caleb borne down with his knees and gentling words.

"Is that meant to impress me?" he said, turning, his voice cold.

She ignored him, kicking forward, and leaned down to sweep up the spent arrow. She sighted along the shaft, checking it for trueness, before slipping it back into the bandolier, then leaned over, her face inches from Caleb's.

"What do you hope to do with this piddling number of soldiers anyway? If I were a man wishing to join, would you still say no? Well, I am a better archer and rider than any man here. Including you."

Caleb closed his eyes.

"I'm not disputing that," he said finally. "But I don't trust you, Neah, and what's worse, you're unpredictable. As a battle group we need to move as one, and I need to be able to rely on that."

"Oh, by unpredictable do you mean emotional?" she scoffed,

straightening in the saddle. "This from the man so in touch with his own feelings. Tell me then, *Commander*, what would you gain if I didn't ride with you?"

"Some peace for a start," he said, swinging around to face her, "and hopefully my *men* and I will be able to take out enough Nuttals to drive them off. That'll only happen if everyone works together. That's why we have the Sworn. It makes for a more efficient fighting machine. Having someone who isn't part of that endangers them and undermines the trust of the unit. It's my job to make sure that doesn't happen."

"That may be your job, but let me tell you what you're really doing. I can read your intent, Commander. It's written all over your face like a poorly written farce. You plan to die—gloriously. Nobly leading your own bunch of slaves, your so-called Sworn, to a redeeming death. Sadly, though, no one gets saved—bar you, of course, redeemed by your perverted way of seeing the world through a blood-hazed blur. Tell me it isn't so.

"Wizard," she called, turning to Mohar, "am I right? You know what he's thinking—more the pity you."

Caleb raised his arm, finger pointing back the way she'd come. "Go. I will not be responsible for you."

Mohar spurred his horse forward, angling it between them. "Before you two kill each other, can I just say, she may have a point," he said, adding belatedly, "Commander."

Caleb felt the blood rush to his head and he was about to order Mohar back when the wizard shook his head wistfully, and raised his hand, palm out. Caleb found that his voice had vanished. He could move his lips, however the sound was trapped somewhere near his larynx, as if the passageway had become too narrow for whole words to squeeze past, only isolated letters, which came out as vowel-type grunts.

Caleb felt his face going red with the effort. Neah, watching, suppressed a chuckle, then, when she realized what was happening, laughed out loud. Caleb became more agitated, which only made her laugh all the more.

"Listen. Both of you," Mohar said, catching the bridles of their two horses in either hand. "Neah is right about one thing, Caleb. We don't stand a chance attacking them, whether head-on or from ambush as you suggested. Once the initial shock is past, their numbers will overwhelm us." Mohar made a gesture and Caleb felt something release at the back of his throat.

He rubbed it before adding with an aspirated croak, "If we hit them hard enough, they'll break and run."

"Perhaps. Though I, like her, won't follow you along any gory glory trail."

"So now you're on her side."

"No, I'm on my side. It's called survival. Think about the alternatives. With Neah's access to magic combined with what little I have left available to me, we may be able to do something. Perhaps create a diversion, or an illusion that will buy you enough time to inflict some real damage without killing everyone in the process. What do you say?"

Caleb ground his teeth together. He didn't know whether he was more infuriated with Neah for calling out what he hadn't allowed himself to be aware of, or Mohar for siding with her.

"Using *magic*?" he spat the word out.

Mohar nodded.

Caleb fumed, logic finally forging a path through to his strategic brain.

"All right—for now. But keep her out of my way. She's your responsibility, wizard."

Tugging his reins away from Mohar, he used knees and heels to guide his horse back to the main group, fury bubbling inside him. Arrowsmith looked hot inside his quilted brown leather vest with mail beneath. He wiped the sweat from his forehead and gave Caleb a quizzical look, anxious to get moving again. Caleb signaled impatiently for him to take the lead, and their small party set off in an easy canter, the emotional afterwash of the clash with Neah still sloshing around inside him.

What was my motivation for coming out here? Surely the witch couldn't be that right? Yet Mohar, who seems to have a direct channel into my brain, all but agreed with her. Am I that hidden—even from myself?

He tried to reason it through. One part of him clearly acknowledged the enormity of the task they faced, however, he was used to challenges, thrived on them usually.

"But they were always calculated risks."

Mohar?

He was finding it more difficult to separate the wizard's implanted thoughts from his own. Not that it mattered in this instance, because the answer was the same. There was no cap to the risk of this mission, and he wondered what price he was truly prepared to pay to ease his shame.

THEY RODE FOR ANOTHER HOUR, reaching a dry watercourse flanked on either side by jagged cliffs. The deep ruts from their caravan's passing the day before were still gouged into the coarse sand. Caleb mentally signaled a dismount; Neah, at the periphery of their party, seemed to catch on and swung down as well, the strangely curved bow in her hands, an arrow already nocked.

"Arrowsmith, get the men to dig here and here, and over there beside those rocks. The Nuttals are certain to come this way. It would take too long to go around, and they won't be expecting us. Get the men to work together, dig holes deep enough for each to lie facedown in. Use one of those hollow reeds to breathe through. Mohar and I will come around and cover you up with a layer of sand once you're in."

Arrowsmith saluted and moved off.

"Come on," he said to Mohar, clambering over the scree and

scrawny bushes at the base of the cliffs. "Let's see how much time we have before company arrives."

They wended their way up, moving across rather than directly up the rocks. The surface was jagged with sharp edges, and whole outcrops were often unable to support their weight and flaked off in shale-like sheets to shatter against the cliff face before showering razor-tipped shards to the sand below.

When they reached a relatively level slab about halfway up, Caleb paused and slipped the eyeglass out his pocket, sweeping the plain.

"There." He pointed, handing the glass to Mohar. "They're still a good hour distant. Judging from the size of the dust cloud, I'd say Chea was slightly out. I estimate there's at least fifty or sixty riders coming, probably closer to sixty."

"Sixty?" Mohar said. "It looks more like an army to me."

"Compared to nine, it is."

Caleb looked down at the strip of sand and the men moving frantically below. "It's a clear field of fire from this spot. I'll station Neah here. She won't like it, but if she is the best archer we have, then let her show us. Her job will be to stop the Nuttals from falling back once the attack begins."

"Like locking the back door," Mohar said, stretching out to look over the edge.

"Exactly. So, what can she really do? Magically I mean—if it comes to that?" Caleb asked.

Mohar shrugged, fingers scratching at his cheek through the matted beard. "If you mean is she all talk, no, definitely not. I saw her and Deva work with that dagger, experienced it, in fact. I sense your question is more how can you use what she has to best advantage, am I right?"

Caleb nodded.

"Well, talent is a funny thing," Mohar said. "I've found it tends to clump toward a specialty of some kind. One person may be fine predictor of the future, but is hopeless when it comes to casting a circular spell or preparing a healing potion. Another the opposite. Some, a very few, are all-rounders able to direct energy with purpose toward almost any end. I believe Neah is one of those, though her ability to direct a lot of power is limited."

"And you?"

"Once I could, which is why I recognize the energy surrounding her. Now," he shook his head, "most of that's been taken from me. I retain the knowledge, and worse the memory of what I once was, but not the power to summon it. It's a cruel and bitter concoction. Part of my punishment."

"For what?" Caleb asked, curious for the first time.

Mohar snorted. "That's a story best left alone. What you need to think about now is how can you enlist Neah's real ability. That won't be easy. I don't know if you've noticed, but she really doesn't like you." He grinned, his strong teeth showing bright against the blackness of his beard.

"Nor I her. I don't know what it is. Every time I see her I get this overwhelming rush of anger. Everything goes red, like I'm looking through blood."

"Like it or not, you need her for this. Go talk to her. Ask her opinion. Remember, the odds are still nine against sixty," Mohar said. "And make her think it's her idea. What is it you want from her, anyway?"

"I want the Nuttals to think that there's a hundred of us when we attack."

"Create a grand illusion?" Mohar nodded. "I like it. You'll need her to cast it though. I can't."

"What would you do if you could? In case she asks."

"Illusion works best when it has something to work from. We will have, what, nine men covered with sand?"

Caleb nodded.

"Then we use that number as a baseboard to create replicas, ten of each. By the time we're finished it will look like you have your full century of troops. At least until the fighting starts—it may even intim-idate them enough to scatter, even surrender."

"Nuttals don't surrender. We'll have to kill them, and the best way to do that is to take them by surprise. The illusion will help with that. Let's get back down."

They retraced their steps down the cliff.

By the time they reached the bottom, all the holes had been dug.

"Good. Good," Caleb said, inspecting each, his boot nudging the edge of one, cascading sand into the hole. "Make this one a little wider and not so deep; we want to hide the men, not bury them."

"Not yet anyway," Mohar mumbled.

Caleb tied his stallion off beneath one of the gnarly, stunted trees that flanked the old riverbed. He poured out a measure of feed for the horse to munch on. In the army men and beasts took their rest where they could. They would hide the horses further back into the gorge when the time came.

He still hadn't spoken to Neah. Mohar was right of course. Much as he hated to admit it, he needed her skills if this mission was going to have any chance of success. One thing he'd learned: putting off hard decisions was a surefire way to turn pain into needless suffering. It was like a deep sword wound. After dressing it needed to be left, allowed to settle and give the healing time to start. After that, action needed to be swift and decisive. If the bandage wasn't changed, the wound would fester and, if still not dealt with, would ultimately poison and kill the whole being.

He took a deep breath and exhaled it slowly before walking over to where she was sprawled, napping in the dappled shade beside her horse. Twenty paces further Mohar was finishing concealing one of the men beneath a thin layer of sand. The distance between Caleb and Neah was less than ten paces, yet it felt like a gulf so wide he could barely sense the shape of the other side.

She started awake as he came close, her hand closing around the handle of a dagger sashed at her waist.

"What do you want?" she snapped, dragging herself into a seated position. Her hand remained on the dagger.

He stopped five paces away and eased himself into an easy squat. Neah's fingers loosened their grip on the knife, but did not move away.

"I'd like to ask your advice." He looked at her in what he hoped was a nonchallenging way.

"What about?"

"Maybe you were right and I was doing this mission for all the wrong reasons. I don't really know, however, I do agree I—we—have a larger responsibility to protect the caravan, which I will do my utmost to respect."

"Go on." Her hand moved, hovering over the dagger for a moment before shifting to her head to tuck a wisp of rebellious hair back through the red bandana.

"Mohar was right," Caleb went on. "The one advantage we have is your, his and your combined abilities. What I'm unsure of is how they can be deployed."

Caleb had been concerned that the words would stick in his throat. So far they'd flowed with relative ease.

She said nothing, staring at her boots.

"He suggested an illusion," he prompted.

"Of what?" she said, finally turning to him, hand moving back to the belt at her waist, lingering close, though not yet on the knife.

"He says I should ask you."

"Your wizard has more sense than you."

"I don't dispute that," Caleb said, surprised to realize it was the truth.

Neah drew her knees up, hugging them against her chest. "You are asking me to put my hatred of you aside."

"For now. For the sake of this mission. For the sake of those waiting back at the canyon. I'd like to put whatever happened that night behind us."

Neah reared up. "Whatever happened? I remember everything

about that night. You took advantage of me. You are no different to any of the others." She snatched the scarf away from her neck, pointing viciously at the scars along her collarbone. "Do you think these are the marks of a victim? No, these are proof of my resistance. I fought these men, each and every one of them, and I came out stronger. I cannot put this behind me."

Caleb felt a rush of red anger wash over him. This time it turned inwards. He had no defenses against Neah's words. The guilt of that day and the disabling doubt surrounding his own inability to resist, or even remember what happened, had already scored deep channels into his self-confidence. Now it rushed in anew, filling the runnels to overflow and cascade down into recrimination.

Caleb felt something shift inside him. The guilt remained. Now there was nowhere further for him to fall. He was at the very bottom, and somehow knowing that gave him strength.

"You're right. It was my responsibility to resist whatever happened that night. That's my job. To resist, to be stronger than the enemy no matter what form it takes. I failed." He paused, then added, "For what it's worth, I'm sorry for whatever I said—and did. However, we are now in a situation where I and my men need your help."

She looked away then inhaled, her eyes closing briefly. When she opened them she returned her gaze to him and nodded decisively. "Very well. For now. But later, when I have the chance, I will still kill you. I rarely forget and never forgive. Do you accept?"

"Yes."

"What is it you wish to know?"

"I know about strategy, and what it takes to lead men into war. However, I know nothing of magic. I don't even know what I don't know. What are our options here?"

The corner of her mouth tugged upward briefly before the full lips compressed into a noncommittal line.

"Imagine," she ventured finally, her voice testing, as if she was unsure of the ground but nevertheless prepared to take the first tentative step. "There are three men in front of you. All are holding a gold ring and each tells you they can make it disappear. They all wave their hands and the rings vanish. The first man has used sleight of hand—the ring is still there, hidden somewhere on his person. The second is still holding the ring in his hand—he has used illusion to make you think you have seen something you have not."

"And the third?" Caleb asked, genuinely interested.

"With him the ring is truly gone, either transformed to some other shape or substance or sent to another place that only he knows the way back from. This third way is what practitioners call the true path. Apart from talent and the ritual in knowing what to do, it also requires time to prepare plus ready access to a reservoir of energy. This, like a flint, will ignite and direct the fuel that the mage calls forth. Hence the need for a coven, or supplicants to draw on. None of which is available to us here."

"Leaving illusion?" he said. "Mohar said something about replication?"

"To do what?"

"My men will be lying facedown covered with sand when the Nuttals ride through. When they rise up I want to make it appear like there are ten of them for each one."

"The burying technique is one of the Nuttals' own strategies. That's what they do."

"Which may be precisely why it might work. They won't be expecting it."

"Perhaps," she acknowledged grudgingly. "For this to work your men will need to have a kill rate of three to one."

"They can do it. Three seconds to aim and shoot is a stretch, I admit. We'll probably get ten seconds before the shock wears off and the Nuttals seek cover. During that time they'll be in close range. It's unlikely any of my men will miss."

"Your men will need that ten seconds to find cover for themselves."

"I estimate four." He waved his arm. "All the holes we dug have been positioned close to rock falls. Easy to roll behind, giving them six seconds to get off an initial two volleys."

"Two, possibly three arrows at best, depending on how well they reload. Assuming all run true, that's only taking down half the Nuttals."

"I'd planned to have you positioned up there. Crossfire is always more devastating; it creates confusion and uncertainty."

"Even that would leave twenty alive. Two to one. From defended positions."

Caleb nodded. "Still manageable. We've dealt with worse."

She shook her head and more hair sprang from the confines of the bandana. "Perhaps, however the bigger issue is that replication won't work with Nuttals. Illusion requires the subject to have an active imagination in order to superimpose one reality upon it. Nuttals have virtually none. Their needs are basic, their minds little better than those of beasts. Apart from the driver of survival, they are governed by the base emotions of need: greed, lust, and fear."

"Surely their fear can be amplified by illusion?"

"To what end? More fighting? Nuttals will not run. Fear will only drive them to fight harder."

Caleb mentally conceded she was right.

"So that leaves what? Sleight of hand?"

"Not just that. There may be another way."

Neah smiled for the first time, staring into the space between them at something only she could see.

ELEVEN

"Form up," Caleb yelled, using his knees to urge the stallion along the ragged line of men.

They were nervous. Through the Sworn link Caleb was often aware of emotions filtering from the other side, like backwash from a full drain. He returned to the front of the column beside Neah and Mohar.

"Are they ready?" she asked, without looking back, her attention caught by the approaching Nuttals now less than a mile away.

"I don't think anyone is ever ready to die," Mohar said in a monotone.

"Then let's hope it doesn't come to that." She tugged off the bandana and shook out her hair. The light headwind caught it playfully, streaming the long wavy tresses behind her as she trotted ahead.

"Move out," Caleb called over his shoulder, following her, a respectful half a horse length behind. Mohar followed suit on the opposite side.

As far as plans went this one was sketchy and reliant on factors totally outside his control. What was more, he realized he was being forced to place all his trust in the one person who'd betrayed him, and he wondered again how he'd come to agree to it.

"Because it's the best chance we have."

Caleb grunted, more to shut Mohar up than agree with him.

In front, Neah slowed Magic to a walk as three large figures peeled away from the Nuttals' pack and galloped toward them, their banshee cries shrill and piercing even at this distance.

"Steady," Caleb called back to the men. "Arms to ready."

The distinctive grate of swords sliding free of scabbards underscored the battle cries from the three Nuttals. Neah reined in and waited patiently for them.

Fifty yards. Thirty, then twenty, and still they didn't slow. Caleb willed his horse to hold. The stallion was strong, though not yet blooded and remained skittish, his nostrils flaring at the eerie battle cries from the frenzied group who seemed intent on riding right over the top of them.

There was jingle of harness behind him, as if a rider was tightening his grip on the bridle. Teetering. On the edge of running. Caleb turned his head.

"Stand and stay, man," he growled.

Closer, Caleb could make out the Nuttals' features.

In front, Neah's back remained straight and erect, hugging the curves of the Shaylene bow strapped to it. The poise of a queen.

Somehow Neah had altered her appearance and her demeanor to become more like Shayla. If Caleb hadn't watched her and Mohar do it, he would have sworn it was the warrior queen herself riding ahead of him.

Barely two horse lengths away, the Nuttals swung their mounts to one side and simply stopped, ceasing their bloodcurdling cries at the same time. A deep silence washed over them, both sides studying each other.

The Nuttals were barely human, with yellow eyes set more to the side than the front of their faces, while long, coarse manes blew wild and unkempt about oversized heads. Their broad nostrils were in constant movement, twitching and flaring, registering—Caleb was almost sure—much more than scents and odor. Around their necks were eyeballs, scooped live from the heads of dying victims. They were strung in ghoulish garlands that swiveled on their cord as if they were somehow still keeping watch.

The largest Nuttal walked his horse forward, looking at Neah critically, eyes narrowing as his quivering nostrils fed back additional information. Suddenly he smiled, or his black lips stretched sideways, revealing long white teeth that had been filed to glistening points.

"Queen Shayla." He made a pretense of bowing from the bare back of his ragged mountain pony. The string of eyeballs dipped and swayed too, giving the impression of being watched by multiple eyes. Caleb had the feeling that several of them were turned toward him and staring.

Neah nodded in response.

"Winterdom, isn't it?" she asked, tilting her head slightly. Her words held an edge, as if she was forcing herself to be pleasant.

"The same." His voice would have been guttural save for a broad roll of the vowels that lent the edges a purring quality. "I am surprised to find you so far from your lines—and in the company of Commonwealth men. Have you been captured and are in need of rescue?"

Neah smiled as one might to a young child. "They are in my thrall. Can you not see the mark in their eyes? I have been seeking you."

"Seeking us?" Winterdom said, looking back, hand to his chest, brow raised. "We are honored indeed, are we not, brothers? Or should we be afraid? Is that why your slaves have their weapons bared?"

"I did not know what reception we might receive. Then I did not know I would be meeting with the Slave Master himself."

Neah made a wave of her hand, and Caleb signaled for the men to sheath their weapons.

"Who else would it be?" Winterdom asked. "I am responsible for supply. Your war is hungry, and stocks are low."

He waited.

Nuttals may not have much imagination, but they were incredibly shrewd and cunning.

"Which is precisely why I have come to meet with you. My men have captured a large caravan just near here. I understand you have one as well. I would like to negotiate to buy yours."

"You have already captured this other caravan?" Winterdom asked, surprise rippling across his face.

"Yes. The rest of my men wait with it in a canyon not far from here."

"This is why you have personally ridden behind the lines of your enemies. To catch slaves? Your army must truly be desperate." He barked out a laugh, its sound harsh and savage.

The other two brothers joined in a fraction later, lending the combined sound a hyena quality. Neah waited until it had stopped. Caleb noticed a twitching around Neah's nose, as if she had smelled something foul.

"Why I do things is of no concern to you. You know I pay well—and reliably. Selling the slaves you have will save us both much time and effort." Neah's mouth stretched into a smile as she touched the purse at her belt.

"They are mostly old. Why would you waste your valuable time with such as these?" Winterdom countered.

"If that is so then I am sure you'll make an appropriate adjustment to the price," she responded.

Winterdom turned his pony with a flick of the reins, and the three Nuttals huddled together, speaking in their native tongue, their voices rough and grating. It was obvious after a time that the other two didn't agree with Winterdom. Caleb wondered which way the power would flow amongst the brothers.

Winterdom finally cut them off with a flick of his hand. Nudging the pony, he turned it until he was facing Neah once more.

"My brothers are curious. Why you are so anxious to have these particular slaves?"

"You mean they want to charge me more because I have come personally."

"Perhaps. I reminded them that you are our biggest customer—"

"I am your only customer," Neah snapped. "The Commonwealth doesn't abide slavery, so your only other markets are across the wide sea, and you have no sea gate for that. Shore is the closest, but its ports are still held by the Commonwealth."

"But under siege from your army. We are hopeful of an early liberation for the ports of Shore," Winterdom said, the purr returning to his voice.

"How much?" Neah asked.

Winterdom glanced behind him, as if he could see the slaves assembled there, assessing their bag worth. "Three thousand. Gold, torians or equivalent weight."

Neah scoffed, holding up three fingers. "Three hundred."

"Two thousand, five hundred."

"What?" Neah said. "I offered three hundred. Two and a half thousand is outrageous. I could buy a whole city for that."

"Then perhaps you should do that. That is our price. My brothers want three, however, I am more reasonable. Unless you'd like to tell us precisely why you want these particular slaves."

Neah said nothing, and the tension ratcheted up. Caleb could feel perspiration slick against his back, pooling, then trickling along his spine. The sun, while low in the sky, was still baking hot. Mentally, Caleb screamed at her to say something. This was going on for too long. *Just pay the beasts what they want.*

"Patience, Caleb. Drain the anger from your face and shift your eyes downward. You are supposed to be in her thrall, there should be no emotion showing."

Too late. Winterdom's sharp gaze caught his, and he pointed at Caleb.

"This man. The commander. He has the look of a free man."

"He is supposed to," Neah said, her tone sharp and commanding. "We are here clandestinely I cannot have them all looking like drones in case we are intercepted by the Commonwealth. The commander is held and completely manageable. That's enough," Neah said.

Caleb felt Mohar push through a mental charge and he started, his face registering sharp pain.

"Damn the man."

The Nuttal smiled and nodded, assuming Neah was responsible. Winterdom's question, however, still hung in the air between them. Caleb's hand tightened on the handle of his battle cutlass as the silence stretched out. There was no good answer to why Shayla would be out here miles from her army, exposed and virtually unprotected. That had been what Caleb had flagged to her and Mohar earlier. Neither had an answer for it.

Finally she spoke.

"Very well. I am told that the Torian's successor is on one of these two caravans. I don't know which. If so, I want to make sure both caravans don't make it to Carmelsara."

The two Nuttal brothers sniggered. Winterdom snorted loudly.

"The Torian's successor? That would be worth three thousand, much more perhaps." He looked back at his brothers, the maniacal grin wide.

"Whoever it is remains undeclared. The new Torian may not be in your caravan at all."

"And if he is, you mean to remove him?"

"Or her. Yes. Once I identify who it is."

"Or you could just kill them all."

"Now that would be a waste. An army needs more than soldiers to be victorious. I'll give you one thousand, five hundred, plus a guarantee of first access to a Shore port and a ship before winter."

"Winter is looming," Winterdom said.

"So is victory. Once I can assure myself that there will be no rival Torian to split the Commonwealth."

Winterdom glanced back to his brothers once more. One nodded, and the other shook his head violently.

Winterdom paused, considering. His nostrils twitched. Finally he said, "Done."

"Good. I have two hundred gold in my pouch. You'll take my mark for the rest and deliver the slaves to Roganshah. My burgher will pay you the rest."

Winterdom nodded, catching the purse and weighing it in one hand when she tossed it.

He nodded again, this time at his two brothers. With an earsplitting cry, Winterdom wheeled his horse and galloped back the way he'd come. The other two followed, their own cries joining with his.

"Always love to see a happy customer," Mohar said.

"Hopefully they'll not come back for a refund," Caleb said. "That was almost too easy."

"What were all those eyes around their necks?" Mohar asked.

"The Nuttals cut them from their victims at the moment of death. Afterwards they are dipped in lacquer to preserve them, and then strung. They believe the soul lingers in the eyes and that wearing them will give them power. They particularly like blue, I'm told," Caleb said, looking pointedly at Mohar.

"Lucky old me," Mohar mumbled. "Anyway, they seemed happy enough.""Why wouldn't they?" Neah cut in, her tone cold. "At open market they wouldn't have made more than twelve hundred."

"What's the matter with you? That went as well as could be expected," Caleb said. "It sounds like you're disappointed that no one died."

"They might once they try and redeem that mark you gave them to exchange for gold at Roganshah," Mohar said.

"It's a week to travel there and another back, we'll be well gone by then," Caleb said. "Besides, Nuttals are pragmatic. They have a purse full of gold and still have the slaves to sell."

"I hate them," Neah said, the words tumbling over each other. "I hate slavery, and they are the ones who perpetuate it. It was all I could do not to unloose three arrows into them, except I'm sure they have no hearts to pierce."

"But you seemed to know them," Mohar said.

"The three that rode out to meet us are brothers. Winterdom likes to think of himself as their leader. Mother always said the one who shook his head has the final say. I was surprised that Winterdom overrode him. He may yet convince the other two to circle back. It was obvious all of them were surprised to find Shayla out here."

"Their noses were twitching. Maybe they could tell you didn't smell like Shayla," Caleb said.

"Nuttals do have keen noses," she conceded. "Smelling is their primary sense, actually."

"Oh, now she remembers." Caleb slapped his thigh in exasperation, irritation slipping through, sharpening the edge of his words.

"Don't worry, they've only ever met Shayla once and that was at her coronation. There were a lot of people—and smells—milling about. It's unlikely they would have laid down a scent signature for her."

"How many times have you met them?" Caleb asked.

"Never. I know them by sight and reputation, that's all."

"That's something," Caleb grumbled.

She bristled. "At least with my plan we all remained alive. I recall that was the big drawback with yours. Why are you always so negative?"

"I'm cursed." He looked at her meaningfully. "Remember?"

Neah's face tightened. It was as if a mask were being pulled over her features, shielding any evidence of emotion.

With a toss of her head she used her heels to nudge Magic away.

"Insufferable witch," Caleb mumbled.

"That may be so, but she did pull it off. I don't think I heard you say thank you for that," Mohar said.

"For what? It could just as easily have fallen apart. You heard her. She hates the bastards. Even I could tell there was something wrong.

Just imagine what emotions the twitching nostril triplets picked up from her."

"You're concerned they might return."

It wasn't a question.

"That's why I don't intend to hang around." He stared across at Neah. "There's something she's not telling us," Caleb said, gnawing at the issue like a dog over a meat-stripped bone.

"Well, if there is I can't see her sharing it now. Particularly with you."

"We better get started back." Caleb swung his horse around and called for the men to come into formation. He turned to face them.

"There'll be a full moon tonight, or near enough to see by. I want to get back to the caravan as soon as we can. We'll ride in pairs; make sure you watch out for each other."

He spurred his horse into a canter. Caleb could feel anger spiking through his efforts at control. Neah was right. They were all alive. Yet this subterfuge of fooling the Nuttals didn't seem right either. Something about it felt unfinished. He just hoped the Nuttals didn't think so too.

THE NIGHT WAS awash with opaque silver and long shadows. The moon, while reflecting sufficient light to see by, held none of daylight's nuanced subtleties, and as a consequence one of the horses had stepped in a hole and broken its leg. They'd had to put the mare down.

This had slowed them, so it was not until midnight that they sighted the concealed entrance to the canyon. Caleb reined in to wait for the rest of the company, the two men sharing one mount trailing. They had spread the extra weight around the horses to preserve their stamina, resulting in more breaks than Caleb would have liked.

Mohar joined him. Caleb was standing in his stirrups searching the horizon. Satisfied, he struck a flint, ignited the taper in a lamp, and swung it twice. After a moment it was reciprocated from within the thick foliage.

"If the Nuttals are out there we'll have led them straight to the caravan."

"They would have found it anyway. No, my bet is they'll wait to see what we do once we make it back to the road. They'll be expecting us to turn toward Roganshah."

"And when we don't?"

"That's when I predict they may get a little too curious."

TWELVE

Neah was awake beneath closed eyelids, allowing the sun to explore her face. They'd ridden through the night and she'd been exhausted when they finally found the entrance to the canyon. After that Deva had insisted she and Mohar join her in performing the full moon ritual to prepare an essence to identify the murdering entities within the camp. All of them had been so tired there was little energy to pour into it, but finally they'd managed to come up with something. It would be a start.

Beneath her the familiar bump and grinding-sway of the wagon told her that the caravan was already underway. The sounds and smells of sun-warmed beasts and men drifted in. She opened her eyes. A patina of fine dust had settled on the cot's counterpane.

Mother must have opened the window.

From outside she heard Caleb's voice, distantly calling. "Tighten up there."

She chanced a look through the window, angling her head so she could see along the line of wagons. The day was already in full shine and there he was, happily giving orders, though he must be just as exhausted as she.

From here he looked fresh. Nothing like she felt.

How does he do that?

Even the uncustomary whiskers on his chin and face were sleek and somehow groomed. Neah just felt grimy. She could smell her own unwashed body, trapped within the weave of the bedding. She hadn't had a full hot bath since leaving Roganshah. Her sleep-deprived mind swayed to sweet memories of daily steaming baths back in the palace, the water right up to her chin with wonderful, foaming soaps. And afterward, fragrant exotic oils, their rich essence released as they were rubbed into her warm and receptive skin....

"Neah. Did you hear what I said?" Deva sounded testy, her head appearing through the curtained flap at the front of the wagon.

"No." Neah flopped back down, irrationally grumpy that she'd been denied even the memory of cleanliness and luxury.

"I said, do you want to eat? I saved you some breakfast. We're not stopping for lunch. Hawke wants to make the road as soon as he can. I think I see it up ahead now."

The road? Have I been asleep that long?

Groaning, she rolled out of bed and pulled on a pair of her least filthy leggings along with a torn blouse. She dragged a red leather jerkin over the top, and was still wrapping the multicolored scarf about her neck when she joined Deva on the bench seat.

Mother had been right. The road was visible in the distance, stretching interminably off in both directions. Heat shimmers made its surface appear like a ribbon of water.

Neah accepted a bowl of cold porridge and knob of crusty bread. She used two fingers to scoop the porridge into her mouth. In between gulps she twisted in her seat, eyes narrowing, dividing the horizon into quartered chunks, examining each of them closely.

"Still worried about the Nuttals?" Deva asked.

"They can't be trusted."

"Caleb sent out patrols several times this morning in case they were dogging us. They found no trace."

"That means nothing. Nuttals are only visible when they want to be. You know that. That fool wouldn't know what to look for anyway." Neah licked her fingers and put aside the empty bowl before tearing off a chunk of the fresh bread.

"And you do?" Deva asked, her cheeks creasing into a smile.

"I need to pee," Neah said, changing the subject.

"We won't be stopping until we make camp tonight. Better use the pot."

Still munching on the bread, Neah eased back into the relative coolness of the wagon and slid the chamber pot from beneath the bed. She squatted over it, idly watching the horizon glide by through the window. A shadow suddenly appeared, blocking the light.

"Ah, there you are," Caleb said, staring in, his eyes widening when he realized what she was doing.

"Get away," she yelled, hurling the last piece of crust at him. It caught his cheek and he disappeared toward the front of the wagon.

Hastily she finished her flow and secured the lid before resuming the seat beside Deva, cheeks burning. Caleb's horse was matching pace.

"Sorry about that," he said, fingers moving to the brim of his hat. "But you did have the window open."

"And that's an invitation for every pervert on this caravan to peer in?" she fired back.

He shrugged. "I came by to say that, well... you were right yesterday. I just wanted to say, you know, thanks."

The word sounded strange, as if his lips and mouth had little practice with shaping it, and even less comfort in allowing it out.

"For what?" she asked, peculiarly irritated.

Why does he always make me feel like I have to justify myself?

"For yesterday. Saving my men," he mumbled, looking away, avoiding her eyes.

They had both been speaking across Deva, who continued to stare directly ahead at the horses' rumps as if she couldn't hear them.

He cleared his throat. "I also came by to tell you—both of you— we'll be making camp by the main road tonight."

"Is that safe?" Deva asked, joining the conversation.

"Safer than turning toward Carmelsara. In case the Nuttals are watching. Chances are, though, they're already back at Strophos Well."

"The moon will still be bright tonight."

Caleb pointed south. Clouds were clumping over the distant mountains. "Hawke said we'll have cloud cover and rain by nightfall." He paused, then asked, "Speaking of full moons, Deva, were you able to come up with anything last night? Hawke is worried about these camp murders starting up again."

Deva sighed. "We distilled a full moon essence after Neah and Mohar returned. Whether it will work...." She shrugged.

"That's something to try at least. I'll tell Hawke."

Caleb rode off.

"You're too hard on him. He came to apologize," Deva said.

"That was an apology?" Neah forced a laugh. "For which insult, I wonder?"

THE RAIN STARTED AFTER SUNSET, just as they'd packed away the pots following the evening meal. It soon worked itself into a deluge, turning the loose dust of their campsite into thick, cloying mud. Water puddled then pooled in the circular center space of the wagons' defensive eight formation. Inside their wagon the drumming of the rain against the shingled roof made it difficult to sleep, so Neah was awake when a loud banging came at the door.

"Mother." Neah glided to her feet, shaking Deva's arm. When she was awake, Neah slipped the knife free of the holster strapped to her forearm.

"Someone is here."

Deva grunted and smacked her lips several times. Snoring always dried out her mouth.

Neah gripped the latch of the door then swung it open, the knife filling the gap. A rush of wind-borne rain sheeted through, as if hungry for the warmth inside.

Caleb jumped back, cannoning into Hawke waiting near the bottom step. "Whoa."

"Sorry, I was asleep. You startled me. I'm cautious about the killers." She kept the knife leveled at them.

"If I was coming to kill you, you'd already be dead," Caleb snapped.

"It's all right, Neah," Hawke said from the bottom step. "We aren't armed." Reluctantly, she sheathed the knife and looked around her wagon. All the available space was stacked with bushel-sized bags of grain and anything else that wouldn't fit into the supply wagons. There was no room for either of the men to enter.

"I'll come out," she said, slipping an oilskin over her head. They huddled beneath the small roof that jutted over the steps, her bare feet ankle-deep in water, toes squelching mud between them.

"The Nuttals didn't go back to Strophos," Hawke said. "They're about three leagues from here, down the road."

"Toward Carmelsara?"

Hawke nodded. "I took Valiant up before the weather closed in. They were already digging in, readying their usual ambush. This rain will have washed that idea out."

"Can we go around them?" Neah asked.

Hawke shook his head, water spilling from the brim of his hat. "Not in this weather, the wagons would bog. No, Caleb and I have been talking. Our best chance is to try and take *them* by surprise."

"Tonight?" Neah looked around. The cloud cover was thick and low, effectively blocking most of the moonlight.

"Yes," Caleb answered. "Look, I know we've had our... disagreements, but tonight I need a good archer. I'd like you to join us. If you're willing."

Neah felt something release inside her. Something tight. It had been nesting there since yesterday's unsatisfactory meeting with the Nuttals, and now she knew what it was.

Relief. She hated Nuttals for all they did and stood for. Neah hadn't been sold through their slave market, though she would have been had not Shayla wanted her to retain her full faculties. *"So she'll remember—everything."* This was an opportunity to settle a score.

She stared at Caleb for a moment. The resentment and boiling hatred toward him was still there, but she could bracket it out for this. "Bows don't like the rain. The wet affects the strings. Arrows don't have the range."

"I intend getting close enough so that might not matter."

She nodded. "I'll get my gear."

"We'll assemble at Hawke's wagon in ten minutes," Caleb called after her. She waved an acknowledgement, slamming the door behind her.

"You're going with them?" Deva asked.

"If you know that, you also know my answer." Neah strapped on the bandoliers of arrows beneath her oilskin, then released the string from the bow and tucked it into her pocket, adding two more. She paused before the small altar in the corner of their wagon, automatically dipping her fingertips into the bowl of warmed sacred oil and touched them lightly to her forehead, lips, and heart as a traditional blessing before battle. She was about to turn away when something caught her eye.

"What is this?" Neah asked, drawing a cloth-wrapped package from where it was resting beneath the carved statue of the Mother.

"The cursed knife I got from Mohar. I've cleansed it and applied the full moon mixture to its blade and handle. It should now be able to detect both those who have the entity within them as well as those who were originally responsible."

Neah flipped the cloth folds open. The double-edged blade gleamed, the metallic threads wound into the handle twinkling in the flickering lamplight.

"It's still cursed, isn't it?"

"The entity is long gone. It's now infused with the blessings of the Mother. Why don't you take it with you? It should give you warning of anyone the entity has infiltrated. There may be some with your raiding party tonight."

Neah stared at the knife, still unwilling to touch it, remembering the cascade of images and sensations it had caused the last time.

"Weapons are neutral, Neah. It is the intention they are infused with that gives them power. I have simply reversed its charge."

Neah reached out and gingerly picked it up. The prickle of charged energy spread up her fingers and into her hand.

"It's like it's vibrating."

"It is mapping you. Its power will now respond to your energy signature."

"Why me?"

Deva shrugged. "It has to be someone, and you are the only one I truly trust. Besides, I feel you will need it. Perhaps tonight. Here, I made a scabbard for it as well. Be careful at first, it may take some time to bond with you completely."

She helped Neah slide the leather scabbard onto her belt. Neah could feel the shape of the blade resting flat against the side of her leg. There seemed to be a faint, steady thrum to it, as there had been that night when the three of them had divined its source. She pushed the feeling of unease aside and tugged on her boots before bending to embrace her mother. Deva felt small in Neah's embrace, as if she had shrunk from the cold of the night. Neah broke away, and without a backward glance stepped outside. The wind buffeted her as she retrieved Magic from the corral and led her back to the wagon.

The wind carried snatches of sound, bouncing some and truncating others: a jangle of harness, a single cursed word, forming a collage of noises within the storm.

A jagged flash of lightning momentarily lit up the camp. Behind her Magic whinnied and dragged against the bridle.

"It's all right, girl." She patted the mare's saturated mane. The wind dropped, as if turned off, as they reached the shelter of the wagon, and in the moment of stillness before the rumbling thunder rolled over the camp, she heard something.

A woman's scream.

The knife against her thigh felt like it was trying to free itself. She placed her hand over it to prevent it falling out and looked around.

Her eyesight was unreliable after the lightning flash, and she ran to the next wagon, pounding on the door.

It opened, framing Mrs. Asake's hunched figure with soft light. "Ah, Neah, what is it, dear?"

"I heard a woman cry out just now. It seemed to come from this direction. Was it you?"

The old woman laughed. "Cry out? Me? Oh not me, dear. Angus and I are well past that." She clutched the scarf about her and chuckled, pausing as she remembered something. "I hope it wasn't Julia. She brought us some dinner over just now. Angus and I haven't been well, you know. Such a lovely girl."

"Julia? The blonde woman from the kitchens?"

"Yes? Is something the matter?"

Neah ran off, searching under and around the wagons. She spotted the body lying on the outside circle of the second one, her blonde hair matted with mud and blood, facedown in a puddle. Julia. Another victim.

Peering through the sheeting rain and dark, she freed the knife from its scabbard. It thrummed against the palm of her hand, the point of its blade moving back and forth like a hound sniffing the air. Finally Neah felt it lurch forward, jerking her arm straight, its blade pointing toward the next wagon. It felt like it was pulling her. She was about to call for help when she sensed something dart from beneath the Asakes' wagon and away from the camp. When she bent to look she could see nothing. As the seconds dragged past, the knife settled. Whoever it was had gone.

Neah returned to the body, wondering about the three daughters.

What will they do now?

Did I really hear anything? Is this knife messing with my head?

She made her way back to her wagon, and escorted Deva over to Julia's wagon to be with the daughters, staying with them until the hysterical cries had receded to a quiet sobbing. Locking the door, she saddled up Magic and rode down to Hawke's wagon.

A gap had been left, and she guided Magic through to join the others clustered in a dripping group outside. Mohar looked like a cat who'd been pulled from the creek, long hair plastered against his skull, rain running off his beard. It made him seem smaller. He tried to smile and failed.

"Where have you been?" Caleb snapped.

"There's been another killing." The others crowded close. Neah touched the knife to check whether any of the men would set it off. It remained still. That was something.

"Who?" Hawke asked.

"Julia. From the kitchens. I just found her. Deva is with her three daughters. Hawke, I haven't touched the body, it's near the Asakes'."

He nodded and moved off to retrieve it.

"Julia?" Caleb asked. His face looked pale in the patchy moonlight.

Is there something more there than surprise? Was I right about a possible relationship between them?

He looked down, hiding his expression. "What's that?" he growled pointing at the knife visible through the side slit of her oilskin poncho. "It's that knife. I recognize the handle."

When he met her gaze she could see the questions, then doubt, forming behind his eyes.

"What? You think it was me?" she said.

"It could be," Caleb mumbled. "We all agreed it could be any of us, and that knife started it all."

"Believe what you like. Are you coming on this mission now, or do you want to wait until the Nuttals come and find us?"

Narrowing his eyes, Caleb mounted up. The wind gusted in, driving rain into their face.

"What about the others?" Mohar asked. "There are only six of us here."

"We need to move quietly, so a small group is best. Our job is to strike fast and deep—then get back here."

"And if they follow?" Mohar asked.

"They won't," Neah said. "Nuttals are cowards at heart. They prefer ambushes rather than outright attack."

"I want them to follow. We'll have men waiting here—twenty counting the auxiliary watch."

"The auxiliary don't have weapons," Mohar said.

"Not conventional ones, no."

"You want to fight the Nuttals with shovels and hoes?" Neah spluttered.

Caleb ignored her sarcasm. He pointed at the space between the wagons. "When the Nuttals come, I've ordered these gaps to be closed. Make sure you're inside before they do. After we hit the Nuttals' camp it'll be a fast run home. Everyone will be on their own. Our primary weapon is surprise, and our only ally tonight is the weather."

Neah imagined Winterdom's arrogant face, and promised herself that whatever happened, the slave master would not survive the night.

They headed out into the storm.

CALEB HELD UP HIS HAND, halting the column behind a copse of trees. He waved the others forward, and they clustered around, hunched and drenched. Magic shook her head, snorting away the water sluicing down her nose.

Caleb pointed to a dark hump about fifty yards away. "Hawke said they were camped just beyond that rise. I'll go over and check it out. Neah, that hill will also be your spot. Remember, your job is just to contain them. Create confusion. The men and I will go in first, hit them as hard as we can, and then fall back. That's when I want you to fire, covering our retreat. Then we'll whip around and go in for a second round. They won't be expecting that. After that's done, we all quit and get going back to the caravan. Got it?"

"There's likely to be sentries up there. It's the logical place to post them," Neah said, wiping at the water streaming down her face.

Caleb nodded. "We'll leave the horses here. The storm and low light should help us if they're up there."

Bent low, they zigzagged from a cluster of rocks to some stunted trees, until they reached the base of the rise. He pointed at her, then jabbed his finger toward the left, touched his own chest, and pointed right. Neah nodded, and Caleb melted into the night, moving up the rise.

She followed the direction Caleb had pointed, moving warily. He was already at the top when she arrived, pressed against a large boulder, an eyeglass steadied against the side of the rock, one hand shielding the glass from the rain. When she joined him, he raised a finger to his lips then pointed down, raising first one finger and then another.

Peering around one of the rocks, she could just make out the dark forms of two sentries sheltering from the rain at the base of the rise. A further hundred yards on was the Nuttals' camp, the low black tents almost invisible in the gloom. The wind tugged at the bandana securing her hair. It was gusting stronger at the top of the rocks. She guessed the sentries had gradually worked their way down to ground level as the storm intensified.

Neah took a deep breath, held it, then released slowly through her nose, stringing her bow and then nocking an arrow beneath her oilskin. When she was steady, she brought her arms through the slit, allowed for the wind drift, trying to keep the bowstring dry. She fired, reloading even as she acquired the dark outline of the second sentry. She loosed the next arrow and heard its satisfying thunk as it skewered his neck. Death slumped them both against the rocks. From a distance it would look like they were still hunkered down out of the weather.

"I'll leave your horse at the base of the rise behind us. Remember, be ready to get back to the caravan after our second sortie," Caleb whispered, before making his way back down the slope. Neah shrugged his presence away. She was here for Winterdom, nothing else.

Tension built inside her. The rain had eased, and the cloud cover was threatening to break by the time Caleb and his four men appeared at the side of the rocky outcrop. At his signal they galloped in, four abreast, straight into the camp, the sound of the horses splashing through mud muffled by the gusting wind. They rode straight into the line of tents, trampling several, crushing the skulls of those who came lurching out.

She waited until the surprise began to abate. Nuttals were snatching up swords and the heavy-headed maces they favored. She spotted a group of them coming up on Caleb's raiders from behind. Ignoring his earlier instructions, Neah released a volley of arrows into the pack. Two went wide, caught by a sudden wind shear. Once she allowed for the drift, the other three struck home. She was too far away to make out Winterdom.

Ducking down, she changed position and replaced the bowstring with a dry one. It was important to keep the arrows coming from different angles to make the Nuttals think there was more than one archer up here.

Caleb and his men abruptly pulled back. The Nuttals, now rapidly becoming organized, chased them on foot, their cries more outraged than the wild whooping noises they'd made yesterday. Neah stood, adopted a wide, grounded stance, and shot off six arrows in quick succession.

Again she changed position, this time to the opposite side of the ridge, just as Caleb turned his horse in a tight circle and led the men in for another attack, his stallion running over and barging past their pursuers. In the brief illumination of a distant lightning flash Neah saw an arm go spinning off into the night, carried by the momentum of its swing as it met Caleb's cutlass.

She shot more arrows.

Something struck the rock beside her and a small rock chip speared against her cheek. Dropping to the ground, she saw a spent Nuttal arrow, its shaft broken where it had struck the rock.

They'd made her.

Keeping low, she weaved between the boulders, finding a better vantage point. Cautiously she peered out. Two Nuttals, kneeling in battle position, bows drawn, were waiting for her to stand again. It was definitely time to go. She clipped her bow to the quiver of arrows and crawled backward off the crest until she could scramble through the loose scree and down the slope.

As she reached the bottom, a Nuttal rounded the outcrop. He was bare chested, skin slippery with water, running red with the aftermath of what might have been blood. He took up a position between her and Magic's dark shape. She silently cursed herself for packing the bow away. With a flick of her wrist she slipped the throwing knife free of the strap around her forearm.

The Nuttal saw it coming and danced to one side, the blade clinking harmlessly against the rocks behind him.

He grinned, his fangs catching a flash of moonlight. The storm had moved off towards the west, taking the rain with it.

With a triumphant cry the Nuttal launched himself up the slope, a broad-bladed gutting knife in each hand. Neah tucked herself into a ball beside one of the black boulders, coiling her strength as she reached for the mystical dagger that Deva had given her. When the warrior was almost upon her, she pushed down through the soles of her feet and exploded up toward him, her shoulder crushing into his groin. A whoosh of air erupted from him and he doubled over. Neah drove the dagger down, deep into his unprotected back. He shuddered as its sharp point found the rear entry to his heart.

Panting, she tugged the dagger free, pushing the body aside before running down the slope and vaulting into the saddle.

From the camp she could still hear sounds of fighting.

What are those fools doing? They were supposed to run after the last charge and lead the Nuttals off.

She chanced a quick peek over her shoulder. Caleb and two of his men had been pulled from their mounts and were cut off, their backs to one other, surrounded by a dozen or more Nuttals. More were coming. It would only be moments before they were swamped.

Kicking her heels against Magic's sides, she headed toward Caleb and his men, bow drawn once more. She fired off three rounds. With a curse of surprise, some of the Nuttals spun around to face her. Using her thighs, she urged Magic to turn sharply, first one way then the other, presenting as narrow a target as she could. It gave her time to unloose another three rounds in both directions.

Caleb took advantage of the distraction and forced his way through the gap she'd created, twin battle cutlasses twirling, his men following, protecting his back.

One was slow to block a blow and a curved Nuttal blade caught him in the belly. He sagged to his knees. The Nuttal was on him immediately, tearing at the man's throat with long, filed teeth. Blood coursed from the corners of his mouth, scarlet mixing with the rain to stain his black lips and run in streaks down his chin. Neah shot him when the Nuttal brought out a shallow spoon and attempted to scoop out the dying man's eyes.

Some of the Nuttals had managed to make it to their ponies. In minutes they'd be mounted. It was time to go.

Caleb found his stallion and hauled his remaining trooper up behind him. Belatedly Neah realized it was Mohar. Before he was fully in the saddle, one of the Nuttals' throwing knives thudded into Mohar's back. Both men jerked, then spasmed, and for a moment it looked as if both had been struck. Mohar slumped against Caleb's back.

Neah swore as more Nuttals swarmed toward them. They seemed mindless of the bodies beneath their feet. She kept Magic dancing to either side, nocking and firing arrows. Her quiver was almost empty.

Something slammed against her and the curved bow shattered, her hands stinging from the impact. If the blow had hit her fingers rather than the bow, they would have been crushed. Beside her a Nuttal was raising his mace for a second attempt. Neah threw herself across the neck of her horse, snatched one of the remaining arrows from her bandolier, and came up under his guard, thrusting the arrow beneath his breastbone and into his heart. He slid from the horse and crumpled to the ground.

Caleb was fighting his way toward her. The mystical dagger sent an urgent tingling sensation against her leg. One of Winterdom's brothers was riding up hard behind Caleb, a mace twirling above his head. With Mohar clinging to his back, Caleb would be taken by surprise. She spurred Magic forward, slipping the blade free.

"Caleb!"

Seconds slowed. Even the guttural cries of the Nuttals became elongated. Time felt like it was being stretched like wet linen over too large a frame as she raced toward him.

He turned at her shout, his mouth open in surprise as she rushed toward him. Perhaps he believed the upraised knife was aimed at him. He stared at it, transfixed.

Neah thundered past, and ducking beneath the arc of the twirling mace drove Magic straight into the shoulder of the smaller pony. She heard a sickening crack and the pony lurched to one side, coming down on its knees before toppling sideways to the ground. The Nuttal rolled clear. Magic stumbled and recovered with an effort.

Neah shook her head as time collapsed back and she drove her heels into Magic's ribs. Just before the knife started vibrating, she'd seen an image of Caleb falling, dead, Mohar dragged down with him. Yet it hadn't happened like that.

Shaking the uneasy vision away, she flicked the reins. The mare needed no encouragement and was in full gallop within a matter of strides. Behind her she could hear the pounding hooves of another horse coming up fast. She chanced a glance over her shoulder.

It was Caleb, Mohar somehow clinging to him, and behind them the Nuttal pack whooping in pursuit.

She could just make out Winterdom in the lead, flicking his reins to either side of his pony's neck with savage force, pointed teeth bared and white in the glare of a flash of lightning.

The Nuttals' shaggy mountain ponies were known for endurance and agility, not speed or acceleration. Their short stocky legs had no chance of catching the larger Commonwealth breed, even with one carrying two men. Neah and Caleb maintained their lead. The caravan came into distant view, a clustered hump against the horizon. Caleb pointed his cutlass at the gap between wagons and they swung toward it. Neah could feel Magic tiring. The mare had been blowing hard for the past league, and her strides were shorter, less sure.

Gradually Neah became aware of a warm wetness against her trouser leg, even more pooling inside her boot. She touched the area with her fingers, and brought them to her tongue, tasting it.

Blood. Her talent told her it wasn't human. Magic must have been hit with one of the arrows. Neah focused her attention and tried to feed her own energy into the mare, urging her on, aiming her toward the gap between the wagons. Caleb's horse was tiring too, but even with the heavier load it had overtaken her. He was shouting, waving his arm, urging her to hurry. She remembered they were going to block the space between the wagons as soon as the Nuttals came into view.

That was now.

Magic staggered and recovered sluggishly. Ahead, Caleb was already off his horse, his shoulder supporting Mohar as he dragged the wizard to the safety of the caravan. Men came out to help.

An arrow hit the ground behind her. A hundred paces to run, and Magic wasn't going to make it. Not carrying her.

Neah drew back on the reins and slid to the ground. Running ahead, she tried to lead Magic, tugging and entreating her to follow. More arrows, but the Nuttals' strings must be wet, because the arrows fell short.

Blood was running freely down Magic's side now. Neah could see the vane of an arrow buried deep beside one of the stirrups.

Two men from the caravan ran out to her. One took charge of her horse. The other, who she recognized as a minstrel, faced the thundering Nuttal pack. He had a bow, his hands shaking as he tried to nock an arrow.

"Give me that," she shouted.

The man thrust it at her, his face reflecting pure relief. She turned to face the Nuttals.

"Now go," she shouted. "I'll cover you."

He hesitated for a moment before running back to the relative safety of the wagons. She still had time to make it back, but she wanted Winterdom more. It was as if all the bloody beatings, pain, and humiliation she'd suffered as a slave were because of him. The Slave Master. No more.

Adjusting her feet, her breath deep and even, she tested the draw on the bow. It was Commonwealth standard issue, heavier and clumsier than her own. A blunt instrument, her father would have called it. But even blunt instruments could kill.

Winterdom was still in the lead. She took careful aim and fired off two arrows in quick succession. Both lost height quickly and buried themselves in the broad chests of two of the leading horses. The ponies stumbled, then fell, spilling their riders. Others directly behind couldn't react quickly enough, and they tumbled over the carcasses, the riders trampled beneath the hooves of those following. The attack faltered, losing momentum, until Winterdom, realizing what was happening, wheeled and with a piercing cry rallied the charge.

Neah mentally calculated the distance back to the wagons. It was both too late and way too far. The gap between the wagons had closed. She could hear the cries of the others behind her, shouting for her to return.

Magic was safe. That was one thing. She and the horse had been through a lot together. Deva would look after her.

She turned to face the Nuttals.

The pack was screaming its banshee battle cry, sensing victory.

She could now clearly make out their faces. Nocking another arrow, she brought up the bow in one fluid sweep and fired. The arrow hung in, striking Winterdom in the shoulder, but the impact was powerful enough to unseat him. He fell, sprawling into the mud. A volley of arrows from the caravan followed, arcing over her and raining down upon the pack. The charge slowed; Winterdom's fall and the concerted defense from the caravan appeared to have stolen the wind from their sails, and the attack faltered once more. They wheeled about and retreated, pulling up just out of range. Winterdom was squirming in the mud like some oversized crab, trying to claw his way back toward his squad. He yelled at them to bring him a horse.

No one moved, his two brothers seemingly content to watch.

Neah smiled, drawing resolutely back on the bow, its arrow squarely aimed at Winterdom's back. She wondered briefly why the Nuttals had been so persistent. They were usually scavengers, not aggressors.

Immediately the dagger vibrated against her leg.

Something was wrong.

In the distance she could hear Caleb yelling.

"Neah. Come back to the caravan. We'll cover you."

She shook her head as if he were in front of her. Time seemed to be stretching again. The tingling from the dagger spread up her leg and into her body. Slowly she lowered the bow and drew out the knife. The vibration was much stronger now. She felt she could release it and it would remain hovering in the air.

"Neah." She felt more than heard the hot rasp of Caleb's voice beside her ear. "You must come now."

"No. I want Winterdom. We need him. Alive." The last word was more like a question. To herself, because she desperately wanted to kill him, though at the same time this other need, to take him alive, was rapidly growing.

"We need him alive," she mumbled. "Look."

She released her grip on the knife and it hovered, a low hum coming from it.

"Alive?" Caleb repeated. "What are you talking about? That is Winterdom," Caleb screamed, as if this in itself was justification. "You wanted him dead. Remember?"

Red bled into her field of vision. She shook her head, trying to clear it. Saving Winterdom was all that mattered. "Look at the knife. It knows him. We need him alive to get answers." Neah's face creased with confusion at her own words. She snatched back the dagger from the air and thrust it into the scabbard.

"What's wrong with you?" Caleb spluttered, gripping her from behind. He yelled over his shoulder for one of his men to come and help.

Neah screamed in frustration. Caleb used his strength to contain her. Struggling, she tried to throw him off, but he was too big.

The familiar whistle of an incoming arrow intruded, thunking into the ground not far from Neah's boot. Another followed, closer this time.

Caleb shoved her back toward the wagons and into the arms of the other soldier who'd just run in. He called a warning, pointing. Several of the Nuttals were advancing tentatively toward them.

"They're getting our range." Caleb motioned to the soldier. "Take her back. If she wants the Nuttal so much, I'll go fetch him."

Time crashed back in. She collapsed against the man's arm. The all-consuming red moment was rapidly disappearing, like water down a drain. Turning, she saw Caleb pick up Winterdom's feet and drag him toward the wagons, the shaggy, misshapen head bouncing along the ground.

Traces of rationality were returning in confusing snatches.

What happened? Why was I so hell-bent on saving Winterdom when I clearly want to kill him?

Behind her she could hear Caleb cursing, the Nuttal growling and screaming like a trapped animal.

More arrows thunked into the ground around them. The Nuttals seemed unmindful that they might hit their leader, and were getting closer.

Hands reached out for her, pulling her through the narrow gap. She flopped into Deva's arms.

THE SWEET SMELL of roasting meat roused her. Neah licked her dry lips, eyelids remaining stubbornly closed. Jagged picture fragments played out against them, some fitting together easily: the sounds of bowls clattering, quiet chatter, sunlight against her closed lids—it must be lunchtime. Others, more bizarrely shaped, found no reference point and roamed aimlessly. Ragged images of marauding slavers and a bloodred haze infusing her eyes.... She sat up with a start, hitting her head against the bottom of the wagon. Mohar, dozing on the ground beside her, jerked awake at her sudden movement.

"What is it?" he asked, looking around.

They were lying on a large red blanket underneath one of the food wagons. Neah recognized the gold-and-green pattern of the blanket as one Deva favored for its recuperative powers. Ten meters away, what looked like the dressed carcasses of a number of goats were suspended on spits above the cooking fires. The smell of roasting meat was almost intoxicating. Neah's mouth flooded with saliva as she tried to remember the last time she'd eaten anything, much less fresh meat.

"Ah, you're awake, good." Deva's voice was evident before her mother, grunting, arrived down at their level. "I wanted to keep you both close while I organized the meal. We have goat today. Several of them got in the way of those Nuttal arrows, so Hawke suggested we make the most of them, though we'll miss the milk in the days to come, I daresay."

Cautiously, Neah slid out from under the wagon. Odd parts of her body protested, as if they'd been used overmuch.

When Mohar attempted to follow, Deva held up her hand to stay him. "Not you, wizard. Not yet, you'll only open the wound if you start moving about. I'll bring you some broth. That's all you'll be able to handle for a while yet."

Neah staggered a little as she walked out of the shadow of the wagon and into the bright sunlight. The air had been rinsed clean of the dust that had billowed about since leaving Roganshah. Everything seemed so much brighter. Even the people; several came up and patted her shoulder, muttering a kind or encouraging word. It felt like a feast day.

"What happened?" She looked about. "Where are the Nuttals?"

"Gone. Oh, they made a half-hearted rush after you and Caleb made it back with Winterdom, but the heart seemed to have gone out of them. They just rode off. Hawke followed them on Valiant all the way back to their captured caravan at Strophos. He said they won't be back. The raiding party lost over half their number, and I dare say the two remaining brothers won't miss Winterdom."

Neah nodded, only half comprehending, satisfied that it was simply one less threat to think about.

"You still look a little disconnected. Here, eat this." Deva thrust a bowl into her hands. It contained three thick slabs of goat hindquarter. The smell of it was simultaneously mouthwateringly inviting and peculiarly nauseating.

Neah picked up a piece. It was steaming, thick with gravy, rich with fat, the smell ripe and strong. Too strong. She felt her stomach heave, and lurching off to one side vomited what little remained in it. Deva hastily relieved her of the bowl.

"Are you all right, love?"

"Fine." Neah shook her mother away.

"Better sit down. You may have hit your head. I'll fetch you some broth instead."

Deva returned soon after with another brimming bowl and an elbow of yesterday's bread. Neah dunked the bread into the broth and sucked cautiously. It tasted delicious. She finished it in moments and held the bowl out for more.

"I'll try some of that meat now too."

"You sure?"

"Sure as can be that there won't be any left if I don't." Neah forced her mouth into a smile, and Deva patted her arm as she left to get more food.

If there was one thing Neah knew about her mother, it was that she loved seeing others eat well. The warm, rich broth had grounded her, enabling the series of events spinning in her head to settle.

When Deva returned, she said, "Caleb told me you insisted on bringing Winterdom back alive. I thought you were hell-bent on killing him."

Neah took a careful bite of the still steaming meat before replying.

"I wanted to kill him. He deserved it. He still does. However, something happened out there. It had something to do with that damned knife you gave me. It's almost as if it has a mind of its own. I felt it vibrate, tingle really, and time seems to, I don't know, stretch somehow. Everything goes red and things happen that I hadn't planned."

"Like saving Winterdom?"

"Yes. What could that mean?"

Deva said nothing, absently slipping another slice of goat into Neah's bowl.

"Mother...," Neah said, her voice rising with impatience.

Finally Deva sighed and pointed at the dagger strapped to Neah's thigh. "It's obviously more powerful than I realized. What were you thinking immediately before this happened?"

"I was wondering why the Nuttals would attack like they did. It's not like them."

Neah remembered the redness infusing her vision, her initial desire to kill Winterdom supplanted by the need to save him.

"But why?" Deva persisted.

"I don't know. I just felt he has the answers."

WINTERDOM WAS SITTING on the ground, his wrists bound at either side of his head to the large spokes of Hawke's wagon. His legs had been spread and secured to the ground.

"He looks restrained." Neah tentatively tested her feelings toward him. Other than an underlying dislike and faint revulsion, there was nothing. She felt Deva's eyes on her.

Hawke ambled over when he saw them. "Ah Neah, up and about again? Excellent. Now if I can only convince that damn wizard to get off his back, we might be able to move this caravan along." Hawke lit his pipe, then taking it from his mouth used the stem to point down at Winterdom. "What's more, I'm keen to get this piece of slime unhooked from my wagon."

"Water," Winterdom croaked.

Hawke motioned one of the men to hold a ladle of water to the Nuttal's blackened lips. He slurped at it greedily, some spilling down his stained jerkin.

"Enough," Hawke snapped. "You'll have more when you tell us what we want to know." He turned to Deva and Neah. "What do you plan to do with him?"

"Neah thinks he has answers." Deva said. "I went through some of the really old scrolls at the bottom of my chest after you left last night, Neah. Remember, Mohar said that the knife was initially invested with an entity?"

Neah nodded. "And after inducing the murder of the first victim it transferred into the host body. Yes."

"Well, he was right. Partly. The scrolls mention that in order for the entity to transfer from the knife into the host body, there needs to firstly be an attraction between the two. It can't be just anyone, not initially."

"Attraction?"

Deva's face crinkled, as she sought the right word. "More like a knowingness. In simple terms they originally must come from the same source. I believe the Nuttals have developed a way to extract the spirit and use its essence to create the entity."

"And you believe Winterdom knows this?"

"Much more than that. I believe he may be the one who created it. See the way he is looking around? He's terrified."

"You're right." Neah said, her index finger tapping her upper lip. "Now that I think about it, he seemed more frightened of being brought inside the caravan than dying out there. Let's show him this." Neah slipped the dagger from its holster and handed it to Hawke.

Winterdom's jaw muscles clenched and his eyes widened when he saw the dagger. Hawke laid it carefully on the ground between the Nuttal's legs. Winterdom cringed away, the boots of his heels digging into the earth as he tried to push himself back against the wagon.

"Get it away," he gasped. The veins in his arms bulged with effort as he tried to lift himself off the ground.

"Where do you know that knife from?" Neah asked.

"It's cursed."

"We know that much. Why are you so afraid of it?"

"It contains power. Dark power." Winterdom's voice was coming out in gasps, his eyes darting nervously from the knife to the people passing by and increasingly those gathering around him. He seemed to be both looking for someone and was desperately afraid of finding them.

"Where did it come from?" Neah persisted.

"It was sent to us. By Queen Shayla."

The onlookers were getting louder, feeding off their own bravado. Neah sensed it could escalate quickly. Crowd mentality was a hard thing to stop once it started rolling, and Nuttals were despised and feared even at the best of times.

She turned to Hawke. "Perhaps you should call Caleb—and some of the men?"

"Good idea."

Hawke called over three of the camp children and sent them off in different directions with orders to bring back Caleb and as many of his men as they could find.

Neah stepped closer to Winterdom. "Do you know who I am?"

Winterdom's eyes met hers, squinting.

"It was you out on the plain, wasn't it? The sister. No wonder the simulacrum of Shayla was so real—you're of the same seed. None of us were sure. Not until we heard from—" Winterdom clamped his mouth shut.

"Heard from who?" Hawke took a step forward and kicked Winterdom's boot.

"You may as well tell us. Or I'll have the knife do it for us," Neah said.

Winterdom's tongue darted out like a snake scenting the air before licking his thin lips.

"All right, just take the cursed thing away."

Neah bent down and removed the dagger. It was vibrating wildly.

"Well?"

"After we left you out on the plain we sent a note strapped to the foot of one of your sister's messenger birds—just to check. When she responded, we knew we'd been tricked."

"What did her message say?"

"That she had mobilized her attack force and was on the march from Roganshah. We were to bring whatever slaves we had and meet her on the road."

The three exchanged a worried look. All knew the caravan's head start would be quickly whittled back by Shayla's fast-moving attack force.

A rock sailed over the heads of the crowd and landed with a thud against the Nuttal's shoulder. He grunted in surprise, dodging another thrown by a young man three from the front.

Hawke barged into the crowd and tugged him out, dragging him by the ear. He turned to face people gathered about.

"This crowd will disperse. Now. Go back to your wagons and get ready to move out. We will take care of this. If anyone else harms the piece of shit tied to my wagon before I find out what I need to know, they'll have to find their own way to Carmelsara, is that clear?"

He spun the youth around and kicked him in the rump, sending him sprawling into the dirt.

"Now clear out."

Grumbling, the crowd began to thin just as Caleb and three of his troopers ran up, Chea following in their wake.

"Is everything all right?" Caleb asked, hand on the pommel of his cutlass, eyes darting around the crowd, seeking possible threats.

"It was just beginning to get interesting," Hawke said, dragging the youth up by the arm and sending him back to his wagon. "But everyone seems to have received the message."

"So what's wrong with Winterdom?" Caleb asked.

They all turned to look. Sweat was seeping from his sloping forehead. It ran in grimy lines down the runnels of his face. Terror was etched across his face.

"Keep it away," he yelled, straining against the restraints.

"What is it?" Caleb asked, looking around. He slid one of his sabers from its scabbard. "What can he see?"

Neah was having difficulty keeping hold of the dagger. It was struggling like a trapped animal trying to get free.

Winterdom screamed, tucking his face beneath his outstretched arm. Neah turned around to see what he was hiding from.

Chea was standing just behind them, his features fixed as if they'd been morphed into a hardened mask. The dagger felt as if it were being dragged from her hand. It flew into the air and hovered between Chea and the Nuttal, blade vibrating. "Chea!" Deva said. "No! It can't be. Not you."

"Stay away," Winterdom yelled as Chea shuffled toward him. "Just keep it away from me. I'll tell you anything. Please. Just don't let him near me."

Neah intercepted Chea. It was as if the boy was in a trance. His eyes were transfixed, locked on the bound Nuttal. She gathered him to her. He felt stiff and unresponsive. Neah could feel the urge within his body to keep moving forward, but at the same time there was no resistance to her holding him.

"Tell us." Neah was running on instinct. "Or I'll release him."

Winterdom closed his eyes and took a ragged breath.

"Before I do, make him promise to kill me." He indicated Caleb with a flick of his head.

"What?" Caleb said.

"Make him promise!" he shouted. "On his oath—as an officer."

"Caleb?" Neah asked.

"I promise, and swear so—gladly," Caleb said.

Winterdom spoke quickly, as if the words were acidic and burned his mouth even as he uttered them. "We found the boy, half dead, in the wreckage of a caravan that we'd ambushed at Strophos. Queen Shayla had ordered us to insert an entity into another caravan that was due out of Roganshah shortly—yours—so we used this child as a vessel."

"You used Chea? How?" Deva demanded.

Winterdom shook his head as if the detail was irrelevant. He answered anyway. "We have a means of extracting the soul. It's an extension on the Swearing we do for slaves. Once the spirit is separated, we join it with a portion of the summoned entity, allowing it to mimic the structure of the essence and then embed itself. The remainder of the entity is wedded within the dagger. When the two are reunited through blood, the entity can then replicate and spread."

"Why are you so afraid of the boy?" Hawke demanded.

"The entity spreads in order to seek its creator. To recover its soul. That is its sole purpose."

"And you are this creator?"

"Yes. If the entity joins with me, I will be damned. My soul will be exchanged for his and be unrecoverable. For all of time."

"Then why come after us at all if that was the case. Why risk it?" Hawke butted in.

"We were ordered to. Queen Shayla threatened to wipe out our whole tribe if we did not obey. My brothers overruled me. For the greater good, they said. They promised to kill me should it come to that."

"They tried," Neah said.

"Not hard enough." Winterdom's voice was heavy with bitterness.

"What will happen to Chea?" Hawke said.

Winterdom's lips firmed. "I have told you everything. Now instruct your commander to do as he swore."

"Tell me what happens to the boy first," Hawke countered.

"He is undead. The entity cannot be separated from him. He cannot be saved. You must kill him. After me."

"Deva?" Caleb asked, his brow wrinkling.

Deva was staring at Winterdom, as if she were trying to divine something from the terrified Nuttal. Finally she turned to Neah, intoning in a clear voice, "Release him, Neah. Let this unfold as the Mother wishes."

"No. You promised," Winterdom whimpered, turning to look up at Caleb. "You are an officer in the Commonwealth. You cannot refuse to obey a bonded oath. You will be disgraced forever."

Caleb chuckled. "Disgrace and I are well acquainted, but don't worry, I do intend to kill you."

Winterdom's face flooded with relief.

Neah released her hold on Chea and he continued his slow shuffle forward, reaching up to take the hovering dagger as he passed.

"Then hurry. He comes."

"I just never said *when*."

"No. NO!"

Chea paused in front of Winterdom, reached out a hand, and cupped the Nuttal's chin. Immediately the man's thrashing ceased. He appeared to be frozen in the boy's light hold. Then, slowly, as if he were emerging into the moment, Chea bent down, pursed his small lips, and blew lightly into the Nuttal's flared nostrils.

Something seemed to transfer from the Nuttal to Chea.

Winterdom stiffened; his breath when it came was a strangled sound from deep inside his throat, as if it were trapped there. Tendons stretched and popped like thick cords at either side of the

Nuttal's neck. The eyes turned yellow, and then red. Something grinned triumphantly from behind the face.

"Now, Commander," Deva said. "Decapitate him."

Caleb brought the sabre through in a smooth arc. The severed head rolled to one side.

Neah beat Deva to where Chea was seated between the Nuttal's legs. His chin was lolling against his chest. When they gently lifted him up, they found the dagger embedded in his gut.

"Is he all—right?" Hawke asked, starting forward, his voice cracking on the last inadequate word as he saw the wound.

Slowly the boy's chin lifted. He looked up at them, his smile innocent and shy, before slumping lifeless, yet whole, into Neah's arms.

THEY HELD a private service for Chea later that day, away from the campsite. Deva suggested burning the body, just to be sure, so Hawke and Caleb broke up some empty water barrels and used whatever other fuel they could find to build a pyre. As the sun angled low, Deva, Neah, Mohar, and Caleb gathered around while Hawke took out the Book of Blessings. When he tried to read from it, emotion broke his voice, and he thrust the tattered pages into Caleb's hands.

Caleb placed his hand on Hawke's shoulder and gave it a squeeze. The big man looked as if he'd aged ten years in an afternoon.

Clearing his throat, Caleb read the service. For him they were words, hollow, bereft of faith, however he was conscious that there were others here for whom the ceremony would be a salve to their grief, and in a way he wished he did believe.

When he'd finished he paused and closed the Book of Blessings and opened the space for offerings, traditionally a time for each mourner to step forward and place something on the body that would symbolically help with the transition.

Deva carefully positioned a packet of honey cakes on top of

Chea's bare chest, Neah placed a yellow flower she'd found in the desert behind one ear, Mohar sprinkled a vial of sacred oil, and Hawke tucked a tail feather from Valiant's cage into his curly black hair.

Caleb stepped forward and placed an apple seed next to the cakes, and one of the copper torians Chea had given him back atop the boy's forehead.

As last to make the offering, he was the first to speak.

"Like Chea, I lost my parents very young. I know what it's like to be alone, on the street, to grow up too early, to be forced to sacrifice innocence for survival." He paused, looking at Chea's face. It looked peaceful. "We'll miss you, Chea. At least you knew love while you were with us."

The others followed, and when they were finished each flared a small twist of twigs from the fire they'd lit earlier and held them beneath the oil-soaked timber. It caught immediately, the flames crackling and clawing their way along the boards, through the bracken beneath the body, and finally roaring, almost in triumph, to engulf it.

They watched for a time, and then one by one they turned away and walked back to the caravan.

THIRTEEN

They entered the foothills two weeks later. The mountains reared in front of them, their rugged blue-rock slopes sheer, cold, and challenging. At their peaks, thick, puffed-up clouds, heavy with coastal moisture, hovered uncertainly. Before the next month passed winter would call them down and turn their fat drops to sleet, then finally snow, effectively sealing off the only pass to Carmelsara.

Already the air was cooling.

Caleb turned in his saddle to look behind him. The twisting road snaked down the slope: wagons, beasts, and people filled it. Many had chosen to walk alongside their wagons to lessen the load up the steeper inclines. In the far distance the wide plain stretched away, brown and dry, and every day the massive dust cloud raised by Shayla's approaching army grew larger.

Hawke had done as much as he could. He'd taken to breaking camp before dawn and travelling as far as the daylight would take them the next day. Even the midday meal had been canceled, to preserve both food and time. Everyone was tired and sore. Despite this, no one complained. They were caught somewhere between the dust behind and the clouds in front.

Caleb urged his stallion up the trail along the line of wagons, waving and touching the brim of his hat as he went. The people had a humbling faith in Caleb and his Sworn. Maybe it was sheer delusional desperation, but like it or not, when the Shaylene attack came he and his surviving Sworn would be their only defense.

Hawke rode up beside him. "They're closer again this morning."

Caleb moistened his mouth. The wind off the mountains was dry. "This trail is steep. It will slow them, like it did us, once they start the climb. I'm keen for us to get as high as we can before they get too close. The narrower the attack path, the better."

"You're planning on making a stand, is that it?"

Caleb nodded, gathering his cloak about him, and pointed into the early sun streaming over the ridgeline.

"I was scouting earlier. See up there where the trail narrows right in, it looks like it's been cut through rocks on either side? We're a way off yet—you may need your glass."

Hawke tugged his eyeglass from his cloak, snapped it open, and brought it up. He nodded. "That's Vale's Arch. There's barely room for a wagon to squeeze through. It's as good a spot as you'll find for that. However, it's at least two days away."

"That'll be about right then. The Shaylene are pushing themselves. In two days they'll be between a half to a full day behind us. That position is highly defendable, and the only approach is through the arch. The rocks on either side are too sheer for a frontal attack. I'm hoping that if we block it off with one of the supply wagons, then bring those rocks down on top of it, some well-placed bowmen may be able to pin them down while you make up some time. With luck we may be able to bottle up their army until the snows come."

"That sounds like a death plan to me," Hawke said, his overlarge nostrils twitching as he weighed distance and risk. "Yours."

"This was always going to be a dead-end trip for me and my men. They know it, as do you. What matters is how many others can be saved in the process."

"It's come to that, has it?" Hawke snapped the glass closed and tucked it away. "I've never agreed with weighing human lives in quantum: one life to save ten doesn't make much sense to me, because it gives no mind to the quality of people—especially the one." Hawke looked at him pointedly.

"The army doesn't focus on the individual, Hawke, it works and runs on numbers, and despite everything, I'm still army. Sacrificing one to save ten still works for me. It has to. Otherwise what use have I been? What use is an army if not to save a greater number through the deaths of a few?"

"You make an excellent point there, Commander; what use indeed is an army." Hawke smiled wryly. "But there may be another way." He pointed up in the opposite direction.

"What's up there? I see no trail."

"There isn't one, not an obvious one anyway. You've heard of the Timpani?"

"Legends only. They're extinct, aren't they?"

"Not quite. I ran into them once, by accident, right here in these mountains. I was lost in a snowstorm, wandering blind, and they took me in. They're short, but their ferocity is fearsome. I learned a lot about them that winter. One particularly interesting fact is that they absolutely hate the Shaylene. If we can make contact and let them know what Shayla plans to do, then we may have an valuable ally."

"How do we find them?"

"That's what I wanted to talk to you about. This is a steep stretch and the animals will need a breather at the end of it. I'll call a break in about ten minutes, once we make that next ridge. Bring Neah and Mohar to my wagon, and we'll talk."

THEY CLUSTERED inside Hawke's wagon, Caleb and Mohar on the bench seat at the front—its burlap curtains pulled to either side—Neah in the patched chair next to the stove, and Hawke filling the space inside the back doorway. Deva had insisted on coming as well and had perched on the side of the cot mounted to one wall.

Valiant, unused to the number of humans in his space, made his displeasure known by fluffing and squawking inside his cage.

"Did Caleb fill you in?" Hawke began, going over to feed the bird some meat strips through the bars.

"He mentioned the Timpani. They're supposed to be extinct," Mohar said.

"They were—almost. The Shaylene drove them from their native prairies twenty years or so back, managing to kill most of them in the process." He glanced over at Deva. "That would have been your husband's doing, I'd guess. It's about that time."

"He called them thieving vermin. They stole crops and livestock —burned farms. My husband gave them many warnings—too many chances, he said. If they still live, my advice is they are not to be trusted," Deva said.

"Maybe so. They saved my life, that's all I know. Plus, I believe they've changed from the time you knew them. The few that managed to escape the slaughter came up here to the mountains seeking out a distant branch of their race. They found them and interbred, taking on the larger group's customs and culture. They act as guardians of these mountains now."

"How many are there?" Caleb asked. He wasn't sold on Hawke's solution. It smacked of both hope and fairy dust, and once the Timpani learned that the wife and daughter of the man who'd driven some of them here were the ones asking for help....

"I counted over a hundred. All fighters. Men, women, and children all are trained from birth."

"A hundred?" Caleb repeated, then chuckled. "There are thousands of Shaylene choking on their own dust down there."

"I didn't say this would be a battle that would win your war for you, Commander, just some time. Wasn't that your plan?"

Caleb grunted.

"I imagine they won't be well disposed to us once they discover who Deva and I are," Neah said.

Caleb grudgingly gave her a mental tick for being on the same track.

What's another hundred when there are thousands lining up to kill us?

"Best not to mention that, I would think," Hawke said.

"How do we make contact?" Mohar asked.

"That's the tricky bit. I can't afford to leave the caravan. This trail is treacherous, and snap decisions need to be communicated fast. Turps hasn't the voice for that, literally."

"So you want volunteers to find your Timpani?" Mohar asked.

"No, I'm suggesting you and Caleb go."

"Not a chance," Caleb said. "Not with the Shaylene this close. They could catch us up any day now. There's no telling how long it will take to find these fairy creatures—if at all."

"More troll than fairy, I would say," Deva said, settling back against the wall, her short legs dangling off the bed. "They're an ugly lot, as I recall."

"Hmm, that leaves me. I don't think so," Neah said. "Why does it have to be one of us anyway? Can't we ask for a volunteer from the caravan? There haven't been any murders since we got rid of the entity through Winterdom. Morale has improved tremendously. I'm sure we could find someone."

"For once, I'm with Neah. I say call for volunteers," Caleb added.

Deva settled herself against the wall. "You may have a point though, Hawke. As I recall, the Timpani were notoriously antisocial. I imagine they may have established other trails through these mountains. Perhaps even right over to the Carmelsaran side."

"None that would take a caravan of this size," Hawke said dismissively.

"I wasn't meaning for the whole caravan." Deva dragged up a corner of Hawke's feather-filled quilt to cover her legs.

"Who then?"

"The future Torian."

Caleb felt Mohar stiffen beside him, as if someone had poked him with a stick. Neah gave an audible gasp. Deva's news seemed to have come as a surprise to them all.

"You've discovered who it is?" Hawke's voice cut through the excited bluster of the others.

"Yes. I've suspected it for some time, mind."

"Why didn't you tell me, Mother?"

"Who is it?" Hawke asked.

"I don't know. Not yet." She held up a hand at their protests. "I can tell you *where*."

She looked directly at her daughter. All eyes turned to Neah.

"The new Torian is waiting to be born. I'd say within the next seven months or so."

Neah jumped to her feet. "Why are you looking at me when you say that? Surely you're not—? That is absolutely ridiculous—"

"You've been vomiting up your breakfast every day for over a fortnight, and haven't had your menses for this past cycle. You're now well overdue," Deva said, her voice rising to be heard over Neah's outrage.

"Most of the camp is vomiting. The damned food is going off. And thank you. Thank you, *Mother*, for sharing my intimate details with these, these—men. For your information—and now everyone else's—I'm not always regular, particularly when I have to go out and kill people. It throws my sensitive female side out for some reason."

"There's something else," Deva added, her voice now calm. "You bear the mark. I saw the start of the Torian's mark this morning when you asked me to sponge your back. I can show you."

Mohar jumped off the bench seat into the wagon. He stood in front of Neah, staring deeply into her eyes, and then took her wrist lightly between two of his fingers. He let it drop after a moment and turned to face Deva and Hawke.

"She's right. Neah is pregnant."

"Are you all insane? I haven't even been with a man for "

Realization dawned in Caleb at the same time as it struck Neah. She spun to face him, hands on her hips. "No! No. This can't be happening. It can't be true."

"She's right," Caleb said. "This is all just hearsay. And just think about what you're inferring: that I've sired the next Torian? Me? Why, I can't even remember bedding her."

Neah lashed out, striking his chest.

He swayed, holding his ground. "And I'm pleased I can't."

She hit him again.

"Enough of this," Hawke snapped. "Neah, there's one way to settle this. Mohar, are you familiar enough with the Torian's mark to be able to tell if what Deva is saying is true?"

"Yes. Yes, I am."

"Neah? Would you? Mind, I mean."

"Aaah. All right! Hold that up quilt, Mohar, and get me a mirror. I want to see this rubbish for myself."

They all waited while Neah slipped out of her jacket and blouse, then turned so that her back faced them. Deva slipped in behind the quilt holding a mirror, angling it so that when Neah looked over her shoulder she could see her back in the reflection.

"Oh no," she said, when Deva managed to find the right angle.

Mohar dipped one corner of the quilt away so the others could see.

The curve of Neah's back was disconcertingly white, feminine, and strong. It was a pity she was so damned infuriating. Down near her hip, just above the long woolen peasant skirt that she favored, was what might have been a large multicolored birthmark, or an ink staining. They all bent to look closer.

Mohar pointed at the top where there was a crescent shape set at a forty-five-degree angle.

"This crescent is the time indicator, or when the Torian is due to succeed. The inking here is a little fuzzy, it's not clear. That's not a good sign."

Hawke, his brows drawn in concentration as he studied the

design, said, "Deva, didn't you say that this mark only appears when the Torian is ready to declare. Surely this child—baby, infant—obviously cannot."

"The mark appears at the appropriate time for the future Torian to be acknowledged. This, I think, is such a time."

Mohar continued, following the curving line beneath the crescent, tracing just above it with his long, sculpted nail.

"This line represents the lineage. The large red dot at the top is the current Torian, the green one below is the one before him, then all the way back through the succession to the very first. This is significant. It's very clear and distinct. This Torian will know his own mind, much as both his parents often demonstrate."

Caleb shot him a filthy glance.

"Anyway," Mohar continued, "right at the bottom is the most crucial identifier. See how it is shaped like a crown? For the Torian to be fully declared, all the arches or points of the crown have to be distinct. These are. In my opinion, there is no doubt. Congratulations. Here's to the new Torian, long may be their reign," he finished, in the ritual blessing.

No one said anything. Caleb sank onto the bed, exhaling deeply. Mohar raised the quilt back up, while Neah, in a huff, dressed herself.

Finally Caleb said, "Surely this means that Neah is the new Torian. How can it be a child if the marks have appeared on her?"

"That may well be. Personally, I doubt it. If the marks belong to the child, they will gradually disappear from Neah's back closer to the birth. They'll then be visible on the child's body once it's delivered."

"You're talking as if this child—if indeed there is a child in there —as if 'it' is making all this happen. Look at her. Surely at this stage any child can only be as big as my thumb—if that. Come on," Caleb protested.

Deva looked over from helping Neah secure her jacket. "Oh, it's already sentient. While the body is not yet formed, the spirit and consciousness are fully in play. The Torian's spirit comes fully matured." She smiled.

"Unlike some," Neah murmured, glancing over at Caleb.

Deva addressed Mohar. "You agree then that either Neah or my grandchild will be the new Torian?"

"Most certainly."

"Very well, then we must do our utmost to ensure their survival and to get them safely to Carmelsara."

"How do you propose to do that?" Caleb asked.

"I think Hawke was on the right track earlier. You and Neah must find the Timpani and convince them to help. Perhaps discover if there is an alternate route over the mountains."

Everyone began speaking at once. Caleb, still reeling with the aftermath of the news, felt strangely disconnected. Something else was niggling at his attention, like a distant voice that he couldn't quite make out.

"Caleb?"

"What, sorry?" He looked up and tuned in. Mohar had asked him a question.

"I overheard you and Hawke speaking earlier about the sacrifice of a few for the betterment of others. I ask you now, is this not just such a situation? We have a new Torian, someone who could potentially ensure tens of thousands, perhaps millions if Deva's prophecy is correct, avoid countless suffering. Is it not your duty to do your part in bringing that about?"

"You cleverly twist my words, wizard—as you do so often. However, I will not leave these people in the caravan defenseless."

"They are defenseless now. Surely you must admit that. You have five men left, and one of them is *me*, for the Mother's sake," Mohar volleyed back. "What can five possibly do against an army? What difference will it make if you two are here or not? A few less dead Shaylene. So what? Their numbers will swamp us ultimately, regardless of how narrow an approach you leave them."

"You're suggesting I should *run away*? To save my own life and leave these people I've been charged with to die?" Caleb spat the words out as if they were a bad oyster.

"This was a voyage of the damned from the start," Mohar shouted back. "You've admitted as much yourself. How we've lasted this long is anyone's idea of a miracle. If you ask me, the people should be grateful for the extra time they've been gifted. Everyone has to die. This is their time, otherwise they wouldn't be here."

"Enough." Hawke intervened. "We can't solve this here, and the caravan, damned or not, needs to keep moving. Let's all think on it and speak again when we camp tonight."

Neah, her lips compressed to a thin pink line, thumped into Caleb as she passed him, far harder than necessary in order to reach the back door.

THE REST of the day passed in a blur for Caleb. He stayed at the rear of the caravan, jumping down once to help change a broken wheel, and again when a dispute arose between the drivers of two wagons. He refused to acknowledge that by staying near the back he was avoiding the possibility of accidentally running into Neah. His world as he knew it was spinning in the opposite direction.

Mohar found him just as the sun was setting.

"Ah, here you are. Hawke asked me to tell you there's another few leagues to travel before we make camp."

"What? It's almost sunset. We can't travel these steep roads at night."

"That's what I told him. Lanterns, he said. One man at the front near the lead team, and another to walk the off side near the drop so drivers can tell how close they are to the edge."

"God's blood, does the man not know how incompetent some of those driving are? Has he not been watching them the past weeks?"

"You're wasting your time railing at me," Mohar said. He paused before adding, "So, have you given any more consideration to —"

"No. And in case you are tempted to ask me again, no."

"Well, I don't blame you, however, I happen to know you are lying. Remember, I know what's going on inside your head."

Caleb shrugged. "Then why even bother asking?"

"I'm naturally polite. Here's something that's not. You must do this, Caleb. If you stay here, Neah and the Torian will be killed along with everybody else." Mohar paused, then added fiercely, "If you do not take her, then I will."

"No one is going anywhere."

Mohar reached over and halted Caleb's horse. When Caleb looked at him, the wizard had a strange expression in his eyes. "You of all people, Caleb, cannot stop me. This is your child you are speaking so dismissively of. Think on that. Your—child. This from a man who, by all that's right and holy, should have been dead the day of the fight on the ridge."

Caleb's head snapped back. It felt as if Mohar had struck him.

"What did you just say?"

"I said your child—"

"No. Not that. You said that by rights I should have been dead that day on the ridge. What did you mean by that?"

Mohar backpedaled. "An expression. Deva said you would have been dead, if you recall."

"No. You said just now that I 'should' be dead, as if you knew something more. You make much of our connection, and I felt the difference just then when you said what 'should' have happened. And come to think of it, I didn't register any surprise from you when Deva announced that Neah was pregnant, either. As if you already knew."

Mohar's eyes slid away. "You're trying to use that underactive imagination again, Caleb. I've told you it's not very good."

"No." Caleb shook his head, staring at the wizard in the diminishing light. "I don't believe you. I'm right, aren't I? You already knew she was pregnant."

"I'm a wizard, after all; we're supposed to know things."

"You're also a bullshitter. Tell me now, or by the lords I'll kick you off the side of this cliff myself."

Mohar's expression tightened. Finally, he nodded. "All right. Yes, I did know. Are you satisfied?"

"No. Now I'm getting something else. Words seem to be flowing through that cursed connection we have."

"It's one-way, remember? And not to you."

"Not tonight." Caleb shook his head. Something was happening, like when that small voice was calling to him in Hawke's wagon earlier today. This was as if Mohar were himself whispering it to him.

"I can hear you telling me. It's your own damned voice. Whispering. A whole bunch of stuff."

Mohar's face went white. "No. That can't happen. It's not possible. Stop." He held his hands to his ears as if this might somehow prevent Caleb from hearing whatever it was.

More and more information flowed, and Caleb's anger grew. Mohar went to ride away. Caleb caught him round the collar of his vest and jerked him from his horse. Finally, when the whispering stopped, Caleb hit him.

"You bastard." He rode away, up to the front of the line.

"HE IS RESPONSIBLE. FOR EVERYTHING," Caleb declared, his finger pointing at Mohar. They were all gathered back in Hawke's wagon. Outside, the camp was settling into its nightly routine: quiet murmurs, the solid click of bowls being stacked, and children being settled. The last puff of woodsmoke as fires were banked ready for the morning."Explain yourself, Caleb, you're making no sense," Hawke said.

Caleb held up his fingers and ticked each event off as he said it. "Stealing the apple in the square back at Roganshah, him being here as part of this caravan, ingratiating himself into this group, even

Neah's pregnancy and my alleged 'drunken rape' of her—that was all arranged by Mohar. Tell them, wizard."

Mohar's face was flushed, whether from the white spirit that Hawke had just passed around, or from embarrassment, it was impossible to say. He cleared his throat.

"Caleb's right. In part." He held up a hand as everyone started to speak. "Allow me to finish. I'll start from the beginning. Deva, as you have pointed out previously, I am, or was, a Third Laurel wizard. I was stripped of my powers by the Torian himself for abusing my... position. I'm not proud of that. However, some time back he offered me a way to redeem myself and regain my access to power. May I have some more of that fine spirit, Master Hawke?"

Hawke gave everyone another full measure, then firmly recorked the bottle. The night was cold despite the crackling fire inside the potbelly. Mohar took a sip from his cup and appeared to be considering his words before continuing.

"The Torian, like everyone, was concerned that his replacement had not declared, and so he sought guidance."

"From who?" Hawke asked, leaning forward, obviously intrigued.

"Each Torian has the ability to speak with the spirit who will succeed him, if necessary. Even if they are still a spirit-in-waiting or, as they are officially called, the Torian Yet To Be Born. He—and yes, it is a boy"—he held up his glass in a mock toast—"identified the two parents he had chosen. Those who would best provide him with the qualities required for his reign. You now know them to be Caleb and Neah. My task was to simply bring them together. To mate. In return, the Torian would reinstate my powers after I successfully delivered the infant to Carmelsara. He also guaranteed to lend me power temporarily during this trip whenever the fate of the child was at risk. At great pain and cost, I have managed that several times."

"Surely in doing this you have manipulated not only Caleb's and Neah's fates, but also many others?" Deva said coolly.

"There is a saying I am fond of. 'Fate is just a sail pointed into destiny's wind. It must be constantly reset to catch its changing direction.' You know this, Deva. Until Shayla usurped the crown, the Shaylene territory was part of the Commonwealth. Caleb was destined to have been posted there—as Territory Commander, a significant promotion, you'll be pleased to know, Caleb. Your destiny was to have been presented to the young Princess Neah, fall hopelessly in love, and eventually both of you would have eloped together to have your Torian love child. Happy endings all round. Unfortunately, Shayla had other plans."

Caleb found his eyes flicking nervously toward Neah. She was staring back at him, arms crossed, mouth set. The warmth from the stove was in stark contrast to the coldness he could feel roiling out from her.

"You make me sound like some farmer's prize sow and him some ranging stud boar. How did you manage our meeting anyway?" Neah's words were sharp.

Mohar looked over at her, his large eyes soft, almost apologetic. "I was there that night, in the tavern where you were working. In fact, it was I who brought Caleb along, having befriended him earlier. I drugged his wine and then entranced the both of you. It wasn't difficult, you were both already highly attracted to one another. After the, er, impregnation, I instituted a memory wash that doesn't seemed to have worked completely on you, Neah, and far too well on Caleb here. Nevertheless, neither of you remembered me, or my part."

"And 'my part,' what of that?" Caleb snapped. "Tell them what was supposed to have happened after that."

The wizard sighed. "When Shayla killed her father and assumed the throne, everyone's fate lines were affected. The new lines revealed that Caleb would die in the Shaylene attack on the Commonwealth-held ridge. That's why I had to bring the two of you together as quickly as I could."

"Go on," Hawke urged.

"Unfortunately, the night of the coupling Shayla was also prowling the taverns, searching for a Commonwealth officer she could psychically infiltrate in order to turn them against their own side at the battle of the ridge. She needed victory to be assured to underscore her claim of invulnerability. After the mind wash, Caleb was a prime candidate; his mind was wide-open. An easy target for her. As a result, he managed to survive the battle of the ridge and—"

"Will now die in disgrace," Caleb finished for him, his voice bitter.

"How did you learn all this, Caleb? I can't imagine Mohar telling you," Deva asked.

Caleb shifted uneasily in his seat. "We are bound by the Sworn link. You know that. I can hear things, sometimes."

Mohar butted in. "The child speaks to him. He even opened some of my closed channels to him, and this information flowed through."

Deva nodded to herself. "Ah. You see, Caleb, even in the womb your boy knows what is best. You must recognize that your duty is to a far higher calling now. It is imperative that you do everything to save your child. My grandson."

"Will everyone stop saying that. I am my own man and know my own mind."

"Pigheadedness is no substitute for insight, Caleb. You have access to that now. I encourage you to use it," Deva persisted.

"I would like to hear from Neah. She is the mother, after all," Hawke said, helping himself to another refill of white spirit.

Neah stood slowly, gathering her thick white cloak about her. It was made from fine wool spun with highlights of gold thread and fringed with large feathers. Eagle, Caleb suspected. Her hair was unbound for a change, hanging well past her shoulders in thick, heavy curls. When she spoke her voice was clear and firm, yet there was a softness underlying it that he hadn't noticed previously.

"I didn't want to believe that I was pregnant. I still find it hard to, yet." She placed her hand lightly against her abdomen. "I have a knowing of it. I feel him in there, even though his physical size is minute. As such, Torian or no, my first duty must be to protect him. There can be no question. If the best chance is to leave this caravan then I will do it, but I am yet to be convinced that walking into the freezing mountains with no shelter, only as much food as I can carry, and no certainty of assistance from the Timpani whom my father chased into virtual extinction is the best solution for that. I will, therefore, be staying right here."

"Well said," Caleb said, clapping. "My vote is that we send Mohar out there to enlist these Timpani into helping us. He seems to be particularly good at getting people to do what he wants. Let's see how it works on trolls."

"I must remain with the Torian-in-waiting," Mohar said doggedly.

"No," Hawke roared. "Your job is to do what you are told, otherwise you can walk back to Roganshah and take your chances with what you find in between. You have signed on to this caravan, made your mark, which as you know, wizard, will bind you, regardless of your 'higher calling.' Do I make myself clear?" Hawke used his full height to advantage as he loomed over Mohar.

Mohar gritted his teeth before providing a tight "Yes."

"Yes, Master Hawke," Hawke persisted.

"Yes, Master Hawke," Mohar repeated.

Caleb was enjoying this, and helped himself to another drink.

"So, as it happens, I think Caleb's suggestion that it be Mohar who seeks out the Timpani makes a whole lot of sense. Given that he is the cause of most of the people's troubles in this wagon tonight, I don't foresee any argument from the floor?" He paused dramatically. "As I suspected. I suggest you make a start at first light. Deva, can you draw him some supplies? The wizard is likely to get hungry before he returns."

THE DAWN BROUGHT A CLEAR SKY. Yesterday's thick clouds had been blown elsewhere, and in their place the promise of blue sky arced over them. The mountains to the east were silhouetted against the sun's tentative rays.

Caleb looked down the trail to the plain beyond. The Shaylene seemed much closer. Through the glass he could now make out tiny dots of color at the front of the ever-present dust cloud.

"You'll need this," Hawke said, handing something to Mohar. The three were at the fringe of the encampment. "It's a whistle the Timpani gave me when I was leaving. They said if I wished to meet with them again I was simply to return to these mountains and blow it. Someone would eventually come for me. I blew it once, out on the plain; it has no sound. I don't know whether they were having a joke with me, or if it's broken, however it's all I have."

Mohar turned the wooden whistle over in his hand.

"Why not blow it now?" asked Caleb.

"The Timpani do not keep to the main trail." He pointed up. "Travel that way. The going is steep. You won't be able to take your horse."

"No horse?" Mohar's eyebrows bunched as he shouldered the pack that Deva had prepared for him. "I must admit, Hawke, that this mission of yours becomes less attractive by the moment."

"Travel until you reach the far ridge. Keep the west to your right. Start using the whistle from that point. If no one comes, then return. We'll be up there." Hawke pointed in the opposite direction. "At Vale's Arch, see, you can just make out where the trail narrows. Caleb and his men will be there trying to delay the Shaylene until Turps and I can get the rest of the caravan up and over the pass. Your new Torian included."

Mohar nodded once and turned to go.

"One more thing." Caleb came around to face him, placing his index finger against Mohar's sternum. "Do not try and dog this caravan. I'll know if you're following us. If you do happen to find the Timpani, then bring their best fighters back. We're counting on you."

They watched Mohar scramble up the steep, rocky face, picking his way along each narrow ridgeline, missing his footing several times. Soon he was far above them.

The howl of a wolf carried over the distance from far up the slope. Several others answered.

"Does he have a hope of a chance?" Caleb asked.

"One thing I've learned about chance is that she always wants to have her turn at throwing the dice. Without her, there is no hope."

Caleb and Hawke turned and walked back to the head of the caravan.

The rocky trail left no room to form an overnight defensive eight, and the wagons were strung out along it. The animals were restless and on close hobbles lest they wander too close to the edge in pursuit of the scarce vegetation.

"There was another passing last night. Along with the seven in the wagon that went over the edge on the way up, that will make eight. Will you conduct a joint service this morning before we break camp?"

Death in all its various guises had stalked them throughout. The ones passing from natural causes, cold, or hardship ended no differently than those caused by arrows, sword, or witchcraft.

"No, there's no time. My aim is to make camp behind Vale's Arch tonight. The Shaylene are coming faster than I'd have given them credit for. What I'm more worried about is that Shayla will have sent a vanguard of her best and fastest ahead of the main pack. My bet is they'll be travelling by night so we won't spot them. If so, they could be upon us at any time."

"Have you been up with the bird to take a look?"

Hawke shook his head. "Valiant and I no longer have the hearts we once did. I have overused both of us too much to get the caravan this far. Neither of us will survive another joining." He paused, his nostrils flaring as he disclosed, "I released Valiant for good this morning. He knows. He won't be back. Not this time." Hawke sniffed, and busied his hands beneath the vast cloak.

"Have you lost your pipe?" Caleb asked.

"No, I still have that, just no tobacco."

Caleb was silent for a moment, then asked, "Is it the leaf or the poppy that you miss the most?"

Hawke grinned momentarily, bringing out one hand to settle on Caleb's shoulder like some great bird perching. "Beneath all that guilt and army bluster, you're a clever fellow. You know that, don't you?"

"I know you're sick. I've seen the pain hit you when you're not expecting it. Is it the canker?"

Hawke tightened his grip on Caleb's shoulder. "I've enjoyed our conversations on this trip, Caleb, but my bad habits and the cause of them are not up for discussion. It's too late for any of that. Deva knows. She's been helping me with some of her herbs." He brought out a packet of dried leaves and laid several beneath his tongue. "They help somewhat. Whatever happens, this will be my last caravan. All that remains is to try and ensure it's not everyone's. Especially that son of yours."

He gave Caleb a lopsided grin, and using Caleb's shoulder as leverage stepped up onto a nearby rock with a painful grunt. He brought out the bone whistle and gave a shrill burst, the signal to break camp.

Caleb said nothing further, simply mounted up and cantered down the line until he reached Deva's wagon. The older woman was already on the bench seat, reins in her hands, a red patterned blanket draped about her.

He touched the brim of his hat. "Is she in?"

She nodded. He slipped off his horse and tied him off to the side of the wagon, before climbing up to sit beside her.

"How are you doing?" he asked. She seemed small and vulnerable huddled within the blanket.

"My grandson lends me new life." She glanced at him shrewdly. "And you? After a night to ponder the ways of the Mother?"

"The Mother, hey? Everyone wants to claim responsibility for destiny, have you noticed? Even though the story changes constantly, you all want to say it's preordained. You and Mohar—and this Torian, whoever the hell he might be."

"Let's hope we all find that out together. Go through, she's expecting you." Deva's grin was mischievous. The gold fillings in her teeth glinted dully in the first light. "The Mother told us you'd be dropping by."

"You're a witch," Caleb muttered fondly, slipping through the curtain.

Inside it was dim, the lanterns still burning, lending the space a cozy feel. Most of the spare food that had been stacked here had either been transferred to the supply wagons or consumed, which meant there was more room to move about.

Neah was lying on the bed, the coverlet tucked around her, the square window beside her firmly shut. She glanced up when he slid through the opening, thumping onto the floor.

She didn't appear surprised to see him. He shook off his great-coat, sending droplets of dew in all directions, some hissing against the hot metal of the potbelly stove. He draped the dripping coat over the chair.

"Most people would do that outside," she said.

"I'm pretty sure you'll have figured out by now that I'm not most people." He stripped off his gloves and held both hands to the warmth from the stove.

"How are you feeling?" he asked over his shoulder.

"Confused. A little afraid. Angry—a whole lot. And embarrassed."

"I can understand the rest, but embarrassed?"

Her words tumbled together. "I wanted to apologize for—for a lot of things."

"That's why I came by too. Mohar has a lot to answer for, and if we ever get out of this, I'll make sure he does. There's one thing I can't abide, and that's being manipulated. We both were."

"That's not what I meant. Not exactly."

He turned and she took a deep breath. He had the feeling she had to force herself to meet his gaze, and when she did her expression was open, almost resigned.

"Mother and I have been talking, and I haven't been honest— with you, or even myself, about... that night."

Caleb didn't know where this was going. He felt confused and slightly uncomfortable. "We've both said things we probably shouldn't. I can blame Mohar for my loss of memory, but not the rest." He looked down. "Not taking advantage of you, anyway."

The wagon lurched into motion and almost immediately hit a large pothole. Caleb made a grab for the sideboard to steady himself.

She sat up straighter, eyes wide and moist. "That's just it. I'm not sure you did. Take advantage. Deva never believed it. That used to infuriate me too, that she wouldn't take my side against you."

"What do you mean?"

"I lied when I said I remembered everything about that night. I don't. Only snatches." Her voice cracked, and she looked down at her hands gripping the edge of the coverlet before continuing.

"I know the memory is inside me, somewhere, because every now and again bits break free and bubble up. There was no forcing."

"None?" He was cautious lest this was another of her tricks.

Neah shook her head. Tears glistened, yet stubbornly refused to form. She shook her head as if denying them. With a deep inhale, she said in a rush, "I can now remember... feeling what happened... even enjoying it."

Slowly, he approached and eased himself down to sit at the end of her bed. The creaking of the wagon and its easy swaying movement settled between them.

Caleb picked at a cuticle on his forefinger. Neah hadn't finished, and to break in now would destroy the tender sharing. When he looked up, Neah was staring out the window. Tears were trickling down her cheeks. She let them run unchecked.

"It was inconceivable that I would willingly go with a man again after—everything I've been through. The only explanation that made any sense was that I was drugged and then forcibly taken." Her voice cracked and she tried to laugh. "I made myself believe it, but when Mohar admitted what he'd done, more memories came. Ones I didn't want to acknowledge." The final words came out with a sob.

"We don't have to talk about this now," he said.

"Oh, yes. Yes, I do. Now especially." Her hand slid beneath the quilt, its outline travelling to her abdomen, resting there as if comforting the child inside.

"The time I was a slave changed me. Irrevocably. The person I'd once been had gone. Warmth, laughter, even hope had died—so I thought. Until now." Neah closed her eyes as if she didn't want to see the effect of what she was saying.

"You mean the child?"

Her eyes opened again and her face flushed. "Yes. I am discovering things, perhaps rediscovering things about myself that are uncomfortable and don't fit with my... story."

The softness he'd witnessed last night brushed briefly across her face. It was tinged with sadness, the long lashes blinking back more tears.

"I didn't know that I could feel again, not after everything that had happened."

"Feel what? Do you mind me asking?"

Bringing her attention back, she watched him for several seconds, as if trying to decide something. Finally she said, "Vulnerable, I suppose. Carrying this child makes me realize how tenuous his life really is. How totally reliant he is on me. There is this almost savage need to protect him."

"And?" Caleb prompted, sensing more.

"Yes, something else. Underneath that there's this other...." She moved her fingers in the air, as if they might pluck the right word for her. "Sort of a rising... tenderness?" She laughed self-consciously. "I'm so unused to it I don't even know what it feels like anymore." She sniffed and looked out the window again.

Caleb knew that whatever he said next would either nourish or crush this tiny shoot of trust she'd exposed. He extended his arm, turning the hand over so that it rested beside her: calloused, strong, and eminently capable. When he spoke, his voice was hushed.

"This arm is there to lean on if, and whenever, you choose. Regardless, it will defend the child until its strength has gone and my arm no longer has the power to move."

Her dark eyes flashed, surprise rippling across her face. He sensed her mentally take a step back toward her shell of self-reliance. He resisted the urge to move the arm, keeping his hand where it was.

Silence closed around them, thickening, closeting the sounds from outside, until all that remained were the echoes of his words hanging in the air and his palm, open and waiting, between them.

Caleb could see her internal struggle. The tightness in his gut added to a shortening of breath. He'd lived his whole life by loyalty; it was a quality he knew well. But this? This was something quite different, untried and untested. If he had to give it a name it came damn close to devotion, and something else. Something far greater that had yet to be spoken.

Slowly, as if even she were unaware of it, her arm moved, drawing out her hand from beneath the coverlet like a small minx in need of nourishment, furtively aware that its tender flesh featured on every predator's menu.

Caleb found himself holding his breath as her hand came down to lie lightly across his. Hers, like his, was battle honed and hard. In between the calluses it was soft.

"This is new to me," she said. "Accepting support. I'm not sure I can—"

Her hand flinched and began to withdraw. His fingers lightly closed around hers, squeezing them briefly before releasing.

"To me as well."

"I make no promises, Caleb. Value that. I will accept your help because of who you are and where we find ourselves. Beyond that I can't commit to anything. Not to or with you—not anyone."

"I accept that. We're all strung between a past that's determined to kill us and a future that none of us can yet see. Survival is all we can try for. Perhaps, if we can do that together—"

Voices and cries intruded from outside. They both started. The unmistakable sound of men fighting was counterpointed with three blasts from Hawke's whistle.

Caleb thrust the window open and looked out. An arrow barely missed his head, smashing through the glass. The wagon lurched to a halt, and Deva yelled,

"Shaylene!" before tumbling through the curtain in a tangle of skirts.

"Shaylene." Her voice was raspy, as if repeating the word was too much.

Caleb bounded off the bed and snatched up his cloak, shrugging into it and roughly pulling on his gloves. "Hawke was right. There was an advance party."

Neah threw back the coverlet and unhooked a quiver of arrows and her bow from the wall beside her.

"What are you doing?" Caleb caught her arm as she fastened her crossed bandoliers, already threaded with extra arrows.

She pulled away roughly. "I said I'd accept your help. I never said I'd be dependent on it. If we're under attack, I'm going to help. Nothing has changed other than I am now defending my child as well."

She pushed past him and nimbly bounded over the bench seat, whistling for Magic. Cursing, he followed.

Outside was chaos. Wagons were in disarray; the one at the front, Turps's, had been overturned. Beasts, some stuck with arrows, bellowed in pain, the yellow-and-blue shafts of the Shaylene arrows bright against their brown hides. The Shaylene must have skirted around the caravan and laid an ambush just forward of last night's camp. When the oxen in the lead wagon had been felled, their bulk had fallen against the wagon's shaft, flipping it to on its side, effectively blocking the road and preventing the caravan from moving out of range.

Caleb drew a cutlass and leaped onto his stallion, activating his Sworn link to the troopers. All appeared to be responding and were returning fire from reasonable defensive positions. The Shaylene were well dug-in, and most of the caravan's return arrows were striking rock.

An arrow thudded into the saddle beside his thigh, failing to penetrate the thick leather. He urged his horse to the other side of Deva's wagon, sheltered from the line of fire. The Shaylene were above them, their archers positioned strategically to keep them pinned them down. He counted five different vectors of arrow flights. Possibly there were more in the rocks over by the right. He looked behind him. The drop yawned off, a sheer chasm spiraling down for thousands of feet. The Shaylene had picked their spot well. Their job was simple: pin them down until reinforcements arrived. He suspected Shayla herself might even lead the larger force, anxious to personally witness the obliteration of any possible new Torian. He wondered if she knew that her own sister carried the future within her.

His mouth firmed as he realized that everyone still alive after this first attack wave would be ultimately be slaughtered, including his child.

They had to get that overturned wagon out of the way.

Using his Sworn link he called the troopers forward, urging them to bring as many men as were able.

He wondered where Mohar was and how he was doing, wishing he had access to his magic, then cursing himself for it. Mohar was the bane of his life, the reason for everything going wrong. Caleb had no forgiveness for him.

"Hawke," Caleb yelled. The caravan master was applying pressure to a woman's wound. Drawing closer, Caleb recognized her as Mrs. Barlowe. She and her husband were travelling with three daughters, and had been trying to marry the oldest off to any eligible male all trip, Caleb included. He could tell from the pallor of her skin and the way her blood was pulsing between Hawke's fingers that she only had minutes remaining.

"We're going to try and clear the blockage ahead. When you're through, I'll need your help to get the rest of the wagons moving again." Hawke nodded and continued to work, undeterred.

Caleb reached the overturned wagon. Turps had been driving when the attack came. The oxen were lying dead in their traces. The arrows had struck in such a way that the animals had dropped in their tracks, toppling sideways; their combined weight had done the job.

Even if they could right the wagon, they wouldn't be able to budge the dead beasts, unless....

"Arrowsmith."

His adjutant squirmed over on his belly.

"Get Hawke up here. I need him now."

The Shaylene archers were trying to advance in the face of a steady stream of defenders' arrows, coming from the midsection of the caravan. From the rate of launch he had a fair idea who was firing them. Damn stubborn woman. He smiled.

Hawke hunkered down beside Caleb. "What is it, Commander— Oh, no. Not Turps too." Hawke's voice cracked. Turps's corpse was sprawled in a heap beside his overturned wagon, the brightly colored fletching of three Shaylene arrows in his body.

"Sorry. I thought you already knew."

"No. No, I didn't," Hawke said, still staring at the ostler. When he spoke again his voice was soft, as if he was speaking to himself. "It was my turn to be in the lead today. I swapped with him because I wanted to make sure Mohar was sent on his way. That should have been me up there."

"Sorry, Hawke. Unless we focus now, there'll be a lot more deaths here today than Turps. There'll be a time for grieving later. First we have to get out of this mess."

Hawke took a deep breath and turned his back on the overturned wagon while Caleb quickly explained what he had in mind.

"See how wagon number three is so close to the edge of the chasm? I'm guessing it slid there when we had to pull up so fast. If we can hook it up to number two as well as the one that's overturned, and then push three over the lip of the chasm, it should pull the next one over as well, and then their combined weight just might drag Turps's wagon, and its dead bullocks with it. Can we afford to lose that many wagons?"

"If it gets us moving again, I'm willing to sign off the whole damn lot. Can you do it?"

Another arrow thudded into the wood beside Hawke.

"We can't stay here, I know that. Come on."

They hooked heavy chains around the axles of all three wagons, and cut free the teams that were still in their traces. The Shaylene archers, seeing what they were doing, unleashed a full assault at the front three wagons.

"Arrowsmith. Take some men, try to get up there behind them and draw their fire. We need some time without worrying about getting hit." After a beat he added, "And find Neah. *Ask* her if she'll go with you."

He felt a curious mix of trepidation and resigned certainty as he gave the order. As an army officer he knew that deploying their best archer on a mission like this made absolute sense; sending the mother of his unborn child out, however, left him... conflicted.

"Put your back into it. Push," he grunted at the man next to him, lending his weight to one of the wheels on wagon three. The drop was only a large stride from the wheel closest to the edge. Getting the wagon moving and then over the uneven ground was proving to be the challenge.

He glanced back over his shoulder. Colored fletchings were now zinging down the slope toward the Shaylene. He smiled. Neah was in position. The intensity of the attack on the caravan lessened as the enemy turned to defend.

Number three resisted for a moment, then lurched forward, gathering speed as its front wheels hit the decline toward the edge. They'd used an extra-long chain to hook up wagon two, so that three

would be well on its way to the bottom by the time the chain tightened and hopefully tugged two with it.

The front wheels rolled over the edge. "Jump clear," Caleb
ordered.

They all waited as the rattling length of chain unraveled, grating
against the granite edge, watching and wondering whether the weight
of one would be enough. The chain tightened with a sudden jerk,
and then the other wagon started creaking forward, bouncing over
the small rocks until it too tumbled down. The men cheered. The
final length of chain was even longer; Caleb hoped the first wagon
wouldn't hit the bottom first. They needed its added weight and
momentum. The final chain jerked tight. It quivered momentarily,
sawing against the section where it met the edge of the rock.

"It's going to break."

The chain looked thick, but like men leading a charge, if enough
force were applied to the weakest section, it would break. The chain
quivered with the tension from opposing weights.

It wouldn't hold for long.

"We have to cut the dead bullocks free," Caleb said, and scampered forward, dodging behind a rock as a Shaylene arrow thunked
into the space he'd just vacated. He sprinted to the first of the
bullocks, shielding himself behind its carcass as he hacked through
the leather traces with his hunting knife. He moved to the second
one, and finally the third. As soon as he'd flung the harness from the
lead bullock the wagon jerked forward, the edge of the overturned
wagon gouging a wide track into the earth as the greater weight at the
end of the chain dragged it inexorably toward the edge.

"It's going over," one of the men shouted.

Caleb, doubled over, skittered back to where Hawke was waiting.

"What about the carcasses?" Hawke said. "We still can't
get past."

Further along the line of wagons, Caleb spotted several live oxen.

"Have someone bring up those beasts, they should be able to
drag them

out of the way. Enough for us to be able to squeeze the caravan past."

Hawke gave the order, and soon the oxen had pulled their dead brethren to one side. He gave a piercing blast on his whistle.

Caleb galloped down the line behind the wagons calling them to get moving. As he neared the end, he sprang from the saddle and dashed over to the rocks, rapidly climbing up the way his men must have gone.

He mentally called to his Sworn. There only three responses. He wondered fleetingly about Neah.

Spotting his Sworn in a cluster of boulders just above, he scrambled over some loose rocks, the small stones slippery beneath his boots, until he reached the next ridge and took a closer look. Fewer arrows were being shot down at the Shaylene, and as a result the raiders had turned their focus back to the caravan as it trundled forward, desperate to stop it.

They were aiming at the beasts. It made sense, they were bigger targets and would cause the most disruption.

He clawed his way up the remainder of the slope and slid into a small space beside Arrowsmith.

"What's the position?" he asked.

"We're low on arrows, and they've moved further along the ridge. We didn't have the firepower to follow."

"Ah, that was inevitable. You did a good job. At least the caravan is moving again."

Arrowsmith brought up his bow, resting it between the two boulders, and released an arrow at the disappearing Shaylene. It fell short.

"We're out of range. Don't waste your arrows," Caleb said. "Let's get back down. Where's Neah?"

Arrowsmith pointed up and to the right. He spotted a flash of her yellow buckskin jacket following a ridgeline, high above. He swore beneath his breath.

She was trying to head them off.

"I'll get her," he said. "Give the men a hand to carry down the wounded. If we lose them, I'll run a service for them tonight. There'll be no sky burials today. Not for these men."

Arrowsmith nodded and went over to help.

They were good men. Caleb didn't deserve their loyalty. At least those who'd died today had done so with honor and hadn't had to face the ignominy of a court-martial.

He clambered up the slope after Neah, then reeled back as an image formed uninvited inside his head.

Mohar: surrounded by tiny men, all with very sharp knives and axes. They didn't look happy. Then Mohar's voice in his head: *"Follow the wolf."*

FOURTEEN

"You're sure?" Neah whispered. She and Caleb had followed the Shaylene raiding party and were now positioned directly above them. There were only three of them left.

"Yes. It was like he took over my consciousness. I was there, seeing through his eyes. His voice said something about following the wolf. I didn't quite catch it."

Neah unleashed an arrow, catching one of the raiders who'd moved past the shelter of a rock. He slumped in a heap, and she selected another from those she'd thrust point-first into the ground at her feet.

"What about now?" she asked, as if nothing had happened.

"No. It's gone. There's nothing. I thought I was linked in to him—"

"He may be dead." She sighted another arrow. When she released it, another man died.

"We can only hope," he mumbled, silently marveling at her skill.

"We should work our way back down. The last wagon is almost past." Neah fired off the last arrow. The Shaylene warrior must have heard it coming, because he tried to duck, but wasn't fast enough. It caught him through the neck.

Caleb snapped out his glass and directed it down the slope.

"There." He pointed at a distant patch of color moving rapidly up the trail. "It looks like another hundred of them. Moving fast. If they can maintain that speed, they'll catch up as early as tonight. Tomorrow morning at the very latest."

"Let me see." Neah took the glass and hissed. "Shayla might be there."

Neah directed the glass further down the slope. "They seem to have their own supply wagons. The main group must be a long way back. There's something strange about them, but I can't quite make it out... oh, no. Caleb, take a look."

He focused on where she was pointing. The wagons were behind the Shaelene soldiers, so the image was hard to make out. It didn't make sense for a time, until he realized that the wagons were being drawn by men. Men in tattered Commonwealth uniforms.

"That bitch. She's shackled our men, turning them into beasts to pull her supply wagons."

"How many?"

"I count twenty, no, thirty. They look dead on their feet."

"Men make poor substitutes for drays. They lack the stamina of horses, much less oxen. There was a shortage of beasts in Roganshah, remember."

"And an oversupply of prisoners," Caleb said, his voice bitter.

"Anything more from Mohar?"

Caleb shook his head. "Good riddance. It was a fool's errand anyway, which is what made him such a good candidate."

"Mohar may be many things, however fool is not one of them. He bewitched both of us to achieve his own ends. Try and retrieve the last image you had of him. I'll help you."

She laid her hand lightly against his forehead. Her fingers felt both warm and hardened at their edges.

"Concentrate," she snapped.

He brought up the memory of what he'd seen before. It flickered uncertainly, threatening to drift off in some other direction, until he felt Neah's steadying presence, as if she were cupping the image, feeding strength into it. Suddenly it reappeared again, strong and almost overpowering.

"I have it," he whispered.

"Good. Now we're going to try and calculate where he was when you received it. Look more closely, what can you see? What do the surroundings look like? Is there a landmark, something we might be able to get a position from?"

Caleb concentrated, finding that he could easily move his awareness around by changing its perspective on the scene.

"It looks like he's underground. In some sort of cave, no, a cavern. It's big."

"Try going deeper still. Imagine where the way out might be, and move your attention toward that." She cupped her other hand around the back of his head.

Caleb's senses swirled, the image seeming to bounce from the front of his skull to the back. He felt like a child being spun round and round until he was wild, giddy, and disoriented.

"What do you see now?"

Caleb made an effort to still the spinning sensation. Several paths led from the cavern. Only one appeared to have any semblance of natural light. He imagined moving toward it. The view changed instantly and he was there.

"I see the way out. There's light at the cave's mouth. I can make out the horizon. And other mountains."

"Good. Imagine moving outside. See if you can identify any landmarks that we can get a fix on."

"I can see the caravan route. It's far below. Higher than we are here. Mountains, everywhere. I'm turning, there's the pass to Carmelsara between the peaks. It seems close."

"What way are you facing when you sight the pass?"

"East."

"And the entrance to the cavern is what, behind you?"

"Yes, I'd say more northwest."

"Look back along the road, do you see the caravan?" she asked.

Caleb physically turned this time, his brows drawing close as if he were looking to the distance.

"Yes. Perhaps a half a day's trek."

"Anything else?"

"There's snow in the air. Flurries of it blowing in from the south."

"Winter comes early to the high peaks. We'll have to hurry."

Neah removed her hands and the images fell away.

"Hurry to do what?" Caleb persisted, genuinely perplexed.

"Mohar has found the Timpani. It doesn't sound like he's been able to convince them to help us. We'll have to try."

"We?"

"Who else? One thing about Mohar, he always seems to get his own way in the end, have you noticed? He originally wanted us to be the ones who sought out the Timpani."

"Then it may be a trick to get us, or rather you, out of harm's way."

"Look back at what's coming. If we stay, we'll be overrun by Shayla's next force. This way we'll have a chance of saving the child as well as everyone else. Besides, if we're really lucky the Timpani may have disposed of Mohar by the time we get there." She looked up. "It'll be a tough climb though."

Caleb followed her gaze, shading his eyes against the light glistening off the snow at the peaks. "Don't snap my head off for saying this, but do you think you're up to it?" He looked meaningfully at her belly.

"Why don't you ask your son? He seems to have the last word on most things lately, and according to Mohar you're in dialogue with him."

When he looked at her she was smiling. It was a sight he found both unusual and distinctly pleasant.

"You should do that more often," he said, and regretted it immediately.

Her jaw hardened, and the lightness left her face. Caleb cleared his throat and looked away. "I should tell Hawke what we're doing. We'll also need some rope."

She nodded and followed him down.

AFTER PICKING up some supplies from Deva, they climbed solidly throughout what was left of the morning, Caleb leading, keeping the landmarks he'd seen earlier within a tight triangulated pattern. As the ravines closed in around them, however, he lost his way.

He paused, waiting for Neah to catch up. They only had one chance to get this right. Overnighting on the freezing mountain held no appeal.

"You're lost aren't, you?" Neah said from behind him.

"No, I know precisely where we are."

"Yes, so do I, we're right here. Do you know where we're heading in relation to it?"

"That way." Caleb pointed up.

"That's a man's answer. Those are snow clouds forming to the east. I need to know if you are lost."

"Thanks for the weather report. Let's keep moving; either way we'll need to find some shelter soon."

He pushed on, easing himself around the next outcrop. Reaching a hand back, he helped Neah steady herself, then made to move on. He paused midstride. The ridgeline they'd been following petered out several steps away. Part of it was broken off, most likely from a recent rockfall because the break in the rock appeared raw and jagged. A wide gap separated the secure footing on either side.

"We'll have to jump," Caleb said. "There's no other way around, and we don't have the time to double back. I'll go first." He unspooled a length of rope. "Put this around you. Loop it around your upper chest and tie it off just beneath the armpits, like this. Make it tight. If you miss your step I'll be able to haul you up from my end. All right?"

"And what about if you miss your jump? You'll drag me down with you?" Neah said, her voice coming with a wheeze. She was struggling, that was obvious. The air was thin this high up.

"Trust me. I won't." He smiled.

"Trust is one of those words. You know. Easy to say, harder to do."

She positioned her feet on the narrow ledge, her breathing still rapid and high in her chest. Finally she up gathered the rope and tied off, handing the excess spool to Caleb.

He mentally measured the jump, transferred weight into his back leg, and launched himself across, landing lightly on the other side.

He turned back. Neah hadn't moved. She was staring down into the gap. The drop was sheer here. Far below, a river snaked through a gully cut deep into the rock. In summer it would be fast-flowing, milky with snowmelt and white-tipped rapids, almost eager to leap from the cliff and cascade in a massive fall on the way to the valley far below. Now, it was sluggish with cold, its surface already smearing with the first smudging of ice.

"Neah. Don't look down. Look at me."

Gradually she managed to raise her gaze. She nodded, and squared the bow and bandoliers of arrows more securely across her back. Pushing off with her back foot, she leaped; her boot slipped and she lost traction. Caleb knew immediately she wouldn't have the distance.

Lunging, he made a grab for her arm, his fingertips only grazing the cuff of her jacket. Throwing himself back against the rock, he prepared for the jolt of when the weight of her falling body would transfer through the rope. When it came, the tightly spliced horsehair bit deep into his back and shoulder. He grunted with pain and the effort of checking her fall while retaining his balance on the narrow ledge.

"Are you all right?" he gasped. The rope cut into the flesh of his shoulder, sawing deeper as she swayed, caught by the wind. If he didn't steady it, she would begin to pendulum and he wouldn't be able to hold her.

"Yes. Can you pull me up?" Her voice sounded weak and distant.

"I'm trying. Can you stop the swinging?" he grunted back, bending at the knees, taking the weight into his legs and pulling up with his right arm. His left maintained the tension, tramping the slack beneath his boot as if that might stop it running back out.

She was a dead weight, and swung more with each puff of breeze.

"Try and stay still," he said through his teeth. The rope was moving easier across his back now. Moisture trickled from his shoulder, running beneath his shirt, and he wondered briefly whether it was sweat or blood. Closing his eyes, he managed to drag up another small section of rope. His left arm was trembling with the strain of maintaining the tension. "Can you reach the lip of the ridge?"

"No. Not yet. I'll try and reach up.... Caleb," she called, her voice urgent.

"What?"

"The rope. It's slipping."

"Put your arms down and look up, not down." He pulled up some more. If he leaned forward to see how she was he would overbalance, her weight pulling him over as well.

"It's still slipping. The knot has loosened."

Caleb closed his eyes, imagining her beneath the ledge, the rope slipping further.

"Clamp your arms down, elbows flat against your ribs, and grip your shoulders with the opposite hand. Can you do that?"

"Yes, all right. It's stopped slipping."

"Good, you're doing great. Remember in the caravan today I was telling you about lending you that arm when you needed it? Well, it's here for you now."

"Right at this minute, I'd take the two of them."

He allowed himself a ghost of a smile and heaved another length of rope up, then one more. Finally the top of her head appeared at the base of the ledge. She reached out, hesitant lest she dislodge the rope from beneath her armpits, and then gripped a protruding rock at the base of the ledge, taking some of the strain. Caleb felt the relief immediately and pulled harder. Soon she was over the lip of the ridge, struggling to rise and stand beside him, her back pressed flat and hard against the rock face.

He could feel her shaking, and could also sense that she was trying to control it.

"If we didn't have to jump over that gap again, I'd suggest we turn back. I don't know where we are," he said.

"Now he admits it. Well, I don't know either— Did you mention a big wolf earlier?"

He followed her gaze. Above them crouched a huge shaggy wolf, its fangs white and bared beneath spotted curling lips.

"Mohar said follow it, didn't he?" she said quietly, not taking her eyes from it.

Caleb nodded. The wolf turned and padded off, turning its head once as if to ensure they were following.

It was midafternoon by the time they made the uppermost ridge.

"There," he gasped, pointing. "That must be it."

From where they stood, the cave was little more than a shadow against the rock. The wolf howled once, then bounded away deeper into the mountains. As they approached the shadow, the entrance became more apparent, its perspective shifting with the angle of the light, layering in depth.

"Are you sure this is it?" Neah asked, peering into the gloom then to either side of the cave mouth. "There seem to be other caves along this ridge."

"I'm sure this is the one I saw. I also now have a sense of Mohar. He's close—and the wolf has gone, if that means anything."

In the distance he heard a howl. It was followed by another, much closer. Caleb's eyes automatically tracked the sound, sighting the animal above them less than two hundred paces away, its gray bristling shape highlighted against the fading light.

"That was the biggest wolf I've ever seen," Neah said.

"Come on. We don't want to still be out here when the light goes." He led the way, striking a flint against the wall to flare a reed torch he found thrust into a sconce near the entrance.

"See," he said, holding the torch high. "There's a torch. Someone has been here."

Neah bent down and picked up some small bones from the curved face of a large flat rock set into one side of the entrance. They looked to be from a body the same size as Chea.

"Yes, someone has been here. But how long ago? These brown lichen stains on the rock look ancient."

Caleb looked over her shoulder, holding the torch closer. The flaring reeds were damp, and cast irregular shadows.

"That's not lichen. It's dried blood. That rock is a sacrificial altar and those bones you're sifting through are likely to belong some poor bastard who was killed on it."

Neah dropped the bones and they clattered hollowly against the rocky floor.

"Do you think it was the Timpani who did this?" she asked.

"The bones look to be a similar size to the trolls who were gathered around Mohar, so, at a guess, yes." He turned and looked deeper into the tunnel, adding, "Of course, we could always ask them." Caleb reached out an arm, gathering Neah behind him. She pulled herself roughly away, determined to face whatever was coming.

Small shapes appeared, stepping straight from the darkness as if peeling themselves away from their own shadows. Soon Caleb and Neah were surrounded.

They appeared to be mostly male, with bare barrel chests, wearing what appeared to be small trousers made from animal skins. The tallest of them barely reached Caleb's waist. Their faces were misshapen, as if the features were assembled in haste or from mismatched parts, with overly large jutting jaws and too-small mouths and noses. Most had long thin bones threaded through the skin of their chests, puckering it like a long needle reinserted through cloth. Some sported brands burned deep into the flesh of their arms and cheeks, others were inked in an intricate pattern of blues and red across their shaven heads. All were armed with short spears, shields, and thick-bladed knives.

No one spoke.

The silence inside the tunnel was eerie. Then, as if from some unspoken command, the host of tiny men began swaying and emitting a low drone, like humming, or the distant sound of bees.

"What are they doing?" Caleb asked.

"I'm guessing its some sort of ritual to determine intent. I remember my father telling me about it once."

"That would be before he attempted to wipe them out, you mean?" he whispered back.

"Caleb. Don't make things worse."

The humming increased in pitch and volume, filling the tunnel and rebounding off the stone, setting up overtones that were both pleasant to hear and difficult to experience.

"I feel as if something is pressing very lightly against me. Like it's trying to get in," Caleb said.

"Don't resist. Let them. It'll be over sooner if you do."

Caleb felt something give, as if the surface tension of a bowl of water had been gently penetrated by an inquisitive and acutely sensitive fingertip. Waves of curious energy followed and then just as suddenly withdrew. The humming and swaying stopping abruptly too. One of the small men stepped forward. He looked no different to the rest other than a narrow circlet of leather around his head. At the point where the band met in the center of his forehead, a large purple stone had been inset—directly, it seemed, into his skull.

"You have no welcome here," he said, his voice unexpectedly deep, sharpened by a jagged accent. "Are you of the wizard who came before?"

Caleb hesitated, unsure whether agreeing would damn them. Neah answered for them both without hesitation.

"Yes. We come seeking the help of the Timpani against the

invading Shaylene army."

"Yet she who speaks is of that blood."

Neah straightened her shoulders, drawing up. "I am the second daughter of Justin, King of the Shaylene."

A wave of sound riffled across the surface of the encircling throng as if a puff of wind across a field of wheat. They pushed in a little closer.

"This daughter is either too brave or overly foolish. Did she not know that Justin slaughtered the Timpani of the plains almost to extinction?"

"That is my shame, yes. However, I am not like my father. Unlike his successor."

"The one who invades?"

She nodded. "Shayla. My sister—who sold me into slavery."

"A bond of blood, no less. I am Nutura. Guardian Elect of the Timpani."

"This is Caleb, a commander in the Commonwealth army." Neah indicated Caleb, who nodded before asking,

"And what of the wizard, Mohar?"

"He waits. Contained—and constrained," Natura replied, his small mouth twitching in what may have been amusement.

"Did he not explain the position?" Caleb tried again. "That Queen Shayla will annihilate and enslave not only the Timpani but the whole known world if her invasion is allowed to succeed?"

"The slave queen seeks opportunity and advantage to grow her power. Neither lie inside the peaks. The Timpani though are content to live within its cracks."

"Shayla will claim the caravan route. You will not go undetected forever. We found you," Caleb said, challenging. "Others will too."

"You followed the wolf at our pleasure, and the wizard our whistle. The Timpani whistle was a gift to the birdman. It was misguided. No other will come or follow. There is nothing of value here."

"If you are unwilling to help, then we will go. We mean you no harm."

The chieftain nodded. "We have determined your intent is pure."

"Then we shall leave," Caleb said, taking Neah's arm, attempting to steer her back toward the entrance. The surrounding mob moved like water, flowing into the space, closing off their avenue of retreat.

"Your purpose, though, is not." Natura continued as if nothing had happened. "You remain. Until the invaders have passed."

"That will be too late."

"For you, perhaps. Not for us."

Several of the men close to Caleb brought up their spears, their points resting against Caleb's chest. The threat was clear.

The group moved as one, further toward the heart of the mountain, Caleb and Neah washed along with it.

THEY WALKED for what seemed a long way. Caleb still carried his torch, but the dancing flames were unreliable, flaring and dulling with the relative dampness of the reeds. He could see only as far as the front of the group. For the past few paces, though, the tunnel had appeared to be widening.

Finally they entered what seemed to be a larger space, the light from his torch unable to penetrate the deep darkness above or around them. Ahead he could hear noises, like the unhurried scuttling of rats inside a well-stocked pantry.

One of the men dug Caleb in the ribs with the blunt end of his spear, motioning to the torch. Caleb lowered it, and the small man snatched it away, thrusting its flame against the rock wall. A few orange embers flared and floated up, before winking out so that the entire space was enveloped in a total blackness. Now not even shapes were discernible.

The group started moving again, shuffling forward with small steps. Caleb resisted the urge to hold his arms out in front of him. He could see nothing, his other senses overcompensating in response: each sound enhanced and unfamiliar, while the combined stench of the surrounding horde became more pronounced. It was almost as if he could taste the smoky, oily sweat rolling off their bodies. He guessed that after months on the trail, he must smell no better.

Something brushed against his face, heavy and furry, reeking of incomplete tanning and dried bat shit. He flinched away, bumping against Neah, who was immediately behind him.

"It's only a curtain, Caleb. Move on," she said into his ear.

He pushed past the heavy flap. As it flopped back into position, bright light assailed his eyes. He had to turn away. When his eyes had adjusted, he recognized the cavern where he'd seen Mohar, now bright with torches. Several cooking pots were set up in one corner, the flames beneath banked to a rich red. The cavern was filled with smell of slow-cooked meat. Caleb's mouth filled with saliva in response. He hadn't eaten anything since breakfast, and cooked meat was a distant memory.

Nutura muttered something to one of the other men, and peeled away. The group ushered them over to the opposite side, toward a large flickering purple sphere. It was almost transparent. Through the shifting purple shades he could make out Mohar sitting on the floor looking over at them.

The ones with the spears came forward again and pointed at the sphere. Caleb and Neah shrugged and walked toward it.

"You can walk in; you just can't walk out," Mohar called as they paused outside. Caleb looked behind him again. The three at the front lifted their spears in encouragement, and he stepped through. There was a flicker of something as he entered. He sat down beside Mohar. Neah joined them, and with a grateful sigh stretched out on the floor. The wizard tossed her a brightly colored blanket.

"I see you fared no better than I," Mohar said.

"Thanks for sending me the personal invite. Why didn't they take our weapons?"

"No need. This sphere is impermeable to everything from inside it, even magic. Try it."

Caleb picked up a rock and threw it at the pulsing light. It bounced harmlessly away.

"I'm thinking that thick curtain you came through contains the energy inside this cavern that then fuels this sphere in a constant cycle. There's one covering each of the tunnel exits."

"They weren't there when you sent me that message. I followed the natural light all the way outside."

"That's what I'm saying. They didn't need to activate this purple thing until I arrived."

"So why send for us?" Neah asked.

"To keep you and the Torian safe. When the Timpani refused to help, it was obvious to me that the Shaylene would overrun the caravan. You would have had no chance."

With a curse Caleb leaped on Mohar, straddling him, his knees pinning Mohar's upper arms. "People will die, possibly tonight, Mohar. People you know. People you have lived, eaten, and slept with. People we have both risked our lives for. Does that mean nothing to you?"

"As I keep trying to tell you, my job is, and has always been, to protect the Torian. Without him there will be no people. No freedom and no future. Not as we know it."

"Get off him, Caleb," Neah said wearily. "You can't change the nature of a snake by talking to it. And besides, for once Mohar is right. The child is safer here. The Timpani also said they'd release us after the invading army had passed. We may still have time to reach Carmelsara."

Caleb grumbled to himself, then rolled to one side, staring up at the glowing arc above him. "How? By flying?"

"Possible, but far too unreliable," Mohar said.

"I can't believe I'm hearing this. Neah, if we do nothing your mother will almost certainly be killed by her own daughter's troops."

Neah turned, snarling. "Don't you think I know that? Or she does? Deva is willing to die in order for this child to live. I just happen to be the one carrying it. All right?" The last two words were shouted. Several of the Timpani glanced up before returning to their tasks.

Caleb simmered, allowing his anger to recede. He was surprised at his reaction. People died in battle every day. Did he feel as helpless and guilty as this when one of his own Sworn was felled? Of course he was pleased that Neah and the child were safe. Should that allow other innocents to die simply so she may live? Other women and children. People he'd been charged to protect. Should they die simply for the sake of an ideology? Yet, wasn't that the job of the army—his job—to defend and protect those in power? He was torn between his past conditioning and the present.

He bolted upright. There was a solution that just might satisfy both.

"Do they know?" he snapped at Mohar.

"You'll have to be more specific, Caleb. My mind reading powers are limited inside here."

"About the child, the new Torian that Neah is carrying."

"No, why would I tell them that? It would just be placing them both at greater risk."

"But don't you see? It's our way out."

He jumped to his feet and rushed to the perimeter of the sphere, yelling for Natura. After a time he appeared. With him were three of the older women, each carrying a wooden bowl. He stopped several paces away from Caleb, motioning the women forward. They knelt and pushed the bowls through the purple barrier. Caleb tried to ignore the delicious smells wafting from the hot stew. His stomach could not, and growled loudly.

Natura nodded. "Eat. We talk later."

"No. Now. I want to talk now. It's important."

The purple stone in the center of Natura's forehead flashed briefly.

"Important to you. Not me. Eat," he ordered, taking a step away.

"What if I could guarantee you title to your own lands. Back in Shaylene."

Natura stopped and turned back slowly, his small eyes narrowing. The purple stone embedded in his forehead was now flashing. He said nothing, and Caleb blundered on.

"I see many Timpani gathered here. Almost too many for the space you share." He pointed down at the bowls. "How long did it take to catch this much meat? The mountains are barren of life. This was scavenged from the dead beasts that we left behind on the trail, wasn't it?"

"It remains fresh in the cold. Do not fear."

"I don't. Wouldn't you prefer to hunt your own, on your own lands once more? There would be enough for all, and the Timpani could prosper and grow.""The old king's court killed the game on our lands—for sport."

"Exactly. That's why you had to retaliate, isn't it?" He flashed a quick glance over at Neah. "What's more, I'm guessing the king wouldn't even talk to you about it."

"The king then decided to hunt our people. For sport," Natura said bitterly. "Many died."

Caleb waved at the large group behind him. "Now your numbers have grown. How long before your needs outstrip this place?"

"Our numbers have swelled, it is true. What is your talk of resuming our tribal lands?"

"This woman"—he pointed at Neah—"carries the new Torian in her belly. If we are able to reach Carmelsara before the Shaylene, she will be declared regent until the new Torian is of age. In return for your help she will deed the lands—your land—back, but we need your people's help to delay Shayla and her army."

Natura studied Caleb's face. The purple gem set in his forehead glowed, then shone. With a grunt, the glow extinguished and Natura motioned to several of his kin who were watching from behind. They huddled together, mumbling between themselves, before Natura turned to face Caleb again.

"You—of the Shaylene. Come." He bid her forward with his stumpy index finger. Neah shot Caleb a filthy glare and approached.

When she was at the perimeter of the sphere, Natura came and stood close until only the flickering purple barrier separated them.

"Does he speak true?"

The gemstone set into his forehead glowed once more; this time it appeared to shine, bathing her in purple light.

Neah appeared to struggle with something and then said in a husky voice, "Yes."

"Does he speak for you?"

"No." She cleared her throat. "I speak for myself. And yes, I will agree to deed your traditional lands if you and your people help us."

Natura glanced back at the older men behind him, and with a clap of his hands nodded. "Then it is done."

IT WAS night by the time they emerged from the cave. There was a moon, barely formed, its glow pale, serving only to deepen the shadows beneath their feet.

The cold was bitter, carried by a wind sharp enough to cut through even the thick cloaks that the Timpani women had hastily sewn together for their larger guests. Regardless, Caleb was grateful and snuggled deeper into its furred collar.

The Timpani moved quickly and confidently in single file along paths that Caleb could barely make out. He'd made a quick count of the warriors before they'd set off. Less than fifty. Natura had been unwilling to commit a larger force in case things went badly. This meant that even with Shayla's advance party they'd be outnumbered almost two to one, not even considering the disproportionate size of the Shaylene troops to the minute Timpani. Caleb wondered not for the first time whether his duty had blinded him, standing in the way of his common sense.

Behind him, he could feel Neah carefully picking her way down the uneven steepness of the slope. He wanted to reassure her, but Natura had made it clear that there was to be no talking. With nothing to impede it, sound carried a long way across bare rock.

He was reminded of this an hour later when the distant sound of men's cries drifted in on a gust of wind. They seemed to be coming from the same direction they were headed.

The column stopped abruptly, and Caleb stumbled into Mohar. "You hear it?"

"Yes. This is a fool's errand," Mohar griped. "They'll be past our help by the time we arrive. You're placing Neah in danger for nothing."

Natura appeared by Caleb's side and motioned him down so he could speak directly into his ear.

"The attack has already begun. Can your people hold? We are still an hour distant."

"Yes. The track is narrow at Vale's Arch. Easy to defend, even with a small number. The Shaylene must be desperate if they are attacking at night."

"Or overly confident. We approach from the Shaylene side," Natura grunted back, before returning to the front. Soon they were moving again, perhaps a little faster.

The sounds gradually grew louder, the familiar cries of men fighting and dying. When they rounded a promontory, Caleb caught sight of the attack. They were still well above Vale's Arch. Several fires were alight on the Shaylene side. They appeared to be supply wagons. As he watched, a volley of fire arrows arced down and into the Shaylene position.

Good call, Arrowsmith.

The fires were creating confusion and would delay a full Shaylene advance. He wondered about the Commonwealth soldiers he'd seen pulling the wagons, whether they'd have still been shackled when the fires started.

I'll find out soon enough.

They skirted the ridge above the Shaylene. While it was an ideal vantage point, Caleb wasn't so sure about launching an attack from up here. They would be too exposed, and the range was marginal for spears. The Timpani didn't seem to favor archers.

Natura paused the column when they were just above the Shay

lene position, and made a parting movement with his hands. The Timpani warriors immediately spaced themselves right along the ridgeline, and then released the straps of the packs they'd been carrying. Each took out a bundle of the short spears, and a curious wooden shaft. Caleb squatted down and examined one of them. It had what appeared to be a handle carved out of the lower edge, and a recessed curve along the top. As he watched, the Timpani beside him slipped one of his spears into the recess, and holding the handle brought the assembly back to his shoulder as if to throw it.

"They're throwing sticks," Neah said from behind him. "They add both range and accuracy."

As she spoke, the line of Timpani loaded spears onto their sticks, and when Natura brought his hand down, a volley of fifty sailed into the air and down onto the unsuspecting Shaylene. Before the first points had found their marks each of the Timpani had another one loaded.

Neah was also firing arrows into the scattering Shaylene pack. A ragged cheer went up from the other side of Vale's Arch. Caleb sent a mental query across his Sworn link. Arrowsmith responded immediately. They were holding.

Below, the Shaylene had scattered, finding cover beneath the overhanging rock. Many of their number remained, lying on the open ground, light from the raging fires casting macabre, flickering shadows against the mountainside.

Natura would have to take the battle down to them now, or risk an entrenched engagement that would trickle away any advantage the surprise attack may have provided. Caleb pulled out his cutlasses, twirling them lightly to warm the muscles in his wrists and forearms, looking skeptically at the steep rock leading to the caravan trail and wondering how he was going to get down there.

Each Timpani warrior watched their leader carefully. Natura finally stood, and taking one end of his spear slammed the shaft against his barrel chest. It thrummed with the deep resonance of a drum. He did it twice more in quick succession; the others along the ridgeline did the same, picking up and joining in the rhythm. Soon the air itself seemed to vibrate with the beat.

It ceased abruptly, and as one the Timpani hastily dug through their packs and withdrew lengths of plaited rope. At one end was a thick metal spike that they tapped, then drove hard into the rock with metal-headed mallets. As soon as the lines were secure, the men scrambled down, dropping onto the trail like spiders falling from a disturbed web. Caleb sheathed his cutlasses and followed, hoping the driven spike would hold his extra weight. He allowed the rope to slide between his gloves. Above, he could see Neah still firing arrows, Mohar beside her. He hoped the wizard could convince her to stay there.

He landed lightly on the road and immediately rolled to one side, finding cover behind a fallen boulder. The Timpani were already attacking, but in a manner Caleb had never seen before. They worked in teams of two or three, leaping and turning somersaults as they darted in and out of the Shaylene's legs until one managed to sever an unprotected Achilles tendon, or ram one of their metal hammers against an unprotected knee, smashing the joint. Their strategy was obviously to bring the taller and stronger Shaylene to ground using their speed and agility. Once down, the trio would fall upon him, using their knives to sever arteries in either the leg or neck, and then in a pack they would move on to another, leaving the crippled warrior to bleed out.

While an effective tactic, the Timpani were already outnumbered, and committing two or three men to attack one only made those odds worse. Already the Shaylene were quitting their entrenched positions and engaging. Caleb waded in, twirling his massive cutlasses in deadly arcs as he carved a path deeper into the battle. Beside him two Timpani balanced on the shoulders of a third, who, like a sapling in a strong wind, swayed with perfect balance to evade the hacking swings from the guard before attacking fiercely from all three levels.

Caleb worked his way over to Natura. "We need to pull back to the arch, join with my men. The Shaylene are recovering from the surprise. We'll be outflanked shortly."

Natura thrust a blade sideways through a thin join in a Shaylene's armor, severing the soldier's spine. The big man toppled slowly, transitioning from life to death like some vast felled tree turning into a lifeless log.

With a ghost of a smile, Natura gripped a whistle that hung on a hide string about his neck and brought it to his mouth. Puffing his cheeks full with air, he appeared to blow three long bursts. It made no sound that Caleb could hear. From all sides, there was an answering chorus of hackle-raising howls. In moments a pack of huge wolves lined the ridge above them. At another blow of the silent whistle, the wolves leaped into the battleground. Natura beat his chest three times, and the boom echoed off the surrounding walls.

"Stay behind me," Natura shouted at Caleb.

The wolves attacked the Shaylene, their massive jaws open and dripping to reveal white fangs that closed around the throats of their victims and tore them open in gory, bloody chunks.

Several of the beasts turned their hungry yellow eyes on Caleb. With a thump to his massive chest, Natura turned them away to find and fell other victims. It was over in moments. The wolves fed from the still warm carcasses. Standing beside the bodies, Caleb could see that some of the beasts were the same length as the men had been.

"What are these? Tame wolves? They are the biggest I've seen." He squatted next to Natura as the small man applied pressure to a sword slash in the leg of one of his warriors. Torches had been lit from the dying flames of the wagons. Caleb could see twisted, blackened forms of men still shackled to their traces in front of the burned-out wagons.

"Not tame and not wolves. We of the plains raised long-haired hounds. When we came here, the hounds mated with the native timber wolves. These are the result. We provide them with food when winter is the harshest; they protect and assist us when required."

"What food would you have to spare?"

Natura met Caleb's gaze. "We are unlike you. We survive only as a group. Sometimes it is necessary for the individuals to make sacrifices—for the survival of the rest. We consider it an honor."

"I saw some bones near the mouth of your cave?"

Natura nodded. "The dedication point."

"And the wolves understand this... arrangement?"

"They even become guides—reluctantly. If we ask them nicely." Natura removed the pressure on the wound as the man gave a massive shudder and slumped back.

Natura said something beneath his breath and closed the man's eyes with his fingertips. He motioned for the body to be placed with the others that had been piled in the center of the trail. The dead Shaylene had been left to lie where they had fallen.

"Your people fought well tonight." Caleb watched as small groups gathered up spent spears and knives. "I haven't seen men work in teams like that before. It makes sense."

Natura grunted noncommittally, and stood to listen as one of his men scampered up to whisper in his ear.

"Others, like you." Natura pointed at Caleb's uniform. "Around that bend. This man will take you."

Caleb squeezed Natura's shoulder, and hurriedly followed the man. A small group of bedraggled men clustered together, still chained to two wagons. Once-white uniforms hung in tatters from their emaciated frames. There were two wagons, ten men to each.

"Who is in charge here?" Caleb snapped, quickly scanning each of the faces. Only one was vaguely recognizable, and he had to look twice beneath the dirt and bloody slashes from the Shaylenes' whips to realize who it was. The man struggled to his feet under Caleb's scrutiny, the chains around his ankles grating. The man's eyes narrowed in recognition and suspicion when Caleb spoke.

"Colonel. I haven't seen you since you testified against me at the inquest in Roganshah."

"Kane?" the man's voice when it came was cracked, betraying a curious mixture of exhaustion, age, and what could have been disbelief.

Caleb motioned to the Timpani. "Can you ask Natura to arrange food and water for these men? And bring chisels to strike off these chains."

The man nodded and ran off, bare feet hardly seeming to touch the rocky ground.

"Colonel. Please sit, you look... done in," Caleb said, taking the officer's arm and guiding him down, noticing the ulcerated skin where the manacle had worn through.

"Who are these midgets, Kane?"

"The Timpani. They are responsible for the victory today. They and their wolves," he muttered.

The colonel appeared not to hear. He was staring into a space only he could see. "They used us to pull their bloody wagons, Kane. Like bloody beasts."

"I know," Caleb replied quietly, lightly patting the older man's back. He could feel the ribs and vertebrae protruding.

Food arrived, and Caleb quickly distributed it to those who could feed themselves. Natura appeared in front of him, followed by Arrowsmith and a gaggle of others, mostly men from the caravan.

"The hounds have fed and left, bar one." He pointed up. A single wolf with white and gray markings waited on the ridge above. He appeared to be studying them.

"We will go now too," Natura continued. "When you require us to join you once more, simply blow this." He handed Caleb the whistle from around his neck. "The hound will hear and come back to tell us. We will come."

Caleb slipped the twine about his neck and bent his head, hand to his chest. "Thank you," he said.

From around the bend a flare of flames erupted.

"Our fallen are burned in honor," Natura said, and with a final thump to his chest he and his men left. Caleb caught sight of them climbing up the ropes to the ridge before melting into the night.

Caleb turned to his adjutant. "Arrowsmith, you and your men did a fine job. Good thinking about the fire arrows. Well done." He pointed to the bedraggled bunch in front of them. "These are imprisoned Commonwealth soldiers. Help strike their chains, and then get them settled in our camp."

Arrowsmith placed his fist to his chest and gave orders to the others.

"Caleb."

He spun at the sound of her voice, surprised to find his chest tightening. She was sitting on a rock, half in shadow. He had to consciously resist the urge to hurry over to her.

"Are you all right?" he asked instead, his eyes moving from her feet to her head and down again, finally settling on her abdomen. It seemed to be getting bigger.

She nodded, a small smile hovering. "Mohar saw to it. He mumbled something and I couldn't move until just now. It was hard enough shaking him off to climb down the rope."

The clang of metal yielding to sharpened steel bounced off the rock and travelled out into the night.

They watched as Arrowsmith's men carried those who could not walk back through the carnage to the other side of the arch.

"They look to be near death," Neah said.

Caleb took the opportunity to move a little closer, pausing several paces away.

"They are. Some may not make it through tonight—what's left of it, anyway. Though at least they'll die unshackled. Unlike the others." He reached out a hand to help her up. "Come, we should eat too."

After a moment's hesitation, she took it.

THE DAWN BROUGHT SNOW. It swirled in seemingly harmless puffs, layering lightly against the windward side of rocks. Caleb lay beneath the thick cloaks, staring up through half-closed lids at the weathered overhang of Vale's Arch that sheltered him. The fire he'd built before sleeping still smoldered, hissing with defiance at errant snowflakes that attempted to land.

"Are you awake?" Neah asked from the other side of the fire. He sat up, noticing that the hollow where Mohar had curled last night was empty now.

"Very. Is everything all right?"

"Will you stop asking that? It's becoming annoying. I'm not made of spun sugar."

He restrained himself from firing a barbed quip back. He saw what might have been relief cross her face.

"What is it, then?" he asked.

She looked away. "Mohar thinks he and I should go on ahead. Move on to Carmelsara."

"Ahead of the caravan?"

"Yes. He feels the men you rescued last night will not be fit to travel, or at best will slow us down too much. He feels that we should get the new Torian to Carmelsara as soon as possible."

"I agree. You two should go on. I cannot, though."

Neah was a fraction slow to mask her surprise.

"But I thought—"

"I have told you before, I have a responsibility to those in the caravan. The Shaylene army remains the only threat, and if you move fast they will be well behind you, slowed even more by these mountains. I have been thinking on this. Not everyone in the Torian's court will welcome your news, particularly given the child's parents—no offense. Even with the Torian's support, they may take some convincing. That will all take valuable time—"

"Kane?"

Caleb glanced around. "Colonel, please sit." He waved a hand toward Neah. "Say hello to former Princess Neah, Shayla's sister... and mother-to-be of the new Torian."

The old man's face had been scrubbed clean of grime and dried blood, however, the color vanished completely as he tried to integrate what Caleb had said.

"What?" he spluttered finally.

Caleb pointed at him meaningfully. "See, this is a small example of what you will be dealing with in Carmelsara. I'm sorry, Colonel. I am forgetting myself." Caleb stood and bowed, his fist to his heart. "Neah is no longer of the Shaylene. I speak truly that she does hold the hope of the Commonwealth in her belly. Please sit and join us."

The colonel looked flustered, and finally shook his head. "I am just an old soldier—made more so by these past months. I do not bother with politics."

"You are honed and hardened, I would say, Colonel," Neah said, kindness softening her words. "It's remarkable that any of you survived at all. I couldn't believe they made you pull their wagons."

The colonel's eyes clouded for a moment. "It kept us strong. Honed and hardened, you say? Well, it did that for our resolve. If what you say is true, Kane, and the new Torian is already amongst us, then it makes what I have come to say even more relevant."

"And what is that?"

"My men and I have chosen to stay."

Caleb made to interrupt, and the colonel placed his hand against Caleb's chest. "Despite everything, Commander, I am still your superior officer, and so I am 'suggesting' you listen. I am only doing this out of courtesy, you understand."

Caleb heard a stifled snicker from Neah, and he took a deep breath. "Forgive me, Colonel, please continue."

"The Shaylenes' main force is up to a week behind us. With good food and rest, that time will allow my men to restore."

"Granted, but why not do that with us, inside the caravan? Why divide our force? I have only three Sworn here that I can give you—"

"I am not asking for the use of your men. You'll need every one of them."

"Then why? I don't understand."

"When you attacked last night, our wagon was at the rear. After the fires started, the overseers forced us to push our wagon back around that bend where you found us."

"Why?"

"Apart from weapons, it also holds a new black powder that explodes with heat. Shayla plans to use it to blast apart the gates of Carmelsara. She gave her advance party a supply in case they needed to blast you out of the way. If it'd been allowed to ignite last night, it would have killed everyone and may even have brought down the arch itself."

"It's that powerful?" Caleb asked, looking up at the solid rock, unable to imagine what the colonel was saying.

"Yes, but as it happened, when those damn wolves appeared the overseers panicked and rode off, leaving us still in our chains. Where the hell did those wolves come from, anyway?"

"Hell is as good a place as any. The wolves seem to have a working arrangement with the midgets that you saw. Go on."

"I've been studying this archway. It seems to me if we can dislodge a few key boulders up there"—the colonel pointed to several —"we could start a rockfall and block the road."

Caleb turned back to the colonel. "Using the black powder? Do you know how it works?"

"For all Shayla's power, her generals are still superstitious and are wary of it. They wouldn't allow their men to handle the powder, so they ordered slaves to test it and fire it. One of my men, a sergeant, was on that detail. I'll speak with him when we finish here."

"And he will know how to bring a structure like this down?" Caleb asked, looking skeptically at the arch rising majestically above him.

"And more, if needed," Mohar stated, striding into their group and flopping down beside Neah.

"You heard us speaking, wizard?" Caleb sniped. He still bristled whenever Mohar was around, resenting his constant manipulations, yet at the same time maintained a grudging admiration for the man's single-minded ruthlessness in completing his mission. Even if it was all for his own gratification.

"I hear always—and in all ways, Commander. You should know

that by now." Mohar's mouth stretched into a semblance of a smile.

"Colonel, do you remember the wizard? He was sentenced with me at Roganshah."

"I do. I've got to say, Kane, that none of us that day expected you to survive, much less—"

"If it's any consolation, Colonel, neither did we." He turned to Mohar. "So you know of this powder?"

"Yes. Though only by reading of it. It's a product of the dark path, which is barred to me."

"So you're saying it's possible to block the pass as the colonel says."

"With enough of it, yes."

"I like your plan, Colonel. It will even allow you enough time to rejoin the caravan after it is done."

"The gods be willing," the colonel said. He placed his hands on his knees and with a grunt pushed himself to his feet. The remnants of his tattered uniform parted, revealing a deep brand on his thigh.

"How many of our men remain?" Caleb asked as the colonel turned to go.

"My count was over a thousand before we were sent on ahead. Many will have died in their shackles since."

"And General Amos?" Caleb asked, remembering the general's amused expression when he sentenced Caleb and Mohar to travel with the caravan.

The colonel scratched his beard as if trying to find an unpleasant memory amidst the gray hair. Finally he said, "The general was seriously wounded in the last battle. Like the rest who weren't fit enough to be harnessed to a wagon, he was hung up and quartered—butchered—and his body parts fed to pigs, who later were slaughtered themselves and then eaten by the Shaylene."

Caleb felt the gorge in his belly churn. He harbored no fondness for Amos, but nevertheless he was one of them, and Caleb silently swore that the general and all his men would be avenged.

The colonel limped off, joining his group once more. Even if they had a month to recuperate before the Shaylene arrived, Caleb doubted whether any of them would be strong enough to put up much of a fight.

"Caleb," Neah whispered, looking furtively over at the colonel, "we must leave. Now."

"We agreed on this earlier," Caleb said. "I will go to the caravan, and you two—"

"No. Didn't you see that brand on the colonel's thigh when he stood up?"

"Yes. What of it?"

"It's the mark of a Shaylene forced Swearing. His mind is linked with a Shaylene who can command his actions. The same has probably been done with all the captured Commonwealth officers, to flag threats of revolt. If his Sworn link is awake, they will know everything that was said just now. It will only be a matter of time, perhaps moments, before Shayla knows everything we talked about."

Caleb shook his head. "Sworn links decay with distance. How could they hear anything this far away?"

"Forced swearings may have been outlawed in the Commonwealth, however, the Shaylene went on refining the technique after Shayla came to power. With their process physical distance is irrelevant."

"Then Shayla will know that you carry the Torian," Mohar said. "Damn it." He drove a fist into the palm of his other hand.

Caleb jumped to his feet. "Prepare to leave. Mohar, you stay with Neah. I'll round up Arrowsmith and the men."

"Caleb!" Neah shouted. He looked up to where she was pointing, and saw the colonel perched atop the arch. As they watched, he toppled forward, his mouth twisted into the rictus of a ghoulish grin, the tatters of his rags flapping about him like the wings of an over-sized flightless bird. As he fell, the colonel managed to throw a draw-string bag into the embers of the fire, scattering ash and sparks. Caleb, realizing what it might be, launched himself at Neah before the world exploded around them.

FIFTEEN

Men were talking. Caleb knew that because when he opened his eyes their lips were moving, but he could hear no words. A high-pitched whine filled the space between his ears, drowning out any sound from outside. Arrowsmith was bent over him, and from the shapes his mouth was making appeared to be shouting. Caleb shook his head, trying to clear the whistling sound, and pushed his adjutant away. He raised his head, and the world tilted. Every part of his body hurt. The smell of scorched cloth capped with a pungent overlay he didn't recognize was trapped inside his sinuses. Ten strides distant, wisps of smoke drifted from a large, deep hole. He remembered with a jolt the bag of black powder falling; the thunderous sound and the feeling of being hurled aside like some discarded toy. And a desperate rush to reach—

Neah!

Frantic, he looked around, belatedly realizing she was beneath him, lying amidst a scattering of clothing, parts of her thick cloak holed, the edges blackened and smoking. Groaning, he rolled to one side and forced himself to sit up. Reaching out one hand tentatively, he took her wrist, seeking a pulse. He mouthed her name, placing the fingers of his other hand at the side of her throat, as if the pulse might better reveal itself there.

He could feel nothing—and, immediately afterwards, everything.

IT MUST HAVE BEEN LATER because the light was different. Slanting with late afternoon, laced with deepening shadows leached of warmth. Caleb shivered. The whistling in his ears was fainter now, allowing through the steady clopping sounds of horses on the move and the mumbled murmur of men talking. He realized he was roped to a litter strung between two of the horses.

"Caleb. Can you hear me?"

The words were spaced and overly enunciated, the voice familiar, but he chose not to recognize it. Not yet.

He didn't feel like responding. Neah and the child were dead. He remembered the desperate search for a pulse, her closed lids, the smoking devastation caused by the accursed black powder.

"Caleb."

That voice again.

He sighed and rolled his head to the right, following the sound. Mohar was riding one of the horses beside him.

"What do you want?" Caleb's voice felt cracked and broken.

"Here, drink this."

Mohar helped him drink, holding the bladder above his mouth and squirting a small quantity of water in. He gulped it back, realizing he was parched, and nodded for more. Bodily needs continued, even when the spirit was gone.

"Where are we?" Caleb asked finally, rolling his head back to the center.

"Still on the way. Now you're awake, we should be able to pick up a little pace. I didn't want to jolt you about too much until we knew how you were. How are you, anyhow?"

"I feel dead. Inside. Does that help you?" Caleb bit back, and tried to sit up. Mohar steadied him.

"Easy. We've got you strapped in. Do you feel strong enough to ride?"

Caleb didn't and said yes anyway. Mohar called out to the front of the column to halt. Men came and untied the bindings, helping Caleb to stand.

He felt shaky, the rocky road beneath his legs dipping and lurching as if he'd been at sea for many days.

"How many of our party were killed?" he asked.

Caleb used Mohar's shoulder to steady himself as he mounted his horse. The stallion snorted and danced sideways, adjusting for Caleb's imbalance. Caleb's other foot found the stirrup, and he settled his seat.

"None, praise the gods. It was an almighty bang. Like being caught inside a thunderclap."

Caleb's head snapped around, and he immediately regretted it. He stared down at the wizard, trying to stop the world spinning.

"None dead? What about Neah?"

"Neah and the child are alive. Thanks mainly to you. You managed to roll her out of the way. Fortunately, most of the blast seemed to go straight up. There were only small chunks of the colonel left though, mostly plastered to the underside of the arch."

"She's alive?" he repeated. "But I could feel no pulse."

"Your senses were overloaded, so I'm not surprised. She sleeps. Her heart, and that of the Torian beat strong." Mohar pointed back at one of the Shaylene supply wagons. "See for yourself."

Caleb cantered back to the open wagon, then rode alongside, staring down at her. She lay on her side, knees curled toward her chest. A canvas shade had been rigged over her upper body to provide shelter, and the splintered boards of the wagon were lined with capes and cloth scavenged from the camp to soften her ride.

He reached out a hand and lightly touched her wrist. A strong pulse met his fingertips, and a flush of relief coursed through him.

"Neah?"

She stirred, her full lips pouting, as if she were a child who didn't want to wake.

"Neah?"

Her eyes opened, blinking as they adjusted to the light and dry mountain air. He watched as memory unrolled, and she jerked up.

His hand steadied her. "Easy. You're all right. Both of you."

Her eyes focused on him.

"Caleb, I had this dream that I couldn't wake from. You were dead and I—"

"It's all right now."

"No. Shayla is coming for us. She knows about the child."

"We're on the way to join the caravan. Deva will know what to do about her," Caleb said, hoping he was right.

Mohar rode up on the other side of the wagon.

"What of the colonel's men?" Caleb asked, looking at the bedraggled men along the column. They were round-shouldered, defeat and malnutrition weighing them down.

"They bear no brands. It's best they come with us."

"Which one is the sergeant, the one who knows the black powder? You surely had him blow up the arch with the remaining black powder, didn't you?"

Mohar motioned toward a man near the front of the column. "That's the man there, not that it matters now. After the colonel took what he needed, he tossed it all into a full water barrel. It is apparently useless after that."

"Damn. That was a good plan."

"It'll be dark soon." Mohar looked up at the sky. "There's snow about. We need to make camp."

Caleb grimaced; his preference was to keep moving.

Cued to him, Mohar added, "It won't matter how far we get. Shayla will still know where we are. We can't outrun her."

"So what, we just wait for some hellish bird to swoop down and bear Neah off?"

Mohar shook his head. "No. I doubt it will be anything like that.

Shayla will want to handle this herself rather than risk what happened when she sent the colonel after us. She gave him the strength and agility to climb those rocks to take us by surprise. Fortunately, your reflexes were faster."

"Luckier."

"That too. Shayla was linked to the colonel, so she'll know he failed. She won't want to take the risk of anything like that happening again. She'll come herself next time."

"And how is that better?" Neah asked, squirming herself up to a seated position.

"It's not. But to transport here physically will take some preparation and a lot of energy. That will take time to arrange."

"How much?" Caleb asked.

Mohar shrugged. "Who knows? It depends on how much power she can gather. One, perhaps two days."

Caleb stood in his stirrups, looking up the road as it snaked through the rocks toward the distant pass at the top.

"We'll be lucky to make the pass by then. There's no telling how far Hawke has pushed the caravan."

"I've called on some help," Mohar said. "They'll be with us by nightfall. That's why we need to make camp."

"Who?"

"Friends. They'll help build a defense around Neah."

"Didn't you say your powers had been stripped away?" Caleb snapped."Not when the Torian's life is threatened. I have that dispensation, remember, though it isn't easy for me to draw on."

"Whatever you say. I'll tell the men to make camp." He rode off, calling to Arrowsmith to swing the horses in beneath a line of boulders. They'd provide some shelter from the wind. He looked up; the clouds hung heavy. He hoped Mohar wasn't right about the snow tonight.

NEAH SHIVERED and snuggled deeper into the thick pelts that the

Timpani had sewn together for her, smiling when she heard the lone wolf's cry drifting on the wind. She'd caught sight of it several times since the Timpani had left, keeping to the higher ground, always there, only a whistle blow away. She found it oddly reassuring to know that help was out there; that they weren't completely alone.

Caleb had ordered the men to stretch canvas across the top of the boulders, securing it to the ground, tentlike, with a series of long sticks prized from the bed of the supply wagon. The rest of the wagon was gradually being broken up to feed the large fire that Mohar had ordered built to one side of the clearing. He circled it, chanting, his feet moving in a curious pattern, their imprints visible in the snow. One man had been tasked with feeding the fire, maintaining it at a constant rate of burn. Even from where she sat Neah could see the strain etched across Mohar's face. Despite the snow driven by a bitter wind, sweat streamed from his forehead and down his drawn cheeks as he pulled in power. Neah could only imagine the strain of connecting with what Deva called "the well" through the thick wall that the Torian had imposed around it. It would be like trying to suck oil through a pinprick hole.

Finally he paused and motioned her over. Neah picked up a bladder of water and went. Mohar looked ready to drop, and at the same time appeared energized, as if being supported by something else. She handed him the water, and he nodded gratefully, gulping it back.

"Are you ready?" he rasped.

"For what?"

"I've managed to connect with the Sisters of the Weave. Their coven is best known for their ability to psychically weave a cage of protection. Two of them have agreed to help."

Neah looked around.

"You'll be able to see them when the ritual starts." He gripped her elbows, positioning her near the fire.

"It begins." He took a deep breath, and bending down, blew it into the fire. Immediately the flames leaped, roaring up as if he'd thrown on a bottle of white spirit. The light reached out, dispelling the night, until the whole clearing was illuminated.

Mohar blew into the fire again, and from deep within something stirred, assembling itself into a shape approximating one, then two women. He blew again and the images separated themselves from the fire, carrying part of it with them. Flames flickered around their ephemeral shapes, as if the very air about them was combusting. They both wore long, flickering cloaks of blue emblazoned with gold and red, the fire surrounding them highlighting the outlines of their bodies against a background of swirling white snow that liquefied at their feet.

The women circled Neah, their eyes shining like lamps from deep inside the blackness of their hoods, locking with hers so that even when one was behind her she could still feel their combined gaze. From a distance she recognized Caleb's voice shouting, followed by a mumbled reply from Mohar. Neither translated to meaning; in her head they remained simply sound. Her world had condensed to fire.

The women paused, one in front and the other behind. Neah seemed to be able to watch both them and herself, as if she were an external observer standing off to one side, simultaneously intensely curious as well as totally detached. The women ran their fingers lightly across the surface of their arms, collecting licks of flames that they wove through the air, fingers moving with speed and dexterity as if they were knitting the fire into the air surrounding Neah.

Their fingers dipped again and again into the syrup of fire along their bodies, as if they were pens and the flames ink, tracing more patterns, leaving in their wake a complex crisscross design that hunkered into a broody red and flared with brilliant orange in the space surrounding Neah, from her head to her boots.

When she was completely encased, they joined the front and back layers of flame with what seemed to be a stitching motion down both sides. Once joined, there was a brief *woompf*, and the fiery cage faded to a smolder before finally winking out. The women stepped back into the center of the main fire and faded away. With a start, Neah felt herself thump back into her body.

Tentatively she reached forward, touching the area where the fire had been.

"You'll feel nothing from where you are," Mohar said, stepping closer, his face animated as he carefully examined the air between them.

Neah sensed Caleb approaching.

"What just happened here? Who were those women?"

"Fire Weavers. From the looks of things they've done a great job; I can't even see the seam where they joined the front and back. Step away, Caleb, and I'll show you."

He led Caleb back several paces, and picked up a rock, roughly the size and shape of his fist. Without warning he hurled it directly at Neah.

She saw it coming. There was no time to react. It slammed into something only inches from her face, exploding into minute pieces, some bursting spontaneously into flame.

Neah only felt the concussion when the rock hit.

"What is that?" Caleb asked, stepping forward, his hand reaching out to tentatively stroke the air where the rock had disintegrated.

"Neah is surrounded by a protective screen that reads intent. You, for example, could touch her and nothing would happen. Go ahead and try."

Caleb slowly brought his fingers closer, finally resting them against her cheek.

They felt warm and somehow welcome. An energy flowed from them. Confused, Neah took a step back and he dropped his arm.

Unaware, Mohar continued. "Had you been intending to strike her, however, the barrier the sisters applied would have activated and, well, you saw what happened to the rock."

"And this flame barrier is strong enough to protect her against Shayla?" Caleb asked.

"For a time. Depending on what the witch throws at her, of

course. It means she has some protection. I suggest we try and get some sleep now. Tomorrow could be difficult."

NEAH LAY AWAKE STARING at the stretched canvas above her, watching the dip between the tent poles deepen, each snowflake weightless as it laid itself down. If it continued, however, the combined bulk would inevitably collapse the canvas. She likened it to how she felt now. The journey that had delivered her here was the result of a series of small, almost insignificant events that on their own could easily be carried, yet now their cumulative force was pressing down upon her. Her survival, that of the child she carried, and ultimately the Commonwealth rested with her.

How did that happen? All Mother and I tried to do was discover the identity of the new Torian, and if possible protect him. The whole thing just seemed to take off on its own from there.

It would be easy to blame Mohar for all his manipulations, and of course his own puppet master, the old Torian, however, that wouldn't be true either. Shayla lay at the center of everything. If it were not for her and her insatiable lust for power, none of this would ever have happened.

Neah found it difficult to come to terms with who her sister had become. While Shayla had always been spiteful and mean to her growing up, Neah could never have imagined that one day her own sister would want her dead.

How easy it had been for Shayla to infiltrate the old colonel's mind, take over his actions through the forced swearing brand on his leg. How many more could she command like that? How far could her power truly reach?

As if he'd overheard her, the soldier on watch rose to his feet and stretched. Taking up one of the long spears, he circled the fire, then slowly walked toward her, his footsteps masked by the wind and swirling snow. The sound of men snoring surrounded her. She was alone. Neah tensed, wondering whether to call out for help or trust the fire shield the sisters had woven to protect her. She could feel nothing of it there now.

Will it really work, and if so for how long?

Stupidly she'd lain down without retrieving her bow and quiver from the saddle. She could see it resting against one of the boulders, a good ten paces away. Too far. The man came closer, hefting the spear in his hand as if testing its balance before a throw. A memory of the glazed eyes of the possessed colonel moments before the explosion sprang to her mind. Caleb was only three sleeping bodies away. She opened her mouth to yell. The sentry paused just in front of the tent, raised the spear, then reversed his grip and used the blunt end to rake away the piled snow from the canvas, dumping it to the ground. Neah realized she'd been holding her breath, and her hand moved automatically to the child, signaling relief and comfort.

"Is the child restless?" Caleb breathed beside her.

She jumped. "You startled me. When I looked you were asleep."

"I was. But the sentry disturbed me."

So he was awake.

That realization filled her with reassurance. It felt both satisfyingly secure, and unfamiliar. Like the patrolling wolf somewhere out in the snow.

"I can't sleep," she said.

"I don't doubt it. That fire show earlier would have put anyone off. Can you feel anything of it now? The barrier?"

"No. And it's hard to trust something so intangible."

"Trust is always intangible. It only works when it flows both ways."

Intrigued, Neah paused before asking, "So who do you trust, Caleb?"

She felt the rustle of clothing beside her as he shrugged. "Most of them are dead now. My Sworn. I betrayed their trust in me and led them into disgrace, so I can't even count them. Of the few that remain, I feel they look at me twice whenever I order them to do something, as if wondering whether I'm affected."

"I don't believe that. Your men adore you. I've seen them. I was wrong before, you shouldn't blame yourself for what happened. I know you can see that."

"You're right, I can. That's the trouble. I can see both, and as a result I fluctuate wildly between the two. One minute I'm tearing myself apart with guilt for what I did, in the next I can accept it all as gross manipulation by Shayla. That flipping back and forth is what I don't have any control over."

"Maybe you're not supposed to. It sounds like the one true stabilizing part is missing."

"And what's that?"

"Forgiveness."

Caleb snorted. "The ones who could provide that are no longer able."

"I meant forgiving yourself, Caleb." She allowed a moment to pass before adding quietly, "And I trust you. We both do."

When Caleb spoke, his voice was thick. He cleared his throat. "I appreciate that. It means a lot. I'm pleased you're here. I feared you were both dead. It felt as if the core of me had gone." He gripped then patted her shoulder awkwardly before rolling back to his bedroll.

MORNING SHUFFLED IN, shrouded by damp mist.

Neah opened her eyes and yawned. The air felt thick and tasted vaguely wet, or that could have been from her furry tongue. She scratched at an itch near her rump, triggering others.

When was the last time I wore clean clothes? And as for my hair....

She sat up and scraped it back, gathering it with a tie that allowed the mane to cascade down her back. Standing, she wandered out from beneath the makeshift tent and tried to see the sky. The mist hid everything. Gray shapes of men and horses emerged from it briefly, before being swallowed again. Visibility was down to several paces.

Mohar emerged out of it holding a bowl. "Breakfast?"

Even that looked gray. She felt her stomach lurch, but took it anyway, using two fingers to scoop the warmed lumpy paste into her mouth. It smelled and tasted like it looked.

"How are you feeling? After the ritual last night, I mean."

"I know precisely what you mean, wizard. And the child is fine. This gruel is purely for him. Satisfied?"

"Not entirely."

"How so?"

"I've noticed your attitude has softened toward our good commander."

"What of it?"

"He doesn't form part of the new Torian's destiny. Caleb lives on borrowed time."

"What does that mean?" Neah snapped. "Speak plainly, Mohar."

"Very well." He turned to face her, dark eyes narrowing. "Caleb's qualities were needed to create the child with you. He was then supposed to die—in battle. The fact that he didn't doesn't mean his destiny has changed, only the timing. You, however, were always meant to be the regent until the Torian comes of age. Caleb has no part in that. In fact, he has no real future, so it is pointless allowing yourself to become attached. Now do you understand?"

She felt her face flush, and hoped the mist would mask it.

"I have no intention of getting 'attached' to Caleb, or to anyone else. Caleb does, however, care about the child. I find that... reassuring."

"Nevertheless, he will not live to see him born."

"Does he know that?" Something knotted in her gut.

"Caleb is a soldier. Death visits him daily. He's always prepared. And if it makes you feel any better, he does know but blatantly chooses to ignore it, as he does with everything I say. However, you cannot afford to do so."

"What do you mean?"

"You will need a mate."

"A what?"

"A partner. Someone on your side. A regent's job is both tenuous and dangerous. Not only must you guide the Commonwealth, you are also responsible for raising and protecting the Torian, seeing that he is educated appropriately in the esoteric arts. You will need help. The court at Carmelsara is a viper's nest of competing and often deadly interests. It won't be safe for you there alone."

"I know how a court operates. I was a princess in one, remember."

Mohar coughed. "Yes, of course you were, however, Carmelsara is on a much larger scale. Believe me, I know what it is like—"

"Ah," Neah said, nodding, understanding at last. "I see, and you are offering your services—as my husband. How kind."

"Arranged marriages are often successful. And it need not be intimate—not right away—think of it more as a partnership."

Neah clenched her teeth, managing only, "I'd prefer not to think about it at all right now. There are too many variables."

"Of course. I merely wanted to float the idea."

He stepped closer and squeezed her arm before slipping back into the fog.

Neah shivered, brushing at the crawling aftersensation on her skin. She'd almost shrunk away when he touched her, and that would have been disastrous. Mohar might be slimy and self-serving, but she needed him nonetheless. She wouldn't be able to defeat Shayla on her own.

Lost in her own thoughts, she didn't see Caleb approach. She jumped when he spoke.

"I was thinking on our words last night."

Neah pasted on a smile and wondered whether he'd seen Mohar's close touch.

"About forgiveness?"

"And other things."

Neah decided to be direct. "I was just speaking to Mohar before. He brought me breakfast."

Caleb stiffened. "That's one person I won't be forgiving. Ever. I'm sick of being manipulated. Unfortunately, though, we need him almost as much as he needs you." He paused, glancing at her before adding, "Need has always been the underbelly of trust."

So he did hear.

She rinsed out the bowl with a handful of snow, avoiding his gaze as she packed it away. "Mohar seems to think you'll die before we reach Carmelsara. He maintains that your destiny will finally catch up with you and that you're here on borrowed time."

"I'd agree, if I believed in destiny—which I don't."

"It's hard for me not to. The reading from the Seer was so clear. It's why Deva and I ended up here."

"Perhaps that's why Shayla did as well. Have you considered that?"

"What do you mean?"

"Well, what if this Seer of yours was herself being manipulated by these so-called dark powers Deva is always on about? What if this whole prophecy started there and was the spark that ignited the fire in Shayla?"

Neah made a scoffing sound, and Caleb held up a hand.

"No, listen. All this didn't just happen on its own, or because some god decreed it. Why would it? No, someone, or something, started it, and I don't believe it was Shayla."

"That's absurd—"

"I asked you to hear me out. What if whoever this is was able to whisper prophecy into a Seer's ear? Would the Seer be able to tell the difference? And could that voice not also divine an elder daughter's desire for a father to see past his sons to her? Maybe even fanning it up into a raging lust for power, and then revenge?"

Neah felt her chest tighten. It was hard to breathe. She knew the sticky seduction of the dark path. *Could what Caleb is saying possibly be true? That all along Shayla has just been a pawn in someone else's game?*

"Shayla always wanted power," Neah countered. "She was an absolute bitch to me—and everyone else—in order to get it."

"What better way to get noticed by a father who focused exclusively on his sons? His rightful heirs. I'm betting that even when she trained in battle he ignored, or even belittled her. Am I right?"

It felt like she was in the midst of a whirling pool, and Caleb's words just made it swirl it faster. Her father had derided them both for wanting to join the army. She remembered his constant taunting, saying what husband would want a woman with sword-hardened hands.

Caleb battered on. "If I were you, the question I'd be asking is who—or what—is behind Shayla, and what do they truly want?"

"We know that. It's the dark—"

"Too vague. There has to be a 'who' and a 'why.' Power has to be directed. You know this. An assassin may use the dagger to kill, however, it's the one who pays for the work to be done who is the real murderer."

Neah couldn't make sense of it. The ramifications were unthinkable, chaotic—

"If what you are saying is true, then it applies equally to our side. Even to Deva and me. If I were to believe you, then everything that's happened has been as a result of manipulation and chance, all driven by delusion."

"*If* you were to believe me," Caleb repeated.

Neah backed away, her hand moving to her chest, shaking her head so that her long hair whipped across her back as if reinforcing her reluctance to accept what he was implying. "Faith is the one thing that has supported me throughout, throughout... everything. If we are not carrying out the Mother's work here, then aren't we just as deluded? This whole war, our mission to save the Torian, even the conception of this child are just someone else's means to an end. No. I can't believe that. I can't."

Caleb took a step closer, taking her hand, halting her retreat. "I'm not asking you to. Just consider it. All I'm saying is we need to know who our real enemy is. As long as they remain hidden behind Shayla, even if somehow we manage to defeat her, the real threat will remain."

Neah shook her hand free.

"I can't prove you wrong, Caleb, nor can you convince me that you are right. This is too confusing right now. My faith is all I can rely on. Through my enslavement, the only thing that got me through was the belief that the Mother would save me. Otherwise I may as well have just killed myself." She gulped the last sentence out. "Is that what you want? To destroy the one thing I've always relied on? Is that it? Why? So you can bind me closer to you? I should have listened to Mohar sooner!"

"Mohar? No. You don't understand."

She struck him across the face, feeling the bristly resistance of his beard, and did it again against the other cheek before turning and mounting Magic, her stomach churning with rage and doubt.

THEY BROKE CAMP SOON AFTER, the mist forming an eerie encircling curtain that echoed some sounds and swallowed others. The rest of the company rode two abreast. Neah had made it clear that she wished to be alone.

As they traveled, Caleb's words kept circling, like crows above a distressed and exhausted lamb.

Not for the first time, she wished Deva were here.

The high pass loomed out of the fog, a shrouded gateway to hell. The column halted, and she sensed movement beside her. When she looked over, Caleb was there again. A haunting specter. His expression was resigned.

"I always seem to be coming to apologize." He gave a self-effacing laugh. "It's new for me, so I guess I must need the practice. Look, I had no wish to upset you—or your faith. In anything. It was neither my right nor place to do so."

Neah took a deep breath. "Faith is meant to be tested. It's how it becomes honed. If mine were strong enough, what you said wouldn't have affected me. I realized that as I was riding. Perhaps my faith has become my way of divesting responsibility for what happened to me, I don't know. Regardless of the cause, though, all of us must deal with what is. I carry a child. Shayla intends to kill him—and me—plus cause immense suffering to others. Faced with this, whether we arrived here through choice or destiny is irrelevant."

"Wise words," he responded.

"You do not have to humor me," she said, her voice as frigid as the air surrounding them.

"I would never do that—" he began, and she halted him, her eyes closing.

"I'm sorry. I didn't mean to bite. Things are... unsettled within me. I don't want to fight, particularly with you. It is too taxing... and infuriating." She smiled briefly. "Besides, there are too many others out there who wish to do so. We must protect each other and respect our differences."

He said nothing, touching the brim of his hat to leave. He reminded her of a ten-year-old who'd just escaped a whipping. In spite of herself she smiled again.

"As usual, we circle each other like distrustful cats," she said.

"We both have territory to defend." He matched her smile, and turned to go.

"Caleb." Neah reached over and touched his upper arm, feeling the bicep tense beneath her fingers in anticipation of a final stinging barb. "I hope that you are right in one thing. That destiny does not stalk you."

He grunted, the muscle relaxing before he rode off.

WHEN THEY REACHED the high pass, Mohar raised his head and sniffed the air. He dismounted, and squatted by what looked like an old cooking fire. He dug through the ashes, then dusted his hands together, looking about.

"The caravan left here yesterday morning," he called over his shoulder. "From the amount of animal dung, I'd say they were here for at least two days. Perhaps they were waiting for us to catch them up."

"That makes no sense," Caleb said. "They had no way of knowing whether we'd even make it through. It could just as easily have been the Shaylene who were on their tail. No, if they waited that long, they were forced to. Let's keep moving. They travel slow, so we should catch them by nightfall."

Neah, impatient with their talk, urged Magic out of the column and toward the mouth of the pass, looking down through the opening before trotting back. "The mist is even thicker on the other side, and large parts of the road seem to have broken away. The drop looks very steep."

"It must have been the combination of storms and the weight of the wagons. I told Hawke some of them were overloaded," Caleb muttered. He turned in his saddle, calling to the man behind. "Post three men with lanterns to the front, one ten paces forward, the other two to either boundary. Tell them to go carefully. Instruct everyone else to keep to the center of that formation until we clear the mist."

They started down the trail, the light from the lanterns enclosing them in a sickly yellow glow against the stark whiteness of the fog.

Neah patted Magic on the neck to settle her as the void yawned away to the right before being swallowed once more by fog. One rider on the drop side had almost tumbled several times where huge holes had been gouged from the edge of the road.

"Can't you do anything about this fog, wizard?" Caleb snapped as they dismounted, leading their horses around a particularly huge crack in the road.

"My powers are limited—"

"I know, I know. To when there is a direct threat to the Torian. Well, I'd class falling thousands of feet a pretty good threat, wouldn't you?"

"There are threats and then there are risks, Commander. You of all people should appreciate the difference."

"Single file," Caleb snarled back at the company, his voice louder than it needed to be. "Stay close against the mountain wall. Fire all the torches." His voice bounded off the rock face. In the distance, a faint echo whispered it back at them.

"This damage was not caused by storms, or wagons," Neah said as other torches were lit, flooding the trail with light. "Look here."

She pointed at the broken remains of brightly colored tiles scattered across the road all the way to the edge. "These are from the roof of one of the wagons."

As she spoke, a low rumble rolled over them from above. She looked up. The whole side of the mountain seemed to be sliding and tumbling down to meet them.

"Rockfall," Caleb shouted. "Dismount! Scatter the horses and take cover."

A smattering of pebbles rained over them, clattering and bouncing.

"Take cover!" Caleb repeated as larger and larger rocks came hurtling down. Neah felt herself being bundled inside Caleb's cloak and slammed against the rock, catching a whiff of his distinctive musk as he covered her back with his own body, Mohar coming in behind him.

She could see nothing through the dark wool of the cloak. Her face was pressed against the cliff, the weight of the two men behind her oppressive and claustrophobic. The stench inside the surrounding cloak was coarse and fiercely male. It brought with it a rush of unwanted memories, and she had to fight the urge to break free and run. Instead she focused on flattening herself against the unyielding mountain face, molding her body to it.

It ended as it began, with a hail of small pebbles.

She felt the press of the two bodies around her ease, and grateful for the release she stood, shaking away the cloak and sucking in air. It was filled with dust, and she coughed deeply.

"Take it easy," Caleb said, slapping her ineffectually on the back. She didn't have enough breath spare to shake him off.

Mohar was in her face too, his blue eyes overbright and anxious, intent, it seemed, on examining her pore by pore. Blood streamed from a gash in his head but he seemed oblivious to it. She pushed them both away.

"I'm all right," she managed to gasp. "See to the others. Mohar, tend to yourself. You are bleeding. Everywhere."

At least the dust seemed to have settled the mist. The road, though, had taken another pounding. Neah wondered whether this was Shayla's work too.

"Tell the men to speak softly," Neah whispered to Caleb. "I've seen loud sounds cause an avalanche of snow. The same might be true of rockfalls."

She heard a whinny from down the trail and saw Magic, dusty, blood staining her white coat. Dodging through the chaos, she reached the mare and gave her a hug, taking a bladder of water from her saddle and washing out the cuts. They were minor and appeared clean. She dressed them anyway from her kit.

Caleb moved between the men, encouraging and prodding where needed. They had to keep moving. Most of the horses had either fled down the trail or been swept off the edge.

WITH THE MIST cleared they could move much quicker, and caught glimpses of the caravan by early afternoon. Even so, they didn't reach the last wagon until just before sunset. Neah's count was only forty-two wagons. She was relieved to recognize Deva's distinctive roofline still intact.

Hawke, his greatcoat flapping about him, strode toward them, arms wide with welcome. He looked thinner, and the lines down his long face were deep.

"I saw you coming. We made camp early to let you catch up. Well met," Hawke said, pulling Caleb into a full bear hug before moving on to Neah. He held her at arm's length, looking deep into her eyes, then drew her gently against him.

"It is truly good to see you, child. Deva was unwilling to come, lest you not be among them." He released her, his brows drawing together when he saw Mohar. "And you, wizard. I had hoped our paths would not cross again. At the least so soon."

"You have the Timpani to thank for that," Caleb said.

"Ah, you found them." He clapped Caleb on the back, as if it were he who'd done so.

"Rather the other way around." Mohar's acerbic tone cut through the bonhomie. "Much has happened since."

"Well, never mind all that now. Come, let us eat. There's not much food, though Deva has been doing wonders with what's left."

He herded them like sheep toward the front.

"There is no space on this trail to gather communally, so we must eat where we can. Let's go to my wagon."

Deva's head popped out from behind a cooking pot, and she gave an excited yelp when she sighted Neah. Snatching up a walking cane, she hobbled over. Neah met her partway, and they embraced.

"Mother, you're hurt," Neah said, pulling away to examine the makeshift splint strapped to Deva's left leg.

"It is a simple break. The rockfalls were... difficult. Many were lost. The Mother smiled on me compared to others. Plus, our wagon is still intact."

"She was injured trying to help others," Hawke chimed in.

"We were caught as well. It took most of the horses," Neah said.

"Two of them ran in earlier today. We stabled them, but it took some doing. Their eyes were still white with terror," Hawke put in, handing out bowls of broth.

Deva eased herself down beside Neah, stretching out her injured leg, grunting. "There is no bread."

All slurped directly from their bowls. The broth was thin and good. Neah recognized the aftertaste of many recuperative herbs.

"I feel the child beating strong within you." Deva removed her hand from the small bulge of Neah's abdomen. "This broth will help. Your face carries the marks of strain, Neah. Be cautious of your strength, lest he draw too much. There are still many leagues between here and Carmelsara."

"Yes, and if Shayla has her way, many obstacles," Mohar added.

"You have much to tell us," Hawke said, his great eyebrows raised, looking from one to the other.

They recounted what had happened, taking turns to speak. In response, Hawke told of the journey since they'd last met. He'd kept the caravan in camp at the high pass waiting for the sleet and driving rain to clear. After two days they set out down the trail. Two hours later, over a hundred of their number were either dead or missing. The heavy, constant rain must have loosened the rock above, and when part gave way it brought down much more.

"It was like the whole section of the mountaintop fell. It cut a swathe right through the middle section of wagons. The ones at the front and back were relatively untouched."

"So," Deva said after he'd finished, "what do you think Shayla has in mind?"

"We were hoping you could tell us," Mohar said. "The Fire Weavers have granted Neah protection."

"Good. How many?"

"Two," Mohar said.

The corner of Deva's mouth twitched. "Shame."

"What's the matter with only two?" Neah picked up on her mother's disappointment.

"Nothing. More would have been better, that's all. The more complex the weavers' pattern, the harder it is to break. A full coven's weave is practically indestructible, however, they rarely agree on anything." She patted Mohar on the knee. "Under the circumstances, you did well. I am surprised though that Shayla hasn't made an appearance yet. This would be the perfect time."

"I wondered whether she was behind the rockfalls." Neah glanced over at Caleb.

"I'd say no," he said. "She needs to know for certain that you and the child are dead. Rockfalls are too random, unless she wipes out everyone, and that would have required many more rocks."

"And a lot more energy," Mohar added.

"The damage should slow down the army's advance anyway, that's one thing," Hawke slipped in.

"Maybe. Though that won't be our main concern, will it, Mohar? There is the matter of the test." Caleb raised one eyebrow at the wizard, making the weariness more visible around his eyes.

Neah wondered at the curious feeling that created inside her, and quickly crushed it, snapping, "What do you mean?"

Mohar straightened as if hit. "I keep forgetting you can enlist the child to look into my mind, Caleb. Yes, essentially you are right. The Torian traditionally must face a test before assuming power. The child is obviously unable to do that yet, so it falls to his regent. Neah, you will have to prove yourself worthy in the Arena of Elements once we get to Carmelsara. It is the way."

Neah bristled. "You and your damned way. So are you saying I must take Shayla on alone?"

"The Arena of Elements test has nothing to do with Shayla. Legend has it that all the gods originated from one of the five elements: earth, air, fire, water, and ether. It is them you have to prove yourself to. Am I right, Deva?"

"Yes. The arena is laid out behind the main temple at Carmelsara. It is said that to walk among the elemental fields, you will identify with the gods. Any new Torian challenger must spend the night there."

"And what if Shayla challenges first? On the road, before I get to Carmelsara?"

"Then we will have to deal with her. Unlike the Arena of Elements, you will have all of us available to help you should she come," Caleb replied.

"Against what?"

"Anything and everything she can bring against you," Mohar added. "You didn't expect a fair fight, did you?" His attempt at humor failed. "Look, if she comes I honestly don't know what form it will take. That's up to her. You claim incumbency with the Torian's mark. If she challenges, well, we'll have to deal with that."

"Why didn't you mention any of this before?"

"Because there is nothing that can be done to prepare, and worry will only weaken your resolve. I suggest we all find sleep now. The next string of days will be long and hard."

SIXTEEN

The weather cleared progressively as the trail shed height, until finally the plains of Carmelsara opened up beneath them, green and fertile.

As the days rolled on with no sight of Shayla, the ratcheted tension eased. Neah had the luxury of relaxing. After weeks of fighting, shivering with cold, and living rough, sitting beside Deva in the wagon was like a long-denied holiday. The sun was warm without being hot. She soaked it up.

"If you'd ever told me that being able to wash my hair and wear clean underwear would one day be a luxury, I'd never have believed you," she said, her head back, enjoying the feel of her unbound hair rippling across her back.

"Simple pleasures. Deprivation lies at the very heart of appreciation."

"You and your pithy sayings," Neah said, delighting in it regardless, scooping up and savoring every morsel of what now passed as normal.

"Pithy or not, it's true."

Deva clucked, and flicked the reins at the old gelding. He found it hard pulling the load alone, and took every opportunity to stop. A stray patch of grass struggling out of a wedge of soil caught between the rocks had caught his eye. Deva let him nibble some more. She'd given away all the other horses in the team to those who'd lost all their own beasts. To not have any meant leaving behind what little was left of their lives, inside abandoned wagons.

"What will we do?" Neah asked after a time. "About Shayla."

"What do you mean?"

"I can't just kill her. She's still my sister."

"She stopped being that a long time ago. I no longer call her my daughter. What she has become is something neither of us knows, or recognizes." Deva's lips barely moved.

"Saying and doing are different. Isn't that one of your pithy sayings too?"

Deva sighed. "You're right. I don't know what I'll do until the time comes. And neither do you. Mohar was right about one thing. Worrying will do nothing. Trust in the Mother, she knows best. We can only do what we can with her help. If it is to be, then it shall."

"Caleb thinks all that destiny talk is rubbish. He believes that Shayla is only a pawn of someone more sinister. That even if we manage to beat Shayla, we will still have some powerful wizard to contend with."

Deva made a noise that could have been surprise, or admiration. "He said that? I always knew that boy was more than just a silly soldier."

"You mean he's right?" Neah spun in her seat to face Deva.

"Ah, what is right? When I was younger I used to know with such certainty. Now...." She shrugged. "Just because I believe in the Mother doesn't make it true for others—or even right. Arguing about something no one can prove is just plain foolish. No, what is interesting is that Caleb sees beneath Shayla's veil. I believe that too. Shayla has unwittingly sold herself to a powerful entity who is lending her power. It is not hers, though she undoubtedly thinks it is. He or it is the true threat, regardless of what becomes of Shayla."

Deva glanced at Neah, her eyes shrewd. "You repeat his views like a parrot I once had. Things have changed between you two."

It was a statement with a question at the end. Neah felt resentful that she had to keep explaining herself.

"He and the child seem linked at a level that I can't tune in to. Of course I listen to what he says."

"Yet you believed him to be a brutish fool previously," Deva persisted, a smile lurking behind her thin lips.

"If he lives, I've told him I will accept his support. That is all. Unlike Mohar, who wants to marry me—and the imperial crown."

"Mohar said this?"

"Yes. It would be a marriage of convenience. His. The worm. He says there are many dangers in the Torian's court. That he is the best one to ensure our protection."

Deva made an annoying clucking sound with her tongue. It meant she was thinking. "He may be right," she said finally. "He has many gifts, and once his power is returned—" She clamped down on the remainder of the sentence as Caleb suddenly appeared beside them.

"Am I interrupting?"

"Always." Neah stretched a smile, managing to extract the force from the word. "I see you have found your razor, Commander."

Caleb rubbed his recently shaved cheek. Parts of it were still red. "All the better to learn my lessons."

She blushed, recalling the springy feel of the beard beneath her fingers when she'd struck him.

"So, is it my turn to apologize? I have lost count."

Caleb laughed. "I think we're even. No, it occurred to me that if I am *fated* to die, what safer place to be than beside the finest archer in the caravan."

"Fine words. Perhaps the question you should be asking is, will she *choose* to save you? Mother agrees with your theory, by the way, about Shayla being used by someone else."

"Ah, vindication, at last." He moved in his saddle, the sound of the creaking leather leaking into the silence. "And what about my borrowed time, Deva?" he asked after a time. "Is Mohar right? Am I destined to die?" Caleb's voice tried for lightness, but Neah sensed the genuine curiosity nested within it. There was no fear though, which was even more interesting.

"We all are." Deva's voice was sonorous. "Dying is the only thing any of us have in common. The only uncertainty, life's big question, is when. Which, incidentally, most of us choose to ignore, pretending it will never happen. Personally, I believe that our destiny can and does change according to what happens around us. So no, the circumstances that were drawing you toward death in the battle for Roganshah changed when Shayla intervened. That is not to say you will not die in the next five minutes, especially if you do not draw your horse away from the edge of the road."

Caleb laughed, nevertheless coaxing his mount closer to the wagon. "That's good enough for me. Do you have any idea who might be behind Shayla?"

Deva shook her head, and some of the graying curls beneath her scarf slipped free. She tucked them back under. "No. I sense it more though as we draw closer, a fierce intelligence. It is well shielded and may not even be manifest."

"A spirit, you mean?" Neah asked.

"More an entity, seeking transmission to the physical. It will probably take over Shayla's body—merge, they call it—if she is victorious."

"An entity? That sounds like something that wouldn't fall to my cutlass."

Deva chuckled. "True. But there are other ways. Entities seek to enter the world of the physical to bring about creation or destruction. They are relative terms in the great scheme, while we here on the path spend our lives searching for conscious oblivion. Do you not find that odd, Commander?"

He appeared to consider the question, finally saying, "It has been my experience everyone always wants what they cannot have."

Neah glanced over and found Caleb looking at her strangely.

Is there a longing there?

She felt her throat flush, and hastily broke the gaze. After a time he rode off without saying anything else.

"He has feelings for you. You do see that, don't you?" Deva said.

Neah watched Caleb's easy movement in the saddle as he worked his way toward the front, stopping to speak with others as he went.

"I don't know what I see these days, Mother. Everything has been so confusing, almost overwhelming when I think back on what has happened. I never believed I'd be pregnant, for a start, much less to someone like Caleb." She laughed. "Particularly Caleb. He's everything I hate in a man."

"Hate and love coexist. One often conceals the shadow of the other, which may be what we truly desire. Caleb has changed since we first met him, and so have you. Perhaps all those jiggled-up parts haven't sorted themselves out yet."

"What do you mean?" Neah felt unsettled by Deva's words, as if she'd walked too close to a fire.

"Ah, don't mind me, child. There are many streams for us to ford before you need concern yourself with what might, or might not, happen afterwards."

"After? Nothing will happen. I tell you as I told him. There can't be anything between us, because I have nothing to give. Him, or any man. Mohar included. My enslavement stripped any hope of that away. I am dead to it. As I said, I accept Caleb's help to protect the child, for as long... well, for as long as that is possible. As you say, we may all die before any of that happens."

"Well, let's not place our hope in that option, for everyone's sake," Deva muttered. "Mohar is right though, in that you will need someone to guard your back. I am not as strong as I once was and may not live long enough to see the child come into his majority. You will need someone."

An uneasy silence settled between them.

"I think I'll walk for a while," Neah said eventually, and climbed down, patting Magic on the rump as she passed her. The mare gave a contented snort in return. The cuts on her body had responded well to Deva's herbal salves, and were almost healed.

Surging emotions swelled within her. With no outlet, they cascaded over each other, mixing and frothing about until the only thing Neah felt for certain was frustration. Words rose up in her mind, speaking with Deva's voice, still dripping with brine. *"You'll need someone, and Mohar is more powerful than most; personally I would not dismiss him."*

Why? And why must it always be men that protect us? Is that fair to the child? Isn't it in his interest that I ensure his safety the best way I can? Does he really speak to Caleb? Why not to me?

Anger and fear in equal measure rolled through her, leading only to more questions, more frustration. Finally she ran back to her wagon, gave Magic a whistle, and leapt up, hands springing lightly off the horse's rump to land on her bare back. Slipping the reins free from the side of the wagon, she dug her bare heels in and they cantered along the line.

"Caleb," she called, drawing rein beside him. "I need to talk with you."

He waited.

"Not here. Ride with me a way."

He shot a look up at Hawke on his wagon. The old man nodded, and together Caleb and Neah cantered ahead. After they rounded the next sharp bend, the caravan disappeared from view, and they were alone.

When they had put enough distance between them and the caravan, Neah slowed Magic to a walk.

"I meant it about neither of us owing an apology," he said.

"Is that a roundabout way of asking why we're here?" she asked.

"It'll do."

"I was wondering... do you really hear him? The child."

"How would I truly know? I've yet to meet him. I hear something,

I know that. For what it's worth, Mohar seems to think it's him, if you can believe anything that lying bastard says."

"What does... what does *he* sound like?"

"Ah, I don't know. It's quiet, so quiet sometimes I think I'm imagining it. It's hard to describe, the words just seem to appear fully formed in my head. They have no intonation that I can pick up."

"Ah, I see." Disappointment rose in her chest. She didn't know what she'd expected, or hoped he might say. They allowed silence to settle over them, punctuated only by the steady, measured tread of their mounts. Neah wondered what it might mean to not only have a child in her life, but also to devote her life to that child—the future Torian. It took her a moment to realize that Caleb was speaking. His voice was hushed, almost hesitant, continuing the thread from before as if this admission had taken time for the words to form.

"I tried speaking back... to him... once."

Neah's interest quickened. She said nothing, waiting for him to go on.

"A question really. I wanted to know, why me? I'm just a soldier. I know nothing about my lineage other than that my parents dumped me when I was six. If the army hadn't taken me in as a cadet, I would either be dead, or a thief—probably both. The army *is* my family. It fed, clothed, educated, and then employed me. In return I follow its orders. You said it yourself. I kill people for a living. So if what Mohar said was true and the Torian-to-be, or whatever, chooses its parents, then why me? You, I get. You're of noble birth; you know what it takes to head up a kingdom. You have beauty, access the mystical arts, you're the best archer I've met—in short, you'll be a magnificent warrior queen and mentor. Anyway, that's what I asked."

Neah touched her hair. *Beautiful?*

"Did you... get an answer?"

"None that I could vouch to. I was probably only speaking to my own insecurities anyway."

"Then perhaps you will let me answer for him. Here are the qualities I would choose from you as a parent. Loyalty, duty, and discipline. The ability to inspire and lead men. To fight with your brain as well as your heart. To recognize the value of holding both strength and vulnerability, often at the same time. Those are just some of the reasons you would be chosen. Believe me, noble birth is no qualification to be Torian. These are rare qualities indeed, Commander Kane."

Caleb cleared his throat, switching the conversation to safer ground. "Have you given any thought to a name?"

"Yes." She looked at him directly. "I'd like to call him Chea."

Caleb nodded. "Fine choice. Hawke will be pleased. Chea was another kid who had a rough time. No one deserved to go through anything like what he did."

He waited for her to say something. When she didn't, he asked, "Why did you really bring me out here?"

She looked down at her hands resting on the pommel. "Mohar has suggested he and I marry. He says it would be best for the child. That otherwise we would be in danger, and once he has his power back he would be able to protect us. Deva thinks so too."

While not completely true, she wanted to hear his reaction. He said nothing. She glanced over. His shoulders were tight, and his knuckles white. Everything else about him seemed shielded.

"Caleb?"

He finally shrugged, though the tension in his shoulders remained. "He's probably right. If you make it through this test, then the next eighteen years won't be easy, for either you or the child. I told you, I'll do what I can—if I'm still around." He tried a weak smile that faltered and failed. "And Mohar is a wizard. His power has the potential to keep the peace inside the court."

"That's what he said."

"There you go. For once we agree."

They let the horses have their heads, walking on, the silence now more strained than companionable.

Finally Neah looked over her shoulder, then up at the rugged ridges.

"Have you seen the Timpani's wolf lately? He seems to have disappeared."

"I sent him home. I blew the whistle."

"You called the Timpani? When?"

"At the high pass. I left Arrowsmith up there as well to wait for them."

Neah realized she hadn't seen Caleb's adjutant for several days either.

"Why?"

"I spoke to the men we freed. What's left of the Commonwealth army is pulling the Shaylene wagons. They're behind the main force, right at the rear. If we can cut them off from the army, we might have a chance of freeing them."

"How?"

"The pass is a potential bottleneck. I instructed Arrowsmith to divide the Timpani warriors in two attack wings. One half will take cover in the rocks above the high pass while the rest are to attack from the rear. If Arrowsmith times it right, the main force will be on their way down the other side by the time the rear guard are hit. The trail is too narrow for them to easily turn back, particularly with the Timpani firing down at them from their holding position in the rocks. If they strike suddenly and swiftly, they should be able to hive off the former Commonwealth soldiers. Once that happens, they can arm them from the supply wagons and make their escape back into the mountains before the Shaylene can use their numbers to force their way back through the pass."

"A bold plan," Neah said, nodding. "For what purpose?"

"If you win against Shayla, you will still need an army. If you lose, they will make a fine guerrilla force. Whichever way you cut it, these men are all you have. The Timpani will bring them back to health, and then we'll see."

"Why didn't you say something before, even last night when we were all gathered around?"

"You said yourself, I'm a strategist, Neah. And the best way for a plan to work is to limit the number of people who know about it."

"You don't trust us?"

"I didn't say that. Besides, I just told you."

"Yes, but now I'm not sure what else you haven't told me."

"Then that really does make us even, doesn't it?"

THE CARAVAN LUMBERED onto the Plains of Carmelsara two days later. In the far distance Neah could see the mountains that ringed the fabled city, their tops shrouded in blue haze along with the two sheer peaks that flanked both sides of the wall. It had been built right into the side of the mountains centuries before, yet the reflection from its white surface was visible and bright even at this distance. It seemed to shimmer in the afternoon light.

"Some say the walls were built by another race. They have never dulled nor been breached," Deva said, her expression wistful, before lifted by a quiet smile. Whenever she smiled, the fine lines on Deva's face deepened and joined, like secret trails to a place rarely seen.

"Do you ever regret leaving Carmelsara?" Neah asked, not sure whether Deva would continue to answer. In the past she'd managed to deflect any deeper questions about her childhood in the capital.

"I think about it sometimes. Whether with regret—well, that's a useless emotion, isn't it. Nothing can be changed by indulging in it."

"Perhaps it has something to teach us. That others can learn from," Neah prompted.

Deva didn't say anything for a moment, and finally made a *phat* sound with her lips, like a child who hadn't quite learnt to make a raspberry. Neah suppressed a smile. Whenever Deva did that, it meant she had given in.

"I was happy growing up there. Back then, Carmelsara was like an enchanted place to us children. We had a large villa, high up, built into one of the foothills outside of the city. Just as well, because my family was a raucous bunch."

She smiled at the memory, her gaze far away. "The house was always filled with noise: music, running, and shouting—you had to be able to shout to be heard above ten other children. And in between, important people would come and go. We kids were like puppies on the stairs, watching it all. My father was away a lot, and Mother was the high priestess in the temple. She initiated all us girls into the order when we were young. I was the only one who went all the way. My mother told me that if I worked hard, one day I might be her replacement...." Deva's voice trailed off, her words lost to memory.

"What happened?" Neah prompted.

Deva shook herself, as if retracing her steps back. "Our family had the old Torian's trust, and as each child came of age we were sent off to a different corner of the Commonwealth. The men to diplomatic or trade postings, the girls married off to secure some treaty or distant kingdom for the Torian. That's how I came to marry your father. Our marriage brought the Shaylene into the Commonwealth. It was the last remaining territory to join."

"And the first to break from it."

"Ironic, isn't it? I may as well have stayed."

"And you never returned?"

"Only once, just after my mother died, not long before you were born. She passed suddenly. My father never quite got over it. I stayed in Carmelsara for three months. They needed someone to fill her role in the temple and initiate a new High Priestess. I was happy to serve. I felt like I reconnected with her spirit during that time."

"Did you ever meet the Torian?"

Deva shifted uneasily. "Yes. A few times. In the temple mostly. A wonderful man. Enough of this. You may get to see Carmelsara for yourself soon." Deva drew herself up on the wagon's hard seat, repositioning her splinted leg with a grimace.

"It heals slowly," Neah said.

"Age does that to the body. It's a reminder that one day it will stop healing itself altogether."

Neah shivered. Something like a shadow had brushed past her.

"You aren't going to do anything silly when I confront Shayla, are you?"

"You mean sacrifice myself so you and the child can live? No. Besides, it would serve no purpose. Whoever Shayla is working with can wield great power. I am just a small spider scuttling between her feet."

"Some spiders can be deadly."

"Only if they remain undetected. I don't think I will have that luxury. Look." She pointed a crooked brown finger. Neah followed her gaze. Something was forming in the midpoint between them and the distant walls of Carmelsara. It shimmered like a mirage. As they continued to watch, it materialized into the shape of a building, growing from the ground up, line upon line, as if being laid down by an invisible team of stonemasons.

Hawke must have seen it too, because he signaled a stop. Slowly the wagons ground to a ragged halt.

"She comes," Deva whispered.

The building was completed within minutes. It was round, like the corner turret of an ancient castle, with a strange orange roof that curled up at the corners. While it was hard to judge the height from this distance, Neah estimated that it must be over a hundred strides tall.

"How did she do that?" Neah asked.

"To identify the best solution, it helps to ask the right question. In this case the better question might be, why?"

Hawke, Mohar, and Caleb all arrived at Deva's wagon together.

"It's time," Mohar said without preamble. "She has thrown down a challenge."

Caleb used his eyeglass to study the building.

"The door at the bottom of the tower is opening, and something is coming out."

He handed the glass to Neah.

When she brought it to her eye, she started. Shayla was framed by the double doors, energy rippling from her as if from a tiny sun. As Neah watched, Shayla walked from the tower, her steps measured, as if she knew she was being watched. She turned back to face the tower and made a beckoning motion with her fingers. Moments later two sleek black horses, their manes threaded with tiny golden bells and silver thread, pulled a brightly painted war chariot edged with gold from between the doors. Neah fancied she could hear the tinkling from the bells even from here.

She handed the glass to Mohar.

He took one look, and gave a satisfied mutter from the back of his throat. "Quite the showman, isn't she?" he said, passing the glass back to Caleb.

Deva's head tilted back and she sniffed the air like a dog. "The air ripples with illusion."

"Quite so," Mohar agreed. He closed his eyes and appeared to be concentrating in the same way she'd noticed with the Fire Weavers. After a moment he made a slashing motion with his arm, scribing what looked to be a large rectangle in the air. When he'd finished, he mumbled several words that Neah didn't quite catch. Gradually what looked like a picture frame formed in the air, its edges glowing with a purplish light.

He motioned the others to gather close in around him. It was as if Mohar had fashioned a window that opened deeper into the scene before them. Through it the plain looked very different. Where the tower had stood moments before, now only a cone-shaped blackness swirled. It slipped in and out of sight, as if constantly shifting between mass and gas.

There was no chariot either, only a shimmering, indistinct image of what might have been Neah's sister.

Neah gasped. "Shayla isn't really there."

When Neah moved away from the frame, the tower, chariot, and Shayla reappeared, as solid and as resolute as before.

"This frame dissolves illusion. Whatever is seen within this frame is what is truly there," Mohar said. "As long as we are looking through it we cannot be subjugated by any of Shayla's projections. She is not here physically, it is only a projection of her energy."

"Which means she can't be killed," Deva said, nodding.

"Not physically, however, I believe she can be energetically damaged."

"What is that black stuff where the tower was... is?" Hawke asked, shifting between the image in the frame and outside it, as if this might make everything clearer.

Mohar extended his pinky finger, the long painfully manicured nail almost touching the image in the frame. "This black cloud conducts and shapes Shayla's power from wherever she is operating from. If we can find a way to disrupt or destroy the flow from it, we may have a chance of making it to Carmelsara's gates before she can construct another."

"That will not defeat her. She will simply lay siege to the city with her army," Neah snapped.

"Hopefully the new Torian will have been declared before that happens. And remember, even if she does lay siege, Carmelsara's walls have never been breached."

"Nor have they ever been attacked by someone as powerful as Shayla, so that is no guarantee. No. We must do as much damage as we can here. She must be destroyed." Neah stared ahead, as if fixated by the scene before her. "The question is, how do we do that if she isn't even there?"

"In battle, I prefer to attack the enemy's strongest position. If that can be breached, then confidence in the rest is shattered," Caleb said.

"You're saying we attack her tower, or whatever that black thing is, regardless?" Hawke asked.

"Yes. Shayla wants a short, sharp victory. And it must be total. Soldiers, particularly the Shaylene, are superstitious. They believe in signs. Shayla can't afford to risk a protracted siege of the city. The outcome is too uncertain. Particularly with winter so close."

"He's right," Deva slipped in. "The winter winds come down off the mountains and sweep right across this plain. While they bring sleet and snow, it's the wind itself that's the worst. We call it the Shiroman, an old Carmelsaran word, because it cuts like a knife."

"Look. Something is happening," Caleb said, pointing at the frame.

The shimmering shape that represented Shayla was floating slowly toward them, the black cloud trailing her, as if attached by invisible strands.

Mohar raised his hand and slid the purple frame to one side. Without the clarity of the screen they saw Shayla resplendent in a gold-and-red cloak, standing on the war chariot, the black horses trotting sedately toward them. Behind her were two massive eagles, soaring in lazy circles above. The tower remained where it was. He flipped his fingers, and the frame returned. Somehow she didn't look so threatening this way.

"She's coming, with or without the trappings," Neah said. "Should I just ride out and try to buy some time? I still have that flame cloak around me—I think. That should hold for a while."

"The flame shield is there only as a last resort, not a primary defense. No, you can't go out there alone. Deva and I will travel with you," Mohar said.

"As will I," Caleb said.

"Not you, Caleb. Your mind has been taken once by Shayla already, remember? We cannot risk that happening again. You must stay here," Mohar said.

Caleb's face flushed, and he looked as if he might argue. Deva reached over and gripped his arm.

"What the wizard says holds some truth. Shayla has already made mental tracks into your mind, Caleb. That makes it easier for her to enter again. Like last time, you would be completely unaware it was even happening. It will be safer for Neah if you wait here with Hawke. Besides, your duty still remains to protect the caravan."

"The caravan is not at risk."

"I disagree," Mohar said, sliding his floppy sleeves up. His forearms were powerful, rippling with intricate tattooed runes. He touched several of them in turn. The points glowed in response, their light strengthening, until with a small flash they linked up, settling into a pulsing circular shape across his arm. "Shayla has no way of knowing whether Neah has disguised herself, so she will annihilate everyone here given a chance. That is why this battle is taking place within sight of Carmelsara. For them to witness her power firsthand —and her ruthlessness."

"What are you doing with your arm, wizard?"

"Preparing myself, Caleb. As should we all. I suggest that you and Hawke form the wagons into a circle, and when you have done so gather everyone inside, beasts as well. Then use this."

Delicately he lifted the glowing circle from his arm.

"Touch this to the inside of the wagon circle. It will create a barrier that will help protect those inside. It, like the fire curtain I provided for Neah, is sensitive to intent."

Caleb opened his palm and Mohar carefully transferred the band of light to him. It floated just above his skin. Hawke took charge of Caleb's bridle and led him back to the front, his stentorian voice already giving orders.

Mohar urged his horse into a trot, past the wagons, leading the way.

Neah exchanged a glance with Deva, who nodded, and together they followed, leaving the caravan behind. They caught up with Mohar, Neah riding to one side and Deva the other, matching his pace, the purple frame floating before them. The bundle of energy that might have been Shayla was still moving toward them.

Hawke's voice floated on the air behind them. A pop followed, like a large bubble bursting. She turned to look over her shoulder. A transparent dome had formed over the top of the caravan.

"It worked," she said.

"Did you have doubt?" Mohar said, the corner of his mouth turning down in that sardonic way she hated.

"Yes. I did. I thought it was a flashy gimmick to get rid of Caleb."

"How do you know it wasn't?"

Neah refused to be baited again.

He seemed content to drop it, continuing to stare straight ahead as if afraid something might disappear unless he did so.

Neah's stomach was cramping; whether from anxiety or the child, she couldn't tell. This slow plodding pace seemed to be taking forever. She wanted to get this over with. "Is there a plan?" she asked finally.

"No. Have you made a decision about my proposal?"

Neah felt a cringe in her belly. "No. And this is not the time to discuss it, seeing as how one or both of us may not make it out of this."

Silence formed a shroud that gathered about them, seeming to form a dome of its own. Inside was only the rhythmic plodding of the horses' hooves atop the road, and an occasional clink of harness.

After an interminable time, Mohar reined in and once more slid the frame to one side.

"You note how the tower appears to have remained where it was, while Shayla's war chariot has moved much closer?" He didn't wait for a reply, simply slid the frame back in place.

"And here, this blackness? What was the tower is really only paces behind her? It's being dragged along behind her. Stare into the image, look between the cloud and the image of Shayla. See if you can make out the tendrils of power that connect her to it."

After a time, Deva replied, "Yes. I can just make them out."

Neah squinted, the sun high and bright above her. It made detail difficult.

"Here, I'll try and contrast the image."

He flipped something over the frame that reduced the glare.

"Yes, I see them now."

"How many?"

"Ten, no, twelve. They keep fading and reappearing elsewhere."

"Deva, how many can you make out?"

"Fifteen."

"I count twenty," Mohar said. "There may even be more. The important thing is to sever as many as we can, as quickly as possible."

"Can Shayla see this frame? Does she know we can see past her illusion?"

"Unlikely. It's invisible from the opposite side. However, she will quickly work it out once we start attacking her power feeders."

"That's something. How do we do this?"

"I'm guessing she will begin with the two massive eagles to try and distract our attention. Once our defenses are directed against them, then she will strike, like a snake."

"That sounds like her," Deva muttered, the corners of her eyes crinkling. Neah sensed her mother drawing power up from the earth.

"We need to split up. The more we can divide Shayla's attention by mounting separate attacks, the faster she will burn through her energy reserves. However, the bad news is this frame will only split into two, not three. Deva, how do you feel about handling those eagles on your own? Remember, they aren't really there, however, they will appear so without the frame."

"You can't leave her here unprotected," Neah protested. "Illusion or not, those things can still kill, am I right?"

"Technically, yes. Though Deva's will is stronger than most."

"No, Mother, you must return to the camp, or come with me."

"If Deva's will remains strong, she won't be harmed. Nothing here can hurt her unless she allows herself to be drawn into Shayla's illusion."

"It's all right. I'll do it," Deva said.

"Mother. No."

Mohar continued speaking directly to Deva. "Good. That's very good. Now remember, once Neah and I leave you, the illusion of the eagles and Shayla will appear completely real. You do understand that, don't you?"

"Yes."

"The important thing is we all work independently and together, each of us doing our best to divide Shayla's concentration. The more we can do that, the harder Shayla will find it."

Mohar pulled his shirt off, revealing his heavily tattooed chest and arms. Again he touched a number of the runes woven through the interlaced designs; this time they fashioned the shape of a large curved blade. He detached one and handed it to Neah. She gripped its handle and immediately felt a flush of power as it connected to her and down through the earth, materializing into a glowing white saber.

"This is the only type of weapon that will sever those lines connecting her image to the black mass. Cut any of them."

Shayla's shape tensed when she saw the long blades form, and instantly the two giant birds appeared above them.

"Ride, Neah. Go. Split up."

They spurred their mounts away, the purple frame separating and reforming in front of each of them as they moved apart. Behind her, Neah could hear the harsh calls of the eagles and the popping sounds of energy exploding as Deva, deprived of the truth from the frame, attempted to defend herself.

Silently Neah tried to generate an image back to her mother of what she could see, hoping to reinforce what was there, not what was being poured into the old woman's overloaded senses.

Shayla's shimmering projection moved to intercept them. Mohar swerved to meet her, raising his curved blade high and slicing through one of the tendrils stretching behind her.

Shayla screamed as the line was severed; fluid, dull red and foul, spurted from the end. From a distance, Neah recognized Shayla's distinctive outraged tone; it collided and crashed into the memories of other times she'd been on the receiving end of her frustration.

"Hurry, Neah," Mohar called, attacking another of the whipping tubes. The octopus-like tentacles varied in thickness; some were vine-thin, while others closer to the ground were as thick as her thigh. Neah decided the larger ones were primary, so would likely be the most important.

Shayla recovered quickly, snatching off chunks of her shimmer and whipping them into flashing spirals and launching them at her two attackers. Neah watched as the spirals separated midair into spear-like projectiles, striking in a pattern of flashing destruction that was hard to avoid. Several splintered and exploded against the barrier the Fire Weavers had placed around her.

Neah spurred Magic forward. The mare tossed her head, nostrils flaring with the burnt stench of spent magic. Neah swung at one of the tubes.

Missed. Damn, the blade's shorter than I'm used to.

A fluttering of static electricity prickled Neah's arm. Throwing herself from the horse, she tumbled across the sand, desperate to keep hold of the blade.

Behind her something bright exploded, the flash making it hard to focus. She could just make out Magic. The horse was terrified. Whatever Shayla had thrown, it had been aimed at the rider, not the horse. Neah decided to present a smaller, if not slower target, and scuttled off to one side, gradually making her way behind Shayla's shimmering shape. Mohar, still mounted, attacked from the other side, managing to cut yet another of the thicker vine-like tethers as he galloped past. Viscous maroon fluid glugged from the slash, forming a glutinous puddle on the earth like oxygen-deprived blood.

A concern about how Deva was coping flashed up. Neah quashed it. This was where she was. Where they both were, separate and together, in purpose if not person. Keeping Shayla's energy and defenses divided was all that mattered now.

The purple frame before her flickered, then brightened once more. She wondered briefly what would happen if Mohar was hit by one of those spiral bolts. Likely the frame would disappear with the consciousness that held it, and then where would she be?

One of the thicker tendrils appeared in front of her. It seemed to pulse with power.

Before it could disappear again she ran over and brought the blade down hard. It was like hitting an oak log with a blunt axe. The blade shuddered, penetrating only deep enough to become stuck. Shayla's voice shrilled across the plain; this time there was pain mixed with the frustration. Neah smiled with some satisfaction. Red fluid gushed around the blade. It stank of corruption. She used her foot against the throbbing tendril to lever the blade free. Taking the handle in both hands she brought it above her head and struck again, this time using the weight of her body to drive it home, the momentum carrying the bright blade deeper. The red stuff sizzled and bubbled against the blade's light, as if it were boiling. The density inside the tendril seemed to increase with depth. Neah was tiring. She managed to dislodge the flickering light blade for a second time, and changing the angle of attack, this time she managed to sever the tendril completely.

Shayla's shape dulled and stilled for a moment, before, with a pulsing surge through the five remaining tendrils, she howled with rage and pain. They were engorged to twice their former size, as if trying to funnel too much fluid. Those that were cut writhed on the ground, reminding Neah of dissected worms mindlessly seeking their other half.

Mohar, his horse slick with what might have been blood or the red from the tentacles, came galloping toward her. Neah expected he would sweep her up behind him. Instead he swerved at the last moment and made a swing for one of the pulsing tentacles. He missed, and Shayla flung two of the spiral spears at him. He swerved again; they sailed past and instead headed directly for Neah. They both hit the Fire Weavers' protective barrier with a sickening thwack and a searing flash of heat.

The impact knocked Neah to the ground. Looking down, she saw that one of the spear points had managed to penetrate the shield. The shaft appeared to hang in the air just above her heart, before suddenly bursting into flame and dropping to the ground, a large chunk of the weavers' shield still attached to it. As she struggled to her feet, she heard a tearing rip, and another section fell away, flaring briefly on the ground before it winked out. Neah had no idea whether what remained would still work, and if so what parts of her body were now exposed.

Another spiral sped toward her, splitting into two, then three separate spears all at different levels and trajectories. She knocked one aside with the white blade and turned her back to the other two in the desperate hope that the rear shield was still intact. They struck in quick succession. Neah felt a flash of heat blast across her back. She rolled away, leaving behind what remained of the Fire Weavers' shield in jagged, smoking pieces.

Over to the right, Neah heard a thunk, followed by a surprised cry. When she looked, Mohar was down, his horse galloping freely away in the direction of the caravan. Seconds later the purple frame winked out, and the writhing tentacles disappeared. The illusion, or what was left of it, reappeared. Parts of the tower's turrets had crumbled, and Shayla's full-length court dress was holed, the edges blackened as if burned. Other whole sections of her golden cloak were missing completely, as if they had been ripped away.

The illusion must be hard to maintain. She has definitely been weakened.

The realization gave her strength as Shayla staggered toward her, a lopsided grin tugging at one corner of her mouth. The other half of her face drooped as if it were palsied.

"Ah, now we can see each other properly," Shayla said, her voice slurred, one eye half shut as if mocking what she'd said.

Neah could see the effort it was costing Shayla. She came closer, stumbling as if her foot had found an unseen hole.

"Your illusion seems to be falling apart," Neah said. "Why not show yourself in the flesh?"

"You'd like that, wouldn't you? Well, let me tell you, you're not worth the effort." The section of Shayla's face that still worked twisted into a scowl of hate as another spiral appeared in her hand. She launched it in one movement, hurling it underhand, like a dagger. Neah was too close to avoid it, and the spear struck, lodging deep in her flesh, just below her shoulder.

She gasped, more in shock than pain. When the adrenaline burned off, she knew it would be excruciating; right now it just felt dull and heavy, tinged with a burning around the entry point.

"What's the matter, little sister? Are you finally getting the point?" She laughed. It sounded harsh and forced.

Numbness radiated out from the shaft of the spear, and Neah wondered whether it might be poisoned. The expectant expression on Shayla's face confirmed it. In one quick movement, Neah gripped the spear and with a savage cry tugged it out. She staggered as the barbs caught and tore at the raw flesh. When it was finally clear she hefted it as if she might throw it.

Shayla laughed. Both of them knew it would be a futile gesture. Neah tightened her grip nevertheless; holding the spear in one hand and the light blade in the other made her feel less vulnerable.

The two sisters faced off, maintaining the distance between them, each matching the other when one took a step, Shalya reluctant to come closer while Neah held the shining light blade. Both knew there wasn't much time. Neah could feel the poison tracking through her body, leaving a trail of numbing deadness in its wake. It moved into her right leg and she staggered, quickly shifting her weight to the left as she lost control over her right thigh muscles. The movement, though, was too sudden, and she lost balance, falling heavily back onto her right side, the blade tumbling from her hand.

Shayla cackled. Kicking the fallen blade away, she came to stand over her, one foot to either side of Neah's body. She snapped her fingers, and a long broadsword appeared in her hand.

"You're not real," Neah managed.

Shayla gripped the sword between her hands, its blade pointed down toward Neah's abdomen. The left side of her face seemed to be working now.

She's drawing power from me.

"Believe what you want, runt of a sister. You will die just the same. It's a shame it will have to be quick. I was looking for some payback for all the trouble you and our blasted mother have caused me."

Deva.

Neah struggled to raise her head, hoping yet scared to see what had happened to Deva.

"Trying to find Mummy? Always the favorite daughter, weren't you? Well, don't bother, I'll save you the energy. My eagles are feasting on her fat thighs."

"Your eagles aren't any more real than you are. You didn't even have the courage to face us in person. Coward. Or is it your puppet master who is afraid?"

"What are you talking about?" Shayla snapped. "I have no master. The power is mine. I earned it. Enough of this sisterly chatter." Shayla lowered the sword to Neah's abdomen. "Get ready for a drastic abortion. Unfortunately, the mother will die as well. Any last words, little sister?"

"Remember what is truly there."

The voice came to her, the words emerging rather than forming, and she remembered Caleb describing how he felt the child spoke to him.

Is it you?

"Remember."

Neah hastily attempted to overlay a memory of the black mass and the five remaining tentacles over Shayla's shimmering form. Whoever the voice was, it was right; the more she engaged with what Shayla was projecting, the stronger the illusion would become. Even the dress and cloak seemed to have repaired themselves in the time they'd been speaking.

She pressed herself against the earth, summoning strength, using her mind to cross the threshold into *Cairos*, or stretched time. It was a risk, for while it seemed as if everything around her was moving in slow motion, it was actually her own metabolism that was speeding up. It would hasten the spread of poison throughout her system, as well as increase the uptake of energy she was drawing from the earth. She attempted to reconstruct what she'd last seen through the purple frame.

From a distance she recognized Deva's distinctive energy signature moving within the flow from the earth. She wasn't dead after all. Neah's heart surged, and it gave her renewed strength.

Shayla's expression changed slowly. Realizing belatedly what was happening, she drove the sword down. For Neah, deep in *Cairos*, it moved in slow motion. Summoning strength, she rolled aside just as the tip of the blade pierced the ground where she'd just been. Quickly flipping the flow of energy, Neah directed her memory of what she'd seen earlier out through the ground and up through the blade of the sword.

Shayla screamed as it travelled up and into her, reversing the illusion. The apparition dropped away, the shimmering image returning along with the black mass and its waving tentacles.

Neah used her quickened metabolism to dive for the shining blade and drive it point-first into the closest tentacle. She heard a high-pitched squeal, and hoped it was Shayla. Neah hacked down, using her body weight to drive the blade deeper, twisting and widening the wound while the tentacle thrashed like a skewered eel.

Finally it lay still. Neah could barely move. Deep within her she felt something stirring, urging her to move while Shayla was distracted by trying to direct the flow through her remaining links to the black mass.

Neah had no strength to slice away at all four remaining tentacles, even if she could somehow manage to reach them. Shayla would be on her by then. No, there was only one solution—one last-ditch attempt.

"Attack the mass."

Yes. Digging the point of the blade into the earth, she levered herself up to kneel on her left knee. Balancing, she drew back her arm and hoisted the light blade directly at the pulsing black mass. It stuck truly and was sucked inside.

Another scream, this time more bestial, as Neah imagined the enchanted blade travelling through the black cloud like a knife through butter. Neah collapsed back to the earth.

A familiar drumming throbbed up from the ground. Neah

couldn't keep her eyes open. Whatever drug was in the poison was too difficult to fight. The throbbing was getting closer, then stopped abruptly. She was lying in the light, the warmth of the sun receiving her. It wouldn't be long now. Idly she wondered whether she had done enough. Her eyes fluttered open.

Blackness blocked the light, shading the heat. A figure stood over her, its shadow stretching across her body, overtaking her as it came closer. The shade felt cool and reassuring. Then she was being shaken. Shouted at.

"Neah." The tone was urgent, voice harsh, rough, and fuzzy at the edges, yet also oddly welcome. Familiar.

Isolated thoughts bubbled up through the pain, daring to be heard. The kindly, cool shadow thrust one of its arms beneath her shoulders and the other behind her knees, and hoisted her up. She felt the light envelop her once more as she cleared the shadow, and she closed her eyes to it.

"Neah?" That voice again, less insistent now. Her eyelids fluttered open briefly. She squinted, trying to see through the light; the face beside her own seemed haloed by it.

Caleb.

SEVENTEEN

Caleb nocked one of the multicolored arrows and waited. Leaning his weight against the gnarly bark of a tree, he allowed some of the tension to ease from him. Overhead there was no competition for light in the canopy; the infrequent trees reached as high as they dared, allowing the vegetation below to bathe equally all the way down to the forest floor, which, as a consequence, was thick with undergrowth.

Ideal for rabbits, but so far his sack remained empty.

It was both frustrating and liberating to be so near to Carmelsara and yet not be able to approach any closer, much less enter. Neah was still too ill to be moved, and leaving her was not an option, though Deva, fully recovered, had urged him to do so several times. The idea seemed incomprehensible to him, yet waiting and being able to do nothing was equally impossible.

Neither Neah nor Mohar had regained consciousness since he had brought them back to the caravan, despite the arrival of a physic from Carmelsara. The Torian's very own, it turned out. Hawke and Caleb had speculated at how the dying Torian would cope without his personal carer, however, that wasn't really their concern. Neah was, but he had quickly tired of waiting—for recovery, or death. Waiting spawned hope, or worse, despair. In a way, he wished Shayla would return and give them a chance to finish this, one way or the other. At least then it would be decided, and this time he wouldn't be sent off to the sidelines to watch like some spectator. At the end, when he saw Neah go down, swinging that glowing blade at nothing —that he could see at any rate—it had all become too much. He'd had to do something, even if it was just riding out and fetching her back.

A rustle in the bushes—off to the right.

He snapped to attention, taking the tension through the bow as he brought the flight of the arrow up beside his cheek. The sound came again. He must have misjudged the distance. It now sounded further away, over toward the small creek. He loosened the tension, keeping the bow ready, taking a cautious step, then another, avoiding the numerous dry sticks littering the forest floor. He'd lost one rabbit like that yesterday. The crack of the dead wood had sounded like thunder, and the hare had bounded away before he'd had a chance to take aim.

Caleb wasn't used to forests; he preferred open space. Not that this narrow belt of greenery could be confused with a forest. It only hugged the narrow transition between the foothills and plain, stretching around the edges of the valley like a lush green belt, less than five leagues deep.

At least coming out here was an opportunity to *do* something. It was a distraction—a diversion—that distanced the need to hope.

He was nearing the creek. It was heavily blanketed by under-growth, so the sound of it came to him first, followed by the smell. Fresh, babbling water produced a distinctive wafting scent for Caleb. He'd only noticed it after once nearly dying of thirst when he'd been a young dispatch officer fresh out of training and had become lost in the desert. Caleb licked his lips, the memory of the relentless heat and scorched dryness of the air searing his lungs still close. He coughed in reflex. Reaching for the water bladder at his belt, he found it empty, yet strangely couldn't remember draining it.

His thirst instantly increased, overtaking him like a dry wave. Stealth and prey were forgotten. The bow slipped from his fingers as he crashed through the tangled bracken toward the illusive sound. The closer he came, the more tangled the bracken, and the more desperate he felt.

The sound of water grew louder. The thirst was now like a furnace in his throat, hot and fierce. Part of him knew this feeling was unreasonable. The weather had been brisk, even cold when he'd started out, yet here it was now blisteringly hot. He couldn't be heat affected, couldn't be this thirsty; the water bladder was empty, which meant he must have drunk from it only recently.

Doesn't it?

Perhaps it leaked? Did I even fill it before coming out?

He used his cutlass to slash at an interwoven mass of vines. They were filled with sticky white sap that spurted across his face and hands. His uniform was soon covered with it. Grunting with pent-up frustration, he barged his way through and finally, there it was. More than a stream, a pool with a tumbling, gushing waterfall at one end and an eddy draining the other.

He threw aside his cutlass, tugged off his boots, and waded in, gulping at the fresh water until his thirst was sated to saturation. He trudged through the mud to the middle of the pond, and turned to float on his back, staring up at the sky littered with long remnants of cloud that drifted like tatters between the distant peaks. He felt satisfied for the first time in weeks. Clean for the first time in months and, he realized with dawning wonder, really free for the only time in his memory.

The pool felt like a sanctuary. Here there was no yoke of responsibility, no crushing weight of lives reliant on a choice that only he could make. Here there was peace without recrimination— or expectation. Only him. He wondered how he had become so lost.

"Caleb."

He started, gulping water, feet pawing frantically for the bottom of the pond as he scoured the surrounding rocks for the source of the voice.

"Caleb." The voice again. It was a woman, he was sure of that, though it was hard to distinguish from the hypnotic sound of water on water. It seemed to have come from the fall itself. He swam closer. The waterfall was not high, the drop deceptively steep, water free-falling in a smooth curtain from the rocky lip directly above the pool.

"Who's there?" he called. The sound of his voice caught in the depression of the mossy rock wall, sounding hollow and empty. "Show yourself."

Something was stirring inside the flow of water, as if a strong wind were blowing it to one side, yet there was not a breath of breeze. A shape was forming. He held his breath as the semblance of a face emerged from the water, its surface smooth yet three dimensional, like blown glass that was still being shaped.

"Who are you?" he shouted, not sure whether this was real or he was really asleep on the bank beside his discarded cutlass, dreaming this up.

"I am a messssenger." The voice was sibilant, the s stretched and dominant.

"What do you want?"

"Sshe wakesss. You mussst go now. To Carmelssssara. Take... the child. Your time isss... returned to you. Ssstay... with child." The words were heavy with pauses, and rushed at the end, like water flowing between obstacles.

The shape of the strange glass face melted back into the flow, and soon there was only the waterfall once more.

What does it mean? Is this water I gorged myself on laced with some drug? Some mineral trace that distorts the senses? Deva will know.

Nothing had been quite right since he'd ridden out to fetch Neah three days ago. Snorting, he thrashed through the water back to the bank. His feet finally finding the muddy bottom, he staggered onto the grass and reattached his cutlass, looking back over his shoulder before flopping to the ground to tug on his boots. The saturated uniform clung to his skin, clammy, his body cooling as a breeze rippled over him. He shivered and struggled to his feet.

Hand resting on the pommel of his cutlass, he left the pool, casting a final, hesitant glance behind before barging back the way he'd come, half of him hoping that whatever had spoken to him was real, that Neah was finally awake, while the solider in him scoffed at his desperation. He shivered.

When had it become so damn cold?

HE GALLOPED INTO CAMP, the road dust overtaking him as he slid from his horse and ran across to Deva's wagon. He sprang up, one foot boosting off the front axle hub, the other finding the bench seat. He slid through the gap in the dividing curtain in one easy motion, landing inside with a thump.

The physic, bending over the body on the bed, jumped at the sudden entrance. Neah was lying there so still....

The air in the caravan felt lighter than before. The back door and side window above the bed were open, creating a flow of air. Caleb, his clothes still dripping, felt chilled, the flesh rising to peaked puckers on his forearms. Deva came through the back door carrying a tureen of steaming water. She pulled the door to and with an acknowledging glance at Caleb, placed the water down beside the physic.

"Has anything changed?" Caleb asked. His lips seemed stiff, making it hard to speak.

"She woke, briefly. About a half hour ago. She was highly distressed, yelling that she needed to get to the Torian. The physic gave her a light sedative—she's sleeping peacefully now. We're just getting ready to re-dress the wound and check the child. Why don't you find yourself some dry clothes and wait with Hawke outside? I'll call when she wakes again."

"She's all right? She is still so pale." His voice was dubious as he squeezed his way through to the back door. Neah's normally full red lips were pale and compressed, as if she was annoyed at something, though she did seem to be breathing easier.

"Yes, or she will be. Now that she has come out of the coma." Deva stopped him at the door, looking closely at his sap-stained shirt. "What is this white stuff?"

He shrugged. "From some vines. I had to cut my way through to the creek."

Deva brought her nose close and sniffed.

Caleb, anxious not go into any more detail, clambered down from the wagon and gently pulled the door to before she could say any more.

Hawke was waiting with questions beside the fire. The afternoon had closed in; the scattered clouds of earlier had clustered together. They reminded Caleb of the face in the water. He decided not to mention anything of it to Hawke either.

Though the voice had said "she's awake." Did that mean it was real? What else might it be?

More to quiet the chatter in his head, he asked, "And Mohar? What of him?"

"He woke just after you left this morning. He was spent though, could hardly raise his head. If Shayla decided to reappear now, there is nothing we could do to stop her."

"The dome he gave us to protect the caravan is still intact. That will be something. Nevertheless, I agree, I can't imagine her giving up. It's the other thing that made me nervous just sitting here. The waiting."

"The caravan is anxious to get moving too. They can see the city teasingly close, just a day's ride away. The memory of what Shayla did out there is still too fresh for any of them to try it alone."

"Is Shayla finished, do you think? Did Neah and Mohar defeat her?"

"You were there. She, or whatever she created, vanished just after you rode out. I can't imagine her giving up though, can you? Deva says that even inside Carmelsara they will still be vulnerable, until the new Torian is officially declared and confirmed."

"She said that?" Caleb asked, confused. In his head it was always the making it through that was important. He'd always assumed that once the gates closed behind them, Neah and the child would be safe. This Arena of Elements Mohar was talking about would surely be a formality.

"So you'll still be needed," Hawke added, "though not if you end up dying of the cold. Your teeth are chattering. Go change those clothes, and I'll fetch you some tea. I may even have a measure of white spirit left too. That'll warm you up. What were you thinking, going swimming with winter almost upon us? It's a wonder you didn't freeze to death."

CALEB SLURPED AT THE TEA, and huddled over the fire outside Deva's wagon. She had reappeared briefly to oversee final arrangements for the evening meal, waving away Caleb's questions. Hawke and he settled down around the fire to enjoy the food. Fresh supplies had arrived from Carmelsara, escorted by a division of the Torian's Imperial guard.

Now that Neah and Mohar had awoken, the physic had deemed them fit to travel as early as tomorrow, so the mood of everyone was light. Several had even unpacked their drums, pipes, and fiddles, and organized an impromptu dance in the center of the wagon ring. It was good to hear music and intermittent laughter after so much hardship and death. Caleb had also stood down his remaining men from the watch, relegating this duty to the freshly arrived Torian guard, who looked in need of proving themselves. Caleb had regarded their impeccable green-and-white uniform topped by brightly shined gold helmets with a mixture of wry amusement and a curious trace of envy. He remembered when such things had mattered to him, acknowledging that one day they might well again if all went his way at the board hearing.

The door to the back of the wagon opened, and Deva's head popped out. She waved him over.

"She's asking for you. The physic has gone to tend to Mohar."

Caleb jumped to his feet and entered the wagon, wary not to make too much noise. The lamps had been lit, and Neah was propped up in the bed. He was pleased to see her color had returned. Her right shoulder was padded and tightly bound. The smell of strong medicants was heavy in the air.

Neah patted the side of her bed with her left hand. He hesitated a moment before easing himself down. Deva hovered near the back of the wagon.

"You look m-much better," he stammered, and wondered at himself. He hadn't stammered since he was a boy. He cleared his throat and pitched his voice lower. "Are you recovered?"

She smiled weakly. "As best I can."

"The child is fine." Deva spoke up from the door.

"I dreamed of you, just before I woke."

"Nightmares?" Caleb joked weakly.

"I dreamed you were at a waterfall, in a pool beneath it."

Caleb's gut spasmed.

"What happened?"

"The Mother was there as well. That's all I can remember."

"Deva?"

Neah laughed. "No, *the* Mother."

"I was. At a pool, beneath a waterfall." He looked over his shoulder at Deva. "Did you say anything to her? I was wet, remember? You must have said something as I passed through that she heard. She was just waking up."

Deva shook her head. She looked as bemused as Neah, before something that could have been slow realization flickered across her face.

"You heard something, didn't you?"

Caleb nodded, telling them in a halting voice what had happened.

"So, maybe I'm off Mohar's official death list now?" He finished with a laugh that no one joined.

"The white sap that was all over your uniform. It is something we use to induce an altered state," Deva said.

"You mean I was drugged? I knew it couldn't be real."

"No. The sap just would make you more receptive. More sensitive. The message, I think, was real. You'll have to make up your own mind about that."

"And if it was, what does it mean?"

"That the numbers have changed," Deva said, coming to stand beside Neah.

"Numbers? What numbers?" Caleb asked, sick of the uncertainty.

"The numbers are cast when reading futures. Sometimes the gods like to have a throw as well. You now appear to be needed by at least one of them for whatever it is that lies ahead, Caleb."

THE GATES to Carmelsara rolled apart as they approached, the immaculate Imperial Guard trotting in formation at the head of the ragged collection of patched and dirty wagons. Neah marveled at the monstrous white walls rising high above her. They appeared to have no joins.

"What are they made from?"

"No one knows," Deva said. "The Ancients built them. The locking mechanism on the gates is equally mysterious. When the gates are drawn shut, each side appears to merge with the other. There is no semblance of separation when they are together, they simply become part of the wall."

Neah looked back around the side of her wagon, watching as the last wagon rolled through. Deva was right, when the doors rolled toward each other they connected with a muffled hiss followed by a solid clunk, then seamlessly joined.

Inside the walls, the city was vibrant, full of color and movement, with all manner of goods on display from both well-tended shops and shaded stalls at the side of the wide cobbled thoroughfare. No one would know that beyond this valley a vicious and bloody war had been raging and would still, though having seen the walls, Neah wondered whether even Shayla's mysterious black powder could make a dent in them, or the bustling life inside.

"See up there." Deva pointed to a white building with four large columns set into one of the surrounding hills. It overlooked the whole valley and the sprawling city below it. "That's the main temple. I'll take you there when you're strong enough."

Hawke rode up beside their wagon. His eyes crinkled with pleasure when he saw Neah sitting at the front.

"Feeling better, I see. Is it bearable?" He touched his own right shoulder.

"Barely bearable." She chuckled. "I'm lucky to be here, Hawke. Nothing could detract from that."

"I am pleased." He looked down at his saddle as if making up his mind to say more. Finally he did. "I've made this journey many times, yet this one has been—special, for many reasons." He looked over at Deva and then back. "I feel privileged to have been permitted the time to share it. There will be no more, and for that I am also grateful."

Deva reached over and gripped his arm. "We too are thankful for you and your wise guidance, Master Hawke, for without you none of us would be here at all. It is the Mother's way to unite lacks and strengths to make a greater whole. Will you still join me at the temple?"

"Yes. I am looking forward to it." He paused. "The road forks ahead. The caravan will go off to the right and the old city. Your wagon, however, is to go left. The captain of the Imperial Guard told me they will escort you directly to the Torian's Seat. His holiness is apparently keen to greet you—all. Caleb and Mohar as well."

"What is this seat?"

"You would call it a palace. It is where the council meets, the seat of power of the Commonwealth."

"Ah," Neah said, nodding. "It sounds as if he thinks the race is won. I wonder if the Torian realizes that Shayla is not defeated, and most of the Commonwealth is lost."

"You'll have to ask him that. I'll see you soon?" He looked meaningfully at Deva. She nodded, and he cantered back to the front of the line.

"What was all that about?" Neah asked.

"Hawke wishes to make his peace. The canker advances slowly. He has less than six months. I said I would help prepare his way while he is still relatively healthy."

Nearing the split in the road, one of the soldiers came over, saluted, and taking the bridle of their remaining gelding, led him away from the caravan to join the rest of his waiting troop. They fell into line behind the escort, rolling through the left-hand archway and up the road beyond. Caleb and Mohar flanked them.

Mohar had barely spoken since leaving the campsite that morning. He hadn't even asked after her health or the child, which was odd in itself. His physical wounds appeared to be minor; however, Neah suspected that deeper ones lay hidden, more on an energetic level. Blastback, some mages called it, where more power was pulled than could effectively be distributed, and so it flipped back on the user. She'd mentioned it to Deva, who seemed reluctant to discuss it, which was also strange.

Caleb too seemed unusually subdued.

The shops fell away almost immediately, giving way to solid-looking homes that flanked either side of the road. The houses featured polished cut stone and intricately carved wooden facades. The upper levels had lavish roof gardens thick with plants that appeared to try and outdo one another. Deva filled the silence with a commentary.

"These houses belong mostly to tradespeople and the more prosperous shopkeepers. Further on it branches again into terraces that lead up a steep hill. Along there you'll see the wealthy merchants' and senior civil servants' homes, much more lavish. The Torian's Seat is built at the very top. The house prices increase the higher up you go."

"Was that where you lived?" Caleb asked.

Deva coughed a laugh. "Oh, goodness no. We were not into that race. Our villa was behind the town, further along the valley."

"How far back does Carmelsara go?" Neah piped in, keen to keep the conversation going. The silence from before seemed charged.

"The valley widens behind the city, stretching back and out for many hundreds of leagues to the distant sea. There are villages, larger towns built around mostly mines, and centers that cater to the larger farmsteads. Carmelsara state is self-supporting, though the city has always been the culmination of the trade route. Before this damned war started anyway."

"When will she come again, do you think?" Neah continued, voicing the question that had been buzzing at the back of her mind like a bee in a bottle.

"Shayla?" Deva grunted. "Now that we're inside the city, all she has to do is find a way of turning up to challenge our claim."

"Can she do that?" Caleb asked. "She has no Torian's mark."

"Ordinarily no. However, her armies occupy all the regions of the Commonwealth. Her claim would be considered. Politically expedient, they will call it. She has to make it through the gates first, and that is extremely unlikely."

"Surely the people will resist if she does succeed," Neah said.

Mohar spoke for the first time. "Why would they? Look around. This is a charmed city. There are no beggars, no poverty. Shayla will make them believe that things will continue as before. And they will, because everyone will desperately want them to. Then with the legendary Carmelsaran treasury behind her, Shayla will expand her empire far beyond the seas. Do you think these people here care who sits at the top of that hill, or what happens to other countries, as long as their lives remain unaffected?"

"So you're saying that it's all right for her to spread the corruption that is driving her," Caleb said. "Doesn't that bit matter? Perhaps you'll be like the rest of them and fall into line if someone returns *your* power."

"I'm at a loss as to why you are even here, Caleb," Mohar snapped, like a terrier to a larger hound. "Surely you should be preparing for your board hearing prior to being cashiered, or better still executed?"

"Mohar!" Deva chided. "That's cruel, even for you."

Caleb overrode her rebuke, his gaze murderous. "Like always, wizard, I am just following orders. Unlike you, though, I go where I am needed most."

"And I do not? It wasn't you that was on that battlefield three days ago. It was my life, my talent, on the line. Not yours."

"Funny, I thought it was Neah's. She seemed to be the one who finished it. From where I plucked you up off the ground, anyway."

"Enough, you two. Each of us is here to contribute our part, and no more," Deva snapped. "There is neither room nor time to strut your silly egos now."

The charged silence settled around them once more. Neah busied herself absorbing the strange and exotic sights surrounding her. The city had opened out beneath them the higher they traveled along the cobbled terraces. She could now see that the streets were laid out in straight lines, like furrows, unlike her home state where houses had grown haphazardly, like weeds alongside a watercourse. The solid homes of the tradespeople had given way to sprawling mansions, with iron-spiked fences separating them from the road and framing the lush gardens inside. Much higher up, she caught a glimpse of the gleaming white tiles of what must be the Torian's Seat. She felt her eyelids become heavy, and allowed herself to drift.

The wagon hit a bump and she started, her hand moving first to her abdomen and then to the pain of her injured shoulder.

"Sorry, I tried to miss it," Deva said.

Neah didn't answer. Ahead was a huge domed palace, spread

across the flattened top of the hill. They were now higher than the massive Carmelsaran gates, the view spilling out to the patchwork plains beyond. She wondered why the palace hadn't been visible on their approach toward the walls.

"It's incredible," Neah said. A pair of white iron gates swung open as the Imperial guards approached, other sentries appearing seemingly from nowhere to check credentials before waving them through.

The palace seemed like a small city in itself. Numerous buildings, all bright with the same white tiles, stretched away on either side, each with their own white-graveled drive. The main broad road stretched ahead of them in a determined line ending at the largest of the structures, topped by a magnificent blue dome.

"That," said Deva, "is the Torian's Seat. The seat of power for the Commonwealth, or what it once was."

The procession pulled up beneath a covered portico. Caleb helped both the women down from the wagon. Mohar struggled out of the saddle, sliding to the ground, waving away help from several of the white-uniformed servants who had spilled through the carved white doors at their approach.

After a small argument, Caleb reluctantly surrendered his two cutlasses to the guard captain, and they were escorted inside. There followed a long walk through a succession of anterooms and grand hallways, all bedecked with artwork and valuables donated from Commonwealth members' collections. Neah even recognized a large painting and sculpture that used to grace the palace in Shaylene.

Mohar drew close, dipping his head so he could speak quietly. "Have you had time to reflect on our earlier discussion? Now is the time to make your decision."

Neah realized she had been trying to avoid this moment, and now it was too late. If she rejected Mohar, she would also create a powerful enemy. Perhaps greater than any within the Council.

"Neah." Caleb approached from behind, placing his hand on her shoulder. She turned around to face him, relief coursing through her.

He'd had time to find and change into a new uniform. He looked almost resplendent in the spotless white with the blue commander's sash, and rakish tilt of his hat.

"The walk through these corridors has been long. Do you need to rest?" He glanced meaningfully at Mohar.

"Perhaps if I could use that ready arm of yours for a moment, Commander?" She smiled, turning to lean some of her weight on him. Mohar, his face smoldering, stalked off.

Finally the small party paused outside another set of double doors. She saw Caleb tug his uniform into place. Mohar shook out the wide sleeves of his elaborately brocaded shirt, and stood a little straighter, his chin rising slightly as if he were pumping himself up for a confrontation. Neah released her hand from Caleb's arm and hooked it through Deva's, wondering at her own rising disinterest. The two women still wore their travel-stained clothes. Beyond these doors was a man like any other, one who was sick, clinging to life until he could anoint a successor. What would he care whether they were dressed in finery or creased leathers?

The doors swung open, behind each more white-uniformed servants. All sported shaven, waxed skulls that gleamed in the brilliant light from an array of hanging lights bedecked with thousands of tinkling pieces of cut glass that reflected and enhanced the glow.

A thick purple rug trimmed with gold led to a raised podium at the end of a very long room, where a diminutive man sat on an elaborately carved high-backed chair, padded with purple upholstery.

As soon as they started forward, the little man launched himself from the podium and strode forward, his white robe flowing about him, its folds sashed with rich purple. A large pendant suspended by a gold chain hung from his neck. He met them halfway, greeting them individually before taking their hands between his and bowing over them. His eyes were intensely blue. Neah felt them boring into her. For a man who was supposed to be dying, he looked remarkably healthy and exuded a lot of energy.

"Commander Kane, I believe we have much to thank you for, and as a first gesture of thanks I'd like to assure you that I've spoken to my remaining general and requested that he drop any charges against you."

Caleb's face flushed as he brought his fist to his chest and bowed his head.

The Torian turned to face Neah. When he turned his torch-like gaze fully on her, she felt like she was the only one in the room, his attention was so complete—but also strangely kindly. He reminded her of Deva's father, her beloved grandfather. She liked him immediately.

"You must be Neah," he said, his brown eyes soft. "You have been through much to be here."

"We have traveled well." She used the old caravaneer term to describe a difficult but successful journey.

He nodded slowly, then placed his right fist to his chest and bowed, before turning to Deva.

The two stared at each other for several moments before Deva stepped forward. The little man opened his arms and they embraced warmly and fully for what seemed a long time. They said nothing when they turned to face the others, the Torian's hand still lightly holding on to Deva's fingertips.

Caleb and Neah exchanged glances.

"We are old friends. Come, let us eat, and we can discuss what must happen next," the Torian said, not in the least embarrassed.

He led them to an adjoining room enclosed on two sides with glass that captured the view of the city and beyond completely. Neah had never seen so much glass in one place before. The Torian clapped his hands, and more of the shaven-headed men brought in several trays of food, mostly fruit and vegetables, but also a tray of various steaming meats in a thick gravy. The rich aroma wafted to her, and Neah licked her lips, swallowing back the anticipation that she suspected was driven by the child inside her. He seemed to love meat, though that would probably change, as the Torian traditionally ate no animal flesh.

They settled themselves along the table, sitting cross-legged atop thin purple cushions. Neah stifled a laugh as Caleb tried to look comfortable, his knees almost level with his chest. Wine was poured from blown-glass carafes into metal goblets that could have been gold. Deva and the Torian sat beside one another, their heads leaning in toward each other as they shared private conversation. Occasionally, a stifled chuckle would float out from them and into the room. Apart from that, Neah could hear nothing.

Deva though looked like she'd shed fifteen years since they'd walked into what she termed the "seat room." As the sweet pastries were served, the Torian settled back, cleared his throat, and using the long nail on the pinky of his right hand clinked the side of his goblet. Neah recognized it as being similar to the one that Mohar was so proud of. On hearing it, the servants took up their empty trays and left the room. When they were alone, the Torian spoke.

"I am aware of much that you have been through and also what remains undone. It is in everyone's interest, therefore, that we have the child declared as soon as possible, so I have arranged to call a meeting of the full council. They should already be gathered."

Neah, unsure of the protocol, spoke anyway. "You are aware, Torian, that Shayla's challenge has not yet finished. She still lives and will possibly find a way to intercede in whatever you have planned."

He nodded. "Shayla cannot gain entry to the city. It is defended by both men and strong magical wards. She well knows this. Her magic cannot penetrate us. Despite that, it is all the more reason to have the council confirm your child's claim. Once that is done no one, including Shayla, can ever challenge the legitimacy of the succession. You have the Torian's mark on your body, I am told." He glanced at Mohar and then back at Neah.

She nodded.

"Then it is as good as done. You will become regent upon my death."

"With respect," Neah continued, "from the healthy glow around you that will not be for many years yet."

With a sideways glance at Deva, the Torian said, "The appearance of health is important to retain the confidence of my people. My life runs out faster because of it."

Neah cocked her head to one side, slightly confused.

Deva's voice slid into the gap. "What the Torian means is that his illness is being masked. The effort of maintaining that illusion is burning through his remaining life force much quicker than it otherwise would. His physic, the one who tended you, estimates that only weeks remain on his span."

"How can that be?" Caleb interjected, then reddened, remembering himself.

The Torian looked amused. "Commander Kane, your input is welcome." He smiled warmly, revealing white teeth. "May I say that you are everything I imagined you to be. And of course, Mohar. We will speak later."

The wizard nodded. Neah saw his chin rise a little more.

"First we must deal with the vipers' pit that is the Council."

"What must I do?" Neah asked.

"I have formally announced that there has been a petition for declaration and that the Council is instructed to attend. After the proofing process, you will be invited to speak of your intentions, and those of your son whom you will govern for. Following that there will be discussion where the vested interests attempt to sway their colleagues, and finally there will be a vote, which must be carried by a majority of fifteen councilors before the Torian can be declared."

"Sounds complicated."

"We will guide you through. I see no difficulty, ultimately. A few will wager their votes for additional merit or gold, however, I think I have accommodated for that. We have ten councilors who have already committed."

"Leaving fifteen to convince," Caleb said. "Shame I had to leave my cutlasses at the door."

Nervous laughter followed as they rose from the table and walked from the room.

THE COUNCIL CONSISTED of twenty-five members, thirteen drawn from Carmelsara's nobility, and the rest representatives from the various countries and states that made up the former Commonwealth. Despite the fact that all the territories bar Shore and Carmelsara were now under Shaylene occupation, it had been determined that all members would still retain their full voting rights.

When the Torian appeared at the top of the steps leading down to the chamber of councilors, the chancellor struck a large gong. The men below quietened and looked up expectantly, standing and bringing their fists to their chests in the traditional salute. The Torian responded, and began descending the broad steps in slow measure, the others following.

The Council was arranged in a semicircle, at the center of which was the Torian's Seat, a replica of the one Neah had seen upstairs. The little man settled himself into the chair, tucking his feet up beneath him, and having done so seemed to grow, filling it with his presence. Neah wasn't sure how he had done that, but it was a handy trick. She was not looking forward to sitting there herself, and wondered idly if she ever would. The selection process seemed convoluted and less sure than she'd imagined.

The chancellor struck the gong again, and everyone resumed their seats. No chairs were brought nor offered to Neah or the others. Instead they were ushered to stand behind the Torian's Seat, two to either side.

"The business is to hear the petition for declaration of a new Torian," the chancellor intoned.

"We shall hear." The Council spoke in chorus.

Neah was waved forward. She walked several paces to stand before the Torian.

"Can you reveal the Torian's mark?"

Neah nodded, and moved to lift her tunic. A white-haired woman scuttled forward and stilled her, hand waving instead for a covering to be brought. Several of the bald servants were instructed to hold the velvet covering up while Neah disrobed. The white-haired councilor pointed at three of her colleagues to come over and bear witness. Finally a grizzled old man with a long beard shuffled into the room, and was also brought behind the covering.

The five all bent over the long multicolored mark, tracing the lineage and murmuring about the crown and the distinctness or otherwise of the various lines. Neah shivered. The breeze coming from the top carried the edges of winter with it. Finally they appeared to come to a decision. The old man with the beard stood before the Council, and in a quavering voice announced:

"She has the mark. It has been confirmed."

Hushed talking and an isolated cheer broke out. The Torian stilled it with the rise of his hand.

"The petitioner may address the assembly," the chancellor said, his stentorian voice loud in the chamber.

Neah dressed quickly and finished adjusting her clothing before taking a wide stance on the tiled floor.

"I didn't ask for this. Indeed, when I found out I rejected the idea. Completely. I am a devout follower of the gods, and am willing to serve where I am called, whether that be as mother to a child who grows up to be a miller, or is destined to be the White Torian. It is not for me to argue. I make no promises. I am Neah: a warrior, former slave, and princess of the Shaylene court—"

A few gasps interrupted her. Neah raised her voice to override the whispered chatter.

"—and the father of the child is a simple soldier." She indicated Caleb behind her, who, she noted, had the good grace to blush. "I believe that was the calling of the gods—for us both. Who am I, or any of us here, to judge or argue?"

Again there were outbursts, more indignant this time.

"Are there any here who would challenge?" the chancellor spoke again, the mallet of his gong already drawn back to strike.

The minutes stretched out.

"I will speak—and challenge."

All eyes turned.

Mohar stepped forward and came to stand beside Neah.

"Mohar!" The Torian's voice rang out through the chamber like the crack of a whip. Mohar ignored it.

This was a challenge and they were all, Torian or no, bound to hear it.

"You all know me. Know of my abilities, before... and now. I was a Third Laurel wizard until I was stripped of my power. In compensation I was offered an assignment to bring this woman and her child safely to Carmelsara. Well, I did that. I did everything that was asked of me, and here she is. I even offered to wed her, to secure her passage through this place and beyond—as *my* service—willing to serve where I am called. Well consider me *called*."

With that Mohar struck the palm of one hand with the clenched fist of the other. Thunder rolled across the room yet the sky, visible through the open chamber doors above, remained clear. Neah heard him mumble several words, recognizing several as forbidden words of power. She skittered away, looking back in horror as Mohar's beard fell out and his hair became longer, changing color even as it grew into a smooth raven finish. The same texture and length as Shayla's. Mohar was turning into Shayla.

"Guards," the Torian commanded. Caleb ran forward, but Mohar seemed to be surrounded by a protective barrier; he couldn't get to him. Instead he moved to stand beside Neah, shielding her with his body. She pushed him aside and threw herself at her sister, but was rebuffed by the invisible barrier. It encircled her completely.

Above, there was a scuffle on the stairs where a dozen or more of the Imperial guards were clustering in confusion, unable to move further down the steps. The same sort of shielding seemed to be in place there as well.

As they watched, Shayla became fully formed. Tall and lithe, her features strong yet still feminine. Neah had always envied her curious combination of beauty and strength. It was what made her a leader that men wanted to follow.

"Councilors of the Commonwealth. Behold. I make my claim as your new Torian." Her voice echoed strongly off the marble walls.

The chamber was silent. Then, like a slowly forming wave, the noise rose until it broke into outraged cries and shouts. The repeated throbbing reverberation from the chancellor's gong as he tried to restore order, adding to the cacophony. Shayla, her arms folded, watched it all and sneered, waiting for the energy in the room to run down, as it must. They had no answers.

Neah signaled Caleb to try and boost her up over the top of the barrier, however, it seemed to cover the top as well, forming a dome. Shayla looked up, lifted an index finger, and wagged it in Neah's face before laughing and walking away, strutting in front of the tiers of councilors. The shield seemed to move with her. Neah slid off the other side to the floor.

As Shayla passed, the talk stopped abruptly, like schoolchildren at the appearance of a teacher.

Finally an uneasy silence settled.

One man, at the back, dressed in an olive-colored shirt with the same wide sleeves that Mohar favored, stood and demanded, "What have you done with Mohar, the wizard?"

"He is beyond you now. I entered his person a day or so back, when he was *indisposed* on my battlefield."

"You possessed him? Then you are not truly here?" the man fired back.

Shayla smiled wryly and gave a small shake of her head before pointing at the councilor, her long crimson nail quivering with power. The man clutched at his throat. Soon the strangled, sucking sounds of someone suffocating filled the chamber. With a flick of the same finger, he was flung back down, the pressure suddenly released.

"Am I still not here, councilor?" Her voice dripped with sarcasm, then hardened as she addressed the full assembly. "Know this. I could kill you all right now and simply take power. No one can get out of or into this chamber until I say so. But I choose not to kill you. Instead I want your endorsement as the White Torian, the one that will lead this Commonwealth to glory throughout the known world and beyond even that. Therefore I repeat my claim."

All eyes turned to the chancellor. Finally he stood and in a quavering voice announced, "As is written, the two challengers, one proved, one not, must meet in the Elemental Arena at moonrise. The winner will be chosen by the gods and confirmed by this Council as the new Torian."

Shayla gave a mock bow, and with another clap of her hands the room filled with smoke. When it cleared, Shayla had vanished.

EIGHTEEN

"How did she do it? How was it that we did not even notice?" Neah stormed from one end of the room to the other, unable to remain still.

Deva and Caleb watched her from one of the elaborately upholstered divans in the lavish suite of rooms they had been given. Trays of food and drink remained untouched on the low table before them.

"That matters little now, daughter. It is already done. I did not see through the deception, did not even suspect it. My mind was deflected by Mohar's energetic wounds, as I suspect was yours. There was no suggestion Shayla had entered him. In hindsight, I can see now how it might be done."

"And what of you, Caleb?" Neah railed at him. "You are supposed to be able to see into his mind through our child. What happened with that?"

"I have heard nothing for some days. He is shielded from me. I consider it a blessing."

"That would be Shayla's influence," Deva added.

"So was that entire battle on the plain outside a hoax to hide this deception?" Neah continued, unable to accept it.

"Not at all. I see her possession of Mohar as one of opportunity and daring, rather than a plan. So like Shayla. Of course, having failed to kill you on the way, she would have much preferred to have ended it with you out there for all of Carmelsara to witness. If your claim was never seen, much less heard, it would have made it so much easier for her."

"Then why not kill me today? Mohar had opportunity. He was riding right beside me, by all the gods. I was unprepared and unprotected for most of the day. He even repeated his offer of marriage."

"And what would that have proved? Simply a defrocked wizard murdering an unarmed pregnant woman? Would that substantiate Shayla's claim? No. As she demonstrated today, she could kill all the councilors. The one thing she needs is legitimacy for what she intends or, rather, whoever is behind her. This puppet master has bold plans, and needs the power or trappings of the Torian to bring it about."

"What form will this challenge tonight take, do we know?" Caleb asked.

Deva sighed, sliding further down the couch. "The Arena of Elements is designed to allow the strength of the gods to move into the petitioner. In this case, both you and Shayla will spend the night there. Whichever gods choose to lend their power to you, or her, will determine the winner. It will be seen as a contest between the one who desires war and those who would have peace in the world of men."

"What do you mean?" Neah asked, a knot of concern in her chest.

"It's as I said when Caleb saw the Mother in the waterfall."

He butted in, waving the idea away. "Allegedly. I'm still not accepting that."

Deva continued as if he hadn't spoken. "The Mother always represents love, while others engorge on the energy of sacrifice and bloodshed. We act out their perpetual fight for dominance. Sometimes, like now, it spills over and threatens to affect the whole race of mortals."

"A fine story," Caleb interrupted. "The only flaw I see, is what if the gods don't choose to intervene tonight—or, even simpler, don't actually exist?"

"The challenge will go ahead regardless."

Caleb nodded. "And so this nonsense continues because no one can prove the gods did, or didn't, intervene. Clever. No doubt put together by some priest with a vested interest. So how does Neah protect herself against what Shayla can throw at her?"

"I managed just fine a few days ago," Neah fired back, pacing again.

"Granted," Caleb agreed. "But that was a physical test. We have just seen what power Shayla can command. Though I am loath to admit it, tonight will require more magical ability than fighting strength; plus you are severely weakened by your wound. We don't even know what the residual effects of that poison are. Am I right, Deva?"

"As always, Caleb, you state the obvious eloquently," Deva said. The old woman appeared distracted.

"Mother?" Neah asked, coming over to place her hand on her mother's shoulder. "Are you unwell? Can I get you something?"

Deva shook her head, patting her daughter's hand before removing it firmly and standing to face her.

"There is something I must tell you. Caleb, will you leave us for a moment?"

"No," Neah snapped. "Let him stay. If this is something that affects the child, then he has a right to know."

"Very well. No one else is to hear of this, though. Yet, if we are careful, what I am about to say may be enough to bring about victory for you tonight."

"Tell me."

"Sit. There is a story I must tell you first." Deva drew Neah down onto the divan between her and Caleb. "It begins when I returned to Carmelsara for my mother's funeral. No, even before that.

Remember when I told you that our family was favored by the Torian?"

"Yes. You said all the children were sent to his service, even you to marry Father."

"Just so. Well we—I—got to know the Torian before he was anointed, when we were still children. We often played together in the gardens behind our villa. His name back then was Jitmah."

"I wondered at your closeness at lunch," Neah commented, a feeling of foreboding growing within her. Deva reached over and squeezed her hand before continuing.

"When it was decided by Jitmah's regent that I should marry into the Shaylene ruling family, I was devastated. Being sent from my home, the city that I loved, to marry a man I had never seen, in a country with customs that seemed barbaric and entirely foreign was horrific to me. But I was young and had been indoctrinated to duty, so I did as I was bid and left. At that stage Jitmah was being prepared to be anointed, so I did not see him again for many years. Our lives went on until I returned to Carmelsara for my mother's funeral. He sent for me after her ashes were scattered, and asked me to stay on, to train the new High Priestess."

Deva paused, looking down at her hands.

"Well?"

Deva's eyes crinkled with the memory and she touched a tear at the corner of her eye with a small kerchief. She sniffed once and went on.

"We became... close."

"Are you saying you had an affair with the Torian? He's supposed to be celibate," Neah shouted, and Deva hushed her.

"That is precisely why no one can ever know."

"That's a fine and sad story, but I still don't see how that can help Neah tonight," Caleb said, his voice measured, some frustration behind it.

"There is more." Deva took a deep breath. "Soon after I returned to Shaylene I found I was pregnant."

"Mother! You're not saying—"

"Yes. Jitmah, the Torian, is your father. I suspect that is why you were selected to bear the child to be the next White Torian."

"I don't believe you are saying this. You knew this all along?"

"Only about him being your father."

"Surely your husband knew?" Caleb said. "The journey is not as long as that from Roganshah, but it is still many weeks before you would have lain with him again."

"It was managed. With herbs and discretion. My husband never said anything, though he was not a stupid man so may have suspected. By that stage he didn't care. We never had feelings for each other, and I had done my part providing him with two fine sons. An heir had been all he cared about. Girls to him were an indulged, expensive nuisance."

Neah felt weak, her head light. Everything she had counted on as being fixed was now tilting and spinning; there was no anchor point for anything.

"Does Shayla know?" Caleb asked.

"No, and of course she must not. This may be Neah's one advantage. If I can establish an energetic connection between Jitmah and Neah, she may be able to channel his power to make it through tonight."

"Is that even possible?" Caleb asked.

"I don't know. In his weakened state, I don't even know if there is anything he has available to give. I will go to him now and try."

A PROCESSION of lamps and torches snaked up the hill to the entrance of the main temple. Overhead, a full moon had risen over the mountains that flanked the city, reflecting off the white marble of the imposing pillars and walls.

Neah and her small party of Caleb and Deva rode in an open carriage drawn by a single black mare, its head adorned with an imperial feather that fluttered in the light breeze. Shayla followed just behind in a similar carriage.

The road was lined with people, up to six deep in places, all eager to catch a glimpse of the two challengers. Neah recognized several faces from the caravan, including Hawke, who stood head and shoulders above those around him. He waved, and she forced a smile back.

They drew up to the broad steps leading into the temple together. Both women ignored each other as they climbed out and up toward the open double doorway above them, Caleb and Deva following.

An unrealness had settled over Neah from late afternoon when Deva, sobbing, had confirmed that she'd been unable to establish a link to Neah through the Torian, though he'd been more than willing. There was no emotional link between them, was the reason they'd settled on. Nothing to set the energetic current flowing.

No wonder. I'm still trying to get around the news that he's my father. How could there be any emotional link when no one spoke the whole truth? She half smiled, remembering what she'd said to Caleb coming down the mountain about not being sure what else he hadn't told her. Not just him, it seemed. Poor Caleb.

He was like one of her arrows, parts of him brightly fletched but overall strong and straight, content to travel life in one direction, intent only on hitting his target. That's how he lived.

Until I came along and complicated it. In these short few months he's adapted, but seemingly without it affecting his essential nature.

Grudgingly she admired the simplicity of that life and what she'd come to recognize as an unflagging simple loyalty to both the child and to her.

Unlike my life, which is an overlapping mishmashed collection of untruths and betrayed trust.

She inhaled, standing before the entrance to the temple, and adjusted her tunic. It had been delivered late that afternoon. A simple white cotton gown without sleeves tied at the middle by a thin purple cord. It came with instructions, read from a parchment that the ornately dressed page unrolled with great ceremony. He must have been all of thirteen, his voice barely broken as he read out:

There are to be no weapons.

Only the two challengers are allowed in the arena; no others would be permitted.

There is no exit from the arena until sunrise by either challenger.

What wasn't explicitly stated was that it was likely that only one of them would be leaving alive. She sensed Shayla standing beside her, the hostility and arrogance rolling from her in waves. Neah steeled herself to it, resisting the impulse to look at her, imagining at the same time the comparison that everyone before them must be making. Shayla the tall, sleek queen, and Neah the stumpy warrior with frizzed hair. The sister-pretender. She felt the child roll, and touched her belly, reminding herself.

It is I who carry the White Torian.

She had to trust in that. Despite all the manipulations and the duplicitous paths that had led her here, this was her child, and she'd do everything she could to protect him. The rest didn't really matter.

They started forward, keeping pace with each other. This was a ceremony, after all. Bizarrely, she felt laughter bubbling up from inside, and clamped down on it. The Council was standing in the middle of the room behind a perpetual oil flame set into an earthen container that was in turn surrounded by a shallow pool, representing the elements. Ranged around the walls in a huge semicircle looking down on them were huge depictions of the gods, all carved from various types of polished stone. Some were white and kindly, while others seemed as if they'd been dragged whole, and chiseled, angry and fierce, from their bedrock of red, gray, or black. One in particular caught her eye, Aguzil holding his mighty silver war hammer. He was carved from red stone flashed with green, his stocky legs black as if mired in mud. He was traditionally placed directly opposite the Mother. They were diametrically opposed in both color and temperament. All the others around the ring of gods were various shadings of one or the other; all could be influenced either way depending on how the power was balanced between the polarities of Aguzil and the Mother.

The back doors of the temple were opening, and a cold wind blew through. Neah shivered in her light tunic. Everyone else was wearing thick cloaks and fur-lined coats.

No one said anything. There was no need. Neah looked around for the Torian, spotting him near the back door. As they approached, he stepped in front of them, handing each what looked to be a golden scepter. One end was capped by a square-headed hammer, the other, a harp.

"These are to be your conduits to the gods," he said. "Use them as you feel you must."

Neah gripped the solid golden bar, trying to detect any vibration. All she could feel was cold, unyielding metal. She tucked it into the sash at her waist. One of the temple maidens, dressed in a similar tunic to her own, brought over two large goblets, handing one each to her and Shayla.

"This is a mixture of herbs and intoxicants. It will assist you in making that connection. You must drink it all," the Torian said, his gaze kind when Neah caught his eye. She took the goblet and drained it. Shayla drank hers and tossed the goblet over her shoulder. The clang of the metal against the marble was loud and discordant.

The Torian led them from the temple down a path of crushed white gravel. It crunched beneath their feet. Neah could feel the sharpness of the stones through the soles of the light sandals she'd been provided. The path brought them to a broad terrace overlooking a large clover-shaped design with four leaves that seemed to stretch for leagues. None of the leaves touched each other, only the central stem. She sensed Deva coming to stand between her and Shayla.

Their mother.

Despite everything, Neah wondered what Deva was feeling now, looking out at a field that two of her children would enter, and from which only one would return. She related it to her own child resting oblivious in her belly. She batted the feeling away.

What is happening to me? It had to be that drink.

She wondered whether Shayla was equally affected.

She focused on the field before her. One of the clover shapes was ringed by fire, the one next to it outlined by a narrow border of water, while the third was defined by turned earth. The fourth, obviously representing air, appeared empty.

"Weren't there five?" she asked.

"Ether, the fifth element, is space. It lies between each of the leaves," Deva said.

As they waited in the shared silence, Neah heard Deva's voice again, this time in her head.

"Daughter, listen. Shayla cannot hear, but do not acknowledge what I am about to tell you. The ether is the in-between. It both separates and supports the other four elements. On it, you cannot be harmed. It is neutral territory. Should you wish to evade Shayla at some stage, step out. Remain aware, though, that if you linger too long in the ether you will become confused and then lost, ultimately unable to return to this plane."

Neah stared straight ahead and wondered whether she'd actually heard anything. She hadn't known Deva to be telepathic before, but the list of "I didn't knows" was becoming ragged and long.

A gong in the temple was struck, and continued unabated, its rippling overtones rolling down the slope to them.

"It is time," Deva said, guiding them toward a flight of narrow stone steps. Gone was the white marble; here stone had been roughly hewn directly from the bedrock of the mountain.

Neah started down, her steps unsure. There seemed to be a disconnect between the muscles that coordinated her descent, and her brain. The gong continued unabated, the sound resonating with some internal part of her and then folding back on itself, until she wasn't sure whether there had even been a time when there had been no gong. From a distance she recognized her awareness broadening, and even her senses seemed to be getting sharper; the perfume from the small purple flowers flanking the path floated up to her, strong and intense, as if she had entered a factory that was extracting their essence. When she gazed ahead and narrowed her eyes, it felt like she could see through the ground beneath her, right into the cloverleaf field and through it. The cold that had bothered her before seemed to have dissipated. If she had to describe the air around her, it would be as rich with promise, untroubled and unaffected by climate.

The whole experience was disconcerting.

Her feet had stopped moving. When she looked down she discovered she was already standing on the field. She could not remember how long she'd been there.

Shayla!

Her head snapped around, looking for her sister, immediately alert for threat. Shayla had disappeared, as had the temple behind her. Only the gong persisted. Even that seemed to drift in and out of focus; she had to concentrate to remain aware of it.

I should keep moving.

She had to think the thought twice before her feet obeyed.

What is happening to me?

As she walked, she had the feeling her feet were sinking into the turf. Yet it didn't feel boggy, more as if she were transcending the boundary between the earth and what lay beneath it.

What part of the field am I on?

Off to the right she could see the fire burning around that section of the leaf, its glow captured by the water of the section bordering it. She remembered that they were the two leaves at the bottom of the configuration. So currently she wasn't standing on any of the leaves. This must be the ether; the in-between, Deva had called it. The urge to stop walking and just stay here and be part of this expanse was enticing.

Neah forced her feet to keep moving, the sensation of dissolving boundaries increasing with each step. She was nearing the leaf ringed by water, and wondered whether Shayla would be waiting for her there. Or something else. She shuddered, the vicious image of Aguzil forming uninvited in her mind.

She shook it away and stepped over the water boundary, and immediately felt herself totally submerged. Looking up, she could clearly make out the underside of the turf forming the clover leaf.

And breathing.

She sank deeper, the cotton tunic floating about her like a shroud. Light filtered up through the clear water. It seemed to be coming from a large clear globe at the bottom of the pond. Using her arms, she stroked toward it. As she drew closer she made out the shape of a golden harp lying on a stone seat, and remembered the scepter at her waist. It had a harp of the same shape and color at its base. Neah drew it from her belt, touching that end to the globe. The same feeling of transitioning that she'd experienced above ran through her, and she found herself inside the globe. Water dripped from her hair and tunic, pooling onto the floor. She reached out to touch the harp on the seat, feeling a tingle from the scepter as she did so.

"Can you play?"

The voice sounded loud inside the globe. When Neah turned to look behind her, a woman's disembodied face was staring back at her, the expression in her green-flecked eyes open and curious. Neah recognized her as Cirra, god of music and the arts.

"Yes," Neah said, curious even at her nonreaction to the appearance of Cirra. She picked up the instrument and strummed it gently. The tones filled the globe, and the woman closed her eyes with what seemed like ecstasy. Neah plucked and strummed her way through a melody she remembered from childhood, the harp taking her rudimentary skills and refining them into something textured and wonderful. It almost seemed it was playing itself. After a time she felt a presence, as if someone or something significant was close by. As she continued to play the sensation grew, surrounding and filling her. She finished the last piece gently, as if withdrawing from something delicate and precious.

The woman opened her eyes. "You play true and are welcome here."

"It wasn't me really... the harp."

The woman smiled, gentle warmth radiating from her. "This harp responds to the spirit that plays it. That is why it sounded so sweet."

Something rocked the globe, and they both looked up.

Shayla. She'd dived into the pool and was swimming hard, heading for the globe, a silver-headed hammer forming in her hand.

"Hurry, child. You must go. She holds the war hammer of Aguzil. If she shatters the globe, you will be unable to breathe. Take the harp. When you need us of the water, play it and we will come."

Neah touched the globe with the scepter and found herself back outside. Shayla was spearing directly for her, holding the gleaming silver hammer straight out in front; it appeared to be dragging her with it, speeding her descent.

What can I do?

"Swim to the surface, child. Hurry."

Neah kicked. The closer she came to the surface, the heavier the harp became. It became increasingly difficult to keep hold of. She considered letting it go so she could swim faster.

To Neah's surprise, Shayla did not follow. Instead she continued her determined trajectory straight down, toward the globe. Neah kicked again, struggling against the pull of the harp. It was as if it didn't want to leave.

A rupture below tumbled her, a gigantic air bubble surging past, seeking release. The globe had been shattered. Jagged pieces floated below her, flaring with a last burst of light before one by one they winked out and settled on the bed of the pond.

Shayla, the hammer raised above her head in triumph, stared up, a malicious, almost hungry smile distorting her face before the light disappeared completely and the water turned black and bitterly cold. Neah could no longer see the surface. All she knew was that with the disappearance of the light she could no longer breathe, and needed to. Desperately. Her lungs were burning. Closing her eyes, she forced herself not to reflexively inhale, instead scissoring her legs. The harp no longer seemed as heavy. Neah clutched it to her chest as if it might give her strength. She had no way of knowing what direction she was swimming in. Her sense of direction had disappeared with the light.

"*Swim, child.*"

The mantra rattled from one side of her head to the other. She tried to focus on it, aware also that Shayla was somewhere close by, circling through the same water like a shark. Blackness smudged the edges of her consciousness, threatening to overtake her.

What of the child. Can he still breathe if I can't?

It lent her legs a final burst of strength. She prayed that they were pushing her toward the surface. The need for air screamed through her; she could no longer resist. She felt her mouth open; the water flooded in; then miraculously a paroxysm of coughing as her head broke the surface and clean, beautiful fresh air fought to find passage past the water fountaining from her mouth and nose.

Sighting the edge of the pond, she struggled toward it, feeling the consistency around her change, transitioning back from liquid until it became solid enough to support her. She crawled the final section, across the narrow channel of water, and rolled onto her back, blissfully accepting the dangerously safe comfort of the in-between, the ether, allowing it to embrace her. Knowing only that Shayla could not reach her here.

The moon was more than halfway across its arc when she woke. She was still on her back, the harp snug, hugged to her chest as if it belonged there. The memory of what had happened beneath the water though was already hazy, and if it had not been for the solidness of the harp, she may have believed the whole thing a dream. The disassociation and complacency that had overtaken her earlier while on the ether had settled deeply upon her. With some effort, she made herself get up. She had no idea what to do next. Sunrise was still some time off, and if she wanted to be here to see it she would have to leave this place and move to one of the other elements, hoping that Shayla did not choose the same one. Neah did not have the power nor the stamina to fight her sister; all she could do was try and survive the night.

CALEB'S HEART wrenched as he watched Neah stagger toward the clover leaf of fire. Several of the councilors standing nearby groaned. They were obviously pulling for her as well. Further along the terrace, others were not as they squabbled to secure better odds on Shayla. Caleb blocked out their noise, making a mental note of their faces for later.

"She looks drugged," Deva mumbled, digging her fingers deeper into his forearm.

Caleb turned his attention back to the arenas. "I can't imagine why she chose the fire ring. It's where Shayla will be strongest."

"Maybe she wants to get it over with quickly. She looks done in; the ordeal in the water took it out of her."

They watched as Neah stepped across the fire border and floated down into the center of a circular arena covered with sand, lit by a raging curtain of fire that sealed the arena, its flames rising to double the height of a man.

"There's nowhere to hide or run in there," he whispered.

NEAH LANDED LIGHTLY ATOP the sand. The weariness of moments before evaporated as she kicked off the useless sandals and sunk her toes deep into the coarse sand, grounding herself. Bending her knees slightly, she tensioned through her thighs, charging her body. One hand still clasped the golden harp, the other the scepter as she shuffled around in a circular pattern, searching the arena for Shayla, relaxing slightly when she found it clear.

The wound beneath her shoulder pulsed in time with her heart. She had overworked both trying to get to the surface of the pond, that much was certain, but from the kicking going on near her belly her son was doing well. That was something.

"I was waiting for you, *sister*, in the earth arena. I felt sure you'd go there next," Shayla's voice rasped from behind her. Neah pivoted on the ball of one foot to face her opponent, evening her weight over each foot so she could spring either way.

Shayla's skin was sheened with sweat and picked up the burnished flicker of the surrounding fire. She still held Aguzil's hammer. Neah glanced at her scepter. The hammer at the top was an exact replica, in the same way the harp was. This was starting to make a bizarre sort of sense. Should she invoke Aguzil? Though it looked like Shayla already had.

In response, Shayla flung the hammer at Neah. It flew directly at her head, flipping end over end. Neah threw herself to the left, landing on the tip of her good shoulder, and bounced back to her feet.

Shayla grinned. "You've learnt something since last we fought. Good."

The hammer was somehow already back in Shayla's hand. It flew through the air again. Neah didn't even see her throw it, managing to duck and roll off to the other side, landing clumsily on the injured shoulder. This time she could only stagger up, the wound pounding in protest beneath its dressing. When she touched it, her fingers came away red. Again the hammer came at her, this time circling in an arc, changing its trajectory at the last moment. Neah dived, sprawling across the sand, unmindful of anything other than getting out of the hammer's way.

How can she keep throwing it so quickly? Does she have more than one of them? If only I had my bow and a quiver of arrows... though I do have the harp.

Frantically she brought it up and plucked at the strings as the hammer came at her yet again. The resulting sound was less sweet, more like an attack than a harmonic strum, but its sound seemed to deflect the path of the hammer. It came close enough for Neah to hear the hiss of its flight through the air before returning to Shayla's hand, lodging there like a trained bird.

Again Shayla loosed it, and once more Neah played a succession of chords, more vigorously this time. The hammer wavered midflight, as if caught by a strong cross current. When it came at her again,

Neah unleashed a full refrain, and the hammer slowed, then stopped, hovering uncertainly in the air. Immediately Neah ran forward, knocking it with the hammer end of the golden scepter. It dropped like a felled bird to the sand and she snatched it up.

The shaft tingled in her hand as the two women circled each other. Another identical hammer was already in Shayla's grip. The heat from the fire was intense, and the throbbing from Neah's shoulder warned her that it wasn't up for many throws. She transferred it to her left and hurled it backhand at Shayla's midsection, but Shayla evaded it easily, throwing her own with deadly precision. Neah realized her mistake as the hammer immediately returned to her right hand. In order to engage the harp's defenses adequately, she needed both hands to play it. She would have to put one down. Dropping the hammer to the sand she fumbled for the harp as Shayla's weapon bore down on her. Neah barely managing a messy strum, which dipped the angle of the hammer's attack so that it struck her squarely on the damaged right shoulder. Her world exploded into stars and flames, radiating pain that flooded her senses. The harp dropped from her paralyzed fingers and she sank to her knees.

Sniffing victory, Shayla closed in, bringing her hammer high, ready to slam it against the side of Neah's head.

The child, perhaps sensing danger, turned, which was enough to bring Neah back from her screaming pain. She forced movement into her fingers, fumbling for the scepter. Drawing it from the sash and holding it before her, she invoked Cirra. Shayla stopped, the hammer frozen behind her head, caught midway through its arc, her face screwed into a mask of hate.

Neah pushed herself to her feet, dragging the harp with her. She searched the sand for her own dropped hammer. It was gone, swallowed by the sand.

"WHERE'S YOUR HAMMER?" Caleb shouted at the scene before him.

"She has lost it," Deva said from beside him.

"Can she get another?"

"I doubt it. Shayla will be more cautious next time. Look, she recovers."

Shayla shook free of the stupor, resuming the hammer's interrupted arc. It flew from her hands and into the space that Neah had just vacated.

They heard Shayla's howl of rage as she turned on Neah again.

Neah was now playing the harp madly, setting up an accelerating melody, a translucent protective screen building around her. The hammer struck it in a shower of sparks. Shayla threw again and then again, each time more forcefully.

Finally she drew her own scepter, and in a frenzied voice called on Aguzil. Immediately another hammer appeared in her other hand. Now she had two, and she unleashed both in a concerted, unrelenting attack.

"How does she have the stamina for that?" Caleb asked.

"It is not her throwing. It is Aguzil," Deva muttered.

"The screen is bending. It's losing power. You have to do something, Deva."

"What?"

"Anything. Try the Torian again. She needs help now," Caleb blustered, his voice hushed and urgent.

Deva turned to the Torian standing beside her. "Jitmah? Can we?"

He nodded, and she placed her hand on the small man's shoulder, closing her eyes, drawing off some of the Torian's power.

Finally she shuddered and removed her hand, shaking the energy out through her wrist and fingers. "It's no good. It won't travel. It's the same as before."

"What do you mean? You're her mother and he's... the Torian. Who else is there?"

"Her energetic field is rejecting Jitmah's charge. I told you that. I don't have the power to do it on my own." Deva's voice cracked as Shayla again battered Neah's shield.

"Try me," Caleb said.

"What?"

"Use me. I can try and link with the child, bypass her natural defenses. Hurry."

Deva replaced her hand on the Torian's shoulder and positioned the other on Caleb's, drawing from one and sending through the other.

Caleb felt a sharp shock from Deva's fingers. It traveled around his body as if trying to find an exit before blasting out through his solar plexus. Once it began to flow, Caleb found it hard to stay upright. The energy was raw and wild, ripping and shuddering through him. He hoped Neah was picking it up at the other end.

NEAH HEAVED IN ANOTHER BREATH. Each seemed to come at a tremendous effort and fueled the pain in her body, whose epicenter was in her shoulder. The harp's strings had become so hot they were almost impossible to play. One had broken under the strain, and her fingers were blistered from the heat. There was a twang as another snapped.

She could feel the shield dissolving around her as the energy leaked away, her link with Cirra and the Mother fading. Shayla, though, looked enervated. Her pace hadn't lessened, the two hammers crashing at Neah without letup. Even the sound of them against the shield was deafening. Grimly she held on, then felt something trickle near her navel. Like water down a dry watercourse it flowed, both alien yet familiar, washing against the floodgates of her awareness.

Caleb. She felt him, and so did his son. They were sending. Gleefully she opened to it and felt the power flow in. She fed some back through the shield and imagined the rest moving in a continuous stream to her right arm and shoulder.

The shield hummed and filled, Shayla's eyes widening as Neah used it to bat away one of the blows, catching the other hammer as it came through, wrenching it from Shayla's grip.

With the strength rippling through her arm, Neah advanced the attack, using the shield as both buffer and weapon, finally swinging her own hammer to land a blow squarely against Shayla's temple. She heard the skull crack, and her sister stopped as if she'd hit a wall, crumpling to her knees and falling onto the sand. As Neah watched, Shayla's form dissolved to reveal the twisted, broken body of Mohar.

NINETEEN

Neah stirred, her awareness returning in reluctant chunks from behind closed lids. The sound of the gong, incessant and loud, came first. She groaned and tried to turn away from it. Pain followed. It seemed as if every part of her had been either shaken, broken, or irrevocably bent. It wasn't excruciating though, rather the edges were dulled as if she were slightly removed from the worst of it. She recognized the feeling; it went with her incredibly dry mouth. Strong herbal remedies.

That can't be good.

It followed that the supporting softness beneath her and the warm gentle drape across her body meant she was in a bed.

How...?

As if they'd been restlessly waiting, the memories rushed in and she started awake, her eyes snapping open. She flinched in the bright light.

"Neah, it's all right."

Caleb. She relaxed back against the pillows, then jerked again, her hands trailing to her abdomen.

"And Deva tells me he's all right as well."

Neah took a deep breath, relishing the return of the pain. It meant she was alive. She turned to look at him. He was scruffy, his uniform collar open, rough curls of brown chest hair poking through. His eyes had the haunted look of someone who'd been reluctant, or unable, to sleep.

Her eyes tracked to a full glass of water on the bedside table. "Can I...?"

Tenderly he slid his arm beneath her shoulders, and held the glass to her lips. She drank greedily. He dabbed some of the excess from her mouth with a corner of the sheet before settling her back.

"Is it true?" she asked, closing her eyes to shut out the light.

"What?"

She heard the sound of him getting up, the drapes being pulled.

"The weird scenes that keep flashing through my head."

"If you mean did you defeat Shayla in the Arena, then yes."

"Then why are they still hitting those damned gongs?"

"They're bells, not gongs. They're ringing all across the city. They're to mourn the old Torian—and welcome the new regent."

She opened her eyes again. "Jitmah's dead? How?"

"We managed to channel his energy to you after all, do you remember?"

"Yes, I do...." She looked at him, eyes wide. "It felt like you." She patted her stomach. "Via him."

"In a way it was. It was the Torian who provided the real oomph; Deva and I were just the connection. In the end he gave everything he had. I saw him die just as I helped you back up to the terrace." Caleb reached over and took her hand. His fingers felt warm and rough, but also familiar and strangely comforting.

There was a light knock at the door. Caleb released her hand and went over to open it. Deva smiled her thanks and pushed through, carrying a large tray.

"Ah, good, you're awake. I've made some of my special broth."

Neah groaned. "Special broth" meant herbal medicine thinly disguised as soup. It was always bitter and chokingly foul. Deva helped her to sit up, fluffing the pillows up behind her before settling into Caleb's seat beside the bed, and spooning the steaming broth into her.

"I should go," he said.

"No, please. Stay."

The words tumbled out, unedited, surprising even her. She slurped on the broth, covertly studying him from beneath lowered lids. He'd crossed to the window and was looking out across the city. He seemed embarrassed, as if he'd been found lurking somewhere he shouldn't. His usual restlessness rippled across him like the fur of a panther, just beneath his skin, and she wondered what he was really thinking.

More to the point, what am I feeling?

Deva spooned in the final dose, dabbing Neah's lips with the cloth. Suppressing a shudder, Neah smiled her thanks. It might taste horrible, but nothing was as recuperative. Kissing her on the forehead, Deva picked up the tray and headed for the door.

"I'll be back in a tick with some real soup."

Caleb came back and sat on the edge of the chair. This time she reached for his hand.

"Are you all right as well? You don't look like you've had much rest."

His smile was tired and unguarded. "It's been a busy time."

"Is she gone, do you think?"

"Shayla?" He shook his head. "I doubt it. Her army is already forming on the plain several leagues from the city. I was just looking at them now. They started coming down off the mountain yesterday and are forming into divisions. They won't stand a chance against these walls though. It's all just chest thumping. I think they're acting on old orders."

"Have you heard from Arrowsmith?"

He grinned, the cheekiness returning as the smile pressed up into his dimples. "That's the good news. He and the Timpani managed to cut off the supply wagons and free your soldiers. Our plan went perfectly. Most of the Shaylene army had already gone through the pass by the time the Timpani and their wolves attacked from the rear. The others who'd been concealed amongst the rocks kept the main force pinned down, preventing them from coming back through the pass to reinforce the vanguard. The Sworn message I received from Arrowsmith said as many as a thousand troops should be available to you once they've had time to recuperate in the mountains. If I'm any judge, by then they'll be keen for payback."

"That's wonderful news, Caleb. Well done. I wonder, though, will it be enough? The Shaylene have many thousands...."

He shrugged, looking toward the window again, his mind calculating. "With the five hundred from the Carmelsara garrison and the three hundred Imperial guards—with the permission of the Torian of course"—he flashed a wicked look at her—"and of course the Timpani, we stand a good chance. Hit and runs on their supply lines at first, that will weaken them. My bet is they'll have to pull back before the pass snows in, otherwise they'll be cut off and locked out until spring. They'll starve. Believe me, there's not enough rabbits in that forest out there to feed me, much less an army. By then we'll be ready."

"Sounds like you've got it covered, Commander Kane. Does the regent have the power to promote you?"

"Only to herself. The army operates at the pleasure of the Torian serving the Commonwealth, and answers only to it."

"I'll have to be content with that then."

Silence settled, the tension of words waiting to be said buzzing between them. Finally Neah sighed.

"I was pleased to see you here when I woke up."

"I seem to be making a habit of it."

"It's one I could get used to."

His eyes widened. The rest of him seemed tightly held. Neah pushed on.

"What I said earlier, that it felt like it was you coming to help me in the arena. I really meant it. Something changed then. I felt something give—inside—when I let you—it, the energy, I don't know—in. It was like a dam bursting. I can't explain it. All I know is that at that moment I trusted you, and for me—" She chuckled, thinking back. "—that's saying something."

"I was just so frustrated at not being able to do anything. Watching you struggle, so bravely. Well, I would have done anything. Will do anything.... Neah— Can I still call you Neah now, Regent? Torian-to-be's mother?"

She laughed, taking his hand again as if it were the most natural thing to do. Perhaps it was.

"Mohar was right about one thing at least."

"Oh?" she said, head cocking to one side.

"Some of the Council are jackals. They will side with whoever promises them the most power. Do you know they were betting on her to beat you?"

"Who was the favorite?"

"She was. They were complaining because the odds were so bad, until I helped them out."

"You what?" She straightened up, then flinched at the pain.

"I won big-time. I put all my back pay on you."

She slapped his arm playfully. "You're incorrigible."

"I'm just here looking after my investment. I got great odds on you getting rid of Shayla within the year." He grinned wickedly.

"Caleb."

His gray eyes turned serious. "Joking aside, I do mean I'd like to look out for you."

She felt herself bristle, and he continued quickly.

"Obviously you can look after yourself, however, as Mohar said, you can't be everywhere. You'll need someone to cover your back. Maybe even help look out for... our son."

Neah felt a fluttering in her chest. "I see. And how do you plan to do that?"

"If I can avoid getting a clutch of arrows in my chest, I'd like to marry you. Torians may have to be celibate, but I'm not sure that applies to regents. I think I love you, Neah."

"What?"

She couldn't decide whether she was pleased or outraged.

Marry?

"You *think* you love me?"

"That came out wrong. I know I love you. You're prickly, but then so am I. Neither of us is ever likely to change."

"I think we already have. This conversation wouldn't have happened two months ago."

"You put a curse on me, remember?"

"It seems to have worked. You are now apparently in love with the woman you swore you hated."

"No. Not hated. That's not true. Well, maybe a bit. I'm just a brilliant actor. Another one of my hidden talents."

"Really. And what are the others?" She stared at him, eyes challenging.

He bent over, bringing his mouth over hers. The first touch of his lips on hers was delicate, incredibly tender. She felt a rush begin in her toes and move up her body. The pressure of his lips increased, and involuntarily she groaned.

This was going to be good.

ACKNOWLEDGMENTS

Writing is not so much a solitary endeavour but a group effort. If being incredibly kind, generous with their time and immensely talented is in any way reminiscent of what a *real* star is then the following people are true 'five pointers' (credits in no particular order).

Kate O'Donnell and Olivia Ventura - editors supreme

Writers in the Ruff - Kathy Stewart, Hazel Barker & Kirsty Cramer

Sue Reynolds - for her keen insight and feedback

Zali Nash - for her encouragement and undying enthusiasm

Russell Cornhill and members of Let's Talk Writing

ABOUT THE AUTHOR

Jack is really Paul but then he is a guy who likes to keep his peas and potatoes separate. Paul has plans of writing non-fiction, is the worker, yoga teacher, yoga therapist and is in the final throes of completing a Masters in psychotherapy (Gestalt) while Jack, well, he enjoys life hiking in the forest, meditating, having fun and writing plot driven genre speculative fiction.

Living on Australia's Gold Coast with his delightful wife Annie combined Paul and Jack have written three books including Last Caravan.

His next Book Mine the Darkness will be released mid to late 2018 by Whistling Book Press (MT, USA).

ALSO BY JACK GARRETY

The Seventh Wave

The Emerald Tablets

www.ingramcontent.com/pod-product-compliance
Lightning Source LLC
Chambersburg PA
CBHW071530110726
47908CB00007B/1823